LINDA
KAVANAGH

The Secret Wife

POOLBEG

Published 2014
by Poolbeg Press Ltd
123 Grange Hill, Baldoyle
Dublin 13, Ireland
E-mail: poolbeg@poolbeg.com
www.poolbeg.com

1

A catalogue record for this book is available from the British Library.

ISBN 9781842236222

Typeset by Poolbeg
Printed by CPI Group (UK) Ltd

www.poolbeg.com

About the author

Linda Kavanagh is a former journalist who has worked for various Irish newspapers and magazines, and was a staff writer on the *RTÉ Guide* for fifteen years. She lives with her partner and dog in Dun Laoghaire, Co Dublin. Her previous novels, *Love Hurts*, *Love Child*, *Hush Hush*, *Time After Time*, *Never Say Goodbye* and *Still Waters* are also published by Poolbeg.

You can contact Linda at **www.lindakavanagh.com** and **linda@lindkavanagh.com**.

Also by Linda Kavanagh

Love Hurts
Love Child
Hush Hush
Time After Time
Never Say Goodbye
Still Waters

Published by Poolbeg

Acknowledgements

Sincere thanks as always to Paula Campbell and all the Poolbeg team; to editor Gaye Shortland, whose expertise and eye for detail has turned this novel into a far more polished product than it would otherwise have been; to my wonderful agent Lorella Belli for her encouragement, support and belief in me.

Special thanks to Denise Hayden-Murphy for inviting me to the inspirational Fuerteventura, where some of this novel was written; to Mike for his support and brilliant cooking, and to Scruff for her devotion and endless supply of licks.

As always, my final thanks goes to my readers, whose support has happily turned all my novels into bestsellers. I hope you enjoy this one!

In memory of my dear cousin Ron,
one of life's great guys.

Your marriage is a disaster

So you end it

You think it's over

He doesn't

Your nightmare is only beginning . . .

CHAPTER 1

"I'm getting married!"

Laura Thornton looked the picture of happiness as she held out her left hand so that her friend Kerry could admire her engagement ring.

"Congratulations, love!" Kerry said, hugging her, and trying to appear happy for her. But truthfully, her friend didn't like the man Laura was planning to marry. Okay, so he was charming and handsome, a stockbroker who seemed to have a knack for making money. Yet there was something profoundly needy about him. Not that being needy was wrong – it just wasn't what you expected to find in a mature successful man. Anyway, Laura seemed happy at last, and convinced that she'd found a man who genuinely cared about her.

"So when is the wedding?"

"Next month – we saw no reason to wait, since we so much want to be together!"

So soon! Kerry experienced a frisson of fear. It looked like Laura was being her usual impulsive self.

"It's going to be a very small wedding – I mean, since neither Jeff nor I have any family – but I'd really like you to be my bridesmaid."

Kerry nodded. "Of course – I'd be delighted."

Nevertheless, she was disturbed at the haste with which Laura was marrying this man whom she hardly knew. Although aware that her friend was impulsive, Kerry wondered if Jeff was the one pushing for this rush into marriage.

Kerry and Laura had met Jeff one evening in a pub. The bar had been crowded, and Laura had been trying desperately to catch the barman's eye. Jeff had witnessed her attempts and, being tall, he'd gallantly ordered the drinks for her, then insisted on paying for them. Laura had been pleased and impressed by the good-looking, blond-haired man, and they'd spent the rest of the evening chatting to each other.

Kerry had disliked him on sight. She'd recognised a smooth-talking chancer, but Laura had quickly fallen for his superficial charms. Before long, Laura could hardly frame a sentence without bringing Jeff's name into it, and Kerry knew that it was pointless to urge caution. Laura was already head over heels in love with him. Instinctively Kerry knew that, if she raised any objections to Jeff, Laura would interpret it as sour grapes on her part, and she'd be the one to lose Laura's friendship. Already she could sense that Jeff was keen to loosen the bonds of friendship between the two women. She suspected he was the kind of man who wouldn't be able to deal with his wife having friends and sharing confidences – maybe even daring to talk jocularly about him behind his back. He'd demand total loyalty, and that loyalty would require him to be the centre of Laura's universe. Would Laura allow that to happen?

"Oh, Kerry, I'm so excited!" Laura said, her face wreathed in smiles. "I never thought I'd meet anyone like Jeff – and that he'd want to be with me, too! He's the most wonderful man I've ever met – I just feel *soooo* lucky to be marrying him!"

Kerry smiled, although she felt that her face was in danger of cracking from the effort, and she quickly steered the conversation away from any further discussion of Jeff's merits. "So what are you going to wear? Have you picked a dress yet?"

"No, so you'll have to come shopping with me!" Laura said impishly. "And we can find a dress for you, too. How about something in burgundy? It would look wonderful with your dark hair . . ."

Kerry nodded. She didn't really care what colour she wore. It was Laura's day, so she'd wear whatever dress Laura chose for her.

In the days that followed, Kerry made a special effort to share Laura's enthusiasm for her approaching big day. Together, they

2

trawled the dress shops during their lunch hours and, with Kerry's approval, Laura blew a month's salary on a gorgeous cream taffeta dress with a detail of tiny pearls.

"Now, I just need to get a matching fascinator!" Laura announced happily. "Oh Kerry, I'm so excited!"

Kerry's dress proved to be a simple and straightforward purchase. She readily agreed to a deep burgundy chiffon dress that Laura discovered in a small boutique, thinking how contrasting the two of them would look at the wedding – Laura's blonde hair and cream dress versus her own dark dress and dark-brown hair. Kerry also opted to wear a simple matching flower in her hair, whereas Laura was thrilled to find a glamorous pearl and feathered fascinator that was an exact match for her dress.

As they relaxed over a cuppa in a city-centre café after their marathon shopping expedition, Laura was still giddy with excitement. But something had been worrying Kerry ever since Jeff had first appeared on the scene. And it was time she said something about it.

"Laura – have you told Jeff about the money?"

Laura looked up from the cream doughnut she was slicing. "No, but I will as soon as we are married."

Kerry sighed with relief. Thank goodness. But how on earth could she delicately point out to Laura that she might soon find herself divorcing Jeff, when she hadn't even married him yet?

"Look, love – I think you should wait a while before telling him," she ventured. "You can't be sure how things will go – none of us can – but what if you ended up divorcing Jeff? He could claim a lot of your money."

Laura bridled. "You seem to be implying that there's something devious about Jeff – that's a horrible thing to say about a woman's fiancé just before she gets married!" Her eyes filled with tears.

Kerry reached across the table and took her friend's hand. "Love, I'm only looking out for you! By all means tell him when you've been together for a year or two – but wait a while, just to be sure. Please?"

Laura looked sullen and offended.

"Look, Jeff has a comfortable home and both of you have good jobs," Kerry pleaded. "You can live happily as you are for the time being. Then when you eventually tell him, you'll have proved that he's the man for you."

Laura's expression became angry. "I know *now* that Jeff's the man for me! Are you implying that I don't know my own mind?"

Kerry raised her hands in appeasement. "Of course not! Sorry, love, I'm just concerned for you. I'm sure you'll be perfectly happy with Jeff – I just don't want you losing half your fortune."

Laura looked slightly happier. "Okay, I won't tell him – at least not for a while. Are you happy now?"

Kerry grimaced. "Love, it's not me that needs to be happy – I'm only concerned about you."

Laura nibbled a piece of her doughnut, then looked at her friend and sighed. "Sorry, Kerry – I know you mean the best. I really do appreciate your concern – but Jeff and I – well, we're in for the long haul. He's the best! But I don't want you and me to fall out, so I'll hold off telling him for a while." She looked at Kerry with a triumphant look on her face. "Then you'll realise that Jeff truly is the man for me – I know he loves me, no matter what my financial situation is."

Kerry nodded, relieved that the fortune Laura had inherited on the death of her parents and brother was still safe from Jeff. She was convinced that if he knew what was in Laura's bank account, there would be little money left by the time she discovered what he was truly like.

"How many guests are you having altogether?"

"At the last count, about twenty."

It would be a small wedding, with around a dozen colleagues from the Sociology Department of the university where Laura was a lecturer, a few of Kerry's colleagues from the engineering company where she worked, and a few friends of Jeff's from his badminton club. Kerry wondered uneasily why no one from other areas of Jeff's life would be attending – even though he'd no family, surely he had work colleagues who were friends? In her opinion, there was definitely something dodgy about him, but she was not about to start pointing out his deficiencies, since Laura was clearly annoyed with her at the idea of keeping Jeff in the dark about the money she'd inherited.

"You'd better stay with me the night before the wedding," Kerry said, smiling, as they gathered up their booty and left the café. "It's supposed to bring bad luck if the groom sees you before you get to the registry office."

Laura nodded, her eyes now sparkling again with excitement. She'd already moved in with Jeff, since they'd decided to make their home in his sumptuous apartment. "Well then, we'll also have to make that our hen night!" she said, smiling. "Since Jeff and I wanted to get married as quickly as possible, there hasn't been time to do a lot of the normal stuff."

Kerry shook her head sternly. "There'll be no hen night for you on the eve of the wedding, madam – I don't want you nursing a hangover on your big day!"

Kerry suspected that Jeff probably wouldn't want Laura having a hen night anyway, since it would mean she wouldn't be focusing all her attention on him, and he'd see danger in the combination of alcohol and male strippers that were usually on the menu. In essence, Jeff wouldn't want Laura having any fun if he wasn't there to share it. Or control it.

The day of the wedding dawned bright and sunny, and Laura was already up and in the kitchen when Kerry padded out in dressing gown and slippers.

"Oh Kerry, I'm so excited!" Laura squealed, jumping up and down, then hugging her friend as Kerry tried to turn on the kettle. "Here, let me get you some breakfast – I'm far too nervous to eat anything myself!"

"You've got to eat something," Kerry warned her, managing to put two slices of bread in the toaster. "Otherwise, you might faint during the service, and that wouldn't look great on your wedding day!"

Laura nodded. Her friend was right, as usual. But there were butterflies in her stomach, and she couldn't sit still. This was the special day that women dreamed of, and she wanted everything to be perfect. Before leaving her room she'd checked and checked again that her shoes, bouquet and fascinator were all lined up and ready. Thrilled, she'd touched the hem of her wedding gown that was hanging on the back of the bedroom door, wrapped in tissue paper. She couldn't wait to be Jeff's wife.

"Here – eat this," Kerry said, pushing a slice of buttered toast across the table towards her. "I'm not letting you leave this apartment until there's something in your stomach!"

Nodding, Laura took the slice of toast and began chewing obediently. She couldn't even taste it because she was so nervous and so excited, but she knew Kerry was right, and was only looking out for her. She had to eat something. Otherwise, she might keel over just as she was taking her vows. And nothing was going to stop her from saying 'I do' to her beloved Jeff.

At last it was time to get dressed.

"I really wish I had my parents and my brother here," Laura said wistfully as Kerry helped her into her cream taffeta dress. "I'm missing them so much right now!"

Her eyes filled with tears, and Kerry hugged her.

"You're the only family I have left," Laura added. "I mean, you're all alone too, since your mum died, so we only have each other." She brightened. "But Jeff and I will have kids eventually, so we'll create our own family over time. And I'm sure you'll have kids some day, too. I hope that, like us, they'll all be friends into the next generation."

Laura brushed away her tears and concentrated on putting on her fascinator and matching pearl earrings. She'd never got over the death of her parents and brother in a tragic car accident when she was twelve. All she had left of them now was a few precious photographs, which she kept in her bedside locker. She regularly took them out and looked at them – it enabled her to remember that she'd once been part of a happy family. And she blamed herself for what happened. Ever since then, Laura had carried around the guilt like a huge weight on her back. She'd gone to check on an injured bird that morning, so she'd missed the planned trip to get new school uniforms for her and her brother Pete. After waiting in vain for her daughter to appear, her mother had finally decided to set off with Pete, and at the last minute her father had chosen to take a lift in her mother's car. Laura was well aware that if she hadn't delayed her mother, they might never have crashed, and her father would never have taken a lift because they'd have left for town already.

Laura stifled another tear. Kerry had been her rock back then and she, too, had been devastated by what had happened. And since Laura had no immediate family left – except a grandfather who hadn't wanted to take on a grieving child – Kerry's mother had taken her in, and she'd lived with Kerry and her mother until both girls had left for university. Sadly, Kerry's mother had died shortly after that, of a suspected heart attack. Without a doubt, the early loss of both their families had brought her and Kerry even closer.

"Come on, dry those tears – you'll ruin your mascara," Kerry said briskly. "There's no time for sad memories today. This is a happy day, and I want to see you smiling."

Laura obliged, giving Kerry a winning smile. Then she picked up her bouquet of freesias and roses, surveyed herself in the mirror, and gave a contented nod. She was pleased with what she saw. Looking back at her was a woman who had the clear eyes of someone in love, and who was just about to marry the man she adored.

"I'm ready," said Laura, taking a deep breath.

CHAPTER 2

As she stood by the graveside, Ellie Beckworth felt completely alone and frightened. Even though the pillars of the local community had all come to pay their respects to her late husband, she suspected most of them were there simply to be seen. It had all happened so suddenly that she could hardly begin to take it in. One minute, John had been laughing at a joke he'd just told her, the next minute he was lying on the floor, dead from a heart attack. How could everything change so quickly? She'd gone from wife to widow in the blink of an eye.

She looked around wildly, almost expecting John to be there in the crowd, reaching out for her, soothing her in her hour of need. But there was no familiar friendly face, and she glanced down into the gaping hole in the cold earth below her feet, where her beloved husband's coffin now lay. Tossing in a single red rose, she heard it land with a thud on the wood below, and the sound seemed to symbolise the end of all her hopes and dreams. She was still a relatively young woman, but a widow nonetheless. Where would she go from here?

She and John had moved to London only the year before, when her husband had been offered a job as a partner in a small accountancy firm in the city centre. They'd packed up and left the north of England behind, intent on making a new life and hopefully raising a family in the London suburbs. They'd even found the house of their dreams, near a village on the outskirts of London but within commuting distance of the city – a small house called

Treetops, with a three-acre woodland garden, just made for half a dozen kids. But no children were forthcoming, and now there never would be.

A few of John's cousins, and a distant relative from her own family, had turned up to offer their condolences, and after the service they'd led her to a local hotel where they proceeded to eat a meal that had tasted like sawdust to Ellie. Then before leaving for their trains to various parts of the country, they plied her with pieces of paper bearing their phone numbers and addresses, and begging her to call if she needed anything. Thanking them, Ellie knew she was unlikely ever to see any of them again. And she was never going to phone them either. An hour later, she was back in her own home, alone and wondering where the future would lead her.

In the hallway, Ellie studied herself in the mirror. Her dark curly hair was still bouncy, her lips full and her body firm. As yet, there were no lines on her face. In fact, she could easily pass for a woman ten years younger. But that brought her little consolation, since her biological clock was still relentlessly ticking. She'd always suspected that the problem lay with her, and she'd been meaning to visit her doctor about it . . . Now, since she was a widow in her mid thirties, there seemed little point.

At last, in the dark brooding solitude of her home, she had to face reality. As she stared through her kitchen window into the woodland beyond, she wondered how she would cope. Owing to the shock of John's sudden death, she hadn't given any thought to her financial situation, and had used up all her savings on an unnecessarily elaborate funeral. But now that reality was setting in again, she was realising that she'd need to get back to work soon.

Since arriving in London, she'd been employed as a chemist in the laboratory of the local canning factory, and the company had been very supportive in letting her take off as much time as she wanted. But she really needed to earn some money. While the mortgage on her house was now paid off, and she'd receive a small pension from John's job, there wouldn't be enough for more than a very basic lifestyle. Besides, returning to work would occupy her mind and distract her from the loneliness that had enveloped her since John had passed away.

"Hello, Ellie – how are you today?"

"Fine thanks, Tony – and you?"

"All the better for seeing you!" he replied, smiling warmly at her.

Ellie ignored the innuendo in Tony Coleman's greeting as she selected samples for testing from the factory production line. While she didn't mind exchanging chat or banter with the factory manager, she didn't want to give him any encouragement. Since he was the only available man in the factory and she was now a widow, he seemed to assume that they shared some indefinable bond. Which she certainly had no wish to foster. Tony was a nice man and she'd be happy to have him as a friend, but nothing more.

At first, Ellie had been secretly pleased that someone found her attractive – it was balm to her ego after becoming a widow and feeling all alone in the world. However, she'd quickly realised that Tony was a plodder whose conversation ran only to football, beer and the factory, and she suspected he'd be awkward talking about personal matters. He'd never be a soul mate, and she needed a lot more than he could ever give her.

Her husband John had been closer to her ideal than Tony could ever be, but even he hadn't been able to fill the gnawing hunger for passion that raged inside her. Nevertheless she'd loved John dearly, and she'd gladly have settled for a mediocre but essentially good marriage if she could only have him back.

The women on the production line were sharing gossip and jokes as the cans made their way along the conveyor belt towards the out-of-date but still functional machine that would finally seal the lids.

One of the women winked at Ellie as she walked past with her samples, announcing loudly: "Our Tony's a fine cut of a man, love – you could do worse!"

Ellie grinned back, well aware that they were only winding her up. But while she enjoyed the women's banter, she wasn't so keen on their teasing about Tony, because he seemed to view this teasing *as some kind of proof that they were ultimately destined for each other.*

It was now almost a year since John had died, and during that time she'd gradually come to terms with her solitary life. She'd worked hard and been promoted – she was now second-in-command in the laboratory, with a salary to match. But coming home each evening to an empty house always made her think of what might have been.

She'd taken to reading to fill the lonely hours, but the books she read only made her feel more dissatisfied. She'd never experienced the heady passion she read about in her books. Did it really exist, she wondered? While John had been kind and loving, he'd never excited her in the way she longed to feel.

It was also increasingly unlikely that she'd ever bear a child. With no man on the horizon and her fertility undoubtedly on the wane, even her desire for motherhood wouldn't allow her to settle for someone like Tony Coleman. Would she ever experience the kind of passion she longed for, or would she go to her own grave a lonely and barren old woman?

CHAPTER 3

In a sumptuous room off the hotel lobby, the champagne reception was in full swing. Laura smiled appreciatively at her new husband, who was talking to some friends of his from the badminton club – Jeff looked so handsome in his dress suit, his blond hair curling over his ears, his eyes a little glazed from all the champagne he'd been drinking.

"Congratulations – you look radiant, Laura!" her lecturer colleague Maria said, giggling as she emptied her champagne glass and deftly grabbed another from a passing waiter. "Jeff's such a handsome guy – and a stockbroker to boot – some women have all the luck!"

Laura nodded. She couldn't be happier, and she loved being surrounded by all her colleagues on this very special day. She smiled as she watched Timmy, another lecturer from the Sociology Department, trying to impress Greta, the department secretary, with his version of the moonwalk, which wasn't an easy feat, given the amount of champagne he'd already consumed. Several of Kerry's colleagues from Sea Diagnostics, the engineering company where she was a partner, were also hovering around the bar. Laura waved across the room to Kerry's colleagues Norma and Jack, who were involved in some kind of shot-drinking competition, and she suspected there would be quite a few hangovers needing a cure the following day!

She glanced across at Jeff, who was now talking to Kerry, and she was glad that her best friend and husband seemed to be chatting together happily. It was so important to her that they got along. She was well aware of Kerry's apathy towards Jeff but, hopefully, once her friend got to know her husband, she'd realise what a sweetie he was.

Professor Darren Coyle, head of the university's Sociology Department, sidled up and slipped an arm around Laura. His thick glasses were askew, his normally neat dark hair was falling untidily over his forehead and he was well inebriated from the champagne. Laura felt a surge of affection for him as they hugged. She was pleased to have him with her on such an important day.

"You look the picture of happiness, Laura!" he slurred, planting a kiss on her cheek. "I hope you won't let Jeff take you away from us? You know how much we all love working with you!"

"Of course not!" Laura told him, smiling. "I love my job too much."

For a moment, Darren looked puzzled. "Oh. I thought Jeff said something about you giving up work –"

Laura shook her head. "Definitely not. I think you might have got that wrong, Darren. It'll take more than marriage to prise me away from all of you!"

On the other side of the room, Jeff was still in conversation with Kerry.

As he looked down triumphantly at her, he raised his glass of champagne. "Now Laura's mine – all mine!"

Kerry smiled. "Congratulations to you both!" she said, choosing not to let him know that she'd got his message. In effect, he was telling her that since Laura was now his, he'd soon see to it that he became the centre of her universe, and that his new wife would have little time left to spend with her friend.

Kerry kept the smile on her face as she walked across to the bar to top up her champagne glass. She'd be there when Laura needed her, as she suspected she eventually would. Kerry had no doubt that Jeff would at some point reach his sell-by date. But Laura would be the last to realise it.

After a pleasant reception, a delightful wedding meal and a cheery send-off from all their friends and colleagues, Jeff and Laura returned to Jeff's luxurious apartment.

"I just wish my family had been there today," Laura said wistfully as she closed the front door. "That would have been the icing on the cake . . ."

"You're lucky to have no family!" Jeff retorted angrily. "My parents beat me constantly, so I'm grateful that *they* weren't there!"

Laura was stunned and more than a little shocked by his remark. It seemed particularly thoughtless to dismiss the loss of her parents and brother so insensitively. But she supposed he himself was hurting and hadn't realised how cruel it sounded. Hers had been a loving family, whereas Jeff had only ever known violence.

Suddenly, being back in the apartment seemed such an anti-climax after all the excitement of the wedding.

"Did you say anything to Darren about me giving up work?"

Jeff shrugged his shoulders. "Well, I might have mentioned that we'll be starting a family soon, and then you won't have time to work."

Laura looked at him incredulously. "Jeff, whether I work or not when we have kids will be a shared decision! I'll probably prefer to keep up my lecturing, and use the university crèche for our children. Anyway, we'll decide that together when the time comes."

Jeff said nothing, then he turned to her eagerly. "But you're going to take my name, aren't you?"

Laura looked at him in surprise. "Well, no, I wasn't intending to. I mean, I'm known in my profession as Laura Thornton – I'd rather not confuse things."

Jeff looked hurt. "But I want us to be a single, loving family unit! Won't it be odd for our children if their parents have different names?"

Laura smiled mischievously. "Well then, why don't you take my name? Then we can all be Thorntons!"

Jeff scowled. "Maybe I should just change my name to 'hen-pecked' and be done with it!"

Laura smiled. "Why is it okay for a woman to change her name, but not a man?"

Jeff shrugged his shoulders, but didn't answer. Then he began hassling her again. "Seriously, wouldn't it be better if we were all called Jones?" he wheedled.

He looked so earnest that Laura had to smile. "Look, I'll think about it," she replied. "But I really don't see why it's so important –"

"Well, if it's not so important to you, why don't you just agree, since it matters so much to me? Oh please, Laura, I want us all to share the same name, and be a real family!"

Knowing Jeff's own history, Laura relented. If creating their own little family unit was so important to him, then maybe she should be willing to give way on this one. After all, wasn't marriage all about compromise? Besides, his insistence made her feel cherished – he was obviously looking towards a long and happy future together.

"Okay, then. I'll become Laura Jones."

"Oh, love, you don't know how happy that makes me!" Jeff said, his eyes alight with joy. "I feel as though you're really going to be mine now! Oh Laura, I love you so much! Let's hope we'll have lots of little Joneses as well!"

Laura smiled as he hugged her tightly. It was really such a small thing to do, yet it made Jeff so happy. And she was pleased that she could make him feel good. After his awful childhood, she wanted so much to make up for it and to help him build a wonderful future with her.

CHAPTER 4

Ellie rode her bicycle home from work, sensing that there was something definitely wrong with the front wheel. It was wobbling too freely, and she decided that at the earliest opportunity she'd take it to the village bicycle store. Perhaps it needed a new tyre, or the wheel frame had possibly become slightly bent. There were so many stones on this stretch of the road, all of them waiting to snare unwary cyclists . . .

Deep in thought, she didn't hear the car approaching until it was almost level with her. It gave her such a fright as it swept past that she and the bicycle wobbled dangerously, teetering for a few seconds before veering sideways and crashing into the ditch.

"Aaagh!" Covered in debris, and with her bicycle clearly beyond repair, Ellie surveyed the mess. Her clothes were dishevelled, and she was having difficulty extracting the twigs that had become knotted in her curly hair.

"Are you okay?" said a voice, and Ellie found herself looking up into a pair of dark-brown eyes.

"Does it look as though I'm okay?" she retorted. "I don't usually choose to dress in muddy clothes, and wear half a tree in my hair!"

As she struggled to extricate herself from the muddy ditch, a hand gripped hers firmly and pulled her up, and Ellie recognised the owner of the factory where she worked – Alan Thornton, or 'Mr Alan' as the employees called him.

"You're Ms Beckworth from the laboratory, aren't you?"

She nodded, raising her eyebrows. "I'm surprised you know who I am. I mean, you've got hundreds of employees."

"Who couldn't help noticing you? You're gorgeous," he said, smiling.

"Well, I'm not exactly at my best right this minute," she said tartly, continuing to pick leaves and debris from her hair and clothes. "But then again, I don't usually make a habit of spending my time in ditches."

Alan smiled down at her, and she noticed how very tall he was. "I'll pop your bike in the boot, and give you a lift home," he said, effortlessly hoisting it out of the ditch. "It's the least I can do – I feel responsible for what happened – it's obvious that I drove too close to your bike and gave you a fright."

"Thank you," Ellie said, climbing into the front passenger seat and hoping she wouldn't leave too much debris and mud in his pristine car. The interior was magnificent, and she looked appreciatively at the leather seat covers and the elaborate walnut-and-chrome dashboard.

"Very nice," she said, running her hand along the edge of her seat. "How the other half live, eh?"

He laughed. "It's not even mine – all the company cars are leased."

"Well, I'd be happy to drive something like this, even if it wasn't technically mine," she replied, trailing her hand along the dashboard's walnut fascia. "Right now, I don't even have a bike!"

"Don't worry, I'll take care of that," Alan said, starting the engine and pulling out into the road. "I'll order a replacement bike right away."

"Well, if you're feeling generous, maybe you'd get me a leasehold car instead of a bike?" Ellie said, smiling impishly at him.

He laughed. "The fall doesn't seem to have affected your brain, does it? You've still got all your wits about you!" He smiled at her kindly. "How are you managing – it's about a year since your husband died, isn't it?"

Ellie nodded, surprised once again that he knew so much about her. Then she remembered that she'd seen him at John's funeral, and had considered it a nice gesture that the company's owner had bothered to attend a mere employee's husband's funeral.

"I'm fine, thanks," she told him. "Anyway, work keeps me busy."

Alan darted a glance in her direction. "If the fall's genuinely shaken you a bit, please don't hurry back to the laboratory tomorrow," he told her. "I'll tell the chief chemist, that it was my fault you're not able to come to work."

Ellie gave him a scornful look. "Do I look like some ridiculously dim damsel in distress? It would take more than a fall off my bike to wind me!"

"Yes," he said softly, "I can see that now. You strike me as quite a remarkable woman."

As Alan turned in off the road and drove up Ellie's driveway, he whistled in admiration. "Wow – I'd no idea there was a house tucked away in here – it's so secluded! And you've quite a bit of woodland behind the house, too. It's lovely! I really like the veranda, too."

"Thank you." Ellie smiled sadly to herself. She and John had bought the house and large garden with a future family in mind.

As the car drew up outside the front door, Ellie hesitated, unsure what to do.

"Would you like some tea?" she asked.

"Yes, please."

In the kitchen she filled the kettle, knowing that Alan was watching her, and it made her feel intimidated and excited all at once. To have such a powerful and attractive man looking at her was a strange yet heady feeling. At the same time, she felt embarrassed at her untidiness, and hurriedly tucked a stray hair behind her ear. She knew she must look a fright.

"Here – there's a bit of grass stuck behind your ear."

Suddenly, he was beside her, removing the offending grass and placing it in her outstretched hand. It seemed such an intimate thing to do, as though they'd known each other for a long time.

"Oh, thanks."

Flustered, she took the piece of grass and dropped it into the bin beside the worktop.

"I must look a mess," she said self-consciously. "Excuse me – while the kettle's boiling, I'll just go to the bathroom and tidy up –"

She felt his hand on her arm, restraining her, and it seemed to sear through her skin.

"You don't need to do anything – you look lovely the way you are," he said softly.

His eyes searched her face, and she felt herself drowning. When he reached out and touched her face, she felt as though her whole body was on fire. He seemed to know it, because he said softly, "I'm married," as though waiting for permission to advance his suit.

She nodded. "I know," she said, trying to smile. "All the best ones are usually taken."

"It doesn't stop me wanting you."

He didn't remove his hand from her arm, and she didn't move from where she was standing – so close to him that she could feel his breath. She shivered with excitement. It had been so long since a man had touched her. In fact, she'd never wanted any man to touch her as much as she now wanted this man to touch her. Desire raced through her like a forest fire, and she found herself longing to be one with him.

He took another step closer, which meant they were actually touching, and she stood still, as though unable to move. Her heart was racing and she felt certain he must hear it.

"I want to kiss you," he whispered, and she had no time to reply before his lips found hers and she was kissing him back.

It was as though that first kiss had ignited a raging fire in both of them. Her hands were suddenly all over his body and his were on hers, and she was aching for more. Like two people possessed, they began tearing off each other's clothes, leaving a trail of garments across the kitchen and hall as she led him upstairs to her bedroom.

In a frenzy of desire, they kissed and explored each other's naked bodies, unable to get enough of each other. And each time he took her, she reached a shuddering crescendo of pleasure.

Later, as they lay sated, their bodies drenched with sweat, they looked at each other and smiled shyly.

19

"I'm not going to apologise," he said, kissing her nose. "You are the most exciting woman I've ever met, and I want to make love to you over and over and over again . . ."

"Then I'll have to make sure my bike breaks down more often!" she said impishly.

Suddenly, his voice was husky again. "Do I need an excuse to make love to you? Please tell me I can visit you again tomorrow?"

"Yes," she whispered.

"In fact –" he said, leaning towards her, "I don't think I can wait till tomorrow."

As he reached for her, desire coursed through her again. And even though she was exhausted from their earlier coupling, he brought her to ecstasy once more.

The following evening, just as she arrived home from work, a delivery van arrived and deposited a shiny new state-of-the-art bicycle with five-speed gears at her front door. An envelope was taped to the front basket, and as soon as the deliveryman had gone, she tore it open with shaking hands and pulled out the note inside. It read: "I'm so glad you came crashing into my life yesterday. I can't wait to see you again." He'd signed his initial at the bottom.

Clasping the note to her chest, she felt a surge of joy running through her body. Yesterday clearly meant as much to him as it had to her. All day at work she'd been thinking of him, and when she'd caught a glimpse of him in his office as she walked by, her heart had leaped in her chest with joy.

Because of her excitement, Ellie didn't give much thought to the fact that this was a seminal moment in her life. There was still time to alter its course. But she silenced the warning bells that reminded her he was married, and the father of a young son. The excitement she felt – the feeling of being more alive than she'd ever felt before – negated everything else.

CHAPTER 5

Darren looked at her uncertainly. "You're changing your name?"

Laura nodded. "Yes. Now that I'm married, I want to be known as Laura Jones."

Her boss chewed his lip as he studied her across his vast desk in the Sociology Department. "Isn't that a bit drastic? I mean, you've been lecturing here for what – nearly ten years? Everyone knows you as Laura Thornton. Why would you change it?" He fiddled with his pen. "Surely you can keep your professional name separate? Can't you just be Mrs Jones in your private life?"

"I'll never be 'just' Mrs Jones!" Laura said hotly. "I'm proud to be changing my name. Jeff and I will eventually start a family, so it'll be best if we all share the same name."

Darren grimaced, hearing echoes of someone else's words. He cared about Laura very much. She'd always been a strong, independent woman – a little impulsive, but an efficient and valuable member of his staff, and he wasn't at all happy about what was happening to her.

Darren made it clear that he wasn't pleased. "This is going to involve quite a lot of paperwork," he muttered. "It might take me quite a while to get it all done."

"It's not that big a deal, Darren – if the passport people can do it, why can't you?" she replied, annoyed.

Darren looked at her incredulously. "You've changed your passport already?"

Laura coloured. "Well no, not yet. But I'm going to. Soon. Jeff and I will probably take a short honeymoon later in the year."

Darren continued to stare at her, his eyes like an owl's behind his thick-framed glasses.

"During the summer break," she added, letting him know that she didn't intend to further inconvenience him by asking for time off.

Laura was growing more and more annoyed at having to defend her decision. She'd encountered surprise and incredulity when she'd announced her change of name to colleagues and friends. In fact, several people had made veiled suggestions that the decision hadn't entirely been hers. It made her very hot under the collar. Surely it was no one's concern but hers and Jeff's?

Kerry had given a short derisive laugh when told of the name change, then had tried to cover it up by changing the subject. Laura wished everyone could just be happy for her. She and Jeff were building a future together – she was simply changing her name to show her commitment to him and to their future together.

Darren adjusted his glasses. "Have you told the others in the department yet?"

"I mentioned it to Maria, and I saw Timmy in the canteen –"

"What did they think?"

Laura felt embarrassed and angry all at once. She didn't need to justify her actions to anyone. "They're happy for me – what else would you expect?"

In fact, both her colleagues had been surprised, although Timmy had had the good grace to try and hide it. Maria had been more direct. "W-haaat?" she'd screeched. "Are you losing your marbles, Thornton? Oh sorry, I mean 'Jones'!"

Darren grimaced. "Well, Laura, I guess it's your decision."

"Yes, it is," she said evenly. There was no point in getting annoyed with her boss, because he was the best in the world and she loved working with him. He'd come round before long.

With a deep sigh, Darren began shuffling papers around on his desk. "Well, I'm always here if you ever want to talk."

Laura could feel the anger rising inside her. "About what?" she asked sharply, knowing full well what Darren meant.

"Anything," he said, looking straight at her. "My door is always open."

Laura nodded as she stood up to leave. It seemed appropriate to thank Darren at this point, but she didn't, since it might imply that she was thanking him for the open offer to talk, which she didn't need. He seemed to be inferring that she might want to discuss Jeff and problems he imagined they might be having. Which they weren't.

As Laura left the room, Darren sighed, finding that a Shakespearean quote summed up his feelings exactly. "*The lady doth protest too much, methinks,*" he muttered to himself as he heard the door close.

As she made her way down the corridor to her own office, Laura felt annoyed and unsettled. She was only changing her name, for heaven's sake. Why did people seem to think it represented a whole lot more? Clearly no one was happy about it. Except Jeff.

As she thought of her new husband, her heart soared with joy. They'd prove everyone wrong. She immediately ordered a new plaque for her office door that would say: '*Dr Laura Jones*'. Eventually she and Jeff would have several little Joneses, and they'd all live happily ever after. At last she'd be part of a family again.

CHAPTER 6

As they curled up together in Ellie's bed, Alan stroked his lover's cheek tenderly. They'd been seeing each other daily for several weeks now, and each bout of lovemaking was just as exciting as the last.

Even going to work each morning was proving exhilarating. Ellie felt like a teenager in the throes of first love, and she lived for occasional glimpses of Alan in his office. He, too, had started coming to the laboratory on flimsy pretexts, and Ellie feared that someone would soon notice how deeply she blushed whenever he entered the room.

"This has got to stop," Ellie begged him. "Someone is going to notice before long. I find myself wanting to touch you all the time."

Alan had agreed with her. "But I can't stay away from you! We're going to have to find a way of spending more time together."

And now Alan felt he'd found it.

"If you continue working at the factory, someone will figure out our relationship before long." He grinned mischievously. "The problem is, I can't take my eyes off you at work. I keep finding excuses to speak to you, and each time I see you on your way to the canteen with your colleagues, I want to whisk you away for a long intimate lunch with me!" His eyes twinkled. "How can I keep myself away from you? You're like a fatal addiction – I want to reach out and hug you every time we're near – and I'm sure someone will cop on eventually." He ran his fingers up and down her naked spine. "On the other hand, if you were to leave the factory, I could visit you any time – at lunchtime, in the afternoon, in the evening – and no one would ever know."

As she opened her mouth to protest, he silenced her with a kiss. "Of course, I'd continue to pay your wages, so you'd maintain the same lifestyle as before. But we could then spend much more time together. What do you think?"

Ellie considered his offer. In truth, she didn't particularly enjoy working in the laboratory. The chief chemist was a dour individual, and the atmosphere wasn't as conducive to jokes or banter as on the factory floor. Yet she needed an income.

"Let me think about it," she said. But already her mind was made up. Why be employed if she could have the same lifestyle with far less effort? She'd be able to devote her life to loving Alan full-time. Because by now, she'd admitted to herself that she was deeply in love with him.

Luckily, she'd never made any close friends at the factory. The laboratory staff were few in number, and contact with the factory workers was limited to the times when she collected batch samples for testing. And since she'd been married for all of the time she'd been working there, she'd gone straight home to John at the end of the day. She'd never made a habit of going to the staff club or local pub as many of the others did. So she'd never really been involved in the sharing of factory gossip and shop talk that formed the basis of so many workplace friendships.

Now all that could work to her advantage. Other than factory manager Tony Coleman – who was always trying to talk to her – the others left her more or less alone. If she gave up working at the factory, she wouldn't need to worry about a trail of visitors to her home to disrupt her secret relationship with Alan.

"Okay, I'll do it," she said, her eyes shining. "I'll leave the factory."

Alan hugged her. "Oh love, it's going to be wonderful! We'll be able to create our own little world here in your home, where no one else can touch us."

Everyone at the factory was surprised to hear that Ellie was leaving to set up her own home-tutoring business, and her departure was the subject of gossip for a day or two, before a juicier topic came along to occupy them. Ellie smiled to herself as she lied to them about her plans to provide one-to-one private tuition classes in science subjects from her home. If they really knew why she was leaving, they'd definitely have something juicy to gossip about!

Ellie opted to work out her month's notice so as not to arouse any suspicion, but those last few weeks in the laboratory seemed to go by so slowly. The chief chemist was his usual dour self, ensuring that she did a full day's work each day right up until five on her last day. Then he smiled for the first time since she'd worked there, and wished her well before heading off home. Clearly, attending her leaving party at the factory's social club was far too frivolous for him!

Not so for the company's boss – Alan was one of the first to arrive, and he bought drinks for everyone before making a short speech about Ellie's value as an employee, how much she'd be missed, and wishing her well in her new business venture. After a round of applause from all her colleagues, Tony Coleman claimed her for a dance as the small combo in the corner began playing. Soon, the small dance floor was crowded, but Ellie could feel Alan's eyes on her as she and Tony jived. She knew he'd be trying his best not to look at her, but he'd be unable to help himself.

Tony was particularly attentive as they made their way back to the bar after their dance.

"Who exactly will you be tutoring?" he asked eagerly. "Maybe I could give you a helping hand if you need to convert a room into a classroom –"

"Thanks, Tony, but it's all sorted," Ellie told him, smiling. Although his attentions were irritating, she was glad Alan could see that another man obviously found her attractive.

Everyone was buying her farewell drinks, and Ellie knew she was drinking far more wine than she should, but this was her own special night, and she was excited at being on the threshold of a new and exciting life.

As the combo switched tempo and began playing jazz, Tony appeared again and dragged her onto the dance floor. Alan was talking to some of the factory workers standing at the bar, but Ellie knew he'd still be watching her.

She was enjoying the heady sensation of being the focus of two men's attention. And she was now deliberately flirting with Tony as he whirled her round the dance floor. She wanted to make Alan jealous. She wanted him to know that she could be with other men if she wanted to, but that she'd chosen to be with him instead.

Exhausted and exhilarated after the dance, Ellie returned to the bar, with Tony still hovering eagerly in the background.

Alan was suddenly by her side, his expression bland although she knew from the intensity in his eyes that he was deliberately affecting a mild demeanour for the occasion.

"You've no idea how jealous of Tony I am!" he whispered. "He seems to be monopolising all your time tonight, and there's nothing I can do about it." He smiled impishly. "But I can't fault his taste in women!" Then he spoke more loudly for effect. "Can I get you a drink, Ms Beckworth?"

"Thanks – I'll have a glass of white wine, please."

Having procured the drink from the barman, Alan handed it to Ellie.

"You shouldn't be looking so happy," Ellie whispered teasingly. "After all, you're losing a valuable employee!"

"Sorry," he said ruefully, although it was clear he wasn't sorry at all, "but I'm starting a whole new secret life with the woman I love. So I'm finding it hard to hide my excitement."

Just then, Tony muscled his way to the bar again, and seized Ellie for another dance. Laughing ruefully, she allowed him to lead her out onto the floor. Ellie could see that other groups of workers were nodding towards her and Tony. She could guess what they were saying – she and Tony were now pegged as a potential couple. Buoyed up by other people's observations and several pints of lager, Tony chanced placing a kiss on her cheek. Pretending not to notice, Ellie began to dance wildly, keeping as much distance between them as she could. She was beginning to regret flirting with Tony earlier, because he seemed to be assuming that there was now some connection between them. And since she and Alan had agreed that it would look better if she left on her own, she'd have to avoid any offer from Tony to share a taxi home.

Professing exhaustion, Ellie left Tony on the dance floor and unsteadily made her way back to the bar. It was now getting late, although there was no sign of the party winding down.

"Can you order a taxi for me?" she whispered urgently to Alan.

"Right away," he whispered back. Then he nodded towards Tony, who was still teetering around on the dance floor. "I don't think your dancing partner is in any fit state to get himself home either!"

"Well, just make sure I'm not sharing a taxi with him," she whispered.

Nodding, Alan went off and phoned the local taxi company from the public phone in the club bar. By now, Ellie was feeling very dizzy. She was aware that she'd drunk far too much because of the euphoria she was feeling at the thought of beginning a new life devoted solely to Alan. But now all she wanted was to get home and go to bed.

When her taxi finally arrived, Ellie slipped quietly out of the social club without saying goodbye. It was easier this way. In the warmth of the taxi, she sat back and hazily considered her future. One segment of her life was finally ending, but another much more exciting one was just beginning.

CHAPTER 7

"For God's sake – what happened?"

Laura looked embarrassed and defensive as she walked into Kerry's apartment.

"Nothing – I hit my head off one of the kitchen cupboards."

"No, you didn't – did Jeff do this to you?"

Laura glared at her. "No, of course not! Why would you think that?"

Kerry ushered Laura into the kitchen, urged her into a chair, and turned on the kettle to make coffee. As she took down two mugs from the rack above the stove, she surreptitiously surveyed her friend, noting the livid red patch, already turning blue, that ran the length of her face, and which Laura was trying to hide by pulling her blonde hair across it. Kerry was well aware that no accidental bump would inflict such a huge amount of damage.

Placing a cup of coffee in front of her friend, Kerry sat down beside her. "Laura, you're a strong woman – you don't have to put up with this!"

At first, Kerry thought her friend was going to continue denying what had happened, but her kind words seemed to cut through the wall Laura had initially tried to build around herself. Suddenly, she was sobbing, and Kerry put her arms around her, saying nothing, just letting her friend cry uninhibitedly. Gently, she patted Laura's back in a gesture that might be used to soothe a troubled child.

"You know what you have to do, don't you?" Kerry said at last.

Laura rested her head on Kerry's shoulder. "I can't leave him –

he's been so cruelly treated by his family in the past – I'm his family now, and if I leave him that will just prove that he can't trust anyone!"

Kerry shook her gently. "But you can't let a man hit you – once they start, it gets worse each time. And there will be another time, believe me. And another. You must get out now, love – before something really bad happens to you."

"I can't, Kerry, I just can't. I made my vows for better or worse – I want to help him through this rough patch. It will be okay, I promise – nothing bad is going to happen. Jeff and I will get through this. All I have to do is prove to him that I love him and won't leave him. Then things will settle down."

Kerry grimaced. "People don't hurt the ones they love. This shouldn't be happening to you, Laura."

Wiping away her tears, Laura looked defiant. "Stop going on at me! I've made my choice – I want to be with Jeff! He's my husband, and I intend spending the rest of my life with him! It was nothing – just a silly argument, and now I'm sorry I said anything to you about it."

"What exactly happened?"

"Oh, nothing really. I wasn't feeling well – I've been feeling a bit queasy in the mornings – and I hadn't squeezed the oranges for our early-morning juice. He got annoyed with me, and one thing led to another."

"So he hit you."

"No, it wasn't like that – I complained about being asked to do it, and Jeff just over-reacted. He was very sorry afterwards."

Kerry was well aware that Laura was giving her a tightly edited version of the truth, but she saw no point in pushing it. Her own imagination could fill in the gaps. But she was instantly alert to Laura's mention of being sick in the mornings.

"You're not pregnant, are you?"

Laura looked surprised. "I don't think so – why?"

"You mentioned getting sick in the mornings, so I was just a bit worried –"

"Why would you be worried?"

"Well, it might be better if you didn't get pregnant immediately, at least until you've sorted things out between you and Jeff. Because if you have a child now, you'll be tied to him forever."

Laura looked annoyed. "I want to be tied to him forever! Jeff wants kids and so do I. He'll probably settle down once we have a family."

"And if he doesn't? You told me what his father was like. Jeff seems to be repeating his father's version of what family life is."

Laura bridled. "That's not fair! Anyway, since when did you qualify in psychology?"

Kerry grimaced. There was only so far she could go in criticising Jeff before she would alienate Laura. Maybe she'd crossed the line already. But she was well aware that things were more likely to go downhill rather than improve. If a marriage wasn't good at the beginning, there was little hope that it would improve later.

"Well, you know that I'm here for you, day or night. If anything goes wrong, lift the phone and call me. On second thoughts, forget the phone – just get out and come here straight away."

Laura shook her head vehemently. "It isn't like that – you're making a mountain out of a molehill. Look, I'm going home. Thanks for the coffee."

Kerry smiled, trying to lighten the atmosphere. "No need to say thanks – you didn't even drink it."

CHAPTER 8

"Ms Beckworth? Ellie, are you in?"

Annoyed, Ellie recognised the voice. It was Tony Coleman from the factory. She'd been going to ignore the knocking on her front door, until she remembered that she'd left her new bike outside, so he'd know that she was in.

Ellie opened the front door. "Yes, Tony? What can I do for you?"

His face red, Tony hopped from one foot to the other, his hands behind his back, and Ellie could see that he was hiding a bouquet of flowers.

"Just checking to see that you're okay, now that you've left the factory," he mumbled. "Everyone misses you, and since I was out for a stroll during my lunch hour, I thought I'd call and see if there was anything you needed –"

With a sigh, Ellie stepped aside and gestured for him to step inside. It would be bad manners to leave him standing on the doorstep, although she hoped his visit would be brief. He was clearly moving his interest in her up a notch, and she knew she'd eventually have to tell him she wasn't interested. She ushered him into the living room.

"Would you like a cup of tea, Tony?"

He nodded, his face suffused with relief. He wasn't being evicted straight away. He might even have enough time to explain his intentions.

In the kitchen, Ellie turned on the electric kettle, wondering how quickly she could get rid of him while leaving his dignity intact. Alan would be calling by in the early afternoon, and she needed time to take a shower and get changed into something sexy before he arrived.

Fortunately, Tony hadn't followed her into the kitchen, and she was grateful for the brief respite it gave her to martial her thoughts. She was fearful that Tony was about to launch into some kind of speech or declaration, and she wanted to make her position clear before he did, thus saving him any embarrassment.

She sighed. On the other hand, how did she explain her lack of interest in him when supposedly there wasn't anyone else in her life? Even if she claimed that she was still grieving for her late husband, she could imagine Tony trying to convince her that an occasional visit to the cinema together would lift her spirits and couldn't do any harm . . .

As she carried a tray laden with tea and biscuits into the living room, Tony was immediately on his feet, trying to help, dropping the flowers and only succeeding in getting in the way.

Without looking at him, Ellie poured the tea, anxious not to give him any encouragement. On the other hand, she had to admit that she'd been guilty of flirting with him at the party in the social club, in order to make Alan jealous. So she'd probably brought this unwelcome intrusion on herself.

Tony cleared his throat, the mug of tea undulating in one trembling hand, the bouquet of flowers now clutched in his other hand. "Ellie, you know that I really like you –"

Ellie's heart gave a jolt. Through the window behind Tony's head, she could see Alan's car turning into her driveway and heading towards the house, and there was no way she could warn him. Tony was babbling on about how much she meant to him, but she was no longer listening. Her heart was beating wildly at the thought of their affair being uncovered. Since Tony was making his intentions very clear, his hurt pride would probably ensure that everyone in the factory knew about her and Alan before long. How ironic to be unmasked after she'd actually left the factory! Ellie was having nightmares at the thought of an unsuspecting Alan entering the house and calling her darling, making some sexual comment or starting to take his clothes off in the hall, as he often did in readiness for their lovemaking.

As Tony continued to waffle, it occurred to Ellie that if she could get him outside onto the porch, Alan would have a chance of seeing him before he got out of his car. Although he couldn't now avoid speaking to Tony, it might give him time to think up some excuse as to why he was there.

"Tony, let's take our tea outside to the veranda," she said brightly, trying not to let her anxiety spread to her voice, and steering him outside before he had a chance to object. "It's a lovely day, isn't it? Oh goodness!" she added brightly. "That looks like Mr Alan's car! I wonder what he's doing here?"

By then, Alan's car was pulling up outside the veranda, and Ellie waited, terrified, to see how things would unfold.

"Oh, hello!" Alan said pleasantly, as he stepped out of the car. He didn't look in the slightest bit embarrassed, and he smiled first at Tony, then at Ellie. "Great weather today – I hope there's a heat wave on the way!" he said, stepping onto the veranda and shaking both their hands.

If anyone was ill at ease, it was Tony. He looked down at the bouquet of flowers he was still clutching, and his face turned red, since his intentions towards Ellie were now perfectly clear.

Alan turned to Ellie, took an envelope from his pocket and handed it to her. "I brought the balance of your wages, and the holiday pay you're owed, Ms Beckworth."

"Oh, thank you, Mr Alan – that's very kind of you," said Ellie, grateful that he'd quickly assessed the situation and slipped into 'boss' mode. "But really, there was no need for you to bring it in person."

"No trouble at all," Alan said smoothly. "I knew I'd be passing by on my way back from the city, and I thought I could save you the journey to collect it."

"Would you like some tea?" Ellie ventured, aware that they were both performing for Tony's sake, yet sensing that it would sound polite to make the gesture.

"No thanks, Ms Beckworth – I've got some contracts to go over with the company solicitors, so I need to be on my way."

"Well, thank you once again," Ellie said, glancing at Tony to see how he was reacting.

He was still standing there, as though frozen, looking awkward and still holding the bouquet of flowers.

"Tony, can I give you a lift back to the factory?" Alan asked, rather pointedly. "I'll be going past there, on my way to the solicitors."

Tony was torn by indecision. He'd come to make some sort of declaration, but it looked as though he wasn't going to get the opportunity.

He looked from one to the other, and seeing no encouragement on Ellie's face, he sighed, silently handed her the flowers and nodded to Alan.

"Okay, thanks, Mr Alan," he said, defeat written all over his face. He turned to Ellie, with a tortured look. "Goodbye, Ellie – maybe I'll call to see you again?"

"Thank you for the flowers, Tony – they're lovely," Ellie said, ignoring his query and smiling noncommittally, and Tony seemed to know that he'd lost the battle. He sighed and followed Alan out to his car.

After giving Tony a lift back to the factory, Alan returned, carrying a large bouquet – a much bigger and more expensive one than Tony's had been.

"Here are the flowers I couldn't give you earlier, my love," Alan said, grinning. "I had to leave them in the car and tell Tony that they were for my wife! Luckily, I had a few unused wages envelopes in the glove compartment, and I was able to fill one of them with the others to create a bulky package – were you impressed by my ability to improvise?"

Laughing, Ellie hugged him. The close call added even more passion to their lovemaking. Without any preliminaries, he took her with a ferocity that delighted her, as he seemed to be re-establishing his right to her body. "You're mine, all mine," he whispered repeatedly, as though he could wish away Tony's intentions towards her.

Afterwards, they laughed at how well they'd performed their roles, and how close they'd come to disaster. Then Alan looked serious.

"I can understand why Tony fancies you, love – what man wouldn't? You're adorable!" he said, his voice husky with desire. "But if he starts calling regularly, it could make things difficult for us." Then his face clouded over. "Unless, of course, you fancy him? If you do, I'll back off. After all, Tony is a good man, and a hard worker –"

Ellie smiled at him tenderly, feeling cherished by his concern. "Don't be silly, love – you're the only one I want," she confirmed, tweaking his nose as they cuddled up together. "Besides, we'll be together eventually, won't we?"

He nodded, still looking worried. "Sometimes I feel bad that I can't give you what you want," he said sadly. "In fact, I can't promise you anything for quite some time. I've incurred large debts just to keep the factory going, and it'll be a while before they can be cleared. Worse still, my debt is to Sylvia's father. Tony could at least offer you marriage straight away. Are you sure you want to wait? I'll understand if you don't –"

"I'm sure," she replied, kissing him passionately.

Never before had she been so excited by any man. Even a limited amount of time with him was preferable to a lifetime with somebody else. Ellie was willing to be available any time he needed her, and he was in her thoughts from each waking moment right through to the end of the day. Now that she'd found the man of her dreams, every breath she took seemed to be just for him. The loss of her husband over a year ago had seemed like the most tragic event at the time, but his death had inadvertently given her another chance to ultimately find Mr Right. And she'd definitely found him in Alan.

She smiled to herself as they snuggled up together, glancing at Alan as he dozed, his eyes closed and a look of contentment on his handsome face. This was the life she'd opted for, and no factory manager could dazzle her the way that her beloved Alan could. It felt good to be important to such an influential man. Besides, she felt certain he'd leave his wife eventually. When he'd repaid the loan to Sylvia's father, he'd be free at last. Then they'd be together forever.

She listened to Alan's gentle breathing, and watched as his eyelids now fluttered in sleep. It was nice to think that he could be a little jealous, but Alan was the only man for her.

CHAPTER 9

A few weeks later, a radiant Laura arrived at Kerry's apartment one evening after work.

"I've got wonderful news!" she told her friend. "I'm pregnant!"

"Congratulations!" Kerry said, hugging her tightly.

"Jeff is over the moon!" Laura told her. "He couldn't be nicer to me – he's treating me like a queen! He brings me breakfast in bed and the morning newspaper before he leaves for work. I couldn't be happier – I feel cherished and very special."

Kerry smiled noncommittally.

"That business earlier – it was just a silly mistake," Laura whispered. "Please forget about it, Kerry – Jeff never meant to hurt me."

Kerry hugged her again. "I'm happy for you, love. Are you hoping for a boy or a girl?"

Laura gave her a dazzling smile. "I'd love a little girl, but Jeff wants a boy. But I'll be happy just as long as it's a healthy baby."

Smiling, Kerry nodded. Perhaps she was being uncharitable, but she couldn't help wondering how Jeff would react if he didn't get the son he wanted. For Laura's sake, the baby had better be a boy.

Darren received the news with equanimity.

"Well, congratulations, Laura," he said, but there was no delight in his voice, and she felt oddly deflated by his response.

He stepped out from behind his big desk and hugged her, but she had the feeling that it was a sympathetic hug rather than a celebratory one, and she felt decidedly disturbed by it.

"I hope you'll be staying on?"

"Of course!" Laura assured him. "You know I love my job, and as long as you're willing to have me here, I'm happy to be here!" She smiled, willing him to smile back. "And when I come back after maternity leave, I'll be able to use the university crèche."

Darren nodded, but there was no smile forthcoming. "I wish you well, Laura," he said solemnly. "I hope that everything works out according to plan."

It was clear that Darren had terminated their discussion, and Laura felt disappointed by what she sensed was his disapproval. Why couldn't he be happy for her? Why couldn't everyone be happy for her?

As she left his office, she felt tense and stressed. It wasn't supposed to be like this. People were supposed to be pleased when someone became pregnant. But even Maria, Timmy and Greta had been less than enthusiastic when she'd told them in the canteen a little earlier. Was it because they suspected that Jeff had hit her in the past? She'd explained away her bruises as an accident, but she'd seen the knowing looks on her colleagues' faces, as though they'd seen straight through her lie.

She sensed that Kerry had reservations too. Well, she'd prove them all wrong. She and Jeff would live happily ever after, and this child of theirs would put the final seal on their happiness.

Returning to her office, Laura sat down at her desk and surveyed the pile of essays that needed marking. Yet try as she might, she couldn't focus her mind on them. She managed to struggle through the first few essays before deciding that it wasn't fair to the students since her mind was on other things. She turned to the window in her office and gazed out across the campus to the sports fields in the distance. She felt very much alone. Somehow her marriage and pregnancy were isolating her from her colleagues. Yet, in another sense, she'd always felt alone, ever since the death of her parents and brother.

But then she smiled, patting her belly. "At least I have you, little person," she whispered. "So I'm not really alone any more."

CHAPTER 10

As the months slipped by, Ellie's life developed a pleasant daily routine. Every workday afternoon, Alan would leave his office for a late lunch, and they would make love in her bedroom. He would stay as long as he dared. They simply couldn't get enough of each other.

But, as time went by, Ellie became more and more jealous of the woman who wore Alan's wedding ring. And she became increasingly unhappy about his vague promises to leave his wife and young son when the time was right.

"Look, love – my wife's father's money is the only reason that I still have the factory," Alan assured her as they lay in bed one afternoon. "If I divorce her now, her father will pull the plug and I'll lose everything." He looked at her tenderly. "Then I won't be able to pay your bills either. We just have to wait until the market's more stable – then it won't matter if they withdraw their capital – I'll be able to keep the business afloat on my own by then. Just have patience, love – please."

Ellie sighed, laying her head on his shoulder. She didn't have any other choice – he meant everything to her, and she would wait as he asked. After all, she was lucky to have someone who truly loved her, even if that love couldn't be publicly acknowledged yet. Many people went through their lives without ever experiencing the kind of love they shared, so she knew she had to be patient.

But Alan had a surprise for her. Reaching into his jacket pocket, he took out a little box and presented her with a thick stylish gold band inset with a huge diamond. On the inside, there was an inscription: 'Alan and Ellie forever'.

"Now you're my secret wife," he told her, sliding off her old wedding ring and slipping on the new. "This ring can be an engagement and wedding ring combined. I doubt if anyone else will notice the difference – but you and I will know what it signifies."

Ellie gazed at the ring, her heart full of love for him. "I doubt if anything this gorgeous will go unnoticed! Thank you, my love – wearing your ring means so much to me," she whispered fervently, raising her lips for his kiss. The ring made her feel a lot more confident about waiting for him now. As she gazed at her left hand, moving it about to let the large diamond catch the light, it seemed to confirm the intensity of their love. Some day very soon he truly would be hers.

She did, occasionally, feel guilty about Alan's wife, and for that reason she always kept her distance. Ellie occasionally saw her in the nearby village, wheeling her young son in his buggy. Sylvia had tried, on several occasions, to engage her in casual conversation – usually about the weather – but Ellie always made an excuse to get away. It was obvious that Sylvia was just trying to be neighbourly, but Ellie didn't want to be forced into an introduction. Nor did she want to acknowledge Alan's child, since the boy would only remind her that another woman had been able to give him something she never could.

Besides, how on earth could she chat normally to Sylvia? She was making love to the woman's husband behind her back, and hoping to take him from her! Anyway, she wanted to keep their own little world separate and private. She didn't want to be part of this other life that Alan lived. In a way, she feared that the contrasting circumstances between his other life and hers might make her bitter. Although they only lived within half a mile of each other, his wife and family lived in a world of opulence compared to hers, no doubt with crystal chandeliers in their drawing room and two cars in the garage. They dined in expensive restaurants and attended grand dinners at city hall. Although she knew he hated every minute of these events, she longed to be the woman by his side, greeting the mayor, dressed in the latest fashions and having all the other women envy her.

But after these events, he'd hurry back to her little house as often as he could, peeling off his formal attire and throwing himself naked onto the bed. "God, how I hate all those stuffy people, and the stuffy clothes I have to wear!" he'd say, and she'd take him in her arms and make everything right again. But then he'd have to dress afterwards, and head home to the woman who rightly expected him to be in her bed every night.

Now, as he kissed her forehead, she felt a new confidence in their future together.

"Someday soon, I'll show you off to the world, dressed in the finest clothing money can buy," he whispered.

It was the waiting for these glory days that was so painful. Occasionally she'd wish that Sylvia and her son would simply vanish into the ether. Then she'd feel guilty, since she didn't actually wish them any harm. But she couldn't help longing for the day when Alan would secure his company's future, and his wife's money would no longer be needed.

CHAPTER 11

"Sea Diagnostics is having a reception next week, and we're invited," Laura told her husband enthusiastically. "Kerry's very excited because one of their design teams has won a contract to develop a new type of sub-sea cable. Isn't it great?"

Laura glanced at Jeff, who stared back at her impassively. He wasn't showing any enthusiasm for this very important event in her friend's life.

"Well, I'm going anyway," Laura said, when she got no reply. "Everyone at Sea Diagnostics is thrilled, and I want to be there to wish them well."

"What are you planning on wearing to the reception?"

Laura smiled, pleased that Jeff was beginning to show some interest.

"I was thinking of the blue dress – you know, the one with the embroidered flower detail around the neck. What do you think?"

Jeff grimaced. "Isn't the skirt a bit short? Why don't you wear your maxi dress?"

Laura raised her eyebrows. "Are you serious? I was going to donate that old thing to a charity shop – it's terribly drab and conservative. I don't know why I ever bought it."

"Well, I love it," Jeff said. "You look very ladylike in it."

Laura raised her eyebrows again. She hadn't heard anyone use the word 'ladylike' in years. It had a distinctly sexist feel about it.

"I have no wish to look 'ladylike', as you call it," she replied sharply.

"Well, now that you're my wife, and going to have my baby, I expect you to dress accordingly," Jeff said stubbornly. "I don't want the woman I chose to be regarded as a slut."

"Jeff!" Laura was appalled. "Why would anyone think that?"

"I'm a man, for Christ's sake – I know how men think! I don't want anyone having thoughts about screwing you. You're my wife, so I have to protect you."

"Jeff, I don't need protection – and certainly not from someone's thoughts! Anyway, none of us can control what other people think."

"Well, there's no point in giving them the opportunity to think about you in that way," he said sullenly. Then he brightened. "Tell you what – why don't I buy you a new dress for the occasion! I'm free this afternoon if you are – why don't we go shopping?"

Laura was pleased to see that Jeff's mood had changed for the better. Luckily, she had no lectures that afternoon – only end-of-term papers to correct, and they could wait.

"Okay," she said cheerfully. "Let's hit the town!"

The reception was in full swing when Laura and Jeff arrived.

At first Kerry didn't recognise her friend in the distance – she didn't look remotely like the Laura she knew so well. At the earliest opportunity, while Jeff was queuing at the free bar, Kerry sidelined her friend and gave her a long hard look.

"Where on earth did you get that dress? It's certainly not your usual style," she said.

"Don't you like it?" Laura said, disappointed. "Jeff chose it for me."

Kerry raised her eyebrows. "I didn't know Jeff was interested in women's fashion."

Laura blushed. "Well, he wanted me to have something nice for the party tonight."

"But you never wear anything like that." Kerry took a deep breath. "If I'm honest, it's downright frumpy. You usually wear much more glamorous stuff."

Laura looked at the floor. "Well, Jeff doesn't like me to look too sexy – he says that other men will think I'm cheap. He doesn't want his wife being looked at in that way."

Kerry laughed harshly. "Next, he'll have you wearing a burqa! He should be proud to be married to a sexy, attractive woman!"

Laura's cheeks were red. It was clear that she wasn't overjoyed about the situation either.

"To be honest, Jeff is a bit insecure," she confided. "You know he's had a terrible childhood, and never felt loved by his parents, so I'm trying to make sure he knows I care. If wearing this makes him feel more confident about my love, then I'll gladly do it."

Kerry said nothing. Jeff was clearly a control freak. Laura had already changed her name to please him, and now he was trying to turn her into a non-person as well.

As Jeff rejoined the two women, carrying two fresh glasses of wine, Kerry gave them a cursory wave and hurried off to greet some new arrivals.

"What did *she* want?" Jeff muttered, staring sourly after her retreating back as he handed his wife a glass of wine.

Laura sighed. It was unlikely that her husband and best friend would ever warm to each other.

"Strangely enough, she wanted to make sure that we were enjoying the reception," she said evenly. "After all, we're here because Sea Diagnostics has won such a lucrative contract."

As they stood among the throng of guests, Laura was trying her best to look happy. But it was proving impossible because Jeff was now criticising everyone's clothing, the finger food being served and the product being launched, although he knew absolutely nothing about sub-sea technology. Laura felt on edge in case anyone else overheard the remarks he was making.

Jeff took a sip from his glass and made a face. "God, I hate this cheap plonk – I'm going to the bar outside to get us a proper drink," he muttered, dumping his glass of wine on a side table and walking off.

Laura said nothing. Although she'd never admit it to anyone else, she was glad to have a few minutes alone without Jeff's snide comments about everyone else at the reception. She wished she'd been able to come to the reception alone, but Jeff had insisted on accompanying her. She really wished he wouldn't bother, since he clearly found such events distasteful. Yet he didn't seem to like her going out alone – perhaps he was afraid she'd meet someone else? It was tiresome having to reassure him all the time that she wasn't looking for opportunities to be unfaithful. She genuinely loved him, but he seemed to have great difficulty in believing her.

As she stood alone, deep in thought, Norma, one of Kerry's colleagues, appeared, with a pleasant-looking man in tow.

"Hello, Laura – I hope you're enjoying the evening?"

"Yes, it's great!" Laura replied enthusiastically. "Thanks for inviting us – we're having a wonderful time!" If only that were true, she thought sadly, thinking of Jeff's permanently miserable frown. "And congratulations to you all," she added. "We're thrilled about your success!"

"Thanks," Norma replied. "But since there are so many industry people here tonight, I thought you might be finding it a bit boring. But Paul here is a trauma counsellor, and you're a lecturer in Sociology – so I figured you two would be bound to have something in common."

"Hello, Paul." Smiling, Laura extended her hand, and Paul smiled back as they shook hands.

"Well, I'll leave you two talking," Norma said, smiling from one to the other. "I see someone arriving whom I've just *got* to talk to."

Rushing off, she left them smiling at each other.

"Your job sounds rather intriguing," Laura added, more out of politeness than interest.

"Well, that's one way of putting it, I suppose!" Paul said, smiling back. "But dealing with people's tragedies can be quite draining."

Laura tried to look interested. But she was edgy, and concerned about Jeff's bad mood. Somehow, he always managed to ruin social gatherings. And she was worried that he'd see her chatting one-to-one with another man. That would be a sufficient cause for the outbreak of World War Three.

"Is yours a nine-to-five job?"

Paul shook his head. "Unfortunately not. I work with problem families – and a lot of domestic violence takes place after hours, primarily fuelled by alcohol. If someone is injured, I may need to liaise with police and the courts."

Laura suddenly perked up. "You deal with families where there's a history of violence?"

Paul nodded.

Laura quickly glanced around. There was still no sign of Jeff.

"Paul, could I ask your advice – on behalf of a friend of mine?" she asked nervously.

Paul nodded. "Of course. What do you want to know?"

Laura took a deep breath. "This friend is married to a guy who hits her. Her husband says he loves her – and she loves him – but she doesn't know how she can get him to stop."

Paul grimaced. "I'm afraid she's the last person who can stop it," he replied. "A violent man usually comes from a violent family. He doesn't know how to love any other way – his only experience of love has been from people who've been violent to him. Love and violence are inextricably linked in his mind – he can't separate intimacy from abuse."

Laura's hands were now shaking. "Is he genuinely capable of loving anyone?"

Paul nodded. "Oh yes – even men who dominate their wives and girlfriends are still very emotionally dependent on them. They hit them because they've been taught that controlling the people they love is the best way to ensure that they themselves won't get hurt."

Laura hesitated. "Can they change?"

Shaking his head, Paul gave her a cynical smile. "Empty promises tend to be the stock-in-trade of violent men. They swear they'll change, but it rarely happens because they must actually want to change. And mostly they don't." He looked directly at her. "Anyway, treatment usually requires years of therapy – too long for your friend to risk sticking around. Violence begets violence – so the next generation become victims too."

Laura shuddered. It all seemed so bleak.

"Does your friend have any children?"

Laura shook her head, guiltily touching her belly at the same

47

time. Why was she denying the child she was carrying? Probably because she knew what Paul's advice was going to be.

"Good – now's the time for her to break the link."

Laura shivered. "It seems awful to condemn someone like that – even murderers can experience remorse, so why do you say these people can't?"

Paul gave a sad smile. "People who are abusive have a remarkable sense of entitlement – they need to be gratified straight away, so they yell, scream, hit, slap and punch, and blame other people for the way they are. They carry a lot of pain inside, but it never excuses what they do to their victims."

Laura bit her lip. Based on Paul's description, Jeff had all the characteristics of a classic case.

Paul looked directly at her, and Laura suspected he was well aware that she was the one dealing with a violent partner. "I presume your friend's husband hasn't shown any inclination to change?"

Laura bit her lip. "Well, er, he usually apologises after he hits m-her –"

Paul smiled sympathetically. "Tell your friend to get out."

"But I – she – loves him!"

"And he may love her too. But that's not a good enough reason for her to risk her life. These situations invariably get worse over time."

In the distance, Laura could see Jeff making his way back through the throngs of guests. "Paul, it's been nice talking to you. But if you'll excuse me –"

"Of course." He patted her arm just before she left. "I wish your friend good luck – and I hope she makes the right decision."

As Paul moved away to join another group, Laura was left reeling as she walked in Jeff's direction. Risk her life? Surely that suggestion was a bit over the top?

Just then, Jeff arrived at her side with their drinks.

"Who was that?" he asked, studying Paul's retreating back.

"Oh, just someone Norma introduced me to."

"But I saw him touching your arm before he left. Why was he doing that?"

Laura shifted uncomfortably. "I don't know – maybe he was just one of those touchy-feely guys."

"What were you talking about?"

"I don't really remember – the weather, I think?"

"Well, it looked a lot more intimate than that!" said Jeff angrily. "Anyway, I don't know why you needed to talk to him – you're supposed to be talking to me!"

"Jeff, stop being ridiculous!" Laura hissed. "You weren't here!"

"I was getting you a glass of decent wine, in case you didn't notice!" he retorted.

"Well, you can hardly expect me to ignore someone I've been introduced to! That would be intolerably rude. People go to parties and receptions to chat to other guests as well, you know. Otherwise we might as well stay at home."

Jeff was sullen, and Laura felt a wave of sorrow for him. He was so terribly insecure. Maybe, when he felt more confident about her love, he'd stop this silly behaviour. She particularly remembered Paul's comment that there was a lot of pain in people like Jeff, and she longed to be the one who would help him to leave his troublesome past behind. Perhaps when he became a father, he'd feel more confident.

But Paul's other words were still ringing in her ears. Surely it couldn't be true that people like Jeff were unable to change – weren't there always exceptions to every rule?

Smiling, she tucked her arm into her husband's. "Jeff, you're the only one I want to be with."

"Then let's go home – this place is boring."

Laura bit her lip. She didn't really want to go, but the evening had lost its magic by now anyway. And somehow she didn't even feel like herself in the awful dress that Jeff had insisted on buying.

"Okay," she said dully.

But Jeff wasn't even listening any more. Already, he'd disengaged his arm from hers and was striding towards the exit.

Abandoning her drink, she followed him out the door.

Later that night, Jeff was vigorous and demanding in bed, and seemed interested only in his own pleasure. He didn't seem to care that he was hurting her – in fact, Laura's cries of discomfort seemed to add to his enjoyment and drive him into a greater frenzy. Perhaps he was angry with her for talking to another man at the party. Or maybe he just hated having to attend the party in the first place. Whatever it was, Laura was left feeling particularly sore and violated.

When he fell asleep afterwards, she lay awake clutching her stomach in discomfort and feeling very worried. Something didn't feel right. Creeping to the bathroom, she noticed several spots of blood on her nightdress. Hopefully it wasn't anything serious.

Climbing back into bed, Laura lay quietly beside her husband, studying Jeff's face as he slept. Never had she felt so alone. Right from the beginning of their relationship, her husband seemed to enjoy violent sex in which he subdued her. At first it had been exciting – a sign that he loved and needed her – but as time went by, she realised that he didn't even seem to be present when they made love. He was in a fury of passion that had nothing to do with her. It was as though he saw her simply as a means to his own release, not a person in her own right or an equal participant in the act of lovemaking. He seemed to be in some other place from which she couldn't bring him back.

She longed to reach out and soothe him, but she didn't dare. Jeff would interpret her gesture as implying that he needed soothing. Jeff's insecurities were becoming very difficult to handle.

CHAPTER 12

A feeling of nausea swept over Sylvia as she surveyed the receipt in her trembling hand. It was for an expensive bouquet of flowers, yet she'd never received them. Racking her brains, she tried to think of a logical reason why such a receipt would be in her husband's jacket pocket. She didn't know of anyone who'd died, nor were any of the factory employees in hospital.

She rummaged deeper in her husband's pocket, hating herself for what she was doing, yet needing to know the truth. She'd led a charmed life up till now – maybe karma was trying to balance the universe, having found her life too cosy and comfortable. Please, she prayed to any unknown deity who might be listening, please don't let it be true. I'll do anything – I'll be kinder, I'll give more time and money to charity – just don't let my husband be cheating on me.

As the wife of a wealthy factory owner, she'd foolishly felt immune from affairs. Since she and her husband maintained a glittering social calendar, and every day he was at the factory, she'd assumed he'd have little time for dalliances elsewhere. Now she wondered just how naïve she'd been.

As her fingers closed around another piece of paper, she pulled it out and stared at it, feeling as though her heart was about to break. This time, the receipt was for dinner for two at an expensive out-of-town restaurant. She hadn't been the beneficiary, and as she looked at the date, she realised she'd been visiting her father and Aunt Maud, her father's sister, that very weekend.

Sylvia shook her head vigorously. No, she was just being silly.

There was bound to be some perfectly logical reason – Alan had probably taken a business colleague out for a meal, and hadn't mentioned it because there was nothing untoward about it.

Feeling a little better, Sylvia slipped the receipts back into Alan's jacket pocket, looking around guiltily since she didn't want him to catch her prying. But her composure had been rattled, and she found herself considering, for the very first time, what she'd do if she ever discovered that Alan really was having an affair. Maybe she should start checking his pockets regularly just to reassure herself that all was well. She knew that lots of the women at the golf club checked up on their husbands, and Sylvia had always felt secretly smug because she'd never felt the need to do such a thing.

But now, she was beginning to realise that she might have been over-confident. Alan was an extremely attractive man, and she'd often seen other women making a play for him. Especially that minx, Janette Walker. Whenever they encountered her and her husband – the permanently inebriated Matthew – Janette was always quick to slip her arm through Alan's, and flirt outrageously with him, regardless of Sylvia's presence. Matthew seemed incapable of reining in his wife, and simply resorted to pouring himself yet another glass of wine or whiskey, and proceeding to get even drunker than he was already. Sylvia didn't think that Alan found Janette particularly attractive. Of course, he might simply be a clever actor . . .

Didn't statistics show that, at any one time, forty per cent of married men and thirty per cent of married women were conducting extra-marital affairs? Why should she think that her marriage was immune?

Mentally, she ran through the list of her friends – well, if she was honest, they were really only acquaintances – women from the same wealthy circle whom she joined at charity luncheons and on visits to health spas or nail bars, or at the golf or tennis club. If not Janette, could it be one of them?

Suddenly she gasped, horrified at the thought that if Alan was having an affair, other people might know about it, and be laughing at her behind her back. Would people at the factory know? Would he ask staff to cover for him when his wife rang, and get them to tell her that he was too busy to come to the phone? Would he nod and wink, and pay extra Christmas bonuses to those who kept his secrets? Her face reddened with shame at the thought of such duplicity on his part, and such humiliation on hers.

Once again, she shook her head in disbelief. No, she and Alan had a strong marriage, and they loved each other, she was sure of it. But there was already proof of a sort, wasn't there, in those two receipts? If only she could ask Alan about them! But she didn't dare, because she desperately feared that he might confirm to her that, yes, he was glad she'd raised the subject because he'd been planning to tell her he was leaving her for somebody else . . .

Sylvia shuddered. How she wished she could confide in her father. After all, he had invested heavily in Alan's factory, so he'd be able to wield some clout with her husband. But she'd feel too ashamed to admit to her father that she was unable to satisfy her own husband. Anyway, she didn't want him to think badly of Alan. Because once she gave voice to her suspicions, she could never take them back. Also, it might affect her father's willingness to lend Alan the money he needed for the factory refurbishment, and that would affect all their lives.

Sylvia sighed. Anyway, confronting her husband would only cause them both grief, and it was unlikely to achieve anything. If he was *having an affair*, she wasn't sure if she really wanted confirmation. And if he wasn't, then her lack of trust would drive a wedge between them. Yet the thought of him with another woman was sheer torture – was she going to have to view every other woman as a potential enemy for the rest of her life? Surely Alan would never do such a thing to her?

Later that night, as she lay in the darkness beside her husband, a tear trickled down her cheek. Lately, sex between them was only perfunctory, and when Alan came to bed he usually pleaded exhaustion when she turned towards him. But recently, there had been one night when he'd turned out the light and reached for her, taking her in silence. Now she wondered if he'd been imagining making love to some other woman instead of her.

Now, as she listened to him gently snoring, Sylvia tried to imagine the type of woman who would appeal to her husband.

Perhaps he fancied someone who was wild and tempestuous in bed – something she could never be, no matter how hard she tried. She suspected that the flirtatious Janette could be a powerhouse between the sheets – she was certainly outrageous enough to try anything. And that might be just what Alan craved.

Sylvia turned on her side and tried her best to sleep. But she found it impossible because her mind was racing and she felt as though her head would explode. If only she had a woman friend she could talk to! Someone who would understand her worries and could advise her what to do. But she'd left her real friends behind when she'd married Alan and moved with him to London. Back then she'd been in the throes of heady romance, and had wrongly assumed that her husband was all she needed.

Suddenly, she thought of Ellie Beckworth. They didn't really know each other, although Sylvia was aware that Ellie was a widow living half a mile from Greygates. They occasionally exchanged a nod when they passed each other in the village, and Sylvia was always intrigued by the other woman's reserve. She seemed totally self-sufficient and not in need of anyone else's approval. Sylvia admired her sangfroid, and longed to be the kind of woman who didn't care what anyone else thought.

For an instant, Sylvia wondered about Ellie and Alan, then felt embarrassed at having even considered such a possibility. Ellie seemed too independent to rely on any man, certainly not one married to someone else. Besides, Alan had always made a point of never socialising with his employees, except for the annual Christmas party and staff retirement parties. He said it wasn't good for business, and that the boss needed to maintain a certain distance if he was to keep his employees' respect.

Sylvia turned over again and stared up at the ceiling. It would be so nice to have someone like Ellie Beckworth as a friend, someone unconnected to any of the golfing crowd, or the gossips she usually had to endure at charity fundraising lunches. It would be great to have a true friend with whom to share confidences, and giggle over silly jokes . . .

With that comforting thought, Sylvia drifted off to sleep.

CHAPTER 13

Laura looked pale as she lay in her hospital bed. She was just beginning to doze off when Kerry burst in the door of her private room.

"My God, Laura – are you alright? Is the baby okay?"

Laura sat up. "I'm fine, and so is the baby. It was a false alarm – I had a show of blood last night, then another at work today, and my colleague Maria drove me here to the hospital. But the doctors say that everything's okay."

Kerry gave an exaggerated sigh of relief. "You don't do anything by halves, do you? I was worried sick when Maria texted me! She just said that you'd been taken to hospital, so I didn't know what exactly had happened. I tried to ring her back, but she must have been on another call."

Laura smiled apologetically. "Sorry, love – I didn't have time to give anyone a detailed account of what was happening."

Kerry looked worried. "Have you managed to contact Jeff?"

Laura nodded.

"Thank goodness for that – because I couldn't manage to contact him myself," Kerry told her. "When I got Maria's message, I thought I'd better check in with him, and make sure that he knew where you were. Since I don't have his mobile number in my phone, I tried to ring his office – I know you told me he doesn't want anyone ringing him at work – but, under the circumstances, I figured he could hardly object." She took a deep breath. "But I couldn't find him."

Laura smiled. "He works at Denham, Goodwood & Clayton. Stockbrokers have such odd-sounding names, don't they? I'm sure you simply missed the order of the names – even I find it difficult to remember which one comes first."

Kerry shook her head. "No, I had the names in the right order, but I couldn't find the company in the phone book or online. It doesn't seem to exist, Laura. But just to be sure, I rang all the stockbrokers in the phone book. None of them ever heard of Denham, Goodwood & Clayton, and Jeff doesn't appear to work for any of them."

Laura smiled again, but this time her smile was forced. "Don't worry about it – I've already texted him, and he'll be here later."

Kerry looked relieved. "Okay – but I think I'd better get his number from you, just in case I ever need it again."

Laura gave her the number, then quickly changed the subject. She was a little perturbed herself, although she didn't want Kerry to notice it. Hopefully, despite Kerry's protests, her friend had simply got the name of Jeff's brokerage wrong.

After Kerry had gone, with promises to ring later and bring in anything she might need, Laura lay back on her pillows and awaited her husband's arrival. She'd chosen to text rather than to speak to him, since his mood could be erratic and she didn't relish an explosion over the phone.

As she waited for him to appear, Laura was worried. Why on earth couldn't Kerry locate him at his stockbrokers? How could the company not exist? And if that was true, where did he go every day? And where did he get the money they lived on? It had to be a mistake! They had an expensive flat in a prestigious part of the city, filled with beautiful antique furniture and a state-of-the-art kitchen – all owned and paid for by Jeff. As yet, Laura hadn't told him about her own substantial inheritance, although logically she couldn't think why. Perhaps Kerry's words of warning were affecting her judgement.

She sighed. There had to be a perfectly logical reason why Jeff couldn't be contacted, and she'd raise the matter with him later. But she'd be careful how she framed her query, knowing how irritable he could become if he thought she was prying or criticising him.

As she relished the silence of her hospital room, Laura thought gratefully of her colleague Maria, who'd deposited her at the hospital before hurrying back to the university to give Laura's afternoon lecture to the first-year students. All the staff at the university were wonderfully kind, and she was lucky to have such a considerate boss as Darren.

Laura was also relieved that she herself had managed to contact Jeff – imagine her embarrassment if Maria had been the one to discover that his office didn't seem to exist.

"Hello, love," Laura said warmly as Jeff arrived at her bedside. Since he always seemed irritated, she hoped he wouldn't view her threatened miscarriage as yet another reason to blame her. For what, she didn't know, but lately, it seemed that she was always to blame for something.

"Is the baby alright?"

Laura nodded, deflated that he hadn't enquired about her own health or given her a hug. But Jeff was never very demonstrative, so there was little point in allowing herself to be disappointed.

"Yes, it's fine," she replied. "Hopefully, I'll be home in a few days."

"What happened?"

"I don't really know – I'd just finished giving a lecture when I suddenly developed cramps. Then I discovered I was bleeding, so Maria drove me straight to the hospital."

Laura avoided mentioning that she'd also phoned Kerry, and that her friend had already been in to visit her. Sometimes it was better to avoid any mention of Kerry when Jeff was around.

"So my little son is definitely okay?"

Laura nodded, exasperated. "The *baby* is okay, Jeff – we don't know whether it's a boy or a girl yet. The doctor said that everything seems fine. I'm just supposed to take things easy for the next few weeks."

"Then maybe you should give up work?" Jeff said hastily.

"Standing on a lecture podium all day can't be doing our child any good."

"Jeff, I only give two lectures a day, and they're less than an hour each," Laura protested. "The rest of the time is spent giving tutorials or correcting exam papers – all of which are done sitting down. Anyway, the doctor says that I can continue working."

This last bit was a lie – the doctor hadn't expressed any opinion – but Laura wasn't planning on spending her pregnancy lying on a couch and being bored. She loved her job too much to stay at home.

Turning to Jeff, Laura took a deep breath. It was time to discover why Kerry hadn't been able to contact him. But she'd pretend that she had been the one trying to get in touch.

"Oh, by the way – during the rush to get to the hospital, I thought I'd mislaid my mobile phone," Laura lied. "Thankfully, it turned up later, but in the meantime I'd no way of contacting you, except through Denham, Goodwood & Clayton. So before Maria and I left for the hospital, I looked up the company in the phone book, then on Google, but it wasn't listed anywhere."

Jeff grimaced. "Ah," he said, looking at the floor.

Laura stared at him expectantly. There was definitely something amiss, and she was suddenly frightened. Had Kerry been right after all? Laura was desperate to prove to her friend that her husband was all she'd believed him to be, but sometimes serious doubts assailed her. Now, the silence from Jeff seemed to confirm her worst fears.

Jeff began pacing up and down the room. Then he thought better of it and sat down on the edge of her bed, lowering his voice as he spoke.

"Look, I'm going to have to trust you. But if you ever tell this to anyone, you could be putting my life in danger. And yours, too."

Laura's heart began to thud painfully.

Jeff glanced around the room, as though to ensure that no one could hear what he was about to say.

"Look, the truth is – I'm not a stockbroker. I work for MI5."

Laura's mouth dropped open. Her husband worked for the secret service!

"You probably wondered why I didn't have any work colleagues at the wedding," Jeff explained. "Now you know. Undercover agents couldn't risk having their cover blown." He looked at her angrily. "You must never tell anyone what I've told you."

Laura nodded. "Of course not. But surely you could have told me? I'm your wife!"

"No, I couldn't – lives depend on the kind of work I do. I had to sign an oath never to tell anyone." He raised an eyebrow. "No MI5 operative ever tells their family. I'd never have told you if you hadn't gone digging. And now that I've trusted you with this confidential information, you must never discuss it with anyone, not even me."

Laura nodded, chastened. She was shocked. Clearly his job required him to keep others in the dark about his life. She felt annoyed at being kept out of such an important part of his life, but she could also acknowledge that there would be good reasons for him to keep quiet. A talkative wife, or a nasty ex-wife, could compromise an agent's position and blow his cover, destroying years of credibility that he'd built up in a community. And already Jeff had trouble trusting people.

"W-what if I need to contact you?"

"You already have my mobile number – memorise it, just in case you mislay your phone again. But only ever call me in the direst of emergencies."

After Jeff had gone, Laura lay back in the bed and stared at the ceiling. She didn't want to read the pile of magazines Kerry had brought in earlier. Instead, she began going over all that her husband had just told her. She felt a frisson of delight at the thought of Jeff doing such important work for national security. He was her very own personal James Bond! It seemed such a glamorous, and also dangerous, life, and now she was part of it. Had she been secretly vetted herself? No wonder Jeff was always tense and worried. He obviously had a lot of responsibilities that she knew nothing about. She'd be kinder, and more supportive, and eventually she'd prove to him that he could trust her.

Laura only knew about covert state services through movies and novels, so she had no idea what Jeff's actual job might be, and he'd made it clear that she couldn't ask him. Since he was home most evenings and at weekends, his job clearly didn't involve travelling, or require urgent changes of plan. Maybe he provided back-up services for agents in the field – as a cryptographer, computer expert or scientist?

Laura also felt a sense of relief. She'd wondered why Jeff only had a few acquaintances at the wedding, and didn't seem to have any close friends with whom he socialised. Now she finally understood why.

Later that evening Kerry arrived in Laura's room with a selection of toiletries and newspapers.

"How are you feeling?" she asked sympathetically.

"I'm fine – just glad this little person is okay," Laura replied, patting her stomach.

"Are the doctors happy enough about your condition?"

"Oh yes, they think it was just a false alarm, and that everything should be okay from now on. But I've been told to take it easy when I go home, and not do anything too strenuous. They're keeping me in for a few days – just to make sure that everything's okay."

"That sounds like a sensible precaution. When can you go back to work?"

"I'm hoping to go back next week. Darren visited earlier today – of course, he's urging me to take all the time I need. But I don't want to mess up the other lecturers' schedules any more than I need to."

"Well, don't rush back – you don't want to put the baby at risk," Kerry told her sternly. "I presume Jeff will take you home when they discharge you?"

Laura nodded, a momentary flicker of something like a frown passing over her face.

"By the way," Kerry tried to look casual, "did you discover why I couldn't contact him?"

Laura nodded, pulling herself up in the bed. Jeff had warned her not to tell anyone, but she knew she could trust her best friend. "I pretended that I was the one who'd tried to contact him – and do you know what?" She looked around her, as though expecting someone to be hiding behind the curtains. Then she lowered her voice. "You must promise me that you'll never tell this to anyone –"

Kerry nodded, looking intrigued.

Laura looked around the room again before speaking. Then she beckoned Kerry to come closer before whispering in her ear. "Jeff told me he works for MI5," she told her. "That's why he didn't want me finding out – because the work he does is top secret!"

Kerry raised an eyebrow. She didn't believe a word of it. But if Laura chose to be gullible, it wasn't up to her to disillusion her. MI5 indeed. She wondered what exactly Jeff was up to. Maybe it was time to find out.

"Of course, I'm sworn to secrecy, so promise me you'll never mention this to anyone!" Laura added worriedly. "I'm only telling you because you're my closest friend."

"My lips are sealed," Kerry said noncommittally.

CHAPTER 14

Sylvia disliked checking Alan's pockets since it made her feel like a sneak. She'd been relieved to find no further incriminating evidence, and was beginning to feel a lot more positive. She decided to abandon her searches – not only was it disrespectful to Alan, but if he ever caught her, she knew she'd die of embarrassment.

Nevertheless, as she prepared to take several of his suits to the dry-cleaner's, she couldn't resist checking the pockets, convincing herself that she was only doing it to make sure there was nothing inside that might damage the fabric during dry-cleaning.

Sliding her hand deep into one of the pockets, Sylvia's fingers came in contact with a rolled-up piece of paper. Extracting it, she unfolded it and stared at it. It was a receipt from a well-known firm of London jewellers, and the item purchased had been a very expensive woman's diamond and gold ring.

For a moment, Sylvia's heart stood still. Then she realised with relief that her own birthday was only two weeks away – no doubt the ring was intended as a surprise for her! Smiling, she put the receipt in one of Alan's freshly pressed jackets – she wouldn't spoil the surprise by letting him know that she'd discovered what he'd bought her.

But, as the days went by, Sylvia found herself worrying. She'd dropped one or two hints to Alan about how much she'd love a new ring, but he hadn't reacted, and she began to worry that he was either a brilliant actor – or the ring was destined for someone else.

On the other hand, her husband would hardly buy a ring worth thousands of pounds for a staff employee – even the longest-serving members of staff only got a middle-of-the-range timepiece along with their bonus when they were retiring. So if the ring wasn't for her – then who was the lucky recipient?

The tension became unbearable as the date of her birthday approached. It was as though time had slowed down deliberately in order to cause her the maximum distress. Sylvia recalled how, as a small child, the joy of anticipation had made every day seem so long. Now, the long drawn-out days were caused by the fear that her birthday might reveal an unpalatable truth.

On the morning of her birthday, Sylvia awoke with a tension headache. At least today, she'd finally know the truth.

Alan was up already by the time she awoke, and she was surprised at how late she'd managed to sleep. Slipping on her dressing gown, she padded downstairs to the kitchen, where she could hear Alan whistling as he prepared breakfast.

He was smiling broadly as he greeted her. "Good morning, love – happy birthday!"

"Thanks – I didn't expect to sleep quite so late."

"Well, this is your special day, so you can do anything you want to!"

Sylvia smiled. If only that was true. If she could really do anything she wanted, she'd wipe away the fear that was currently poisoning her marriage. She'd become a different, more exuberant and exciting person. Then Alan wouldn't need to look elsewhere . . .

Warily, she eyed the breakfast table. Alongside the morning papers, Sylvia could see two gift-wrapped boxes, and she guessed that the bigger one was a gift purportedly from young Pete to his mummy. A smaller box stood beside it, and Sylvia's heart did a quick somersault. Thankfully, it looked exactly like the kind of box that would contain an expensive gold and diamond ring. Relief flooded through her. She'd been silly to worry, and everything was going to be fine.

Smiling, Sylvia sat down at the table, just as Alan began singing 'Happy Birthday' carrying two plates of scrambled eggs and buttered toast to the table.

Leaning forward, he kissed her. "I'm hoping we might manage to have breakfast together before Pete wakes up." He looked at her expectantly. "Go on – open your presents!"

Taking a deep breath, Sylvia picked up the bigger gift box, the one whose label read: 'To Mummy from Pete xxx'.

She smiled as she unwrapped a pair of pretty gold filigree earrings, ornately shaped in the letter 'S'.

"Obviously, I had to help him," Alan joked. "I mean, he hasn't learnt his alphabet yet!"

"They're lovely," Sylvia replied, standing up and crossing to the mirror where she slipped on the earrings and stared at her reflection. Her hands were shaking, and she was anxious to delay the moment of truth as long as possible, fearing the results might not be to her liking.

"Aren't you going to open my present?"

"Yes, of course."

Returning to the table, Sylvia's heart was beating so wildly that she felt certain Alan must hear it. She smiled as she lifted up the small box. All she had to do now was open Alan's present, find the ring inside, and all would be well again. She could abandon all her silly suspicions and enjoy the rest of her birthday. Flowers had already been delivered from Daddy, and she knew he'd slip her a cheque later that evening when they all met for dinner. It would be for a generous amount too but, right now, all she was concerned about was the contents of the box she held in her trembling hand.

Her fingers shook as she tore off the gift-wrapping, and her heart sank like a stone as she gazed at the bracelet lying on a bed of soft tissue paper inside.

"Oh!"

"Don't you like it?" Alan asked anxiously.

"Yes, yes – of course. I love it," Sylvia assured him. It was beautiful, but it wasn't the ring she'd been expecting, the ring whose receipt she'd found in Alan's pocket.

"Are you sure you like it, darling? If not, I can change it for something else, you know that."

Although her heart was breaking, Sylvia reached up and kissed her husband's cheek. "It's perfect!" she told him. "It'll go beautifully with the new dress I'm wearing tonight. What time have you booked the restaurant for?"

She knew she was gabbling, but she felt out of control and in danger of breaking down.

"Eight thirty."

Sylvia nodded. "Is Daddy bringing Aunt Maud?"

"I think so – he rarely goes anywhere without his sister these days. I've booked a table for six – and I've arranged for the table you like. You know, the one over by the window."

Sylvia raised her eyebrows. "Six? Who else is coming?"

"Janette and Matthew." Alan grinned. "Janette was most insistent that they be present to wish you a happy birthday."

Sylvia's heart gave a jolt. Janette, with her red mouth and long talons, was the woman she considered most likely to be having an affair with her husband!

"Must we have them there?" she answered peevishly. "After all, it's my birthday! Shouldn't I be the one to choose the guests?"

"Sorry," Alan said sheepishly. "I actually thought you'd enjoy their company – I mean, your father and Maud aren't exactly party animals, are they? And you know what a madcap Janette is – I thought she'd add a bit of fun to the occasion."

Sylvia grimaced. "I suppose there's nothing can be done about it now – but I wish you'd asked me before inviting them."

"I didn't actually invite them – I bumped into Janette as I was coming out of the jeweller's carrying your gift bag. She wanted to know what was inside, and who it was for."

Sylvia bit her lip angrily. She was beginning to realise that from now on she'd have to view everything Alan told her as a lie. Janette had probably been with him at the jeweller's – no doubt the beautiful ring had been bought for her.

"When I told her the gift was for your birthday, Janette invited us for drinks at their house," Alan added. "When I politely declined, and told her we were having dinner at La Strada with your father, she insisted that she and Matthew join us."

Sylvia bit her lip. Perhaps Alan was flattered at being singled out by 'old money'? She felt like crying. Her birthday was already ruined – Alan's gift seemed to prove conclusively that the ring had been given to someone else, and now she was expected to spend the evening with the woman who was probably her husband's mistress.

In La Strada, the wine flowed freely, the conversation was lively and everyone seemed to be enjoying themselves. It was impossible to fault the restaurant. The table Alan had booked was situated exactly where Sylvia liked it, the waiters were attentive, the food delicious. As expected, her father had slipped her a cheque as soon as they arrived at the restaurant, and even Sylvia had been surprised by the large amount. Her father seemed pleased by her surprise, and Sylvia wondered if he'd somehow guessed that she needed cheering up.

Aunt Maud had knitted her a sweater, in a hideous yellow colour that Sylvia instantly disliked. But she gave an Oscar-winning performance, assuring her aunt that it was a colour she adored, and that the style would go perfectly with either jeans or skirts. Her aunt's face was pink with pleasure, and Sylvia could feel the tears forming as her heart filled with affection for the older woman. It was good to be surrounded by people who would never hurt you. But as she glanced across the table – at Alan and Janette, who were engrossed in a private conversation – her heart contracted. She'd always believed that Alan would never hurt her – now she wasn't so sure.

Sylvia glanced around the restaurant. Every other table was full, and all the other patrons seemed to be enjoying themselves. As the waiters delivered several extra bottles of wine that Matthew had ordered, Sylvia wondered how long she'd have to endure the proceedings. But as the guest of honour, she could hardly leave before the party cake was brought out and she was forced, child-like, to blow out her candles. Her only hope of surviving the evening was to get pie-eyed. This was something she usually avoided, believing that her position as Alan's wife demanded a certain level of decorum in public. But to hell with Alan tonight, she thought. Let him dare comment!

Sylvia sneaked a glance at Janette's husband. Clearly Matthew had a head-start on her – he was already well oiled, and pontificating to anyone who would listen about some theory of his for converting water into fuel. Sylvia watched, both fascinated and horrified, as he slurred his words and gesticulated wildly. Then her gaze moved to Janette again. Or more specifically, to Janette's left hand. The woman was wearing what looked suspiciously like the ring listed on the receipt in Alan's pocket!

Sylvia took a deep breath and leaned across the table. "I love your ring," she said loudly, and was gratified to see Janette blush. She glanced quickly at Alan, but he was already deep in conversation with her father and didn't appear to have heard her comment.

"Oh, thanks," Janette said off-handedly, then quickly changed the subject, seizing the nearest bottle of wine and topping up Sylvia's glass. "Do you like this Grenache?" she asked eagerly. "It's a bloody nice wine, isn't it? Personally, I prefer Chateauneuf-du-Pape, but Matthew always orders what he likes, regardless of what I want. Before we left home this evening, I made him promise to go with my choice this evening, but oh no, he has to start showing off his knowledge of wines every time!" She smiled at Sylvia as she took a gulp from her glass. "Although I can't fault him on this one – it's really good, although I'd never let him know that!"

Sylvia was both embarrassed and relieved when the birthday cake finally arrived. She felt embarrassed because all eyes in the restaurant had turned towards her, and relieved because the candle-blowing episode signified that the evening was drawing to a close. Sportingly, she blew out all her candles in one go, and was rewarded by a round of applause from her own table, and catcalls from inebriated diners across the room.

At the end of the night, as Alan helped her put on her coat, Sylvia watched carefully for any interaction between her husband and Janette. But other than a perfunctory kiss on the cheek, they had no further contact before Alan steered his wife outside to the waiting taxi.

"I haven't seen you drink so much in a long time," Alan said mildly as they settled into the back seat of the taxi.

Sylvia arched her eyebrows. "So?"

Alan laughed, holding up his hands in appeasement. "I didn't mean anything by it – I'm just glad to see you enjoying yourself."

Sylvia said nothing. If Alan thought she'd enjoyed herself tonight, he was very much mistaken. But maybe, when a man had eyes for only his lover, he could hardly be expected to notice that his wife was suffering.

The following morning, Sylvia was surprised to receive a phone call from Janette.

"Hey, Birthday Girl, how are you feeling today?"

"A little hung-over," Sylvia admitted. In fact, she had a monumental hangover from all the wine she'd drunk. But it had helped her to get through the otherwise intolerable evening.

"Look, about the ring –"

"Sorry?"

"You admired my ring last night –"

"Did I?"

"Yes, and I'm sorry I changed the subject so quickly. But Matthew doesn't know I've bought it – I mean, he got me the new Merc convertible earlier this month and I didn't want him to think I was ungrateful. But when I saw the ring – well, I just couldn't resist it. And the jeweller said that VAT was going up again next month, so it was going to be a lot dearer if I waited. So I put it on my gold card –"

"I'm sure you did," Sylvia said dryly, remembering the night before, when she'd watched Janette coquettishly whispering in Alan's ear while Matthew swayed drunkenly in his seat, waffling incomprehensibly to anyone who would listen to him.

"You won't mention it to Matthew, will you?"

"Of course not," Sylvia replied, unable to think of anything else to say. But now she no longer believed a word that Janette – or Alan – told her. And she surmised that the mistress was now cleverly asking the betrayed wife to help keep knowledge of the affair from the mistress's own husband!

"Let's do lunch some day soon?" Janette added brightly.

"Of course – that would be lovely," Sylvia replied, thinking to herself: *Over my dead body*. She had absolutely no intention of having anything to do with the woman who was probably screwing her husband.

"I'll call you, okay?"

"Okay."

Since she loved Alan, Sylvia was still willing to find any excuse that would explain away the mystery of the ring. She persuaded herself that she was being ridiculous in equating a missing ring with an affair – there was undoubtedly some other reason why Alan hadn't given it to her.

On the days when she decided that Janette wasn't his lover, she'd think that perhaps, like Janette, Alan had made the purchase to avoid the forthcoming VAT increase. He was probably keeping the ring for her fortieth birthday next year. Equally, she accepted that it might be intended as a gift for Maud – wasn't her seventieth birthday coming up soon? Although Sylvia couldn't think why her husband would give an aunt by marriage such an expensive gift. Then Sylvia felt ashamed. Why did she think that she was a worthy recipient of the ring, and poor Maud wasn't?

At other times, she'd scold herself for her naïvety. Why shouldn't Alan be among the forty per cent of men who cheated? He was reasonably wealthy, handsome and ran his own business. All of which made him highly attractive to other women. She'd often seen women coming on to him but, like a naïve fool, it had never occurred to her that he might respond to any of these overtures. Then she shook her head vehemently, aware she was letting her imagination run riot. Besides, Alan spent so much time at the factory that there was hardly time for an affair! He was such a conscientious employer that he was always going back to the factory after hours, to ensure that everything was in order for the following day's production. By now Sylvia didn't even question his regular late-evening trips – she just accepted that this was part and parcel of who Alan was, and that lonely evenings were the price of being the boss's wife.

Sylvia vacillated between hope and despair, convinced one minute that Alan wouldn't cheat on her, then swinging back to the certainty that he was carrying on with Janette. At other times she convinced herself that he was involved with some other woman – perhaps someone from the golf club – and she vowed to watch all Alan's interactions with other women from now on. On the other hand, she knew she couldn't live like that – it would be sheer torture. And throughout it all, she had to suffer in silence – there was no one with whom she could share her fears or count on for support.

CHAPTER 15

Kerry found it astonishing that Laura trusted Jeff so implicitly, and didn't need to check up on the man she'd married. Unlike her, Laura was a trusting and gullible soul, taking people at face value and assuming they were who they said they were. Kerry was well aware that this was often far from the truth.

Without telling Laura, she decided that she was going to follow Jeff one morning as he left their apartment, and see where he went. She'd be surprised if he went anywhere near Whitehall, where she knew that most of the covert services were located. Of course, if Jeff *was* telling the truth, she'd never be able to prove it anyway, because of the very nature of the secret service. But she didn't believe for one minute that Jeff had anything to do with it. He was too volatile, for starters. Agents would need to be capable of staying calm in difficult situations and, in her opinion, Jeff would never have got past the first interview.

She also knew that in books and films about spies, the secret service always provided its agents with a cover story. So if Jeff really *did* work for MI5, the fictitious stockbrokers would have had a phone number and someone would definitely have answered when it was phoned.

She also thought back to what Laura had told her about Jeff's violent parents, and she found herself wondering if there was any truth in that story either. Violent parents wouldn't look very good on a CV for special ops and, even if he'd lied in his application, MI5 wouldn't be long sussing out the truth.

The following morning, Kerry was lurking outside Laura and Jeff's flat in Islington by eight o'clock. When the alarm had gone off at six, all she'd wanted to do was turn over and go to sleep again, but she reckoned it would be easier to follow Jeff while Laura was still safely in hospital. She'd wondered if he'd bother to leave the flat at all – since Laura wasn't there, he didn't need to pretend that he was going on some MI5 assignment.

After forty-five minutes shivering in a doorway opposite their flat, Kerry watched as Jeff stepped outside and closed the door. Keeping a safe distance behind him, she followed, thinking yet again that if he truly was a secret agent, he wasn't a particularly good one, since he didn't seem to realise he was being followed.

As she tried to keep up, she was hoping that he wouldn't suddenly sprint for a bus, since she was already having trouble matching his long strides. She had some hope of following him if he took the Underground, although even there it was easy to lose someone on a crowded platform.

Luckily, Jeff headed down into the Underground, and Kerry was able to lose herself among the people waiting for the next train. She'd taken the precaution of wearing a dark hooded jacket and had altered her hairstyle and make-up, so she felt confident that Jeff wouldn't notice her. If he did, she'd have to make up some excuse for being there. In theory, her job as an engineer entitled her to be anywhere, so she could be on her way to meet a client to discuss one of Sea Diagnostic's projects. Besides, it wasn't any of Jeff's business where she went, and the streets were public areas anyway.

As the train roared into the station, Kerry kept her eye on Jeff, managing to get into the same carriage, although she made sure to stand behind other commuters while watching to see what station he got off at.

When the train reached the city, the crowds began to thin out and the carriage became decidedly empty. Kerry quickly sat down and tried to partially cover her face. She began to worry about her situation, since without the protection of other bodies he'd surely notice her before long. Fortunately, when he stood up to get off just two stations later, he moved to the forward door of the carriage, and she hung back until he'd left the train, leaping off just before the doors closed. By now, Jeff was making his way up the escalator, and Kerry followed, her hood pulled up, poised to look away in case he turned and looked down the escalator.

They were now in the East End Docklands area, and Kerry held back as Jeff headed towards a large modern hotel and entered the foyer. As she lurked outside, peering in through the heavy glass doors, she saw him step into the dining room. Taking a deep breath, she lowered her hood and followed him inside. She knew she was taking a risk, but if he spotted her, she could always claim to be meeting a business associate herself. She was dressed a little too casually for work, but she'd no choice but to go ahead and hope for the best.

Luckily, the staff at the reception desk were dealing with guests who were arriving and departing, and she was able to walk past without being queried. Outside the dining room she paused, trying to spot Jeff inside, and finally she saw him sitting at a corner table with another man. Luckily, Jeff had his back to the door, but Kerry frowned as she looked at his companion. He was a tall, dark-haired, well-dressed man, and Kerry knew she'd seen him somewhere before. Who on earth was he?

As the man caught her eye, Kerry quickly looked away, embarrassed. It was time to get out of there, before the man drew Jeff's attention to her presence. She hoped she simply looked like a hotel guest in search of her breakfast companion. She hurried back to the foyer and left the hotel, still puzzled. She'd definitely seen or read about this man quite recently. Could he be a politician?

Hurrying back to her apartment, she changed into more suitable work clothes and headed off to the offices of Sea Diagnostics. She'd research the situation further just as soon as she got the chance.

CHAPTER 16

Ellie was excited, because today was the day that Alan was going to end his marriage.

"I'm going to ask Sylvia for a divorce," he'd told her determinedly as they'd lain together the afternoon before. "This morning I paid off the final instalment of the loan from Sylvia's father, so I don't owe Dick Morgan anything any more. I've approached the bank for working capital, so it should be plain sailing from now on."

Ellie's heart had soared with joy.

"I'd also rather split from Sylvia sooner rather than later," Alan added. "It'll be easier for Pete to adjust while he's still too young to understand what's involved."

"But you'll still make sure to see him regularly?" Ellie asked, more than willing to make this small concession, now that she was gaining a much bigger one.

"Of course," Alan replied, flashing her a grateful smile.

As he held her close, she revelled in his nearness, his smell, his masculinity. She was so excited to think that soon he'd be hers completely!

Excited, Ellie watched from the window as Alan's car drove in the gate and down the driveway. As it disappeared from view, she waited anxiously while he parked it out of sight behind the house. It was just occurring to her that, from now on, he wouldn't need to hide his car any more. They'd be a proper couple, and they could be seen together at last. They could shop together, eat out together, go to the theatre together . . .

Briefly, she thought of Tony Coleman, who was still inviting her to go out with him. When she'd been feeling alone and neglected by Alan, she'd actually considered saying yes. After all, it would have involved nothing more than a trip to the cinema, and would have served as cover for her affair if she'd been seen publicly with him. Now, of course, there would be no need for any cover ever again! In fact, she'd love to see Tony's face when he discovered that she was about to become Mrs Thornton!

She felt a brief pang of guilt for poor Sylvia, who must, by now, be reeling in shock. One woman's joy was bringing another woman so much unhappiness. But Ellie couldn't afford to feel sorry for someone else – it was her special time at last, and she couldn't wait to tell the world that she and Alan were finally going to be together.

The previous morning in the village, she'd been tempted to blurt out her news to one of the shopkeepers who'd enquired about her good humour. Luckily, the outward reserve she'd cultivated during her time with Alan had kicked in, and she'd simply smiled sweetly. Besides, out of respect for Sylvia, she needed to wait until Alan had made his separation official. At this stage, she could afford to be magnanimous, since she was the one who was winning the prize. There would be time enough to let them all know that she was about to become Alan's wife.

Anxiously, Ellie hovered at the door, wondering why Alan was taking so long to step inside. Today, of all days, she'd expected him to come bounding through the door, since he was finally coming to her as a free man. Usually there was an urgency in his stride, since both of them would be anticipating the joys of making love together.

But something was different. As Alan stepped into the hall, his shoulders were stooped and he seemed reluctant to face her. She had a horrible feeling in the pit of her stomach. Something was clearly wrong.

He gave her a sad smile as they embraced. "Oh, my darling, darling love," he whispered as he held her tight.

"What's wrong?" she asked, almost afraid to know the answer, but needing to know it anyway.

"It's the factory," he answered, and she was relieved that it wasn't an accident.

"Well, if no one's dead, it can't be that bad," she said, smiling to lighten the atmosphere.

He looked grave. "But I'm afraid it's bad news for us," he replied. "My negotiations with the bank have fallen through – I thought they were happy with my business plan, but they've refused point blank to lend me the money I need for expansion. So I'd no other option but to ask Sylvia's father for another large cash injection."

She bit her lip, because she knew exactly what that meant.

"I'm sorry, love – I can't possibly ask her for a divorce now – not while I'm taking her father's money."

She buried her face in his jacket so that he couldn't see her tears. She knew how difficult things were for him, and she didn't want to add to his burden. But her own dreams were now being put on hold yet again.

"I know this is awful for you, love, but please remember that I'm torn too," he whispered. "Although I'm not in love with her any more, I do care about her and I respect her. After all, she's given me a great kid." He kissed her nose. "But none of us can help who we fall in love with. That first day I met you, when I caused you to run into the ditch on your bicycle, I instantly fell head over heels for you."

He held her away from him and gazed at her earnestly.

"Can you wait, love? It won't be forever, I promise. I'm expecting to sign a contract with one of the largest wholesalers in the country very soon. I'm hoping the bank will then reconsider its position when it sees the substantial increase that the contract's going to make to our turnover."

Ellie nodded, glancing down at the gold and diamond ring that confirmed Alan's love for her.

"I also have to go away on business for a few days," he told her gently. "I need to meet with some of our fruit and vegetable suppliers – unless we can negotiate a better price for their produce, we could have a serious problem on our hands." He smiled at her sadly. "I know this wait is disappointing for both of us. But we still have each other, and we'll eventually manage to be together full time." He kissed her tenderly. "You'll be okay while I'm away?"

Ellie nodded. "But I'll miss you terribly," she whispered.

"Good," Alan whispered back. "I couldn't bear it if you didn't miss me!"

CHAPTER 17

Kerry sat on the edge of Laura's hospital bed, holding her hand sympathetically.

"How do you know all this?" Laura demanded, tears in her eyes. "You couldn't possibly find out so much by simply following Jeff!"

"No, you're right – when I got home after work this evening, I checked through the last few weeks' newspapers on-line, because I'd a hunch that I'd seen a picture somewhere of the guy who was with Jeff. And there he was – smiling as he left court after his acquittal. He'd been prosecuted for importing and supplying Class A drugs like heroin, and cocaine." Kerry grimaced. "But somehow, the informer who was to testify against him disappeared – presumed dead – so he got off." She reached into her pocket and took out a folded piece of paper. "Here – I printed off the page, so you can see for yourself."

Laura looked at the picture of the smiling man, but it meant nothing to her. She certainly didn't recognise him.

Kerry looked at her earnestly. "What worries me is – why would Jeff be meeting with a guy like that?" She took a deep breath. "Aren't you worried that whatever Jeff is doing, it looks decidedly illegal?"

Laura could feel the anger building up inside her. "You've no business following my husband while I'm here in hospital!" she said hotly. "I'm sorry now that I told you about his work for MI5 – he's clearly on some kind of mission. He probably has to deal with these people for reasons of national security!"

Kerry looked apologetically at Laura. "I'm sorry, love – I accept that maybe I shouldn't have followed him. But I'm worried about you, and I just want you to be safe and happy."

Laura looked slightly less angry, so Kerry decided to tell her what else she'd looked up.

"I also Googled Jeff's father's name – there were lots of old newspaper reports about his family at the time of his parents' deaths. The coroner ruled that Jeff's mother had been murdered by his father, then the father hanged himself."

Laura turned pale with shock. "Oh God! I knew his parents were violent, but I'd no idea his father was a murderer! Poor Jeff – that explains so much."

Kerry grimaced. "I just thought you should know. You'd have been livid with me if you found out later that I'd known all this and hadn't told you."

Laura nodded. "Okay, I get that. But I'm not happy that you followed Jeff. It's almost as though you expected to find something wrong. And Jeff can hardly be blamed for his awful parents, can he? It's not his fault that his father was a murderer. I know Jeff is scarred by his childhood – he probably didn't tell me all that because he's embarrassed by it."

Kerry squeezed her hand apologetically. "Promise me you won't let him know that I've told you all this."

Laura looked at her truculently. "Of course I won't! He'd be so humiliated. You know how insecure Jeff is – he'd be mortified if he knew that I'd found out about his family background, and that my closest friend had been following him! Besides, Jeff is my husband. I signed up for better or for worse, and I'm expecting his child. So I have to make a go of it."

She looked at Kerry defiantly.

"Besides, I love him."

Kerry smiled sympathetically at Laura. Still gullible. Still seeing the best in her husband, despite the fact that he'd told her a pack of lies from day one. Love truly *was* blind.

When Kerry left, Laura lay alone in her bed feeling shell-shocked and very vulnerable. No, Kerry had to be wrong. Laura was also loath to accept that her own judgement about Jeff could be off. But this new information of Kerry's – that he'd been having breakfast with a well-known criminal – was certainly worrying. Undoubtedly he was doing it as part of his job for MI5, since it seemed perfectly reasonable that secret services would want to infiltrate the drugs world. Jeff was probably working on some kind of sting. Now she was even more worried than before, but all she could do was hope he'd be safe. No doubt his threatening outburst to her had just been a stressful reaction to the dangerous work he did.

Feeling exhausted by it all, Laura lay back and patted her belly. At least the baby was okay, so she could look forward to the family that she and Jeff were creating together. And her number one priority was this little person growing inside her. She owed it to this child to make the best of her marriage, and to create a happy home environment for it to grow up in. If she was to start questioning everything her husband did, she'd have no marriage left. Jeff had to be allowed to do his job without her interference – hadn't he told her that she wasn't ever to question him about what he was doing? Presumably that was for her own protection. Jeff wouldn't want any of the unsavoury characters he dealt with intruding into his family life. She felt a warm glow of contentment. He was only trying to keep her safe.

Feeling relieved, she picked up a magazine and began flicking through the pages.

CHAPTER 18

When she missed a period, Ellie paid little attention. Even after a second period was missed, it still never crossed her mind that she might be pregnant. Since she'd never conceived during her marriage, Ellie had always assumed that becoming pregnant wasn't ever going to happen for her. But now she finally – and joyously – was confronted with the truth. She was expecting!

She was excited and frightened all at once. She hadn't told Alan yet – in fact, she was only getting used to the idea herself. And since she was now in her late thirties, she wasn't going to miss the opportunity of having this child.

Ellie was bubbling with a mixture of excitement and tension as she waited for her beloved Alan to arrive. She'd now passed the first trimester of her pregnancy and she'd finally decided that the time was right to let him know. Giving Alan a child would put her on a par with Sylvia, and she'd been anticipating this moment for weeks. In her own mind she'd played the scenario over and over like a continuous newsreel, and in it he'd expressed his delight and excitement at her revelation. She'd gone through the scene so often that she felt certain it would play out exactly the same way in reality.

Nevertheless, a shadow of doubt briefly flickered across her face. Perhaps she'd also delayed telling him until her pregnancy was far enough advanced that he couldn't suggest any alternative course of action . . .

As she watched his car coming up her driveway, she felt her heart thumping uncomfortably in her chest. She seemed to be waiting for an eternity as he parked his car behind the house, gathered up the bouquet of flowers he often brought her, and stepped into her hall. She'd planned to wait until they were in bed before telling him, but she was so nervous that she blurted it out the minute he arrived.

"I'm pregnant!" she announced, watching his face closely to gauge his reaction. She'd hoped to see delight, but instead she saw confusion, followed by a look of guilt as he struggled to say something appropriate.

"B-but I thought –" he said at last.

"You thought I was taking precautions?"

"Well, yes, I assumed . . ."

"I never managed to conceive during all the years that John and I were together, so I assumed I wasn't able," she told him, disappointed by his initial reaction. But she wouldn't give up this child, even if he begged her to. This was probably her last chance to be a mother, and she would keep the child regardless. She looked at him from under her eyelashes. "You don't mind, do you?"

"No, of course not!" he said quickly. "If that's what you want? If you do, then that's wonderful!"

"But is it what you want? To have a child with me?"

"Yes, yes, it's just that –"

He took her in his arms, but since she knew him so well, she was aware that something was definitely wrong.

"What is it?"

"You know I can't leave Sylvia yet."

Ellie nodded, relieved that this was all that was bothering him. "Of course I understand – I know by now how heavily in debt you are to your wife's father. But this pregnancy was totally unexpected," she assured him earnestly. "I don't want you thinking I'm putting a gun to your head. I know our time hasn't come yet. But this impatient little person," she patted her stomach tenderly, "has moved things up a notch."

He still didn't look convinced.

"I know I must wait for you," she whispered, slipping into his arms. "But this may be my only chance to have a child – I'm not getting any younger, you know."

He kissed her forehead tenderly. "You'll always be young to me," he said.

"So you're happy for us?"

"Of course."

Ellie allowed him to hold her in silence, aware that it would be financial suicide for her to try to rear this child alone and without his support.

He seemed to read her thoughts. "Your child will want for nothing," he whispered. "I'll make sure that you have everything you could possibly need. And all the medical care you need during the pregnancy."

Deflated, she said nothing. He'd referred to 'her' child – already he seemed to be distancing himself from the baby she was carrying.

He smiled as though to placate her. "Don't worry – I'll love this child just as much as –"

She silenced him by resolutely placing a finger on his lips. "Don't say it – I don't want to hear you refer to this child as the illegitimate one."

"I wasn't going to –"

She bridled. "Well then, how were you going to refer to it? By referring to your other child as legitimate, you'd be implying that this child isn't!"

"Oh love, please don't split hairs – I know this complicates things, but we'll get through it."

She sighed, her dream now slightly tinged with sadness. She'd hoped and dreamed of a more positive reaction from him. If only the three of them could be a family! But since she had to share him, then that's the way it would have to be. She'd decided long ago that it was preferable to have a small amount of time with someone she loved rather than a whole life with someone like Tony Coleman.

"Well, I'm not prepared to live on the fringes of your life. I want this child," she touched her belly, "to have all the advantages her child will have."

"Of course – anything you want," he said, kissing her gently.

With that, Ellie had to be content. She knew he'd ensure that her child would have the best of everything – after all, she'd now forged a lifelong connection with him.

The following day he bought her a car – a brand-new, blue, four-door saloon – and had it delivered to her door. He was beaming when he arrived later in his own car, and saw it parked outside her house.

"To match the colour of your beautiful eyes," he told her tenderly, watching with delight as she fingered the keys to the new car in wonderment. "It's fully taxed and insured – I don't want you walking, or taking that damned bike anywhere while you're carrying my baby! I want you to take things easy, and not take any risks with your health, okay?"

As she nodded gratefully, he leaned down and kissed her belly through her dress.

"I want our baby to come into the world happy and healthy, and that means you must take care of yourself!"

Overwhelmed with love and gratitude, she kissed him hungrily. As always, he'd already set her body on fire for him, and she couldn't wait to hold him close to her.

Without speaking, she led him upstairs, where they eagerly undressed each other and fell onto the bed where she climbed on top of him. She was feeling both powerful and very loved as she took him to the heights of ecstasy.

Afterwards, they made love again, more languidly this time, then they lay contentedly in each other's arms.

"Hello, little baby," he whispered, addressing the slight swell of her naked belly. "I don't know you yet, but I love you already." He turned to face her. "And I love you, my darling Ellie, the mother of my child, so very much!"

Ellie smiled, feeling cherished and content. She was now feeling more positive about the future. Alan had accepted the baby, and the dark clouds that had threatened to engulf her had finally been blown away.

CHAPTER 19

Laura was relieved to be going home at last. But during visiting hours, Jeff had offhandedly informed her that he wouldn't be available to collect her the next day, and that she'd have to take a taxi home on her own.

After he'd left her hospital room, Laura couldn't stop the tears. She felt wretched, and hurt that her husband couldn't be there for her. She assumed that it was the demands of his job that were keeping him away, and she suddenly wished Jeff had an ordinary nine-to-five job. Other people had offered to bring her home – Darren was first to offer, then Maria, followed by Kerry. But she'd turned them all down – pretending that Jeff was collecting her – because she couldn't bear to see the pity in their eyes.

Once back in the apartment, Laura looked around at all the magnificent fittings, state-of-the-art kitchen and sumptuous furnishings, and felt her heart almost break. On the surface, she and Jeff had everything. But where it mattered, they seemed to have very little. Laura wondered if she was lacking somehow. Maybe Jeff needed a much more dynamic woman than she was. Clearly, she wasn't enough to make her husband happy. Was Jeff as disappointed with their marriage as she was? Nevertheless, she was expecting a baby with him, so she'd make the best of it in order to create a good home environment for their child. And she'd try to be the best mother she possibly could.

The following day, Laura returned to work. Her colleagues were surprised to see her back so soon, complimenting her on being so keen, and urging her to take it easy. They all volunteered to ease her workload, or bring her coffee or food from the canteen. Their kindness overwhelmed her, and she felt a sense of peace in her work surroundings that she never seemed to feel at home. Why couldn't Jeff express those same caring feelings? He was supposed to love her, whereas her colleagues, who were simply acquaintances, had shown more humanity and kindness to her than he ever had.

Darren fussed and flapped like a mother hen, urging her to put her feet up at every opportunity, and insisting that she give only one lecture a day instead of two.

It felt good to be pampered, but Laura was keen to pull her weight and get back to her full-time schedule as soon as possible.

"I'll be late home this evening," Laura said, hoping Jeff wouldn't throw a tantrum. "There's a debate organised by the students of the Literary & Historical Society, and Darren has asked me to attend. All the staff in the department will be going, to give moral support to our students."

Jeff shrugged his shoulders as he sat in front of the TV. "What's the debate about?"

"That drugs should be legalised immediately by the government."

Jeff looked up, his eyes narrowing. "How could anyone be so stupid?"

"It's only a student debate," Laura said mildly, not sure what exactly he meant by his comment. But she felt that it was safer to avoid any further discussion.

Yet Jeff suddenly seemed keen to keep the conversation going.

"What's your opinion?" he asked, and for a second Laura hoped they were about to have a pleasant discussion about it.

"Well, I'd favour legalisation," she said, smiling. "Governments have been fighting the drugs war for years, without any success. Like Prohibition, once you forbid something, it goes underground. If drugs were freely available, it would reduce crime, and save taxpayers the money that's currently being spent on keeping people in prison. The quality of the drugs would be better too – they wouldn't be cut with dangerous substances like chalk and flour."

Jeff was getting angry. "I might have known you'd feel that way," he said disgustedly. "That's what you lefty, university types think – yet people like me know the harsh reality! Drugs should never be legalised!"

"Jeff, it's only a debate!" Laura said quietly. "My opinion doesn't count – it's the students who are debating the issue."

She could see how agitated he was becoming. She touched his shoulder in a calming gesture. She could guess why Jeff would oppose decriminalisation – his parents had probably been drug-users as well as being violent psychopaths.

"I'll be back about ten tonight."

Jeff looked truculent. "Why aren't you coming home first?"

Laura smiled to lighten the tension that she realised was building. "It's hardly worth it – I'd barely be here for half an hour before I'd be leaving again. I'll just grab something to eat in the canteen before it closes," she said, avoiding mentioning that all the lecturers were meeting there before heading off to the debate. Jeff would become angry if he knew that other men would be in her company. It was ridiculous that she had to watch everything she said – it was like being a teenager again, and needing parental permission to go anywhere.

By now Jeff had risen to his feet, and too late Laura recognised the manic gleam in his eyes. "Are you saying I'm hardly worth spending half an hour with?" he asked, his voice deceptively gentle.

"No, no – of course not!" Laura said anxiously. "I love spending time with you."

"Then why are you going to this stupid debate?"

"Because Darren asked all the lecturers to attend," she explained anxiously.

Jeff's voice was low and menacing. "So what Darren says is more important than what your husband wants?"

"No, of course not!"

"Then stay here, with me, tonight."

"Jeff, be fair! I promised Darren I'd go –"

"And we can't break a promise to good ol' Darren, can we?"

Laura was torn by indecision. She shouldn't have to beg, but she was actually afraid. In fact, she was suddenly terrified.

"Jeff, it's part of my job! I have to be seen to support my own students –"

The blow, when it came, was almost a relief. She'd been expecting it for several minutes, and she was momentarily blinded by its impact. At first, she thought her neck had been dislocated, but as the pain receded she found she could still move her head. Her hand reached up and felt a deep gash along her cheek. Already it was beginning to throb.

"Why do you make me so mad?" Jeff screamed. "You're the most infuriating and self-centred woman I've ever met! The only thing that matters is what you want!"

Laura longed to verbally retaliate, but she was too terrified. Jeff was actually blaming her for his own behaviour. Touching her stomach, as though to reassure the child within, she rushed into the bathroom. Immediately locking the door, she surveyed her pale red-eyed face in the mirror over the sink, and watched as the blood dripped from the open gash and ran down the length of her cheek. There was no way she could go to the debate now. Tears filled her eyes, blurring the image of her face in the mirror. She felt so tired that she hadn't even the energy to open the bathroom cabinet and find ointment and a dressing. As her legs gave way, Laura sank to the floor and wept.

CHAPTER 20

As Ellie's pregnancy progressed, she sometimes became emotional and insecure, and Alan tried to spend as much time as possible with her.

"I'm sorry we can't go places together – at least, not to the places where I have to go with Sylvia." He looked earnestly into her eyes. "But, my love, we already have our own special places."

True to his word, he regularly took her to out-of-town restaurants, private dining rooms and hotels, where she felt that they were a real couple. He always took her to expensive places that none of the factory employees could afford to patronise. They also went to places where a nod, a wink and a large tip would ensure complete discretion.

It was agreed that if, on any of these occasions, they encountered anyone who knew Alan, he'd introduce her as a supplier with whom the factory was doing business. They even invented a new identity for Ellie, so that she'd have a name and a fictitious company if such an occasion arose. Often, they'd play silly games based on her new identity, and she'd pretend to be a stranger, meeting him for the very first time and propositioning him. It all felt very exciting and cloak-and-dagger-ish, and she enjoyed the fillip that the element of danger added to their time in public together. Being on edge always kept the magic alive.

And when his wife and son were away visiting family, Alan was able to stay overnight, and for Ellie these were the best times of all. On those occasions, she almost felt as though they were a married couple. Alan would do small repairs around her house, like fixing a leaking tap or mending the gutter. They would prepare meals side by side, she frying the steaks while he prepared the salad and rice. Then they would sit down at the kitchen table and eat together before cuddling up on the sofa in the dining room to watch TV. Sometimes one thing led to another, and they wouldn't manage to reach the bedroom. The floor in the living room would quickly be strewn with their clothing as the urge to make love overwhelmed them.

As they sat down to dinner in Ellie's house one evening, contemplating a night of passion later, Ellie couldn't resist bringing Sylvia into the conversation. She didn't really like asking Alan what Sylvia thought about anything, because it brought a third party into their midst, someone whom she wished didn't exist. But she was curious to know how he was managing to get away for an overnight with her, since Sylvia wasn't away this time.

"Where does Sylvia think you are tonight?"

He laughed guiltily. "She thinks I'm taking a group of our fruit and vegetable suppliers to dinner, and staying over at the hotel rather than risk driving back after drinking too much wine. She seems to have forgotten that I did that deal with our suppliers months ago. Remember that time when I was away for several days?"

Ellie nodded, remembering that time only too well.

"Luckily, Sylvia doesn't take much interest in the business, so it's easy to ply her with reasons to be out of the house." His eyes twinkled, and he looked for all the world like a naughty boy. "She's incredibly trusting, and sometimes it makes me feel very guilty."

Ellie didn't like Alan feeling guilty, especially where Sylvia was concerned, so she quickly changed the subject.

"I've had my first check-up today, and the doctor says everything's fine," she told him, caressing the slightly swollen mound of her belly.

"That's marvellous," Alan said warmly, "I just know you're going to be a wonderful mother!"

Ellie nodded smugly. Having this baby would tie her to Alan in *a way that even a marriage certificate couldn't.*

Alan began pouring her a glass of the expensive wine he'd brought, but Ellie looked at him apologetically. "I don't think I should," she said, placing her hand over the glass. "I don't want this baby ending up with foetal alcohol poisoning!"

Her comment had a sobering effect on both of them, as they contemplated all the changes their relationship was about to undergo.

"We'll be okay, won't we?" Ellie asked softly, twisting her gold and diamond ring.

Alan nodded, knowing exactly what she meant. "We'll be fine," he said gently. "All relationships change, but we're both in this for the long haul."

"And we will be together some day, won't we?"

Alan stood up and hurried round to her side of the table, crushing her in a hug. "Of course we will!"

CHAPTER 21

As Laura hurried along the university corridor, hoping to sneak into her office unnoticed, her heart sank as she saw Darren approaching from the opposite direction. It would be churlish to ignore him so, keeping her head slightly tilted, she gave him a cheery wave before quickly unlocking her door and stepping inside. She'd covered this new gash on her cheek with make-up as best she could, but it was still obvious, and she didn't want anyone commenting on it, least of all Darren. Despite those thick glasses of his, he didn't miss a thing.

Fortunately, she didn't have to give any lectures until the afternoon, and she hoped that by then, any swelling would have gone down. This morning, she intended staying in her office and getting on with all the papers she had to correct. Hopefully, she could do that without having to see anyone.

But it was not to be. Laura cursed silently as she heard the rap on her door. Briefly, she considered ignoring it, or pretending she hadn't heard it. But she was meant to be a professional, and in a work situation she couldn't simply ignore it.

Turning her head to hide the scar, she pretended to be studying a pile of papers as she called out: "Come in!"

Her heart sank as Darren stepped inside and closed the door.

"Laura, I didn't see you at the debate last night – are you okay?" he asked anxiously. "I also noticed you were holding your head rather oddly out in the corridor, so I thought maybe you'd hurt your neck –"

He gulped as she turned to face him. "Oh, my God. What happened?"

"I-I walked into a door."

"Ah."

He said nothing more, and Laura could feel the tears stinging in her eyes. He didn't believe her. He was allowing her to save face, and that made her feel even worse.

They stared at each other, Darren unsure what to say next, and Laura almost daring him to say anything else.

His brown eyes clouded with concern as he crossed the room and silently took her in his arms. His kindness and support was Laura's undoing. The floodgates opened and she wept, her tears soaking the shoulder of his jacket.

"Was the door's name Jeff?" Darren whispered.

Laura was about to shake her head, but then she realised it was pointless. It was obvious to anyone with half a brain that a door couldn't have inflicted an injury like that, and her tearful demeanour wasn't helping either. She was finding it hard to pretend that everything was okay when it clearly wasn't.

"It was an accident," Laura told him.

"Yeah, they're always accidents," Darren added dryly. "Is there anything I can do? I think you should go home – you're in no state to give lectures today. In fact, you shouldn't have come in at all."

Laura shuddered at the thought of going home. That was where it had happened. And even though Jeff wouldn't be there, just being in the apartment would make her jumpy and insecure.

Darren rubbed her back affectionately. "Look, I'll get Maria or Timmy to take over your lectures today. In fact, for the rest of the week."

"No, honestly –"

"That's an order, Thornton – sorry, Jones – and it's not negotiable." He suddenly grinned. "It's occasions like this that make me love being the boss!"

Laura couldn't help smiling back through her tears. Darren was such a sweetie.

Then his face darkened. "If you don't want to go home, I can give you the keys to my place," he said. "You can stay there as long as you need to –"

Vehemently, Laura shook her head. "I'm okay. Thanks, Darren, I'll go home."

Darren released her from his embrace and stood back, looking at her sadly. "Are you sure that's wise? Maybe a break for a few days would be a good idea."

Laura shuddered. She could imagine Jeff's reaction if she told him she was staying in another man's apartment.

"No, it'll be fine."

Darren studied her injured face. "Have you seen a doctor? Just in case you've broken your cheekbone. Or I can drive you to the hospital –"

"No, no – thanks, Darren," Laura said firmly. "I'll take your advice and leave the lecturing to Maria or Timmy. But I'll stay on here and get the students' essays corrected –"

"Don't even think of it, Laura. You need to rest, and give your cheek a chance to heal."

Laura nodded, overwhelmed by his kindness. "Thanks, Darren – I'm really grateful. But I'm going to insist on taking the essays with me."

"Okay, but take it easy for as long as you like," Darren said gently. "I don't want you back here until you feel fit and well again. And if there's anything I can do – just pick up the phone. You know I'm always here for you."

Nodding, Laura turned away. Darren's kindness had brought tears to her eyes once again. It was good to know that somebody cared, because she felt terribly alone and vulnerable.

"Laura –"

She stopped in her tracks, but didn't turn back to face him, knowing what was coming.

"You don't have to stay with him just because you're pregnant," Darren said softly.

Laura didn't answer, because she didn't know what else to say.

CHAPTER 22

As Tony Coleman made his final nightly check on the machinery in the factory, ensuring that everything was turned off and the safety switches turned on, he wondered yet again how he might advance his suit with Ellie. Perhaps he should make another attempt at asking her out. After all, a widow must get lonely, and he was comfortably off and could give her a good time.

He'd fancied Ellie ever since she'd arrived at the factory, but back then she'd been married, so he hadn't given any serious thought to a relationship with her. But after her husband died, he'd begun looking at her in a very different way. She was gorgeous – any man could see that. He'd tried to attract her attention any time she visited the factory floor, but she'd never shown any interest in him. His heart had plummeted when he'd heard she was leaving the factory, but then it occurred to him that he was being handed an even better opportunity. If he offered to help her establish her new business, he might gradually worm his way into her affections . . .

But Ellie hadn't seemed interested. Although she'd danced with him enthusiastically on the night of her leaving party, she'd left early without making any arrangements to see him again. Unless she was playing hard to get? He was still smarting from his first abortive trip to Ellie's house. Just his bad luck that his boss should turn up at precisely the same time with her holiday pay. But he managed to convince himself that his visit had simply been bad timing – Ellie was hardly going to profess any feelings for him with her former boss present, was she?

He'd eventually risked a second visit, and had been surprised when she'd accepted his invitation to the cinema, but that hadn't ended particularly well. After going out of his way to drive her home, he'd left her house with a flea in his ear. All he'd wanted was to make his feelings clear, but Ellie hadn't seen it that way. And although she always maintained that she was single, he'd got the distinct impression that there might be another man somewhere in the background . . .

Nevertheless, Ellie didn't seem to go out much – he'd never seen her socialising in any of the local pubs, nor did she attend the weekly bridge club where he played every Monday night. Then again, he was relieved that she wasn't out socialising, since undoubtedly she'd have been snapped up by now. She was a stunning-looking woman, with those luscious lips, big blue eyes and the figure of a goddess. Perhaps he should make another move soon, before some other guy set his beady eyes on her. Surely his position as factory manager must count in his favour?

He'd rarely seen her in the intervening months, although she was seldom out of his thoughts. But since she never seemed to go out, there was little opportunity of bumping into her casually. The only hope of seeing her was to call to her house, and he was wary of doing that yet again.

As he shut the main door of the factory, turned on the alarm and headed for his car, he decided to make one more attempt at declaring his intentions. Ellie was a prize worth winning, there was no doubt about that.

Tony nursed a pint – and his bruised ego – in his local pub, as he tried to come to terms with the events of the evening. Earlier, he'd risked another visit to Treetops, but Ellie had let him know, in no uncertain terms, that his attentions were unwanted. He supposed he'd only got himself to blame – he'd behaved stupidly on that previous occasion when they'd gone to the cinema together. He now knew that he should have played it cool and taken his time in courting her. It was never a good idea to declare yourself too eagerly where women were concerned.

Tony took a swig of his pint angrily. Anyway, she looked as though she was putting on weight. He'd been astonished at how rapidly her waistline had expanded since he'd last seen her. She certainly didn't look as attractive to him as before. Tony preferred slim women, so perhaps it was all for the best, he told himself. He didn't need a shrewish overweight woman in his life. At the rate she was putting on weight, she might reach twenty stone by the end of the year! Then he'd be too embarrassed to be seen with her. He slammed down his now empty glass. All in all, he'd probably had a lucky escape.

CHAPTER 23

The following week, Laura returned to the university. She hadn't told Jeff the real reason why she had the week off – he'd have been livid if he thought any of the university staff were aware of what had really happened. Instead, she simply told him she was correcting papers at home, which was perfectly true. She was glad she'd insisted on taking them with her when Darren had ordered her home to rest – otherwise she didn't feel she could justify taking her salary.

She still felt overwhelmed by sadness. She'd done as much as she could to help Jeff cope with his demons, but she seemed powerless to lessen his pain. Even when he'd been rude and offensive, she'd bitten her tongue, hoping that by refusing to react, he'd calm down and realise that she wasn't his enemy. Jeff had a gigantic chip on his shoulder, and it seemed to be getting bigger. Blithely, she'd believed that marriage would give him the security he craved – and which she craved too – but nothing seemed to pacify the monster within him.

She was also becoming frightened by his sexual demands – what she'd initially believed to be passion had degenerated into a form of violence. But she was too embarrassed to discuss his demands with anyone else. Not only did it seem like a betrayal, but also her own personal pride was preventing her from admitting that her marriage was less than perfect. She'd hoped that if she cared enough, and put up with Jeff's tantrums enough, he'd eventually calm down and become secure in his marriage. But in solitary moments of contemplation, she had to admit that this prospect was looking decidedly unlikely.

She was also deeply worried by what Kerry had told her. Her friend seemed convinced that Jeff was involved in some kind of criminal activity because she'd seen him with a drug-dealer. But Jeff hated drugs – he'd already made that very clear to her, so he couldn't possibly be involved in selling them. She preferred to believe that he was simply doing his job for MI5, and that his bad humour resulted from the precarious and dangerous situations in which he had to work. Nor could she forget the words of Paul, the trauma counsellor. But now, whether she liked it or not, she and Jeff were having a baby together.

The previous night, he'd come home in a temper, and despite her efforts to cheer him, he'd turned on her again. "What do you know about problems?" he'd sneered. "You haven't got a clue!"

"Well, that's because you won't tell me anything!" she'd retorted, angry that he could negate her own suffering so offhandedly. She'd lost her entire family, yet he treated that monumental event as though it counted for nothing.

"You know I can't tell you!" he'd screamed, lashing out with his hand, catching her across the cheek with his wedding ring. The gash on her cheek from his previous attack had now been split open again. As she reeled from the blow, she could feel wet on her cheek, and her fingers found blood as she touched the broken skin. Storming out of the room, Jeff slammed the door and retreated to the TV room.

Laura's eyes filled with tears. Was it always going to be like this? She was carrying his baby, yet even that didn't seem to affect his attitude to her. Why wasn't she one of those lucky women whose husbands cherished them during their pregnancies? Her heart was breaking, but still she wasn't prepared to give up on Jeff. If only she could break through the wall of pain that surrounded him, she felt sure all would be well.

Later, he'd begrudgingly apologised, although he hadn't attempted to examine her injury, or offer any help. Laura said nothing when he'd mumbled his apology. There didn't seem to be anything worth saying.

Later that night in bed, he'd turned to her, and she'd hoped their coupling would bring them emotionally closer together, and help to heal some of the damage that Jeff's temper was doing to their relationship. But he'd taken her in anger, not heeding her cries of pain. It was as though her confusion and pain turned him on, or satisfied some terrible need deep within him. When she'd screamed and begged him to stop, he'd held her down, ignoring her protests.

"Shut up – don't think I won't kill you, too!" he'd muttered, as he continued to thrust violently into her.

Despite the pain, Laura's mind was buzzing. What did he mean by 'too'? Had he killed someone before? She didn't dare raise the issue with him – she was too terrified. She was seeing a side of Jeff that she didn't know at all. Kerry had tried to warn her but, as usual, she'd been stubborn and wouldn't listen. Could Kerry be right? Or was killing part of Jeff's job – could he be an MI5 assassin?

Afterwards, as she lay there wide-awake and unable to sleep, she rationalised it away as something he'd simply said in anger, on the spur of the moment. Nevertheless, his threat didn't augur well for their future. As she lay beside him while he slept, she wondered what demons were chasing him, and whether he could run fast enough to get away from them. A tear rolled down her injured cheek, and she wiped it away as gently as she could. Then she touched her belly, as though to assure the little baby within that she'd look after it, no matter what the future held.

CHAPTER 24

Sylvia sat on her bed and studied the thin blue line on the pregnancy test kit. She should be feeling elated, but instead she felt flat and uninvolved, as though this pregnancy was happening to someone else. If she felt anything, it was resentment. This should be a joyous time, but Alan's affair was taking away any pleasure she might feel. It was ironic that despite their rare and loveless coupling, nature had intervened with a plan of its own.

She wondered how Alan would view the news. Maybe it would be a blessing in disguise – surely no mistress would want to be with a man whose wife was pregnant? Maybe this pregnancy could be a turning point for them as a couple, and she could reclaim her husband's love. Perhaps forty years from now, she'd view this time as a brief and temporary glitch in an otherwise long and serene marriage. Maybe some day she'd laugh about this little hiccup, having weathered the storm and sailed into calmer waters.

Sylvia sighed. If only life could be that straightforward.

As he retired to an armchair with his newspaper after dinner, Alan noted the same depressing headlines as every other day. Interest rates were going up, profits were coming down, and protesters were taking to the streets over wage cuts. Didn't business people ever learn? If employees were properly paid, they wouldn't feel the need to protest. He allowed himself to gloat a little since he'd always made a point of looking after his employees, and they gave him their loyalty in return. If only the bank could be equally supportive!

Sylvia suddenly broke into his reverie. "Darling, what exactly does running private tuition classes involve?"

Alan immediately knew why his wife was asking.

"I've no idea," he said, shrugging his shoulders and hoping that would be an end to the subject.

But Sylvia was determined to keep it going. "I heard that's what Ellie Beckworth does now – she must be making good money – why else would she leave a permanent and pensionable job?"

There was a question implied, and Alan felt that some reply was necessary, but he didn't want to involve himself in any conversation about the merits or demerits of Ellie's departure from the factory.

"Hmmm," he mumbled, pretending to be completely engrossed in his newspaper.

"You're not remotely interested, are you?" Sylvia said, poking him playfully in the ribs. "You should be concerned about what your former employee is doing now – if too many of them leave to start their own businesses, you could end up running the factory on your own!"

Alan grinned. "Very funny, Syl. Anyway, I thought you were playing tennis this evening?"

Sylvia nodded, pleased that he'd remembered. "Yes, I was, but I've decided against it," she replied. "Given that my last pregnancy wasn't easy, I don't want to take any unnecessary risks."

Alan nodded approvingly and Sylvia felt a surge of hope for their future together. Maybe things would work out for the best. Alan had been surprisingly kind when she'd told him about her pregnancy. But he'd looked worried too and, as he'd hurried off to attend to some problem at the factory, she'd wondered if he was thinking that another child was one too many, given their precarious financial situation. To outsiders, they appeared to live well, but Sylvia knew how much Alan worried about the factory and its future. On the other hand, Daddy wouldn't let Alan's business fail, would he? And he was going to love having a second grandchild!

"Alan . . ." Sylvia hesitated, "are you genuinely happy about this pregnancy?"

"Of course I am!"

Sylvia still wished she'd had the courage to confront him with the evidence she'd found in his jacket pocket, and ask him who the beneficiary of the expensive ring was. But every time he looked at her so openly and unflinchingly, her courage failed her. On the other hand, did she really need her suspicions confirmed? As long as they could keep up a seemingly happy demeanour with each other, it was probably easier to maintain the lie that all was well between them. Hopefully the other woman would finish with Alan anyway, when she discovered that his wife was pregnant. Although if it was Janette, she'd probably enjoy the situation and use it to her own advantage, flaunting her tiny waistline in contrast to Sylvia's thickening one.

Alan abandoned his newspaper and crossed the room to where Sylvia was clearing the table, slipping his arms around her. "Are you happy about it, Syl? Is it too much for you – I mean, I know Pete's birth was difficult –"

"I'm fine," she said firmly. "I just needed to know that you were happy to have another child."

"Happy? I'm delighted!" he said tenderly.

His show of kindness brought tears to her eyes. Maybe she was wrong about his affair – how could he look at her so caringly if he was involved with another woman?

Breaking away, he looked at his watch. "I've got to check something at the factory," he told her cheerfully. "I'll be back in an hour or two, okay?"

When he'd left the room, Sylvia sighed to herself. They hadn't been intimate since the baby had been conceived, and Sylvia wondered if they ever would be again. Surely they were a little young to have abandoned marital relations already? Perhaps it was just that Alan was always so preoccupied with the running of the factory. He took his job so seriously that he was always going back there to check on some machine or catch up on paperwork.

Crossing to the window, she watched as he got into his car and drove away. She always detected something odd in his demeanour before he left for the factory. There was usually a spring in his step, *as though he actually enjoyed going there and dealing with all the problems.*

Sylvia sighed as she headed to the nursery to check on Pete. In a way, she envied Alan his devotion to his career. She just wished that he could have that same gleam in his eye when he was coming home to her.

CHAPTER 25

The following morning, Laura didn't feel well, but she got up nonetheless and went through the motions of getting ready for work. She felt a dragging sensation in the pit of her stomach, but she didn't want Jeff to start fussing, so she said nothing. Instead, she made toast and coffee for them both, and chatted as pleasantly as she could manage while they had breakfast together. Then, with a brief absent-minded grunt, Jeff gathered his keys and briefcase, waved goodbye and headed out the door. Laura sighed. The fresh cut on her cheek was throbbing, and although it had sealed itself again overnight, she was worried in case she'd be left with a scar this time.

As soon as she was certain that he'd gone, Laura sank down gratefully onto the couch. She didn't think she could go to work today. The dragging sensation had turned into severe pain. Despite reassurances from the hospital, she was worried that something might be wrong with the baby. Gripping her middle, Laura rocked from side to side, hoping that the pain might ease if only she could distract herself. She longed to take a painkiller, but she didn't dare in case it would have a detrimental effect on the baby. Maybe if she tried to read . . . grabbing the previous day's newspaper from the coffee table, Laura tried to focus her mind on the headlines. But she felt light-headed, and the print seemed to dance before her eyes. And the pain wasn't easing. If anything, it was getting worse. Now she was really beginning to worry.

Reaching for her phone, Laura called Darren, explaining

apologetically that she wasn't well enough to come in today. Perversely, she wanted Darren to bite her head off, but as usual he was kind and concerned, urging her to take as long as she needed to get well. There was no problem, he assured her. He'd ask Maria to take over her lectures until she felt well enough to return to the university. Laura had tears in her eyes when she came off the phone. He was such a sweet, kind man. Why on earth couldn't Jeff be a bit more like Darren?

A little while later, as severe pains began ripping through her abdomen, Laura grabbed her mobile phone and rang Kerry. She hated imposing on her friend and taking her away from her job at Sea Diagnostics, but there was no one else she would trust to help her. She didn't dare phone Jeff. Apart from the fact that he'd start fussing, right now she needed Kerry's calm authority to help her get through whatever was happening to her.

When she heard Kerry's voice over the intercom, she could barely struggle to her feet to press the entry button, and by the time her friend reached the apartment she'd collapsed onto the sofa again.

"Christ, you look awful!" Kerry whispered, as she hugged her friend. "And your cheek – it doesn't seem to be healing yet. What can I do for you? Will I make you a cuppa?"

Laura nodded, glad for some semblance of normality in her life, since right now everything else felt totally alien. She listened to the familiar sounds of tea-making coming from the kitchen, grateful for Kerry's presence. Maybe the tea would help to ease the terrible cramps that seemed to be getting worse.

When Kerry returned from the kitchen with two mugs of tea, a sudden look of dismay crossed her face as she placed them on the coffee table.

"Laura, I don't know if you realise it, but you've got blood on the sofa and it's dripping onto the floor . . ."

As Laura leaned forward to look, Kerry urged her to lie down again, and she rushed off to the bathroom to get some towels.

Laura bit her lip. Jeff would be furious with her for ruining the sofa and the carpet. She'd better ask Kerry to bring her a damp cloth, in the hopes that she could mop up the blood before it stained permanently . . .

"Listen, love, I think we'd better call an ambulance," Kerry said as she slid several towels under her friend.

Laura could detect the panic in her voice, although she was trying to hide it. "Do you think I'm having a miscarriage?" she whispered, pleading for a negative answer. But in her heart she already knew.

"I-I don't know, but something's definitely not right," Kerry told her as she dialled the emergency number. "You need professionals who'll know what to do."

Giving all the relevant details to the dispatcher, Kerry disconnected the call and sat down again beside Laura on the couch.

"It won't be long now, love – the paramedics will be here in a few minutes," she said reassuringly.

But Laura already suspected that it was too late to save the baby. And she felt guilty because she should have told Jeff how badly she was feeling before he left for work. If he'd stayed home and called the ambulance earlier, the baby might have been okay.

A tear rolled silently down her cheek. On the other hand, she had to face the fact that she hadn't wanted Jeff anywhere near her. He'd have started fussing, and somehow he'd have blamed her for what had happened. In fact, he'd probably blame her anyway. Somehow, with Jeff, everything seemed to be her fault.

"Would you mind getting me a wet cloth from the kitchen?" Laura asked anxiously. "I need to get the blood out of the sofa and the carpet –"

Kerry looked at her incredulously. "Stop worrying about the damned furnishings, Laura! I'll do my best to clean it up once the paramedics have taken you to hospital. Do you want me to call Jeff?"

Laura shook her head. "Let's see what the medical people say first. There's no point in bothering him until we know what the verdict is."

"But he'd want to be with you."

Laura looked at her unflinchingly. "Well, I don't want him there. He'd only fuss. Besides, you know he doesn't like me to ring him during the day."

Kerry raised an eyebrow. "Well, I think, under the circumstances, he'd expect you to call."

"Too bad," Laura snapped. She was beginning to feel angry with Jeff, feeling certain that his violent sex of the previous night had been a contributory factor in this already fragile pregnancy. But no doubt he'd blame her for the miscarriage.

Kerry said nothing, aware that this was the first time since her marriage that Laura had openly acknowledged that her husband might be less than perfect. It seemed that Laura was becoming a bit more realistic about Jeff.

The intercom rang, and Kerry leaped to her feet.

"That'll be the paramedics," she announced, her voice suffused with relief.

As Laura lay resting in her private hospital room, the door burst open and Jeff was suddenly at her bedside.

"Why didn't you phone me?" he screamed, furious. "Why the hell did you ring that so-called friend of yours? It was my baby you were having! I should have been there!"

Laura closed her eyes. She was too tired for arguments. In fact, she was too tired for anything. After the trauma of her miscarriage, she just wanted to go to sleep.

"Look, Jeff – firstly, you don't want me ringing you during work hours," Laura said at last. "Secondly, when I knew there was something wrong, it was a woman's advice and support I needed."

"That bitch never had a kid – what the hell did you expect her to know about it?"

"Jeff, please – I'm not in the mood for an argument," Laura said quietly. "There are times when only another woman can understand what you're going through, that's all. And when I needed an ambulance, Kerry was able to pack the kinds of things that I'd want in the hospital. Please don't take everything so personally."

"But I could have packed your nightdress and toiletries," Jeff said stubbornly.

A tear slid down Laura's cheek. Jeff hadn't even asked how she was feeling. All he could think of was his own loss. Well, she was devastated too. According to the doctors, there was no specific reason why she'd lost the baby, and they felt certain she'd carry any future baby to term. So that was good news really, although right now she just felt bereft and alone. She wished Jeff would put his arms around her and ask how she was coping. She wished they could share their pain with each other, and support each other through it. But instead it felt as though Jeff saw her as his enemy rather than his ally. She wondered if his aggressiveness was due to guilt – perhaps he, too, was remembering his vigorous sexual activity of the night before.

Laura's eyes filled with tears. "They told me it was a little girl," she said softly.

Jeff's eyes narrowed. "What? But I told you I wanted a son!"

Laura felt overwhelmed by sadness. "Surely you'd have been happy with a healthy baby? Anyway, it doesn't really matter now."

Jeff said nothing, but Laura could see that he was making a supreme effort to control his temper. He was far too clever to lose it in the hospital.

"When are you coming home?"

Laura shook her head. "I don't know yet – the doctor will be around later, and she'll give me her verdict then."

Jeff nodded, rising to his feet. "Well, phone me on my mobile when you find out," he said curtly, before leaving the room.

Alone in her bed, Laura could feel the tears coming, and she angrily brushed them away. It was as though Jeff was punishing her for losing the baby, and for daring to conceive a girl. He hadn't even brought her flowers – then again, flowers were for celebrations and they had nothing to celebrate. Suddenly, she couldn't stop the tears any longer, and they poured down her face as she sobbed bitterly. Since the very beginning of her pregnancy, she'd loved the baby she was carrying inside her. She'd dreamt of holding it in her arms – now, she'd never have a chance to tell her how much she had cared.

CHAPTER 26

Ellie caressed the soft material lining the bassinette. It was a glorious wickerwork creation lined with oodles of soft luxurious fabric and trimmed with lace. But, she thought, surely a baby would outgrow it very quickly? A cot would undoubtedly be better value. On the other hand, Alan had told her to spend as much as she liked on whatever items she needed – he'd said that only the best was good enough for their baby. "And have it all delivered," he'd insisted, "I don't want you carrying anything in your condition."

Already she'd been wandering around the baby section of the big department store for most of the afternoon, and she still hadn't managed to see all the items on offer. It was astonishing how many beautiful cots, prams, car seats and clothing were on display, and how much money you could spend on a tiny baby! She supposed that people went wild because a child's birth was a major milestone in their lives, and they wanted others to know how much the event meant to them.

She suddenly thought of her late husband John, and wondered what he'd make of her present situation. It was a very different life from the one she'd envisaged. Strange that she should think of death when she was in the process of creating new life, but thinking of all the expensive baby accoutrements made her think of her husband's funeral. She'd paid a fortune for his coffin, choosing the most ornate and expensive one in the catalogue to prove to herself and others how much she'd cared for him. Now she acknowledged that there had also been an element of guilt in her gesture because she feared that maybe she hadn't loved him enough. Certainly, she'd never felt for him as passionately as she did for Alan, and she knew if it hadn't been for John's death, she'd never have met the man whom she now loved more than life itself.

Feeling that someone was watching her, Ellie suddenly turned and found a pair of gentle brown eyes looking into hers.

"Oh hello," said Sylvia Thornton, "I thought it was you. You're Ellie Beckworth, aren't you?"

Ellie nodded, perturbed at this unexpected encounter. "And you're the factory owner's wife." She couldn't bring herself to mention Alan by name.

"Yes, I'm Sylvia. I sometimes see you shopping in the village, but we've never had a chance to talk before now."

Ellie felt self-conscious about her growing belly, especially when Alan's wife made a point of looking down at it.

"How far on are you?" Sylvia asked.

"Six months," Ellie murmured.

"You look the picture of health," Sylvia said approvingly.

Ellie tried to smile in acknowledgement, all the while wondering how quickly she could make her escape.

But Sylvia seemed determined to chat. "The stock here is wonderful, isn't it?" she said, fingering a tiny hat and matching mittens that hung on a display panel beside them. "I'm hoping for a girl this time – there are so many pretty dresses available!"

She smiled warmly at Ellie, who suddenly felt as though the world was crashing in on top of her. She felt dizzy and feared she was going to faint.

"Y-you're pregnant?" Ellie whispered.

"Yes!" Sylvia replied cheerfully. "I'm only three months gone, so nothing's showing yet. And we've no idea what sex it is either."

Ellie could feel her eyes welling up and she turned away, pretending to cough so that Sylvia wouldn't see her tears.

"I really shouldn't be browsing," Sylvia added, unaware that Ellie's world was collapsing all around her. "After all, most of the baby stuff we bought for our son Pete will be usable again. But I simply couldn't resist buying something!" She smiled, delving into a shopping bag bearing the store's logo. "If I have a girl, I'll be guilty of stereotyping, because I couldn't resist buying this gorgeous little pink outfit!" She waved the little dress and matching socks in front of Ellie, who longed to reach out and throttle her.

Sylvia suddenly noticed Ellie's white face.

"Are you alright?" she asked, alarmed. "Do you need to sit down? Look, they have a coffee shop on this floor – let's get you over there immediately."

Leaning on Sylvia and feeling ridiculous, Ellie allowed herself to be led into the coffee shop, where Sylvia found her a chair and asked the woman behind the counter for two coffees.

"Would you like something to eat?" Sylvia asked anxiously. "I find that I'm always ravenous when I'm pregnant."

Ellie shook her head, unable to speak because of the huge lump in her throat. She felt betrayed by Alan, and winded by what she'd just heard. At the very moment when Sylvia had revealed her pregnancy, something inside her had died. She'd never asked Alan about his sex life with his wife, but it had always been there, hanging over their relationship like a dark cloud. Perhaps the same issue hung over every illicit relationship. What lover didn't want to be the only one in their beloved's life?

She bit her lip to hold back the tears, recalling all the nights when she'd lain alone in her bed, wondering if he was making love to his wife. She'd longed to ask him about his marriage, but the words always got stuck in her throat and, besides, she didn't want to spoil the brief time they had together with queries and recriminations.

Logically, Ellie had always known that Alan and his wife must have some physical contact – otherwise Sylvia's suspicions would be aroused. Now, as she looked at Alan's wife across the café table, she was having to confront his other life head on. She'd never allowed herself to consider that the logical outcome of their occasional sexual activity could lead to another child.

Suddenly, Ellie realised that Sylvia had been talking to her, but she hadn't heard a word.

"P-pardon?"

Sylvia looked embarrassed. "I'm sorry for loading this on you, but I've no one else I can talk to, and somehow I feel I can trust you."

Ellie nodded, since it seemed the easiest thing to do.

Sylvia took a deep breath. "I think my husband's having an affair," she said softly.

Ellie gasped, wondering for a split second if Sylvia knew about her, and was about to confront her.

"Yes, I knew you'd be shocked," Sylvia said, looking miserable. "I was shocked too. I've no idea who it is – well, actually I did suspect someone we socialise with, but now I'm not so sure – and anyway, I've no idea what to do about it."

She looked imploringly into Ellie's eyes. "I've always felt that you're the kind of strong independent woman who'd be worldly about this kind of thing. Have you any advice to offer me?"

Ellie felt as though she'd stepped into an alternate universe.

"N-no, not really," she managed to say at last, but her voice sounded strangled and totally unlike hers. "I mean, it's probably best to do nothing," she added lamely.

Sylvia nodded, seeming to hang on Ellie's every word.

"It'll probably blow over," Ellie added again, trying to sound helpful, "These things usually do."

Sylvia grasped Ellie's hand gratefully. "Thank you," she said, a look of relief on her face. "You've no idea how relieved I am to hear you say that." She suddenly looked guilty. "I hope you'll keep what I've told you to yourself –"

Ellie nodded, unable to speak. She felt she was suffocating, and she found it impossible to drink the coffee that had suddenly appeared in front of her. She began to rise up from the table, knowing that if she stayed there any longer, she was in danger of breaking down.

Sylvia looked startled. "Are you feeling sick? Do you need something to eat? I could ask the waitress to get you a scone or a sandwich –"

"No, I'm fine thanks," Ellie said, stumbling from the table. "But I have to go – it was nice meeting you."

"And you, too."

I've embarrassed her, Sylvia thought sadly to herself. *Although I hardly know her, I've crossed the line by unfairly involving her in my problems. But I was desperate for some honest womanly advice. No wonder she doesn't want anything more to do with me.*

"Goodbye," Sylvia said sadly, wishing that Ellie could have stayed longer. "Good luck with your pregnancy."

"And you with yours," Ellie replied. Then she rushed out of the coffee shop and down the escalator as fast as she could. She desperately needed to get out of the store. She was overwhelmed by the need for fresh air . . .

In the local park, Ellie sat down on a bench and cried. She felt totally betrayed by Alan. He'd known for at least a month, maybe even two, that Sylvia was pregnant, yet he'd said nothing. He'd led her to believe that her own pregnancy was the most exciting thing that was happening in his life – whereas now he was also having a baby with his wife!

As long as she hadn't actually met Sylvia, Ellie had been able to imagine her as a vain, controlling, selfish woman, worthy of her hatred. But having discovered how genuinely nice she was, Ellie felt wretched at being the one who was cheating with her husband, and also bearing his child behind her back. Sylvia seemed so innocent, so genuinely interested in Ellie's pregnancy, and Ellie had the impression that she would have liked to make a friend of her. But there was no way she could bear to maintain contact with the woman she was deceiving.

This meeting also made her angry and insecure about Alan. How could he not love such a really nice woman as Sylvia? Perhaps he did love his wife, and he was lying when he told her that she was the only one he cared about? He clearly liked his wife enough to have sex with her. Maybe it was Ellie he was deceiving, and that he'd no intention of ever leaving his wife. Insecurity rose up inside her like bile. Had she mistaken intensity for intimacy? On the other hand, how could she claim to be a decent person herself, when Alan's wife was the innocent victim of their appalling deceit?

CHAPTER 27

When Jeff collected her from the hospital a few days later, they drove home in silence. Already, Laura had a headache from the sheer dread she felt at being alone with her husband. The silence in the car was oppressive, the atmosphere loaded with tension. She darted a glance at Jeff's profile, and could see that his lips were tightly pressed together and he was frowning – a sure sign that there would be hell to pay when they got home.

Then her anger reasserted itself. She hadn't done anything to provoke his ire! She hadn't lost the baby deliberately. If anything, Jeff should be consoling her, and showing her some kindness. Losing the baby had been a horrible and devastating experience, and her husband should be capable of understanding that.

When they reached the apartment, Laura fully expected Jeff to come round and open the passenger door for her, given that she was still a little unsteady on her feet. But Jeff remained in the driver's seat.

"You'd better get out," he told her. "I'm putting the car in the lock-up."

Biting her lip, Laura gingerly alighted from the car. This wasn't the homecoming she'd been hoping for, although perhaps it was the one she should have expected.

Alone, she let herself into the silent apartment. Instantly, she longed to be back in the hospital, where the medical and nursing staff had been kind and caring. Checking the sofa and the carpet underneath it, she sighed with relief. Thankfully, Kerry had managed to get almost all the bloodstains out, and what remained wasn't really noticeable. Jeff would have been livid if his designer furniture and Axminster carpet had been damaged, and right now she didn't want to give him any reason to complain.

When Jeff entered the apartment a few minutes later, Laura heard him cursing as he threw down his keys on the hall table. He was clearly in a temper. She felt too tired to cope with his mood, and hoped he'd either go back to work or go into the TV room and just leave her alone.

As she lay on the couch in the living room, Laura longed for a cup of tea. But she didn't dare ask Jeff, and she didn't feel well enough to make it herself.

To her relief, he disappeared into the TV room, but before long she heard the sound of things being thrown about. When she heard something large hitting the wall, she feared it was the TV set – or could it be her computer?

Struggling to get to her feet, Laura called out. "Jeff – what's wrong? Do you want to talk about it?"

The door of the TV room was suddenly thrown back on its hinges, and as Jeff strode over to the couch as she sat down again, his face was like thunder. "Talk about it? Of course I want to talk about it! I was trying to restrain myself, but if you want me to talk, I'll talk!" He stared down at her, rage and contempt in his eyes. "You stupid bitch, you couldn't even manage to hold a child in your belly! Other women manage it, so why can't you? What sort of woman are you, anyway? And not only that – you had to carry a female child when you know I want sons!"

Laura was shocked by the venom in Jeff's voice, and by his totally irrational views. Although she knew he was disappointed, she'd expected some sympathy for her situation. She felt weak and very tired, and all she wanted to do was sleep.

"Can we save this discussion until I'm feeling better?" she whispered.

"No, we can't! Anyway, you're the one who suggested we talk about it! So what the hell is wrong with you?" Jeff shouted, standing over her. "Did the doctors say why it happened?"

Laura was annoyed now. "Why do you assume it's my fault? The doctor said that these things happen sometimes – if there's something wrong with the foetus, nature decides to get rid of it, so it's for the best in the long run."

She was tempted to suggest that his recent violent sexual behaviour might have been a contributory factor, but the look on his face made her quickly change her mind.

Jeff's eyes narrowed. "I hope you're not implying that my genes are faulty –"

"No, of course not –"

The blow caught her across the side of her head, and suddenly she was seeing stars. What had just happened? Laura found herself on the floor from the impact of the blow, and when she put her hand to her mouth, blood came away on it. She felt something gritty inside her mouth, and realised that part of a tooth had broken off. Her head and her mouth were throbbing, and she realised that Jeff had hit her. Again.

As he stormed out of the room, Laura continued to lie on the floor, in pain and disbelief. She felt too lethargic to get up. Her insides hurt, and she wondered vaguely if she'd started bleeding again. The doctor had told her to rest for the next week, and to allow her husband to pamper her. Laura felt the tears forming – the doctor couldn't possibly imagine the kind of relationship she really had.

She must have passed out, because suddenly she opened her eyes to find Jeff smiling down at her tentatively, a mug of tea in one hand, a wad of tissues in the other.

"I'm sorry, love," he whispered, placing the mug on a small table beside her, and helping her up off the floor. Gently guiding her back onto the couch, he began dabbing her bleeding mouth with the tissues. "I don't know what came over me – I suppose I was just so disappointed. But we'll try again, won't we, love? And you'll give me a son next time, won't you?" He gave her a wheedling smile. "Isn't there a test that can tell what sex it is early on in the pregnancy?"

Laura was appalled. Was Jeff expecting her to abort a perfectly healthy baby just because it happened to be a female? She wished that a giant hole would open up in front of her and that Jeff would disappear into it. Right now, she didn't want to be anywhere near him. Because she knew that it wouldn't take much for his violence to flare up again.

"Of course we'll try again," Laura lied, "but I need time to recover before then. The doctor said I must heal before I can become pregnant again."

In truth, she had no intention of ever making love to this man again, if indeed her experiences with him could be called lovemaking – their sex life had always been on his terms. She'd just made up her mind to leave him, but she didn't dare tell him, because she knew what the consequences would be.

Although her lip and tongue were hurting badly, Laura took the proffered mug and downed the contents, enduring the pain rather than risk displeasing him.

By now, Jeff was kneeling down in front of the couch, weeping and begging her to forgive him. "It's just that I felt so disappointed," he sobbed. "But I shouldn't have taken it out on you, love. I'm so sorry."

Laura said nothing. Everything felt weird and out of synch. It was like living in a real-life Punch and Judy show, where she was in favour one minute and out the next, and there was no rhyme or reason as to why she was being punished.

"Do you want to tell me what else the doctor said?" Jeff asked, gently lacing his fingers through hers.

Laura shook her head. The last thing on earth she wanted was to discuss her miscarriage with Jeff. Or anything else, for that matter. "Not now, if you don't mind," she said dully. "I'm feeling very tired –"

Suddenly, Jeff's mood reverted to anger again. "But I'll bet you've discussed it all with your so-called friend!"

Laura sighed, no longer caring how he reacted, because as far as she was concerned, her marriage was now over. "If you're referring to Kerry, yes, of course I talked to her about the pregnancy – she was thrilled for us, by the way – and since she came to the hospital later, naturally she knew that I'd lost the baby."

"You mean, *we* lost the baby! And how dare you discuss our relationship with that – that – creature!"

Laura was furious now as well as tired. "For heaven's sake, Jeff – it's perfectly natural that I'd want to discuss the miscarriage with her."

He glared at her. "I suppose you've told her about our arguments, too?"

Laura grimaced, aware that yet again Jeff was refusing to accept responsibility for anything he'd done. 'Arguments' implied equality between the participants, whereas Jeff was always the angry one, and the perpetrator of the violence that inevitably followed.

"Yes, Kerry did notice the bruises, and asked me about them."

Jeff snorted. "How dare you tittle-tattle to someone else! It demeans our relationship! That's what my mother used to do – she'd run to the neighbours, humiliating Dad in his own street!"

Despite her injuries, Laura no longer felt afraid of expressing her own anger. "But your father hurt her! She needed to get help!"

Laura could see that Jeff's face was turning red again, and he looked as though he might burst a blood vessel. Suddenly, she worried that his anger might bring on a heart attack. Then she realised that she didn't actually care.

"My mother deserved it," Jeff said, his voice dangerously low. "She used to make Dad so angry that he'd take it out on me as well. Then she'd have another go at me when he'd left for work."

Jeff left the room, slamming the door after him. Shortly afterwards, Laura heard the door of the apartment slam, and she was relieved that he'd gone before his anger boiled over again. In effect, Jeff had tried to justify what his father had done, and was blaming his mother for her own suffering. Was that the way he viewed their marriage, too? It was little consolation that his anger was directed at the parents who'd physically abused him, and that she was merely a convenient vehicle through which he could act out all his pent-up rage. But she wasn't going to be his victim any longer – otherwise, she might end up dead, like his mother.

At last she was facing the unpalatable truth. She wasn't free to say anything she wanted, or have an opinion that was contrary to

119

his. Everything she said had to be passed through a filter in her brain, in order to ensure that it wouldn't offend him and result in her being battered.

Kerry and Paul the counsellor were right – it was time to get out. She'd tried to be the woman Jeff wanted – she'd done her best to restore his faith in human nature by being there for him, through thick and thin. But defending his father's violence didn't augur well for their future together. And if she had children with Jeff, she'd be trapped in a violent marriage. Because even if she left him, the courts would award him visitation rights, and she'd never be free of him. Now was the time to go, before another pregnancy linked them together forever. She felt sad for the baby that might have been, but also relieved that now she had no physical ties to Jeff. She could make a clean break.

Mopping her bleeding lip, Laura made her way to the bathroom, locking the door behind her in case Jeff should return.

Kerry answered immediately, listening as Laura told her that she was leaving Jeff.

"I'm phoning from the bathroom," Laura whispered, a tremor in her voice. "I feel guilty about going – I vowed to stay through sickness and health, and now I'm abandoning him, and leaving him to his demons!"

"Forget about Jeff, and get out this very minute!" Kerry urged her. "Will I come over and help you pack?"

"No – I don't want to risk another confrontation," Laura whispered. She could imagine Jeff's fury when he found out she'd left him. He'd see it as a massive betrayal, and he'd never forgive her. "Besides, I have a better idea," she added.

Laura explained to her friend what she intended to do, and Kerry reluctantly agreed.

"I'll make up your bed in the second bedroom," she replied. "And I'll be over first thing tomorrow morning – after Jeff's gone for the day – to put the first stage of your plan into operation."

"Thanks, love," Laura whispered, tears in her eyes. As always, her dear friend was there for her when she needed support.

CHAPTER 28

"Why didn't you tell me?"

"Tell you what?"

"That your wife is also expecting your baby!" Ellie spat out the words venomously, hardly waiting until he'd stepped inside her front door before verbally assaulting him. Her eyes were red from crying, and she looked as though she wanted to tear him limb from limb.

Alan had the grace to look embarrassed. "How did you find out?" he asked. When there was no reply forthcoming, he sighed and looked at her uncertainly. "I just didn't know how to tell you," he said. "I'm sorry."

"Sorry you slept with her or sorry I found out? I thought you told me you didn't find her attractive?" Ellie said angrily. "Then how the hell is she three months pregnant?"

He licked his lips nervously, unable to find any words that would make sense. "Look, you know I have to sleep with her occasionally," he whispered, reaching out to stroke her back as though soothing an upset child. "But it's never like the way it is with you."

Swatting his hand away, Ellie folded her arms and said nothing.

"Ellie, you know her father holds a huge stake in the company now –"

"To hell with you and your damned factory!" Ellie shouted. "What about me? What about the child I'm carrying? It'll be born three months before your precious wife gives birth, but I doubt if there'll be any fanfare of trumpets for us, will there?"

"You know the score!" he protested. "I thought you said it was enough just to be pregnant? I thought you were so happy about it –"

"I was, until I found out that your wife is up the duff too! It makes a mockery out of all your declarations, doesn't it?"

"Don't be ridiculous!" he said angrily. "You know I love you, and you also know I'm looking forward to our baby. But you have to accept I have another life as well!"

"Oh, go to hell!" she shouted, pushing him out the front door and slamming it behind him.

It was the first time he'd left without making love to her.

Later that evening, on a pretext of needing to check something at the factory, Alan left Greygates and hurried back to Ellie's house.

When she opened the door and saw him on the doorstep, she burst into tears and tried to close the door on him again. But he ignored her protests and he pushed past her into the house.

"I'm so sorry, love," he whispered, trying to take her into his arms. "I just couldn't find the right words. But we'll make this work, won't we?"

"I really liked your wife!" Ellie said accusingly as she succumbed to his embrace.

Alan sighed. "Yes, Sylvia's just told me that she bumped into you in one of those baby stores."

"How could you treat us both so badly?"

"I never intended to hurt either of you," Alan said guiltily. "And I'm genuinely excited about our baby –" He patted her stomach gently. "I never lied to you about that."

"But what about Sylvia? She's really nice!"

"Of course Sylvia's a nice person," Alan said gently. "I just don't love her the way I love you." He sighed. "It's very much a marriage of convenience – but you know all this already. I've explained to you that her father's invested heavily in the factory – I'd be out of business by now if it wasn't for him." He kissed Ellie's tear-stained face. "So while I'm grateful to Sylvia for her family's money, my heart and my body belong to you."

"But you still sleep with her!"

He kissed her forehead. "Well, I can't afford to fall out with her, since it's her father's money that keeps the factory going."

Tears pricked Ellie's eyes. "It's always about money, money, money! Why can't you be happy just to live here with me?"

Alan looked at her bleakly. "Love, whether you like it or not, I already have a son – and now two more children on the way – all of whom I'll love and protect. I want them all to have a good upbringing and a good schooling." He looked at her angry face. "If there's no money, then it won't be possible to give them a decent education. And if the factory closes, hundreds of people will be out of a job. Is that what you want?"

"Don't you dare make me responsible for people losing their jobs!" she retorted, stomping out of the room. She hadn't told him about Sylvia's worries over his affair – she felt a peculiar loyalty towards his vulnerable and insecure wife. In fact, she felt totally confused about everything that had happened.

As she stood alone in the kitchen, Ellie wondered if she was a fool, and if it was time to take back ownership of her life. Perhaps, she thought spitefully, she would have been better accepting the attentions of Tony Coleman. At least he could have offered her marriage straight away. On the other hand, she deeply regretted accepting his invitation to the cinema that time Alan had been away, because it had led Tony to believe once again that she was interested in him. And despite making it clear that she'd never think of him that way, he'd called again recently, inviting her out to dinner. But before long his eyes had been drawn to her expanding waistline, and she'd seen a query in his eyes. Then he'd retreated quickly, the invitation abandoned. She wondered if he suspected she was pregnant? At least then, he wouldn't bother her any further!

Ellie sighed. Anyway, it was Alan that she loved, and it always would be, so help her. As she gazed unseeing out the window, she felt the fluttering of the child in her belly, and knew that there was no greater joy than knowing she'd soon fulfil her dream of becoming a mother. She'd made her choices, and she must learn to live with them.

She heard Alan coming into the kitchen, but she didn't move until he pressed against her and slipped his arms around her. She could feel the tension in his body, and since she knew him so well, she was aware that there was something else he needed to say to her.

"I can't leave Sylvia now, love," he said, holding her tight.

She longed to scream at him: But what about me? I'm pregnant too! Why is it acceptable to leave me all alone? But she said nothing, allowing herself to be held as she considered what all this meant for her own future as well as that of her unborn child. His wife's pregnancy felt like a huge betrayal to her, yet who was betraying who? She sighed, surrendering to her fate as she turned to face him, acquiescing by resting her head on his shoulder.

CHAPTER 29

"You sneaky bitch!" Jeff hollered down the phone. "You moved your clothes out bit by bit, so that I wouldn't notice! You planned this whole thing with that so-called friend of yours!"

"I'm sorry, Jeff, but there was no other way," Laura said, gripping her mobile phone tightly. "If I'd told you face to face that I was leaving, you'd have tried to stop me."

"Damn right I would've!"

Laura felt brave enough to state her case now that she was in the safety of Kerry's apartment.

"That's what I mean – I can't live in fear all the time. I really did love you, but I couldn't keep letting you hit me. You need to get help."

There was a pause at the other end of the line. "Will you come back to me if I get help?"

Laura sighed. "No, Jeff – I'm sorry. You've killed any feelings I had for you. You made me so afraid that all the love I had for you got pushed out of the way."

She could hear him crying in the background, and her own eyes filled with tears. It would be tempting to run back to him and try to soothe his pain, but it would never work.

"Look, you need to get long-term therapy if you want to have a truly equal relationship with someone in the future," she said gently. "But you've got to come to terms with your past before you can do that."

"I won't give you a divorce."

Laura sighed. "I haven't even thought that far ahead, Jeff.

Besides, when one person wants out of a relationship, it's over anyway."

"I love you, Laura – more than I've ever loved anyone. I'm so sorry for what I've done to you – I'll get help immediately. But please come back to me."

Laura wiped away a tear. She could hear the anguish in his voice. She could picture the little boy, terrified of his parents' wrath, but who had nevertheless absorbed their violent way of dealing with problems.

"Sorry, Jeff – I can't. I wish things didn't have to end this way, but I don't want to be scared any more."

She heard a sob at the other end of the phone.

"Okay, I can understand that," he said. "And I'm desperately sorry for what I put you through. But tell me there's hope for us."

Laura sighed. "No, Jeff, there's no hope. We could never get back to those carefree early days. Even if you got help, I'd still be worried that something I'd say would make you snap. I'm not prepared to take that risk any more. Anyway, it's better if we both start our lives afresh."

"Please, Laura – give me another chance."

He sounded so contrite, and momentarily Laura caught a glimpse of the old Jeff, the man who'd been tender and affectionate when they first met. He'd been so anxious for things to go right, and she'd needed to assure him that she genuinely liked his company and wasn't going to drop him. But before long, the boot was on the other foot, and she'd learnt how quickly he could switch from being nice to being nasty.

"No, Jeff – it's over," she said firmly. "You've hit me too many times, and you've even broken one of my teeth. I can't risk anything else happening to me. We haven't even been married a full year yet – what state would I be in if I stayed with you for another year? Accept it, Jeff – it's over."

"I'm so sorry for what I've done – I know it's pointless to tell you that I never meant you any harm."

Laura said nothing. She just wished the phone call would come to an end.

"I presume you're staying at Kerry's?"

"Yes, I am. For the moment anyway."

That afternoon, a huge bouquet of freesias and roses arrived for Laura at Kerry's flat. The attached card said '*Sorry*' and Laura felt tears welling up in her eyes as she thought of what might have been. Jeff had even remembered her favourite flowers – the ones she'd also chosen for her wedding bouquet. For a moment, Laura was touched. Then her tongue caught on her broken tooth, and she remembered the reality of her marriage.

CHAPTER 30

Sylvia felt exhaustion creep over her as she settled gratefully into the large armchair in the living room while Pete took his afternoon nap. Although she was hardly showing yet, this pregnancy was making her feel more tired than she'd ever felt before. Perhaps the problem lay in the fact that her previous pregnancy had been a joyful one. But now, having become convinced of her husband's infidelity, Sylvia felt the immense weight of her sadness bearing down on her. How could she feel joyful, or look forward to the birth, when it was clear that her husband no longer cared about her?

All the congratulations, and all the baby gifts that were already arriving, couldn't ease the pain she was feeling inside. She'd heard that the workers in the factory were also organising a collection for a baby gift, and she wondered how many of them knew about her husband's infidelity, and pitied her. Perhaps this planned gift of theirs was merely a sop to their consciences, and she longed to tell them where they could shove it. But, as always, she'd be the gracious boss's wife, thanking them for their thoughtfulness when she'd really rather scream and curse at them all. It was hard to bear all this anger and exhaustion without having someone with whom she could let off steam. She was used to people trying to become her friends simply because of Alan's position, but this was not the kind of friendship she wanted.

Sylvia was still puzzling over her recent meeting with Ellie Beckworth in the department store. Despite the fact that they were both pregnant, and could have been supportive of each other, for some reason the other woman wanted to keep her at arm's length. Did she feel that their social positions were too different? Surely nowadays, people didn't let things like that keep them apart? She could have helped Ellie by introducing her to a whole range of influential people, the kind who might have proved useful contacts for her tuition business. Being rebuffed was a new and hurtful experience for Sylvia – surely Ellie must get lonely too? Nevertheless, her tuition business was obviously doing well, Sylvia thought approvingly, since Ellie had recently bought herself a brand-new blue car.

When she'd broached the subject of befriending Ellie Beckworth with Alan, he hadn't thought it a good idea either. "You've lots of friends at your tennis club, and at the golf club too – surely that's enough for you?" he'd said gruffly. "I'd have thought you had more than enough people in your life already."

Sylvia felt annoyed. Who was he to tell her whom she could befriend? He hadn't consulted her when he'd taken a mistress, had he?

Sylvia sighed. Since she'd become convinced of Alan's affair, her skin had broken out in pimples and her hair had become lank and uncooperative. It was ironic that just when she needed to look her best, her body seemed to have turned against her. She felt exhausted by what she'd discovered, and unable to fight back. The pain of loss was so great that she no longer felt capable of engaging in witty repartee with her husband, or offering any sort of challenge to the woman who was taking over her position. She felt herself dwindling into a non-person, whom her husband didn't really see any longer, because his mind was filled with images of the woman who'd taken her place.

Apathy and anger were her twin bedfellows as she struggled to make sense of what was happening. What had she done – or not done – that had been the catalyst that altered Alan's feelings towards her? She tortured herself endlessly, wondering what it was that the other woman had that she didn't.

She wished she could know for definite who this other woman

was, so that she could see what she was up against, and hopefully find fault with her. She still wasn't certain if Janette was the guilty party, or if some other unknown woman had captivated her husband. Whoever it was, she hoped her eyes were too close together, and her laugh was grating, and that eventually her husband would realise it too. But Sylvia sadly concluded that the other woman's hair was undoubtedly glossier than hers, her breasts more pert than her own slightly pendulous ones. *As her star is rising,* Sylvia thought sadly, *mine is on the wane.*

Perhaps this was one of the reasons that she longed for a close woman friend, someone she could joke with and confide in – someone who'd distract her from her present woes and help her to appreciate what was good in the life she already had.

Sylvia wondered about the father of Ellie Beckworth's child. Since it obviously wasn't her late husband's, could it be someone from the factory? There had been rumours about Ellie and Tony Coleman, so he seemed most likely to be the father.

Sylvia's reverie was quickly cut short, as Pete began to scream. Clearly, his afternoon nap was over, as was her own chance to rest. "Coming, love!" she called soothingly as she dragged herself out of her comfortable chair and headed towards the nursery.

CHAPTER 31

"Stay here for as long as you like," Kerry told her. "Don't even think of moving into a place of your own yet. You need time to get your head together – I mean, it must all have been a terrible shock. And with the miscarriage, too, you're bound to be feeling down, and in need of some TLC."

Laura smiled gratefully. "Thanks, love – I really appreciate all your support. But I can't impose on you indefinitely –"

Kerry laughed. "Hang on, you've only been here for a few days! When you've been here for a few months, I might think about throwing you out!"

"Seriously, I feel I should start making plans – I don't want Jeff thinking that I'm a weakling who can't stand on my own two feet."

Kerry frowned. "You're still letting him rule your life – he's gone, so to hell with him. You must do what's best for you."

"Well, I still think it's best if I get my own place – you know what they say about guests and fish?"

Kerry laughed. "By all means start checking out places – I'll gladly look at apartments with you – but there's no rush." She squeezed her friend's arm in an affectionate gesture. "You don't want to push yourself too hard. You've been through so much lately, and I actually enjoy having you here."

Laura shivered. "Thank goodness I never told Jeff about the money – you were right as usual, and I was a great big fool! I could have made such a mess of things if you hadn't suggested I delay telling him –"

Kerry patted her shoulder. "There's no point in stressing yourself about it now – you did the right thing and that's all that matters."

Laura nodded, looking at the bare third finger of her left hand. Before leaving the apartment she'd shared with Jeff, she'd taken off her wedding and engagement rings and left them in an envelope with a note explaining why she'd gone. Now that she'd experienced his dark side, she was grateful to have a caring and generous friend like Kerry. Then she grimaced, remembering the wedding presents she'd had to leave behind in the flat.

"I'm sorry about leaving that fabulous coffee machine you gave us," she said ruefully. "It was a lovely gift, and I know you went to a lot of expense. But I don't ever want to set foot in that flat again, and I doubt if Jeff will surrender it willingly."

Kerry hugged her. "Don't give it another thought – a coffee machine is nothing compared to your safety. There are plenty of coffee machines in the world, but there's only one you."

"All the same, it's mean of him to keep everything –"

"Look, you're safe, and you're a free woman again," Kerry said equably. "It could have been a lot worse – imagine if you'd had kids, a car, and built up a whole series of memories together."

Laura nodded. "How was I so easily fooled? You saw through him early on, but I was such an idiot."

Kerry grinned. "I'd imagine your hormones had a lot to do with it! Jeff's a good-looking fellow, and he did more or less sweep you off your feet."

Laura nodded sadly. "How could I have thought you weren't happy for me?"

"I wasn't happy for you – I was certain that you were making a terrible mistake, and in my own clumsy way, I tried to tell you so. But there's only so far that a friend can interfere – I mean, it's your life. I just hoped that you'd delay the wedding for a while, so that you'd discover what Jeff was like before you actually married him."

Laura laughed ruefully. "But of course, I didn't listen – I couldn't wait to sign on the dotted line! But how did you know what he was like?"

Kerry shrugged. "I didn't – there was just something about him

– a kind of possessiveness that I didn't like. But for all I knew, that might have been a trait you admired. No one can ever know what goes on in someone else's relationship, so I just had to hope that you knew what you were doing."

"Well, I think you've proved conclusively that I didn't," Laura said ruefully. "I really did love Jeff at the start, and I genuinely thought we'd be happy together. I suppose I identified with his pain – he'd lost his parents at a young age too, so we had a lot in common. I think we were both lonely, and longed to create our own family unit." She grimaced. "I'm embarrassed to think that I fell for him because he seemed so needy – I thought I could give him the stability he craved, and that in return he'd never leave me. Now I know that we couldn't have been a worse combination."

She turned and looked searchingly at her friend.

"Why on earth did I stay with him after he'd hit me? I'm an intelligent, independent, educated woman, for Christ sake!"

Kerry looked away. "Probably because you're still riddled with guilt over the deaths of Pete and your parents. I think you probably let Jeff punish you for it."

Laura bowed her head. There was a ring of truth in what Kerry said – she'd always felt responsible for her family's deaths, because if she hadn't delayed her mother that fateful morning, their journey mightn't have led to such catastrophic consequences.

Kerry stood up and went to make coffee. "Let's stop talking about Jeff right now – he's in the past, and you don't ever have to see him again. He doesn't deserve any more space in your head."

Laura nodded. "Let's go out on the town tonight – there's a new bar open on Flower Street, and I'd like to give it a try. What do you think?"

Kerry punched the air. "An excellent idea! Let's paint the town red!"

The new bar on Flower Street was already packed when they arrived. There was a pleasant air of camaraderie among the customers, and the staff seemed efficient and friendly. There was a range of introductory drink offers written up on boards, and a group of young men were standing near the counter and downing shots in some kind of drunken competition.

"This place could become our local," Laura said approvingly, as she sipped her gin and tonic. "There seems to be a nice crowd here, and it's within walking distance of your place, Kerry. If I get an apartment near here too, we could meet up for drinks after work on Fridays."

Kerry nodded, glancing around approvingly. "Yeah, I like the design and layout of the place too – they've made the best use of the limited space, and I love the way they've disguised the reinforced steel joists holding up the mezzanine floor over the bar –"

"Can't you ever stop thinking about how things work?" Laura said, exasperated. "There are some nicely built guys here too! Needless to say, I'm off men myself for the foreseeable future!"

Kerry suddenly gasped. "Oh Christ, no – you're not going to believe this. Don't look now, but Jeff has just come into the bar!"

"Then we're leaving!" Laura said resolutely, downing her drink in one gulp. "I don't want to be anywhere near that – that –"

But it was too late. Jeff suddenly materialised beside them.

"Well, hello!" he said, smiling at them both. "What an amazing coincidence!"

"We're just leaving," Laura said abruptly.

Jeff looked hurt. "There's no need to go on my account," he said, using his most reasonable voice. "I'll stay at the other end of the bar if that's what you want. But there's something I wanted to ask you, Laura – would you like to have the coffee machine and the dinner service back? I feel it's unfair for me to keep all our wedding gifts. I could drop them off for you at Kerry's place –"

Laura found she was unable to speak. How weird that Jeff should be thinking about the very same thing that she and Kerry had been discussing earlier!

"No, thank you, Jeff," she said at last, her voice trembling, "I don't want you anywhere near Kerry's apartment. You can keep them."

Jeff looked crestfallen.

Kerry grabbed Laura's arm. "Come on," she said firmly. "We'll be late for our appointment. Goodnight, Jeff."

Strong-arming Laura out of the bar, Kerry marched her along the street, still holding onto her arm tightly, as though trying to control a recalcitrant child.

As they turned a corner, Kerry finally let go and the two women stared at each other.

"Is it always going to be like that?" Laura whispered. "Am I going to keep bumping into him everywhere I go? I feel sick – I really loathe him at this stage."

"Don't worry – it was just bad luck this evening," Kerry said firmly. "I'm sure he was just as surprised as we were. Besides, what else could he do but say hello?"

"But he came right over to us!"

"Well, he wanted to ask you about the wedding gifts."

"If he'd just stayed at the other end of the bar –"

"Well, he did offer to, in fairness," Kerry pointed out. "Look, maybe that bar isn't the best place for us to make our local – I mean, it's quite near to where you and Jeff used to live, so he could turn up there at any time."

Laura was shivering. "Don't you find it strange that we were talking about Jeff hanging onto the wedding gifts – then he turns up and offers to return them? It's as if he could read our minds . . ."

Kerry smiled, linking her arm through Laura's. "Now you're really becoming paranoid!" she said. "Come on – let's go over to the Irish bar in Cook Street."

Kerry glanced behind her. "Hopefully, Jeff will stay in the Flower Street bar – but you've got to face the fact that you're bound to bump into him from time to time."

CHAPTER 32

"*I want you to have the best of doctors, and the best care during your pregnancy,*" Alan told Ellie firmly. "*Let's book a private room for you at St James' Private Maternity Unit – it's reckoned to be one of the best in the country.*"

"*Is Sylvia going there?*" Ellie asked, then wished she hadn't mentioned his wife, but the words were out of her mouth before she'd had time to censor them.

"*No,*" Alan said mildly. "*That's why I suggested there. Sylvia will probably be referred to one of the teaching hospitals, because she's having even more complications than when she had Pete. She may eventually need another Caesarean section.*"

Ellie nodded smugly. "*It's a pity, isn't it, that some women aren't really cut out for giving birth naturally?*" Her tone implied that real women didn't need all this medical intervention.

Alan sighed. He knew how jealous and hurt Ellie was feeling about his other life, and he was anxious to keep her as content and even-tempered as possible, even if that meant swallowing her barbs about Sylvia. He was well aware of how irrational she could be while her system was flooded with hormones. He'd already seen her fly off the handle for nothing at all, and cry over the silliest of things.

"*Our baby is going to have the best of everything,*" he told her, holding her tight. "*I can't wait to hold this little person of ours in my arms.*"

"*Well, I've decided I'm having a home birth,*" Ellie announced triumphantly, watching to see his reaction. "I think any healthy woman should be able to give birth naturally, don't you? Women have been doing it for thousands of years!"

Alan refused to be drawn into answering such a loaded question. "Fine, if that's what you want –" he said. "But I want us to be sure that you can get the care you need if anything goes wrong."

"Why should anything go wrong?" Ellie asked archly. "I'm a healthy woman – not a wimp – and I'm only doing what nature designed me to do." She looked at him defiantly, daring him to disagree.

Alan held up his hands in appeasement. By implication, Sylvia had been excluded from this category of 'natural' women. But he knew by now when to let Ellie have the final word.

As her pregnancy progressed, Ellie bloomed. She was one of those women who developed a special glow – her skin became dewy and her hair and nails took on a lustre that the hormones of pregnancy supplied. Although she complained of feeling tired and unattractive, it was really only a ploy to focus Alan's attention on her. She was well aware of how good she looked, and that Alan's desire for her never lessened. If anything, he was even more attentive than before. And she never tired of hearing him affirm that she was even more desirable to him now that she was pregnant.

But a dark cloud nevertheless obscured her happiness. He'd made another woman pregnant too. She longed to know more about Sylvia's pregnancy, although she didn't dare to spoil the moment when he was with her. Alan seemed so content being in their own little cocoon that she didn't want anything from the outside world – or his other life – to intrude. But sometimes, thoughts of his other life broke through the tight control she tried to maintain, and somehow, try as she might, she simply couldn't regain her earlier feelings of euphoria.

The spectre of Sylvia's forthcoming baby would sometimes haunt her dreams at night, and blot out every other thought during the day. At these times she'd feel irrationally angry at the woman whose pregnancy was lauded and congratulated by everyone in the locality, and regarded as the natural order of things. She, on the other hand, felt unable to talk publicly about her pregnancy. And when she went shopping and saw people from the factory in the distance, she'd hurry in the opposite direction, since she'd no idea what she would say to them. She could imagine the snide remarks being made behind her back as they speculated on who the father of her child could be.

She'd sacrificed a lot to be with Alan. Her role as his secret wife had prevented her from doing a great many things, particularly from enjoying the benefits of other friendships, since there were too many aspects of her life that needed to be kept under wraps. She could never risk gossiping with friends over a cuppa or having a few drinks with them in a pub. There was too much at stake, too much she could never share with them, too much they might try to wheedle out of her, too much she might inadvertently confess.

One day she'd spotted Tony Coleman in the distance, and although she'd tried to avoid him, he'd seen her and come running after her.

"You're certainly looking well," he said, looking rather pointedly at her swollen belly. Ellie knew he was dying to ask her who the father was, but something prevented him from crossing that line.

Nevertheless, he'd been able to bring her up to date on his boss's wife's pregnancy, and since Ellie had been avid for word about Sylvia's condition, she'd put up with his otherwise unwelcome presence.

"I've heard that the poor woman isn't well at all," he told her. "She's developed really bad morning sickness, and they've had to send for the doctor several times. There was even talk of her having to go to hospital." Smirking, he looked closely at her. "I guess pregnancy suits some women better than others."

Ellie glared at him, but secretly she felt glee at Sylvia's discomfiture – it seemed to confirm that she herself was a more natural mother, and therefore a better candidate for Alan's devotion. Briefly she hoped that Sylvia might lose the baby, then she felt mean for wishing the poor woman any harm, since she really liked her. It was just that they were both vying for Alan's love, although Sylvia had no idea she was in any competition.

The day after meeting Tony Coleman, and in an effort to banish destructive thoughts, Ellie devoted herself to satisfying Alan with renewed vigour.

"My god, you're a right little goer today, aren't you?" he said delightedly as they disentangled their limbs for the third time that afternoon. "Pregnancy definitely suits you, my love!"

Ellie smiled outwardly, but inside she was still a seething mass of jealousy. She quickly stepped out of bed, hoping to compose herself in the privacy of the bathroom.

"I'm missing you already, love," he complained good-naturedly. "Don't be long – I'm longing to hold you again."

In the bathroom, she tried to think positively about her life, rather than spending her time thinking of the other woman who shared his life. She loved this man deeply and he reciprocated her love – what more had she any right to ask for? And she was fulfilling her lifelong dream of becoming a mother – the fact that she'd never conceived during her marriage to John seemed to indicate that her relationship with Alan was meant to be.

Placing a smile on her face, she returned to the bedroom.

CHAPTER 33

Laura had an appointment at her local dental surgery the following morning. She'd asked Darren for a few hours off, explaining that she'd broken a tooth, but not telling him how it had happened. As always, her boss was understanding, and he'd agreed that Maria could give her morning lecture instead.

She was anxious to get her broken tooth fixed, because its jagged edge was cutting the inside of her lip, and proving extremely painful when she ate or drank. Luckily, the dentist's receptionist had given her a priority appointment and, as she sat in the waiting room, she hoped that the tooth could be dealt with immediately and that only one appointment would be necessary.

In the waiting room, Laura flicked through a series of out-of-date magazines before abandoning them. There were two other people in the room – an elderly woman and a man who was hidden behind the folds of his newspaper. Laura instantly felt a flicker of fear – could it possibly be Jeff? Right now, she felt that he was capable of turning up anywhere she went. Then the man put down his newspaper, and she was relieved to find herself facing an extremely attractive dark-haired man who appeared to be in his mid-thirties. They smiled at each other, and at that precise moment the elderly woman was called by the receptionist.

As they sat together in the waiting room, the man ventured a remark.

"Nice day, isn't it? What a pity we're stuck in here while the sun's shining!"

Laura nodded. "Nevertheless, I was very grateful to get an appointment today – I've broken a tooth, and it's really irritating. What are you having done?"

"Just a filling – the old one fell out and I've been meaning to get it sorted." He grinned. "It took a really bad toothache to get me here!"

The receptionist popped her head round the waiting room door. "Mr Rudden? Dr Brady is ready for you now."

The man seemed disappointed to be called so soon. "Best of luck with the tooth!" he said, smiling at Laura as he left the waiting room.

"And to you, too," she said, smiling back. She felt a pang of disappointment as he left the waiting room. She'd been surprised and pleased to find herself enjoying another man's company, even though it was only days since she'd left Jeff. After all she'd been through with her husband, it seemed a positive indication that his cruelty and violent outbursts would soon be a distant memory. She felt almost light-headed when she was eventually called into the dentist's surgery.

"Are you okay to take on the second years for statistics?"

Laura nodded as she stood in front of Darren's big desk in his office. She was glad of the opportunity to help him out, since he'd been more than good to her over the previous few months. In fact, he'd been looking out for her for years.

Darren smiled, nodding his approval. "It'll only be for a month – until Timmy gets back – thanks, Laura."

"No problem."

"How's the tooth?"

"It's fine thanks – luckily, I just needed it to be filed down a bit and a filling put in."

As yet, she hadn't told any of her colleagues that she and Jeff had parted. The break-up was so new to her that she still woke up in the mornings with a feeling of dread in her stomach, until she realised she was safe in Kerry's apartment.

She was also embarrassed about how short her turbulent marriage had been, although she guessed that most of her colleagues had been well aware of Jeff's unsuitability long before she had. Right now, she couldn't quite face the thought of proving them right. She knew they'd all be relieved for her, but that didn't make her feel any better.

Darren took off his glasses and wiped his eyes. He looked tired, and Laura's heart went out to him. She was deeply fond of him, and wished he could meet someone special. He was such a wonderful man, and it would be a lucky woman who finally snared him. But he seemed to devote all his energies to running the department.

"If there are any extra courses you need me to cover, just let me know," she said. "I have plenty of time on my hands." She could see a question forming in Darren's eyes, but she quickly deflected it. She didn't want to entertain any queries about Jeff right now. "I'm giving first and second-year Sociology lectures every morning next week," she added, "but I can fit in extra lectures in the afternoons, if you need me to, or if anyone else needs a break."

"Thanks, Laura – I might just take you up on that. Maria wants some time off soon, so that might dovetail quite well with your offer. I'll talk to her about when she wants to go." He looked at her shrewdly. "You okay?"

Laura gave him a convincing smile. "Of course. But *you* look tired," she added, turning the attention away from her own situation.

Darren wiped his eyes again. "Yeah, I'm a bit knackered right now. Running this show can be a headache sometimes. I've meetings with the Vice Chancellor and the board all this week."

Laura nodded sympathetically. "Review time?"

He nodded, then put on his glasses again. "Are you sure everything's okay with you?"

For a moment, Laura almost decided to tell him that she'd left Jeff. Then she changed her mind. "Yes, fine thanks," she said airily instead. "Just let me know what weeks Maria wants off."

Leaving his office, Laura headed down the corridor towards her own room. As she opened the door to enter, she glanced distastefully at the plaque above her head. At her own insistence, it read '*Dr Laura Jones*', but now she longed to rip it off the door and throw it in the bin. But it would have to stay there until she decided to inform her colleagues that her marriage was over.

CHAPTER 34

When Ellie experienced the first few contractions, she wasn't unduly worried. She'd read all the books and faithfully attended her antenatal classes, so she knew these were probably Braxton Hicks contractions – the ones that sometimes happened in the weeks preceding the actual delivery. It was as though the womb was in training for the big event, and was flexing itself in preparation. Besides, she wasn't due for another two weeks, and it couldn't happen now anyway, because Alan was away, and he'd promised to spend as much time as he could with her during her labour. He was planning on telling his PA, and anyone else who needed to know, that he'd be attending important meetings all that day. Since the midwife wouldn't need to be present for most of her labour, Ellie was looking forward to long periods in Alan's company while she waited for their baby to be born.

She hadn't slept very well the night before, probably due to the storm that had raged outside. But now all was calm again, although some of the trees in the garden had been divested of branches, and she could see that the grounds outside were strewn with debris.

"Ow!" A jolt of alarm shot through her as a really severe contraction rendered her breathless. Fifteen minutes later, it was followed by another one just as strong, and Ellie wondered if it was time to phone the midwife.

Making her way to the phone in the kitchen, she looked in vain for the address book where she'd written the midwife's number. Dammit! She now remembered that she'd brought it upstairs the night before, and left it on her bedside table beside the telephone extension. How could she have been so stupid as to fail to bring it down again that morning, especially at such a critical time?

She began crawling up the stairs on her hands and knees, pausing to puff after every few steps because the pains were becoming more regular and severe. Ellie experienced a wave of panic. If she went into labour while upstairs, how would the midwife manage to get through the locked front door?

Crawling back down again, Ellie sat on the bottom step. Then another strong contraction gripped her, and she knew she had to get help urgently. But there was no one she could phone and ask to go upstairs on her behalf, because she had no friends. She'd given up everything to be Alan's secret wife, and now she feared that she and her baby might suffer because no one was on hand to help her.

Alan had recently had one of those new-fangled car phones installed in his BMW, but since he was overseas, it was useless to try and contact him. Why on earth did he have to be away now, just when she desperately needed him?

Resolutely, Ellie stood up and staggered towards the phone in the kitchen. She'd ring Directory Enquiries and ask them to locate the midwife's number. As a last resort, she could ring for an ambulance, but she was still determined to give birth at home. A vision of Sylvia pushed its way into her mind – she was determined to out-do Alan's wife by giving birth naturally, and not relying on medical intervention, as Sylvia needed to do.

Leaning against the kitchen cupboards, Ellie picked up the receiver and began to dial. But there was no sound from the phone at all. Not even a dial tone. Puzzled, Ellie looked at the receiver, then shook it. Why wasn't it working? What was wrong? Then it hit her like a ton of bricks. The heavy storm the night before must have caused a local cable to come down. Now she had no way of contacting anyone. She was all alone and about to give birth, and she was terrified.

She cursed the isolation of her house – its private and tranquil setting meant that no one was likely to hear her, even if she screamed at the top of her voice. There was only one thing she could do – she'd have to make her way down the driveway and out onto the road, where hopefully she could flag down a passing motorist or pedestrian.

Leaving the house, Ellie made her way gingerly down the driveway through the fallen branches, stopping every few minutes as another contraction gripped her. Never had her driveway seemed so long, and help so far away . . .

She sighed with relief as the gate and the road came into view. All she needed was for a kind Samaritan to come back to the house, locate the address book then go off and phone the midwife from a working phone. Then it crossed her mind that letting a total stranger into her house mightn't be the brightest idea. They could rob or murder her, or . . .

She gasped as another contraction winded her. These were no Braxton Hicks contractions. These were the real deal. Panic set in as she contemplated having her baby by the side of the road.

As she faced the oncoming traffic, Ellie wondered how she was supposed to attract attention. Should she stick out her thumb like a hitchhiker? She must look a sight – nearly eight and a half months pregnant and flailing her arms by the side of a very busy road. Maybe people assumed she was a madwoman, and best avoided. A few drivers looked at her curiously but drove on, and Ellie concluded that she wasn't far enough out on the road to get their attention. Yet if she stepped out any further, she risked being struck by the cars speeding by.

Ellie was crying quietly in desperation when a large car drove by, then slowed and pulled in a few hundred yards further down the road. The driver's door opened and Ellie's heart plummeted as Sylvia jumped out and ran back to where Ellie was standing, her own pregnancy now clearly evident.

"Are you okay?" she asked, a concerned look on her face. Ellie quickly explained the situation, relieved to have help, but wishing it could be anyone but Alan's wife.

"Let's get you back to your house, then I'll drive home and ring your midwife from there," Sylvia said briskly. "Here, lean on me – I can see you're having a contraction. How far are they apart?"

Ellie explained how increasingly close they'd become, gratefully clutching Sylvia's arm as they made their way slowly back up the driveway of Treetops.

As they reached the front door, Ellie experienced a sudden jolt of fear. There would be evidence of Alan's presence all over the house! Since there had never been any need for him to hide his belongings, his shaving kit and aftershave were in the en-suite bathroom, his dressing gown hanging on the back of the bedroom door! But there was no time for any further reflections as another contraction seized her just as she was opening the front door.

Inside, Sylvia helped Ellie to the sofa in the open-plan living area, then looked around her. "Now, Ellie – where exactly is your address book?"

Ellie bit her lip. There was no way to avoid letting Sylvia go upstairs to the bedroom where she and Alan had made love only two days earlier. She was also thinking of the ring Alan had given her – lately, since her finger had become too swollen to wear it, she'd left it on the dressing table. If Sylvia saw it and read the inscription on the inside, their secret would be out and there would be hell to pay. Hopefully, she'd put it in the drawer of the dressing table and not left it on the top, but she couldn't be certain where exactly it was . . .

"It's in my bedroom – on the bedside table."

As Sylvia headed upstairs, Ellie was filled with trepidation. What would she do if Sylvia found the ring, or something else incriminating, and came down the stairs screaming at her? She could hardly expect her help after that. Ellie also didn't want to leave her address book in Sylvia's possession, even briefly, since Alan's phone numbers were in it, and Sylvia might accidentally – or curiously – look through it. Frantically, she looked round for a piece of paper and a pen, so that she could write out the midwife's number for Sylvia when she came back downstairs. Ellie was quietly freaking out, especially as Sylvia seemed to be taking an awfully long time . . . Had she spotted something incriminating up there? Alan used a particularly expensive brand of aftershave and if Sylvia spotted it she might start to put two and two together . . .

146

As Sylvia began descending the stairs, her demeanour looked normal enough, and Ellie held out her hand for the address book. "Here – let me write the midwife's phone number on this piece of paper for you," she said brightly, producing the pen and paper she'd located on a nearby bookshelf. "That'll make it more convenient, won't it?"

Sylvia nodded, handing over the address book, and Ellie sighed with relief at having it in her possession once again. Having looked up the number, she wrote it down and handed the piece of paper to Sylvia.

Sylvia tucked it into her pocket. "If I can't contact your midwife, will I call an ambulance?"

Ellie shook her head. Although it was probably foolhardy, she was still determined to give birth at home.

Sylvia bit her lip. "I don't like leaving you here on your own – why don't you just come back to my house? Then I wouldn't need to keep asking you where everything was –"

"No!" Ellie had to stop herself from shouting, but the thought of delivering Alan's baby in Alan's house was like being in some futuristic nightmare.

Sylvia nodded apologetically. "Sorry – I should have realised that you'd much rather be in your own home. I'll gladly stay with you, but Pete will be finished at the crèche by three, so I'll need to collect him then." She looked at her watch. "But that's not for several hours yet. I'm sure the midwife will be here long before I need to leave." She smiled impishly. "Hopefully, you might be holding your baby by then!"

Ellie nodded through the pain of another contraction. Sylvia really was such a nice woman.

"I'll be back as quickly as I can," Sylvia assured her. "Is there anything I can get you? Any treats you'd like me to bring back?"

Ellie shook her head. Even if she'd been desperately craving for something, she couldn't have borne the guilt of having Sylvia bring it to her.

When Sylvia had left, Ellie tried to make herself as comfortable as she could. She'd be relieved when the midwife arrived, at which point Sylvia could leave and Ellie would have one less thing to worry about. She wondered if the strain of coping with Sylvia's presence and her own combined guilt and fear was causing her contractions to become even more severe.

Fifteen minutes later, Sylvia was back.

"Our phone line is down too, so I had to go into the village to make the call," she told Ellie. "Unfortunately, two of your midwife's other clients are also in labour, so she's notified another midwife on your behalf. But it seems that the second midwife is also delivering a baby over on the other side of the village – but she'll get here as soon as she can." Sylvia smiled apologetically. "I'm afraid you're stuck with me, for a while anyway." Then she smiled impishly. "Thank heavens I'm not due for another few months myself – you seem to have chosen a very popular time to deliver, Ellie!"

While Ellie rested between contractions, Sylvia busied herself in the kitchen, making tea to accompany the freshly baked scones she'd brought back from the village bakery. Initially Ellie refused to eat, but hunger and the delicious smells wafting from the kitchen eventually got the better of her. But it felt bizarre to be eating food supplied by her lover's wife, and she wished, yet again, that Alan's wife was anyone but Sylvia. Then she could have a guilt-free friendship of her own as well.

As Sylvia collected the plates after they'd eaten, she cleared her throat. "Look, I'm sorry for – well, for pouring out my troubles to you when we last met. It was unfair of me – but I really was grateful for your advice. You were right, too – all I needed to do was sit it out."

Ellie tried to look nonchalant as she spoke. "Really? I mean, are things better now?" She felt a total hypocrite. But she was also avid for any information about her lover's marriage. If Sylvia was happy, what did that mean for her own future with Alan?

Sylvia shrugged her shoulders. "I'm still convinced he's having an affair – but he's a lot calmer lately. You were right when you advised me to say nothing. It's true what they say – 'least said, soonest mended'."

"How did you discover he was having an affair?" Ellie asked, hardly daring to ask, yet keen to find out how Alan had slipped up, so they might ensure it didn't happen again.

"The usual way, I suppose. I was sending his suits for dry-cleaning, and I discovered receipts for items that definitely weren't intended for me!"

Ellie nodded. She must warn Alan to be more careful. But she also felt sick at the thought of Sylvia uncovering her own duplicity. For some reason, she didn't want to disappoint this woman, whom she liked very much. It was clear that Sylvia would also like their tenuous friendship to continue. But Ellie knew she'd have to cut off any contact with Sylvia as soon as her baby was delivered. She felt dreadful at the thought of using Sylvia, then discarding her. And her blood ran cold at the thought that the poor woman was actually helping to deliver her own husband's baby!

"Is there anyone you'd like me to contact?" Sylvia asked. "I can easily drive into the village and use the public phone again. What about your – I mean, your child's father?"

"He's away."

Sylvia smiled. "Men, eh? They're never around when you need them! My husband is away too, and I really wanted him to come with me for my check-up tomorrow."

"Will you mind terribly if you have a second boy?" Ellie asked.

"No, not as long as the child is healthy," Sylvia answered. "But a girl would be nice this time." She grinned. "Well, you know that already, since you've seen the gorgeous pink outfit I've bought!" She looked closely at Ellie." What are you hoping for?"

"Like you, a healthy child."

"And your – I mean, the father of your child – would he prefer a boy or girl?"

"Aaaagh!" Ellie groaned suddenly and gripped Sylvia's hand. She hadn't expected to be glad of a contraction, but the severity of this one prevented her from replying to any more personal questions.

"Can I get you some more cushions?" Sylvia asked as Ellie's contraction eventually subsided. "They might help to ease the pressure on your back."

"Yes, please," Ellie replied gratefully "You'll find some in the drawing room – just out the door and to the right."

Ellie suddenly froze. She'd just remembered that she'd taken delivery the previous day of a beautiful floral arrangement from Alan, and it was on the drawing-room table! Had she removed the card that came with the delivery? Luckily, Alan had only signed his initial, but the message had been quite racy!

Returning with several cushions, Sylvia placed them behind Ellie's back. "I see you've got a beautiful array of flowers in there – clearly someone cares for you very much."

Ellie's mouth was dry, so she nodded, too nervous to say anything.

"I see your man friend has the same initial as my husband," Sylvia added, smiling at Ellie, whose heart was now in her mouth.

"Er, umm, yes – his name is A-A-Anthony."

Sylvia gave her a triumphant look. "Aha – I guessed as much! He wouldn't be called Tony for short, would he?"

Relief flooded through Ellie as she realised that Sylvia thought Tony Coleman was the man in her life! What luck that she'd picked the name Anthony. It had simply been a spur-of-the-moment choice, but it had worked out perfectly. She smiled noncommittally, hoping to create the impression that Sylvia was right.

But Sylvia's expression had now darkened. "But surely he should be here – with you? I didn't realise that his job involved travel . . ."

Ellie feigned a contraction, hoping she could distract Sylvia from probing any further. She was genuinely feeling very uncomfortable, and desperately wishing that the midwife would hurry up so that Sylvia could leave.

"Do you think I could have another cup of tea?"

"Of course!"

Sylvia rushed into the kitchen and Ellie lay back on her pillows, relieved to have even a few minutes on her own, without having to continuously play a role. But it wasn't long before Sylvia was back, and this time she wore a big smile on her face.

"The phone's working again!" she told her. "What a relief!"

Ellie nodded in agreement, until it suddenly dawned on her that this reconnected phone could cause her even more problems. What if Alan rang and Sylvia answered? They'd managed to fool Tony Coleman in the past, but it would be impossible to think up some excuse that would fool Sylvia. As Ellie drank her tea, she found that her hands were shaking. She felt out of control and on the brink of disaster. Where the hell was the midwife?

As a series of severe contractions ripped through her, Sylvia came and sat beside her, holding her hand, rubbing her back and mopping her brow, and for a while, Ellie managed to forget the peculiar relationship that existed between them. But anger towards Alan welled up inside her. Why wasn't he here when she needed him? No doubt he was off wining and dining while she was struggling to bring his child into the world.

"Have you ever helped anyone to give birth before?" Ellie asked, as she tightened her grip on Sylvia's hand during a particularly strong contraction.

Sylvia shook her head.

"Well, I think you might be about to have your first experience –" Ellie roared at the top of her voice as she felt a sudden urge to push. "Oh God, I can't stop –"

She felt a burning sensation, followed by a feeling of total relief. Sylvia stared in astonishment at the tiny baby who had just appeared, then she galvanised herself into action. Turning the child over, she gently tapped its back, then removed mucus and blood from its mouth. As it began screaming, she handed it to an exhausted Ellie.

"Congratulations – you have a beautiful daughter!" she said, her face a picture of wonder and delight.

It was a strangely intimate moment, and the women smiled at each other, each of them experiencing a gamut of emotions.

Instinctively, Ellie opened her blouse and held the baby girl to her breast, and she began suckling almost immediately.

"Have you chosen a name for her yet?"

"Yes, I – we – are going to call her Kerry."

"What a lovely name!" Sylvia said enthusiastically.

Just as the afterbirth arrived, so too did the midwife, and the spell was broken by her cheery no-nonsense attitude.

"Well, I can see that you two have managed perfectly well without me!" she said cheerfully, cutting the cord and checking Ellie and the baby thoroughly. "What a fine healthy baby!" she added. Then she glanced at Sylvia's stomach. "I can see you'll be next," she said, smiling. "How nice for you two friends to be pregnant at the same time! When are you due?"

"In three months," Sylvia replied, smiling back.

"Well, you've done a great job here today, but now it's time for you to go home and rest," the midwife told her. "You've had enough excitement, and I don't want another early birth on my hands!"

Sylvia looked at her watch. "My goodness – it's almost time to collect my son from the crèche!" She took Ellie's hand in hers. "Are you sure you're okay?" she asked earnestly. "Is there anything else I can do for you before I go?"

Cradling her baby, Ellie shook her head. "You've been wonderful," she said, tears in her eyes. "I don't know what I'd have done without your help."

Blushing, Sylvia shook her head in rebuttal, but Ellie could see that she was pleased to have her role in Kerry's birth acknowledged.

"The midwife's right," Ellie added. "After you collect your son, you need to go home and take it easy."

"Well, if you're sure there's nothing else –"

"Thank you – for everything," Ellie whispered fervently.

The following day, a floral arrangement of lilies and pink carnations arrived for Ellie, and the card accompanying it was signed: 'Congratulations from Sylvia and Alan Thornton.' How ironic, Ellie thought, that Sylvia should be the one to send it.

So far, there had been no word from Alan. But after the stress of the previous day, Ellie was content to nurse her daughter alone. She didn't want visitors as she bonded with her baby. She'd fulfilled her dream of having a child, and she didn't need anything more. Except Alan, of course. She longed for his arrival, and to see the joy in his eyes when he held his baby daughter in his arms. Now they were a family at last.

She thought once again of John, her late husband, and wondered what he'd make of the present situation. He'd always known how much she longed for a child, so perhaps he wouldn't be too shocked by what she'd done.

As Ellie thought of Sylvia, she was aware of how awkward the situation would be between them now. Since Sylvia had played such an intimate and important role in Ellie and Kerry's life, it would appear churlish to cut her off without even a backward glance. Yet she'd no other choice. At least she could rely on Alan to support her in keeping her distance from Sylvia.

But it made Ellie sad. More than ever now, she longed for the friendship of another mother, someone with whom she could share the milestones in her child's life, and chat about the important and the inconsequential things that were part and parcel of motherhood. Much as she loved Alan, Ellie was well aware that his eyes would glaze over if she tried to tell him about the minutiae of her daily life. But such a friendship with Sylvia could never be. She'd sacrificed that comfort and support for Alan's love and a child of her own. And it was a price she was more than willing to pay.

CHAPTER 35

During her lunch break, Laura decided to stock up on some basic foodstuffs and toiletries. She'd been eating Kerry's food and using her mouthwash since she'd arrived at her flat, and it was time she repaid her friend's kindness. Since she had to give tutorials that afternoon, she'd avoid buying items for the freezer, but she'd be able to select plenty of fresh fruit and vegetables, bread, tea and coffee, kitchen towels and dishwasher tablets.

As she wandered through the aisles of the nearest supermarket, Laura filled her trolley with the various items on her list, as well as a Black Forest gateau as a treat for her and Kerry.

"Well, hello again!" said a deep male voice, and Laura turned to see the good-looking dark-haired man whom she'd spoken to in the dentist's waiting room.

Smiling, she returned his greeting. "How's the filling?" she asked.

"Oh fine – I don't know why I left it so long," he replied, patting his cheek. Then he grinned cheerfully. "But I wouldn't have met you otherwise!"

Laura's cheeks turned pink, and she cursed her tendency to blush.

"I presume you got your broken tooth fixed okay?" he asked.

Laura nodded, pleased that he'd remembered. "Yes, thanks – it's a relief to be able to eat without feeling that my mouth is full of pins."

He smiled. "Speaking of eating, it's lunchtime and I'm planning on going to the café across the road as soon as I've finished my shopping. Why don't you join me if you're free?"

Laura felt a bubble of happiness welling up inside her.

"Thank you, I'd like that."

The man gave a pleased grin. "Okay, I'll see you there in, say, fifteen minutes?"

"Okay – great."

In a pleasant daze, Laura continued with her shopping, hardly able to concentrate on what she was supposed to be buying. She smiled to herself. Wouldn't Kerry be surprised to hear that she'd already got a date! Well, a date of sorts. Lunch was a neutral, getting-to-know-you sort of date. The guy seemed very nice, and Laura was glad she'd worn her new blue T-shirt, since it brought out the colour of her eyes, making them look a really deep blue. Then she laughed to herself – she was only going to have lunch with a nice guy, and there was nothing more to it than that. Nevertheless, it seemed to augur well for the future – Jeff was firmly in the past, and some day soon she'd have a very different and hopefully better life.

After placing the groceries in her car, Laura quickly checked her appearance in the driver's rear view mirror, locked the car then crossed the road to the café. The man was already there, and he waved to her as she made her way to his table.

"The courgette pie looks good," he said as she sat down. "By the way, my name is Steve Rudden."

Shaking hands, Laura introduced herself and took a seat opposite him in the red banquette. They both spent a little time consulting the menu, then Steve ordered the courgette pie while Laura opted for a cheese and tomato club sandwich. When the waitress had taken their order, they caught each other's eye, and both laughed.

"Okay, I'll go first," Steve said. "I run a small accountancy business, I'm single, I live in Hammersmith, and I like football, tennis and vintage cars. I own a 1929 Rolls Royce, which is my pride and joy. I nearly got married once, a long time ago, but she met someone else and dumped me. I grew up in Yorkshire, and my parents and sister still live there."

He looked expectantly at her.

"Now it's your turn," he said.

Briefly, Laura summed up her own life, explaining about her career, the death of her parents and brother in a car crash, her plan to move into a new apartment after her brief but unsatisfactory marriage. She didn't mention Jeff's violence. It didn't seem appropriate to tell someone she barely knew.

At which point their food arrived, and they both tucked into it with gusto.

"Hmm," said Steve between mouthfuls, "this is really good. How's your club sandwich?"

"Great," Laura told him. She was enjoying Steve's company, and secretly marvelling at how easy it had been to meet another man. He'd almost fallen into her lap! She'd had no intention of dating again for a very long time, but fate seemed to have deposited Steve at her door. Well, at least, at the dentist's door! Of course, Steve mightn't want to see her again, but she was already starting to hope that he would.

Her phone rang, and Laura grimaced. She glanced at the number – Jeff was hassling her again. She rejected the call and continued with her meal, but she noticed Steve watching her closely.

The café was beginning to fill up with lunchtime diners, and so far they hadn't been expected to share their banquette. But knowing they could be joined by other people before long, Laura decided to tell Steve about Jeff before they acquired an audience.

"My ex is proving tiresome," she confessed, "That was him on the phone just now. He can't forgive me for leaving the marriage – he keeps ringing me all the time and, believe me, it's scary. I don't answer any more, because when I do he just starts being abusive."

As if to prove the point, Laura's phone rang again, and they both laughed.

"I guess it's time to change your number," Steve said.

After an enjoyable lunch, and the table all to themselves, a waitress cleared the table and left their bill.

Steve picked it up as Laura reached for it. "I asked you, so it's my treat," he said, smiling. "But if you really feel I've compromised your dignity as an independent woman, you can always invite me to lunch another day?"

Laura nodded, smiling back at him. She liked the idea of seeing Steve again.

"Anyway," he added, "I was going to ask if you'd like to come out for a meal with me some evening next week? I know a great Italian restaurant – old-fashioned and basic, but with marvellous food."

Laura nodded. "I'd really like that."

CHAPTER 36

As Alan left the airport and hailed a taxi to take him home, he felt
hugely relieved that the business week was over. He'd finally
managed to get the contract with a new tin supplier signed, and on
very favourable terms too. But he was tired from all the
negotiations. He'd had to bluster and make endless objections to
their initial proposals before eventually hammering out a very
satisfactory deal – one that augured well for the future of the
factory. But now, all he wanted to do was sleep.

In the back of the taxi, he yawned, wondering how Sylvia and
Pete were. And Ellie – he was longing to see her, too. If anyone
could make him forget how tired he was, it was his secret wife, and
he felt himself hardening at the very thought of her. Even though
she was close to giving birth, and her bump made it awkward to get
close, they still made love at every opportunity. He adored that
woman, and he was looking forward to being there to support her
during the birth of their child.

"Hello, darling – did you have a good trip?"

Alan nodded as he kissed Sylvia's cheek. "Yes, everything went
well. I eventually got the deal I wanted, but it was hard work
getting there!"

Pete appeared from the playroom, and ran into his father's arms.
"Hello, little man!" Alan said affectionately.
"Toy for me, Daddy?"
Alan grinned, producing a package from his briefcase. Despite

Pete's tender years, he already understood all about presents! As the child ripped the gift-wrap from the plastic fire engine his father had brought him, Alan presented Sylvia with a pair of diamond earrings. Thanking him, she slipped them on, but he could see she was bursting to tell him something. Perhaps the hospital had been able to tell her the sex of their baby?

"What is it, Syl?"

Sylvia looked at him, her eyes shining mischievously. "You're not going to believe what I did this week –"

Alan nodded, encouraging her to go on.

"I helped Ellie Beckworth to give birth!"

Alan could feel his heart almost coming to a standstill. Yet on some level he was conscious that outwardly he had to appear calm and in control.

As he stood silently, unable to speak, Sylvia assumed he needed reminding about whom she was talking.

"She's that nice woman who lives half a mile away at Treetops, and runs a tutoring business from home – she used to work at the factory?"

Alan nodded slowly, needing to call on all his reserves of control. "Oh yes, I remember now," he said at last. "She worked in the laboratory, I think." He took a deep breath, not sure how to play the situation. "She's had a baby, you say?"

Sylvia laughed. "Oh Alan, dear, you're so unobservant! You must have seen her around – she was very big towards the end! When women carry all to the front, it usually means they're going to have a girl. Well, now she has a beautiful little daughter – and I helped her deliver it!"

"So, you've taken up a new career as a midwife," Alan said lightly. "How did that come about?"

Keeping a tight rein over his facial expression, he listened as Sylvia talked, her eyes alight as she explained what had happened. All Alan could think of was how close he and Ellie had come to disaster, but it was obvious that Sylvia hadn't suspected a thing. Nevertheless, his two separate lives had come alarmingly close for comfort.

"Well, since you seem to know so much about these things, do you think we're having a boy or girl?" he asked, eyeing Sylvia's bump and hoping to move the discussion away from Ellie.

Sylvia looked at him coyly. "Well, what do you think? I'm getting rather large in the front, aren't I? So I'm betting on a girl."

Alan took her in his arms, and hugged her so that she wouldn't see his expression. He was afraid his excitement might be showing. He had a daughter! He was longing to see Ellie and this new child of his.

"Well, I'll be happy with either a boy or a girl," he told her, wondering how soon he could slip away to visit his secret wife.

At Treetops, Ellie was waiting eagerly for Alan's visit. He'd phoned briefly while Sylvia was feeding Pete in the kitchen, and had promised to call later that evening. As soon as she saw his car coming up the driveway, she had the door open and was waiting for him to step inside.

"Come and meet your daughter!" she said proudly.

"You're wonderful!" he whispered, kissing her hair as he held her close. "I'm so sorry I wasn't here for you when you gave birth."

"Don't worry – your wife was," Ellie said, giving him a cynical smile. "I presume she's told you all about it?"

Alan nodded, stepping into the living room, and Ellie proudly led him over to the cradle in the corner where young Kerry was sleeping.

"She's beautiful!" Alan whispered, gazing in awe at the tiny baby sleeping peacefully, her thumb stuck firmly in her mouth. "But I wish you hadn't had to go through all this without me. How did it happen?"

Ellie explained about her early labour, the disconnected phone line and how his wife had stopped to help. Now that the stress of Sylvia's involvement was over, she was able to laugh about her initial fears. "I never expected to have your wife in my home," Ellie told him, smiling. "There wasn't time to hide anything incriminating, so I was terrified she'd spot something belonging to you!"

Alan shuddered. Just thinking about what could have happened gave him palpitations.

"But I'm also deeply grateful to her," Ellie added humbly. "Without her, I don't know what would have happened. She may well have saved our baby's life."

Smiling, they slipped into each other's arms. Their relationship was different now, and they both acknowledged it. They were a family, albeit a family that couldn't proclaim itself in public.

Ellie then told him about the flowers, and how, on the spur of the moment, she'd used the name Anthony to explain away his initial on the accompanying card.

"I hope Sylvia doesn't snub Tony Coleman, because I managed to give the impression that he might be the father," Ellie added, smiling. "But that made Sylvia very annoyed on my behalf – she thought Tony should have been present at the birth."

Alan chuckled. "Luckily, Sylvia is too polite to behave badly in public, so I don't think we need worry on that score." Then he suddenly remembered the gift he'd bought for her, and produced a package from his pocket. "Thank you for my adorable baby daughter," he whispered, as she unwrapped a magnificent diamond pendant. In the glow of the chandelier overhead it sparkled as Ellie lifted it out of its box.

"It's beautiful!" she told him, turning her back to him and urging him to fasten it around her neck.

"No, you're the one who's beautiful!" he whispered, nuzzling her neck as he fixed the clasp. She felt the quickening of desire, and knew he was feeling it too.

Suddenly, the peace was broken by the sound of crying from the cradle. "It's feeding time!" Ellie announced, smiling. "Kerry and I have already established a routine – every three hours she wakes up hungry, she feeds for fifteen minutes, then goes off to sleep again."

As Ellie lifted the baby out of the cradle, and brought her back to the sofa to breastfeed, Alan couldn't help eyeing Ellie's beautiful breasts, now bare and tantalisingly full of milk, as his tiny daughter began suckling contentedly. He marvelled at Ellie's beauty, and he longed to suckle those full breasts himself.

Ellie smiled, knowing exactly what he was thinking. She always knew when Alan was ready to make love. Which was nearly always. They could never get enough of each other, and giving birth hadn't changed those feelings one iota. If anything, she wanted him even more now.

When the baby eventually fell asleep, Ellie gently extricated her and laid her back in her cradle. Then she approached Alan, making no attempt to cover her breasts, and she could see his erection straining through his trousers.

His expression was a mixture of tenderness and excitement as she stood provocatively before him.

"Ellie, I'm not sure if you realise what you're doing –"

But her wanton expression told him that she knew exactly what effect she was having on him.

"Please, Ellie – don't make me want you so much –"

As she kissed him, Alan groaned.

"Stop, Ellie –"

But she didn't stop, and her hands became even more adventurous.

"Isn't it too early?" he whispered. "I mean, I'm longing to make love to you again, but are you sure you're ready?"

She could feel his erection pressing against her.

"I'm sure," she whispered, taking his hand and leading him upstairs.

CHAPTER 37

That evening in Kerry's apartment, Laura couldn't stop smiling.

"He's really nice, and he's even got his own accountancy business. I like a dynamic, independent man, don't you? He asked me to have lunch with him – and he's invited me out next Friday evening!"

Laura was in a bubbly and animated mood and Kerry was amazed that she'd come through her tragic marriage with her happy and impulsive nature still intact.

Taking their dinner out of the oven, Kerry grinned at her friend. "I'm pleased for you, love, but promise me you won't be rushing down the aisle again for a while yet? I don't think I could handle two weddings in less than a year!"

Laura laughed as she placed cutlery and plates on the table. "Don't worry, I'm just going to have fun. Anyway, I need to apply for a divorce from Jeff first. But more important –" she grinned mischievously, "I'm sure Steve has some nice friends, and maybe we can find one who takes your fancy."

Kerry gave her a sarcastic look as she placed the pizza and garlic bread on the kitchen table. "Let's find out what this Steve fellow is like before you start fixing me up with one of his friends!" she said.

"Oh he's really great!"

"I seem to remember you saying the same thing about Jeff," Kerry added dryly.

Laura looked guilty. "You're right. But honestly, I'm only going out for a meal with this guy. I'm not going to rush anything." She looked sincerely at Kerry. "I mean, I wasn't even looking for anyone, but fate seems to have intervened."

Kerry looked doubtful as she sliced the garlic bread. "Fate produced Jeff as well. Please be a bit more critical this time, won't you?"

"Of course. But Steve seems genuinely nice, and it's a relief to be able to express my opinions without worrying that he'll throttle me if I don't agree with him."

Laura looked affectionately at her friend. She'd really like Kerry to meet a nice man, too. But Kerry hadn't had much luck with men so far. She'd had a boyfriend during her final year at university, but that relationship had fizzled out after they'd graduated and he'd emigrated to Australia. Laura suspected that her friend was either too shy or too absorbed in her work to make any real effort at attracting a man. When they went out socialising together, Kerry would invariably wind up in a corner, talking shop with other engineers, although nothing romantic ever seemed to develop from these encounters. Laura longed for her friend to open her eyes to all the eligible men around. She was genuinely hoping that Steve might have a friend who'd take a shine to Kerry, and whom Kerry might like, too . . .

"He really *is* nice!" Laura enthused to her friend as she arrived back from her Friday-night date. "He took me to a cosy little Italian restaurant – it was really old-fashioned, with check tablecloths and candles in Chianti bottles. But the food was fantastic! It's run by an elderly Italian couple, and Steve says it's the best Italian restaurant he's ever been in."

Kerry smiled. "Are you seeing him again?"

Laura nodded. "He's taking me to a French restaurant next Friday night. He says it's got great write-ups. And we're going there in his vintage car! I'm really looking forward to seeing this 1929 Rolls Royce – he's picking me up outside the apartment, so you'll be able to see it from your bedroom window."

"I can't wait," said Kerry dryly. She was surprised at how quickly Laura had bounced back from Jeff's behaviour. Clearly, this Steve guy had given her back her joie de vivre.

CHAPTER 38

Sylvia sighed as she bent to pick up the trail of toys that Pete had left in his wake. He was now having his afternoon nap, and she intended dozing in a comfortable chair while she had the chance. She could be sure of an hour before he was likely to wake up again.

After placing the toys in the toy box, Sylvia eased herself into one of the club chairs in the living room. She felt large and cumbersome, and even the slightest exertion winded her. But she was coming near the end of her pregnancy, and for that she was grateful. Soon, the tiredness and the bloated ankles would hopefully be a thing of the past.

In the silence of the room, Sylvia tried to relax, patting her bump and hoping that the birth would be quick and hassle-free. As far as she was concerned, it was definitely a girl, because this pregnancy felt decidedly different from her last, and she was carrying all her extra weight to the front. Hadn't she made that very comment to Alan, about Ellie Beckworth?

As her thoughts turned once again to the enigmatic woman who lived only half a mile away, Sylvia shook her head in mystification. She'd hoped that by helping Ellie to give birth, she'd managed to forge a bond with the other woman. Afterwards, she'd hoped that an invitation to tea might be forthcoming, or even a phone call to suggest they meet for a cuppa in a local café. But Ellie had retreated into her shell again, and Sylvia was left feeling that she herself was somehow to blame.

As she lay back in the chair, Sylvia reviewed her behaviour while in Ellie's house, concluding yet again that she hadn't done anything to warrant being dismissed so summarily. The only conclusion she could reach was that Ellie Beckworth was simply a very private person, and didn't need or want friends.

Sylvia sighed as she contemplated her own final visit to the obstetrician the following day. She wished she had a friend to accompany her, because Alan was taking the afternoon off to mind Pete. It would have been nice to have Ellie there, reassuring her that all would be well. Alan did his best to be supportive, but a man couldn't possibly empathise in the way that another woman could.

A wail from the nursery broke the peace of the afternoon, and Sylvia struggled to her feet. Pete had woken much earlier than usual. She wondered if somehow he was aware that changes in their family dynamic were imminent, because the more she longed to rest, the more he seemed to demand her undivided attention.

In the nursery, Pete was standing at the bars of his cot, his face red on one side from sleeping, his curls matted with sweat. His mouth was open in the rictus of a scream, and Sylvia tried to comfort him as she lifted him out of his cot. His nappy was wet and he seemed to weigh a ton, and Sylvia wished she'd accepted Alan's offer of a live-in nurse during the latter stages of her pregnancy. But she'd been determined to be independent, hoping it might cast her in a more favourable light with her husband. There had been no other way she could hope to compete with Alan's mystery lover, since she looked ungainly and invariably felt tired. Since Alan didn't even bother to make love to her any more, she could only hope that things would improve when her body was back to normal again. She also continued to hope that the news of her pregnancy might have dispatched the other woman, but she'd no way of knowing if her rival was even aware of it.

As she placed Pete on the changing mat, Sylvia gave a start. Had she just had a contraction? She wasn't due for another two weeks! As Pete continued to cry, Sylvia felt her patience snapping, and she experienced what definitely felt like another contraction as she removed the child's soiled nappy. She felt a moment of panic – she was alone with a crying baby, and feeling as though she'd definitely started labour. After putting a clean nappy on the child, Sylvia placed her screaming son back in his cot, despite his very loud protests.

Hurrying into the hall, Sylvia lifted the phone and dialled the factory.

"Alan," she told him peremptorily, "you'd better come home. My labour has definitely started."

When Alan arrived at Treetops the following afternoon, he tried to hide his elation, but Ellie could see how secretly thrilled he was. "Sylvia had a seven-pound baby girl," he told her, trying to sound unconcerned out of respect for Ellie's feelings, but he was finding it impossible to stop smiling.

"So I heard – congratulations," Ellie replied, trying to keep the note of sourness out of her voice. The birth was already being talked about in the village. She'd been told all about it that very morning, by a woman whose husband worked at the factory.

Ellie felt decidedly jealous of this new child – the one born on the right side of the blanket – who was now heralded with gifts and welcomed into the community at large. Even the workers at the factory had already made a collection and bought a gigantic teddy bear for the little girl. Needless to say, there had been no such gifts after the birth of her own daughter.

"What are you going to call her?"

Alan hesitated, not wanting to seem too excited and involved with this new child of his. "Sylvia wants to call her Laura."

Ellie nodded. "That's a nice name," she said stiffly. "I think I should send Sylvia some flowers – after all, she sent me a bouquet when Kerry was born."

Alan nodded. He supposed Ellie had no other choice. He knew Sylvia would be pleased to receive them – he just hoped she wouldn't see them as an opportunity to reconnect with Ellie.

"Wouldn't you like to see your eldest daughter?" Ellie said tartly, reminding him that he already had a female child.

"Of course! That's one of the reasons I'm here," Alan replied, chastened. He was well aware that Ellie's nose was out of joint, and that he needed to appease her.

In the living room, young Kerry was sleeping in her cradle. Alan caressed her cheek as she slept, then bent down to kiss her, aware that Ellie was watching his every move. He felt as though he was on a tightrope, caught between the two women in his life. One wrong move and he could plummet to unimaginable depths.

"Will you be visiting us later this evening?"

Alan knew he was being tested too. If he spent too long with this latest child of his, there would be hell to pay from Ellie. But he had to spend time with Sylvia and baby Laura in the hospital, while Aunt Maud minded Pete. Sometimes he found it difficult to manage these two very separate lives.

"I can't manage tonight, but I'll be here tomorrow afternoon. Is that okay?"

Ellie nodded, relieved that at least he wasn't forsaking their usual arrangement. But it was clear that she was far from happy. Alan made a mental note to buy her a special gift – one that would make her feel cherished and appreciated – and something for Kerry. If he forgot a gift for the child, his head would be on the block.

Much to Ellie's chagrin, Alan left shortly afterwards. This was only the second time they hadn't made love the minute he arrived, and Ellie knew that he was controlling his passion for her out of respect for Sylvia.

Damn the woman, Ellie thought, as Alan's car drove out the gate. She now felt diminished by Sylvia's ability to produce the perfect family – a boy and a girl – for Alan. In her daydreams, Ellie had imagined Sylvia having a second boy, while she would have a daughter, who'd therefore have a special place in Alan's heart by virtue of being his only female child. But now, her child was effectively ousted by this new, tiny interloper.

CHAPTER 39

The man stood in the shadows as Kerry left the offices of Sea Diagnostics and began heading for home. He glanced at the photo again. Yes, it was definitely her. There could be no doubt about the likeness.

He followed at a safe distance, comfortable in the knowledge that she had no idea who he was. Even if she turned around, there would be nothing suspicious about him being there.

As she reached the entrance to the Underground, Kerry began to experience a prickly sensation running up her spine, and she got the distinct impression that someone was watching her. Swinging around quickly, she was just in time to see a man ducking into the shadows of a shop doorway.

As she continued on down the steps to the Underground, Kerry couldn't resist another quick glance back. No one seemed to be following her now, and she sighed with relief. Maybe she'd just imagined it. After all, there was no logical reason that anyone would be following her. Lately she'd been working so hard on the barrage project that her brain was probably fried, and she was letting her imagination run riot.

On the other hand, this wasn't the first time lately that she'd felt someone was following her. The previous week, she'd experienced the same uneasy feeling as she'd left work, and several evenings when she'd been alone in her apartment her phone had rung, but when she'd answered no one had replied. But she'd got the distinct impression that someone was on the other end of the line.

Kerry glanced around her, but none of the other passengers on the platform seemed remotely interested in her, and she sighed with relief as her train clattered into the station and she got on board. Was she imagining it, or had that man genuinely been following her? Maybe it had simply been a coincidence that he'd chosen that precise moment to step into a doorway. She was being ridiculous. But it gave her the creeps to think that someone might be spying on her. And even though she was in a public place, with people all around her, Kerry suddenly felt very scared.

Outside the Tube station, the man was feeling very annoyed with himself. He shouldn't have behaved like an amateur. By stepping into the doorway, he'd only drawn attention to himself. But when she'd turned around so decisively, he'd been worried for an instant that she might be about to challenge him. He'd have to be more careful in future. He wasn't ready to make his move yet. He slipped into the shadows once more, deciding to abandon his mission until another night.

Laura was watching TV when Kerry arrived home, and she jumped up, shocked at Kerry's slumped shoulders and worried expression.

"Are you okay?"

"I'm fine," Kerry replied abruptly. She no longer wanted to talk about what had happened. She just wanted to go to bed and seek the oblivion of sleep.

"You look a bit –"

"I'm just tired," Kerry lied. "We had a lot of meetings about the project today."

"You poor love, let me make you a cuppa – have you eaten this evening? Let me cook something for you –"

"Stop fussing – I ate earlier, with Norma and Jack," Kerry lied. "I'm just going to have a bath and an early night."

Laura looked anxious. "Are you sure I can't get you anything?"

Kerry shook her head. "Right now, I just want some peace."

Laura got the message, and left her friend alone.

As Kerry lay in the bath, letting the warm water wash over her, she was annoyed with herself for not making more of an effort to hide her distress from Laura. Her friend was clearly aware that something was wrong, but Kerry didn't want to be quizzed about it. She saw no point in telling Laura about the man until she'd assessed the situation for herself and decided what to do about it.

Kerry wondered if Jeff could have arranged for someone to follow her. Perhaps he'd actually spotted her that day when she'd followed him to the Docklands hotel. She was also well aware that, by showing her support for Laura, Jeff would see her as a threat to his chances of getting back with her. Equally, Jeff's drug-dealer breakfast companion might have alerted Jeff to her presence in the hotel that morning, and she suspected that neither of them would have been happy that she'd spotted them together. Perhaps they were giving her a warning. Kerry shivered, remembering the newspaper cuttings she'd looked up. People due to testify at the drug-dealer's trial had conveniently disappeared . . .

Could her follower be a rival from another engineering company? Kerry was well aware that competition was fierce for the contract to design the new estuary barrage. Everyone at Sea Diagnostics was pulling out all the stops to get the submission ready on time. But what would be the point of following her? It would make more sense to break into their offices or hack into their company computers. Unless the plan was to unnerve her. Did they think that by frightening her, she'd become ill, take time off work so that the submission wouldn't be finished on time? Kerry smiled to herself despite her fear. This person or persons hadn't reckoned on the Sea Diagnostics team! Even if one member of the team were down, the others would work around the clock to ensure their submission was in on time.

Kerry climbed out of the bath and reached for her towel. She wasn't going to let anyone unnerve her! Nor would she let Jeff or his drug-dealing friends alter her life . . .

The following morning, Kerry arrived, bleary-eyed, at the Sea Diagnostics offices.

"You look as though you've had a rough night," Norma said, surveying her colleague's look of exhaustion as she headed for the coffee machine.

"I didn't sleep a wink," Kerry admitted. She hadn't intended to say anything to her colleague about the events of the previous evening, but she was so on edge that the words suddenly came tumbling out. "I was followed last night," she blurted out. "When I left here, some man was hanging about, and he followed me as far as the Tube station!"

Norma grinned. "Oh, don't mind him – he's just the local pervert, but he's totally harmless."

Kerry's eyebrows shot up. "What? Then why haven't I seen him before?"

"He only comes out in the evening – if you'll forgive the pun – you're only seeing him now because you stayed late to work on the project."

Kerry's heartbeat was returning to normal. She felt rather foolish now – after all, she was a woman of the world, not an innocent schoolgirl. It was an immense relief to discover that there was a simple explanation for her concerns, not the complicated scenarios she'd been envisaging in the early hours when she couldn't sleep. She was almost feeling affectionate towards the neighbourhood pervert now. Since he wasn't targeting her specifically – just any passing female – she could afford to feel magnanimous towards him. What a relief that she could forget about Jeff and the drug dealer! And the silent phone calls had probably been wrong numbers.

"You're such a fusspot!" Norma said affectionately, mussing her colleague's hair.

Kerry laughed good-naturedly as she poured herself a cup of coffee. She was also relieved that she hadn't said anything to Laura the previous evening – if she had unburdened herself to her friend, she'd now be left with egg on her face. And that was something Kerry could not abide. She always took pride in being sensible and fearless. At least now there was no longer any reason for her to worry.

CHAPTER 40

"Oh, hello, Ellie. Do you mind if we join you?"

"No, of course not. How nice to see you!" Ellie tried to hide her discomfort as she saw Sylvia, with baby Laura in her arms, looking down at her. She was sitting in the busy village café, with Kerry balanced on her knee, awaiting the arrival of her coffee and scone after doing her weekly shopping.

Sylvia pulled her buggy alongside Ellie's, lifted Laura out and sat down facing her. The two women smiled at each other.

"It's rather crowded in here this morning, isn't it?" Sylvia said. "It must be the miserable weather that's brought everyone inside!"

Ellie nodded, unsure of what to say next. Since she'd only just ordered, she couldn't exactly get up and leave. Yet she dreaded having to spend half an hour making small talk with Alan's wife. She owed the woman a huge debt of gratitude, but she hadn't banked on spending any further time with her. She and Alan had agreed that Sylvia was best avoided, but now Ellie would have to make the best of a difficult situation. It seemed churlish not to be friendly to the woman who'd helped to deliver her baby, and possibly saved Kerry's life.

"Your daughter is lovely," Ellie said lamely. "And so big for – six months?"

Sylvia nodded, pleased that Ellie had remembered the child's age. "Yes, doesn't the time just fly? It seems only yesterday that you and I –"

This unintentional reference seemed to highlight the length of time since they'd last seen each other. It increased their mutual embarrassment, which Sylvia tried to cover up by pointing out how time flies when you're caring for a young baby.

"How is Kerry doing? She looks the picture of health!" Sylvia said, smiling at the serious, dark-haired baby on Ellie's knee. Kerry gave her a disdainful look, and turned her attention to Laura, whose blonde curls seem to fascinate her. She reached out her chubby little arm, but Ellie deftly moved her before she could lean across the table and grasp the younger child's hair.

"Yes, she's doing great."

"And her father – is he helping out?"

"Yes, of course."

Sylvia flushed, wondering if she'd overstepped the mark by mentioning this unknown man in Ellie's life. She still wasn't certain if it was Tony Coleman, and she seemed to be always putting her foot in it where Ellie Beckworth was concerned.

By now, Ellie's coffee and scone had arrived, and the busy waitress had taken Sylvia's order for tea and a pastry.

"Please go ahead," Sylvia urged Ellie, "otherwise your coffee will be cold by the time mine arrives."

Nodding, Ellie took a sip of her coffee, suddenly realising that Sylvia was bound to notice her gold and diamond ring. It was such a beautiful and distinctive ring, and normally she loved showing it off. But she didn't want to risk Sylvia commenting on it. Horror of horrors – she might even ask to try it on. If she looked at it closely, she couldn't miss Alan's loving inscription on the inside.

Luckily Sylvia was smoothing down Laura's hair and didn't notice as Ellie deftly twisted the ring around so that the diamond was no longer visible. From the back, it simply looked like a broad gold wedding band.

"I presume your son's at a crèche?" she asked, hoping to find a neutral topic they could discuss with relative ease.

Sylvia nodded, smiling impishly. "Yes – having him out of the way for a few hours gives me the chance to bond with Laura, because when Pete's around, he's terribly boisterous, and demands lots of attention."

"How does he get on with his new sister?"

"Oh, he thinks she's wonderful! It's just that he doesn't realise how fragile she is. I have to watch him in case he might whack her with one of his toys. He's too young to understand the harm he could do."

Ellie smiled. If only she could keep this topic going . . .

"Have you noticed much difference in your children's personalities?" she asked, sussing that Sylvia was happy to chat about Pete and Laura.

"Oh, yes. Even though Laura is only six months old, I can see already that she's very impulsive. And in some ways, she's more outgoing than Pete – he's a more demanding child, but hopefully that will change as he gets older."

Sylvia looked at Kerry. "And your daughter? What traits have you seen developing?"

"Well, she loves concentrating on things, and is very determined," Ellie replied. "If she decides she wants to do something, she'll see it through, no matter what. If her building blocks topple, she'll keep going until they're all stacked up again, even if it takes hours. She just won't give in. It seems an odd trait in a child so young, but it does keep her occupied for ages!"

She and Sylvia shared a conspiratorial smile. They both knew how nice it was to get an occasional break from the unending task of minding a small child.

Sylvia smiled eagerly. "I've been dying to ask you about the business you run. I admire any woman who can set up on her own – I'd be hopeless at anything like that."

She seemed to be waiting expectantly, and Ellie racked her brains to think of something plausible to say.

"Well, actually, I sold the business a while back," she said at last. "It was doing well, and I was offered a good price for it. And, of course, my late husband left me with a good pension." All of which was totally untrue, but she could hardly tell Sylvia that her own husband was keeping Ellie and her child in comfort!

"I think you're amazing," Sylvia said, looking admiringly at Ellie, who blushed, feeling a total fraud. "It must have taken great courage to leave the factory – where you had a secure permanent job. I'm so glad it all went well for you. I wish I had the guts to do something like that, but I'd be hopeless." She laughed deprecatingly. "Luckily, I had a rich father, and I found a rich husband as well!"

In the silence that followed, Ellie felt that she should really ask Sylvia about the details of Laura's birth. It would be the caring, womanly thing to do, since it was a topic that united women everywhere. But she was afraid that by talking about the birthing process, it would re-establish that earlier bond they'd shared when Sylvia helped her give birth to Kerry. And she couldn't allow that to happen.

By the time Sylvia's tea and pastry arrived, Ellie had almost finished her coffee and scone. She was dying for another coffee, but that would mean staying in Sylvia's company even longer. Maybe the time was now right to extricate herself and leave the café on some pretext.

Sylvia almost seemed to read her mind. "Will I order you another coffee? You're not in any rush, are you?"

"Actually, I am," Ellie said apologetically as she stood up from the table. "I have to meet a friend at –" She looked at her watch and saw that it was twelve twenty.

"I'm meeting someone at twelve thirty," Ellie said apologetically." "I'd better get moving, or I'll be late."

As Ellie strapped Kerry into her buggy, Sylvia began reaching for the bills that the waitress had left on the table.

"No, I'll get these – it's my treat." Ellie snatched the bills off the table, and Sylvia conceded defeat.

"Thank you," Sylvia said, smiling. "My treat the next time, okay?"

As soon as the words were out, Sylvia knew she'd said the wrong thing. Ellie had frozen, as though the idea of another coffee in Sylvia's presence would be intolerable.

"Yes, of course," Ellie said eventually, but the gap had been too long for Sylvia to believe her reply.

When Ellie had paid and left the café, Sylvia gestured to the *waitress for another pot of tea. As she bounced little Laura on her knee, she gazed sadly out the café window, watching as Ellie wheeled Kerry's buggy towards her car. She was always on edge when she met Ellie Beckworth, sensing that there was some undercurrent she didn't quite understand. She liked Ellie, but clearly the feeling wasn't entirely mutual. Try as she might, there seemed no way of breaking down the shell that seemed to surround the other woman.*

Sylvia sighed. At least Ellie had answered her query about the business she'd been running. When she'd helped Ellie give birth, she'd seen no evidence of a business being run from her house, but now it was clear that Ellie had sold the business before Kerry was born. Clearly, she didn't need the money – her late husband's pension must be a good one, because Ellie and her child seemed to live in reasonable comfort.

Sylvia wondered if Ellie's distant manner could be because she was embarrassed about having a child outside marriage. But did anyone care these days? Well, Sylvia didn't care a damn – as far as she was concerned, it was no one's business but Ellie's. And presumably Tony Coleman's. But it would be difficult to make that point to her without embarrassing them both.

As she strapped Kerry into her car seat, Ellie felt sad, guilty and on edge. She hadn't been able to relax in Sylvia's company. Her conversation had been stilted, since she'd been worried about accidentally letting something slip. She couldn't risk holding a normal conversation, or truthfully answering any of the perfectly reasonable questions Sylvia had asked. Every question became a minefield that required a split-second delay while her brain processed and reformulated the answers. She hoped Sylvia wouldn't consider her continual hesitation to be rude – hopefully, she might think of it as a mannerism or personal peculiarity. Ellie didn't want Sylvia to think badly of her. She liked the woman very much, yet of necessity, she was treating her appallingly. Sylvia must think her a smug, distant and self-centred bitch – although being such a nice person, Sylvia probably wouldn't even allow herself to articulate such unworthy thoughts. How she wished Sylvia could know that her aloofness was nothing personal. On the other hand, it *was* personal, wasn't it? How could sharing the woman's husband not be personal?

Ellie felt unreasonably angry with Alan. It was all his fault that she couldn't have a woman friend. Living a lie meant making all sorts of sacrifices, and she was tired of them. Why did loving someone have to be so painful?

CHAPTER 41

Laura surveyed the clothes she'd hung in the wardrobe in Kerry's spare room. She was trying to decide what she'd wear for her Friday date with Steve. She planned to go for something really sexy – maybe the sequinned black dress with matching shrug? Or she might opt for the pink taffeta skirt and off-the-shoulder matching top. As she flicked through the hangers, Laura grimaced as she remembered the brown dress that Jeff had insisted she wore to the Sea Diagnostics reception. She'd left both the brown dress and the maxi dress in the wardrobe of his apartment. Shuddering, she wondered how she'd ever let him dictate what she should wear. She never intended wearing anything like those frumpy things ever again!

Suddenly, her mobile rang, and without checking the number she answered it, assuming that it might be the new man in her life. A second later, she bitterly regretted her decision.

"You fucking whore!" Jeff screamed down the phone. You couldn't wait to get your knickers off for another man, could you? You lousy bitch – you seem to have forgotten you're still my wife – I'll kill you for this!"

"Jeff, please!" Laura was horrified. "We didn't –" She stopped. She would not demean herself by answering his accusations. The fact that she and Steve hadn't had sex was irrelevant. She'd left her marriage and was a free agent as far as she was concerned. She'd told Jeff it was over, so it wasn't as though she was sneaking around behind his back.

"You never intended staying with me, did you?" Jeff raged.

"You're a liar and a cheat, just like every other bloody woman I've ever met!"

"Jeff, that's not fair!" Laura replied angrily. "I expected to spend my entire life with you – but you wrecked our marriage with your violence! Now, I'm hanging up – please don't call me again."

No sooner had she ended the call than her mobile phone rang again. Looking down at Jeff's number again, Laura suddenly lost her temper. "You bastard, Jeff!" she screamed, answering his call, "I am sick to death of you – don't make me do something I'll regret! You're nothing but a pathetic loser!"

Exhausted from her outburst, she turned off the phone and flung it across the room.

Hopefully Jeff would now realise that she meant what she'd said. There was no going back for them as a couple, and the sooner he accepted that, the better.

Laura was shaking as she entered the kitchen.

"What's wrong, love?" Kerry asked, looking concerned. "I thought I heard you shouting –"

"Jeff just phoned," Laura said, her voice trembling. "I didn't look at the number, so I answered it. Oh Kerry, he called me a whore!"

The tears came, and she wept as Kerry held her tightly.

"He said I was still his wife, and that he'd kill me for dating someone else – but how on earth did he know I'd been out with Steve?"

Kerry bit her lip. "He must be watching the apartment."

Laura's tears were now replaced by anger. "The nerve of him! Anyway, when he rang back, I gave him as good as I got – I told him to take a hike, so maybe he'll realise that I'm not 'meek little Laura' any more!"

"Good for you, love."

Kerry could see that Jeff's behaviour was seriously distressing her friend. "It was probably just bad luck that he was watching when Steve collected you last time," she said reassuringly.

"Maybe, but it's the not knowing that's so frightening," Laura said angrily. "He wants me to be on edge all the time, and he's succeeding."

CHAPTER 42

One little dark-haired girl and one blonde-haired girl eyed each other as they queued for the tuck shop on their first day at prep school.

"I know you – you live in Greygates, don't you?" the dark-haired girl ventured.

The blonde girl nodded, looking surprised. "How do you know that?"

"I live not far from there – on the Tefford Road. Do you know where Treetops is?"

The other girl nodded. "Isn't that the house hidden behind all those big trees?" Then she grinned sheepishly. "I suppose that's why it's called Treetops!"

Nodding, the dark-haired girl smiled back. "The house itself isn't very big, but it's got loads of woodland on all sides. I've built a platform up in one of the tallest trees – you can see for miles from up there. I can even see your house!"

The other girl raised an eyebrow in disbelief. "Wow! That sounds amazing. Did you really build a platform without any adult help?"

The dark-haired girl nodded. "I'm pretty handy at things like that," she said, without a trace of modesty. "I'll probably be an engineer or an architect when I grow up – I like working on practical things. I can build a platform in your garden too, if you'd like me to."

"Would you really?" The blonde girl was in awe of her new friend.

The dark-haired girl nodded. "In the meantime, you can play in my garden any time you want," she said. "By the way, my name is Kerry."

"And mine is Laura."

The girls looked at each other shyly. They seemed briefly to consider shaking hands, then decided against it.

Kerry smiled. "Your dad owns the canning factory, doesn't he?"

Laura nodded. Sometimes it was embarrassing to have so much more than other people.

"My mum used to work at the factory years ago – she was a chemist and worked in the laboratory," Kerry added. "Of course, she had to give up working when I came along."

"What does your father do?" Laura asked.

"I don't have one – my mum's a widow. My father died before I was born."

"Oh." Laura was puce with embarrassment, but Kerry didn't seem bothered. In a way, not having a father seemed to lend her an air of mystery, and it occurred to Laura that having one less parent would mean a great deal more freedom, since there would be one less pair of eyes scrutinising everything you did.

"Will you be in Mrs Bishop's class, too?"

Laura nodded, relieved to have a new friend in the same class. Mrs Bishop, who was both large and loud, would be their teacher for beginner's French. Already, Laura was terrified of her.

"Are you taking cookery?" Laura asked.

"God, no!" Kerry shook her head disdainfully. "I'm taking woodwork. I couldn't bear to do all that girly stuff." She grinned. "Although I'm happy to eat all that tasty food once it's been cooked!"

By the time the queue reached the tuck-shop counter, the girls discovered that they'd be sharing most subjects.

"If you like, you can come to my house and play with my dolls," Laura said generously. "I've got about a hundred."

"Eeuch!" Kerry wrinkled her nose. "I hate dolls. I'd rather play cops and robbers up in the trees, or pirates, or go on my skateboard." She looked at Laura's disappointed expression. "I'll

183

show you how to skateboard, if you like. It's much more fun than dolls – you can go really fast, and you can even learn to flip the board over, and do all kinds of exciting things – it just takes practice."

"Okay," Laura said tentatively, warming to the idea the more she thought about it. Skateboarding sounded like fun. The large courtyard behind her house would be perfect for practising in. Wouldn't Pete be surprised – and jealous – if she could demonstrate some clever moves? As the younger sibling, she was always trying to outsmart her brother, and this might be the very opportunity she was waiting for.

"Will you really *teach me* to skateboard?"

"Of course. It's easy – just a matter of balance. You won't be long getting the hang of it."

Laura smiled, her eyes alight. "Thanks – that's great. I'll ask Mum and Dad for a skateboard for my birthday."

"When is your birthday?"

"Next month. I always have a party – I hope you'll come?"

Kerry nodded. "Thanks. How old will you be?"

"I'll be eight," Laura announced.

Kerry smiled triumphantly. "That means I'm three months older than you! But don't you have to be eight already before starting prep school?"

Laura lowered her voice confidentially. "I know, but my parents asked the principal to make an exception for me, since I didn't want to wait another whole year."

Kerry nodded matter-of-factly. "People always make exceptions for those with lots of money." She squeezed Laura's hand. "But I'm glad they made an exception for you – because I think you're going to be my very best friend!"

As the family finished dinner, Laura decided to bring up the subject of her new friend.

"Mum, there's a girl in my class that I'd like to invite to my party."

Sylvia nodded approvingly. "Of course, darling – I'm glad you're making new friends. What's her name?"

184

"Kerry."

Alan's head shot up. "Did you say Kerry?"

Laura nodded. "And the great thing is – she lives near here too."

"Really?"

Laura nodded again. "Yes, she lives at Treetops, on the Tefford Road. She's such fun!"

Sylvia looked hesitantly at her husband, realising that Kerry had to be Ellie Beckworth's daughter.

Sylvia still wondered who the father of Ellie Beckworth's child was, although she'd never dare broach the subject with Alan, since he'd say she was simply being a busybody. She also remembered how, all those years ago, Alan hadn't been keen for her to befriend Ellie. Nor had Ellie responded to her overtures either. Now, ironically, their daughters seemed to have taken matters into their own hands.

Sylvia still felt a deep affection and gratitude towards Ellie. It seemed strange to think now that while she and Ellie had both been pregnant with their daughters, she'd been convinced Alan was going to leave her for someone else. But that affair had clearly been over for many years now, if indeed it had happened at all. Sometimes she wondered if she'd misread those receipts? Only for Ellie, she might have confronted Alan, perhaps with dire consequences, since he'd have abhorred her lack of trust, and it would have permanently damaged their relationship.

Sylvia wondered briefly how Ellie could afford to send her child to such a prestigious school, but of course she'd no idea about Ellie's financial circumstances. Years earlier, Ellie had told her that she'd sold her business, so maybe she'd made a lot of money from that. She'd also mentioned a pension from her late husband, so presumably he'd left her very well off.

"I'm sure it's very nice for you to have a friend who lives so near," Sylvia said to her daughter, glancing at Alan to ensure his approval. It was one thing to discourage an adult friendship with Ellie, based on their differing social positions, but it would be unfair to discourage Laura, who was shy and impulsive, and needed to learn about the give and take of friendship. Pete was far

185

too boisterous for his younger sister, and was always plotting ways of frightening her. It would be good for her to have a friend of her own age. She looked at her husband. "It'll be nice for Laura, won't it, dear? Having someone nearby to play with?"

Alan nodded, trying to look absent-minded, but his feelings were far from vague. He supposed that since both girls were attending the same prep school – both paid for by him – it was inevitable that they'd discover they lived within half a mile of each other. He should have insisted that Kerry be sent to a different school, but Ellie was adamant that her daughter would receive exactly the same standard of education that Laura did. Hopefully, the girls would discover that they were like chalk and cheese, and they'd outgrow their friendship with the passing of time.

"Can Kerry come to my birthday party, Mum?"

Sylvia darted another glance at her husband, but didn't wait for his approval this time.

"Of course, darling – what a lovely idea!"

CHAPTER 43

The following day, Laura's mobile phone continued to ring every hour on the hour until finally she turned it off. Since she was meeting Steve again that evening, she'd wanted to keep her phone on in case he needed to contact her. But Jeff made it impossible. She really did need to change her number. Which was very annoying, since all her friends and work colleagues used the number she already had, and it would mean having to let everyone in her address book – except Jeff, of course – have her new number.

She'd decided to wear a white top and tight black trousers for her date. She felt a surge of excitement as the time when Steve would arrive was drawing near. To hell with Jeff if he was watching – what could he do but make more abusive phone calls? But she wouldn't answer, and she'd change her number the very next day.

On the dot of eight, Steve arrived in his magnificent black 1929 Rolls Royce, and as she stepped out of the apartment lobby and into the street, Laura was blown away by its sleek lines and impressive finish. "Wow! It's fabulous!" she told Steve, her eyes shining. "I can't believe I'm about to travel in such style!"

Steve was clearly pleased by her response and, smiling, he held open the passenger door for her. Casting a glance around the street, Laura was relieved that there was no sign of Jeff. She settled herself in the passenger seat, and soon they were off. Laura was equally impressed by the car's interior. She loved the smell of the old leather seats and the crafted walnut dashboard. As Steve drove along, Laura found herself gradually relaxing with each mile they were putting between her and Jeff. She glanced at Steve's profile. He really was a good-looking man. She wasn't really looking for a serious relationship yet, but there was no harm in seeing what might happen between them.

The restaurant proved every bit as delightful as Steve had claimed. The French cuisine was wonderful, and the maître d' was both efficient and flirtatious towards Laura. She was amused by his gallantry, banter and innuendo, and Steve didn't seem to mind that he kept kissing Laura's hand at every opportunity. But it crossed her mind that if Jeff had been with her instead of Steve, he'd have punched the maître d' by now.

During the evening, Laura's phone rang, and glancing at the number, she cursed silently. Reaching into her purse, she turned it off. She wasn't going to let Jeff ruin her dinner.

Steve looked at her. "Is that your ex again?"

Laura nodded, embarrassed.

Then Steve suddenly grinned. "Well, I can understand how he feels – he's not with the most gorgeous woman in London any longer – I'm the lucky guy she's with now!"

Laura was secretly delighted by his comment. Steve was making it clear he thought her attractive, and that he was enjoying her company. She also found it pleasant and relaxing to be with someone who didn't require her to monitor everything she said. She and Steve found lots of topics to discuss, and were pleased to discover that they had quite a few interests in common.

After a beautiful meal and two bottles of wine between them, Laura was feeling full and happy. As Steve paid the bill and they prepared to leave the restaurant, she tucked her arm through his. "Thanks for a really lovely evening, Steve," she said warmly. "Next time, it'll be my treat, okay?"

Steve smiled back. "I'll hold you to that," he said, kissing her lightly.

Laura felt content and at peace with the world. It sounded like he intended seeing her again. Things could only get better between them . . .

As they strolled arm in arm through the car park, Laura was

wondering what she'd do if Steve suggested a nightcap back at his place. Was it too early in their relationship? Would he think she was easy if she said yes? Or would he be offended if she refused, and think she wasn't interested in him? She did really like him. He was a lovely guy, and she was growing more and more fond of him . . .

"*Holy shit!*"

Laura was awakened from her reverie by a roar of anger from Steve. They'd reached the Rolls Royce, and she could hardly believe her eyes as she stared at the vehicle. The word '*Whore*' had been scrawled across the sleek black bonnet in some kind of white paint.

Her heart beating wildly, she looked all around her. She knew who had done this. Rage filled her heart. Now he was destroying her future as well as her past.

Steve was already on the phone, talking rapidly to someone, but Laura had no idea who. It could have been the police, his insurance company, or a friend. Although the evening was warm, Laura was shivering. Probably from shock, she thought. I can't believe that Jeff would go this far.

When Steve finished his phone call, he walked around his car again, caressing it as though it was a wounded person whom he was reassuring. It was obvious that the car meant a lot to him, and Laura felt overwhelmed by guilt as she watched his stunned expression and haunted eyes.

Eventually, he left the car and ventured over to where Laura was standing. In silence, they looked at each other. Laura felt shaky and miserable, and didn't believe that anything she could say would help the situation or make Steve feel any better.

At last Steve spoke. "Look, I like you, Laura, but there's clearly something weird going on here, and I don't want to be part of it." He shrugged his shoulders. "If you haven't already gone to the police, you should do so now. Your ex is a psycho, and I don't want my car damaged any further. Nor do I want to end up injured or dead because your ex doesn't want you dating anyone else. So I'm out of here. Sorry."

"Oh Steve, I'm the one who should be sorry for what's happened to your car," Laura said humbly. "Please let me pay for the repairs –"

Steve's smile was bitter. "Forget it, Laura. It's not your fault. Luckily, I have vintage-car insurance, which should cover it after I report what happened to the police. And you'll have to go to the police, too. Otherwise this guy will keep ruining your life."

Laura nodded, feeling awful.

Steve took out his phone. "I'll call you a cab, then I'll get this baby of mine home."

Steve called a taxi, and when it arrived he paid the cab driver and helped Laura in.

"Goodbye, Laura," he said sadly. "I'm sorry it had to end this way. Please notify the police about your ex, won't you?"

Feeling numb, Laura nodded. As the taxi drove off, Laura wept quietly. It wasn't just the loss of such a nice guy that bothered her so much, but the fact that Jeff was still ruining her life. She'd do what Steve had suggested. It was definitely time to contact the police.

CHAPTER 44

Laura's party was going well, and the magician hired to amuse the children had proved very popular. Afterwards, the youngsters had descended on the food like a plague of locusts, and only a few sandwiches remained, now well trodden into the floor. Alan smiled. He had to hand it to Sylvia – she really did seem to know what kids liked. The children attending the party were a mixture of their friends' children, the sons and daughters of his factory workers, a few of Laura's new classmates – and, of course, Kerry.

The downstairs of the house looked as though a bomb had hit it. Gift-wrap lay everywhere, abandoned by Laura as she'd excitedly opened her presents. She was so thrilled to be eight! Toys, jigsaws and birthday cards littered the living room. Her new skateboard held pride of place in the middle of it all, and she'd been so excited as she'd unwrapped it earlier that morning at the breakfast table.

Since the weather was still warm for October, the children were now running wild in the gardens, and everyone seemed to be enjoying themselves. As Alan joined Sylvia outside, he slipped an arm around her. "You've done brilliantly," he told her. "Laura's having a ball!"

But Sylvia looked worried, and Alan followed her eye-line to where Kerry was playing at the swing, and some of the other children were trying to push her off.

"Oh dear, she's rather a tomboy, isn't she?" Sylvia said anxiously. "Kerry has actually taken the seat off the swing and is

191

now hanging from the top by her arms! Surely she'll hurt herself? And if the other children start copying her – well, I'm not sure what to do."

Alan laughed. "Don't worry – she looks as though she knows what she's doing."

"But if she falls and breaks her arm – how could I ever face her mother?"

Sylvia's comment made Alan realise that a calamity like that would mean even more contact between Sylvia and Ellie, so he strode over to Kerry and peeled her hands from the top of the swing and placed her on the ground. Had he imagined it, or had she just kicked him in the groin?

Hands now on her hips, Kerry glared at him with a mixture of anger and contempt. "Why did you do that?"

"Because you might fall, and I don't want to have to explain to your mother that you broke your arm or leg at our party."

"You can't stop me – you're not my father!"

"Well, I am one of the people organising this party," Alan said mildly. "That gives me quite a bit of authority."

Kerry looked at him scornfully, and he had to hide his smile. She looked exactly like Ellie did when she was annoyed. The child was becoming a replica of her mother!

Alan smiled at her, trying to diffuse the tension. "Laura tells me you're brilliant at skateboarding – any chance you could show me how you do it?"

Kerry's fierce expression was disbelieving at first. "You really want to watch me?"

Alan nodded, pleased when her face brightened.

"Okay – c'mon. I've left my skateboard over in your courtyard."

Without hesitation, Kerry took his hand and they began walking towards the courtyard behind the house. Sylvia smiled quizzically at him as he went by, clearly grateful that he'd managed to distract the child from her daredevil antics.

In the empty courtyard, Kerry collected her skateboard and stepped on it.

"This is where I'm going to teach Laura," she told him.

Alan nodded approvingly. "She's really looking forward to it. Is it true that you travel everywhere on your skateboard?"

Kerry nodded. "Yes, it's a really fast way of getting around. When I'm older, I'll probably get a bike. But Mum says I'm too young for one yet."

As Kerry demonstrated her ability around the courtyard, Alan marvelled at her skill. She really was good at it! He could see the determination on her little face as she concentrated on her moves, particularly her back flip, clearly keen to impress him.

"Bravo! You really are talented!" Alan said, clapping as she came to a stop in front of him.

Kerry looked at him shyly. "Thanks," she said. "Laura could be just as good as me – if she sticks with it, that is. She starts something but doesn't always finish it."

"Well, with such a good teacher as you, she's bound to succeed," Alan told her, and was pleased to see her little face flush with pleasure.

As they walked back to the garden where the party was in full swing, Alan had a sudden thought.

"Kerry, would you like me to teach you how to ride a bicycle?"

The little girl looked quizzically at him. "But I haven't got a bike!"

Alan smiled down at her. "Well, I could teach you when you do get one."

It was an impulsive and ill-thought-out idea, but the more he thought about it, the more he liked it, and the more he wanted to do it. And he welcomed the idea of spending some one-to-one time with his secret daughter.

Kerry nodded, but in her own mind she dismissed his offer as just another of those empty promises adults made and later forgot about.

"I really mean it," Alan said, looking down at her sceptical little face. "But don't tell Laura, because she might be jealous." He grinned. "Anyway, since she's three months younger than you, she can learn to ride later."

Kerry looked pleased that the three-month age difference had been acknowledged, and Alan smiled to himself, knowing how much even a few months mattered to a small child.

He also suspected that Kerry was shrewd enough to appreciate the value of secrecy. But even if she did eventually tell Laura about the lessons, while he'd be disappointed in her, it wasn't as though the sky would fall. He'd simply tell Sylvia that he'd felt sorry for the girl and had spent a few afternoons helping her. In fact, he wondered if he might even tell Sylvia upfront. She was a generous woman, and would probably applaud him for his kindness. On the other hand, maybe not. Sylvia might want to become involved as a way of seeing Ellie again . . .

As they walked back to the party, Alan was filled with resolve. He really did want to teach Kerry to ride a bike. Perhaps he wanted a little time to bond with his secret daughter, and he knew Ellie would be pleased. Of course, he and Ellie would merely be polite to each other in Kerry's presence. It amused him to think that they might even address each other as 'Mr' and 'Ms'.

"Bye, Mr Thornton," Kerry said, as she ran off to join the other children.

Alan smiled, watching as she and Laura quickly singled each other out, Kerry taking her place in the game beside Laura. They were so different, yet they seemed to get on very well. He supposed that if they did stay friends, there was nothing much he could do about it. He and Ellie would just have to be extra-careful.

As the party ended, the usual chaos ensued as over-excited children rushed to their parents' cars, clutching their goodie bags.

"It's been fun, but I'm very glad it's over!" a relieved Sylvia whispered to her husband.

It had been arranged that Alan and Sylvia would each drive the few remaining children home. Alan made sure that Kerry was one of the children who got into his car – he didn't want Sylvia and Ellie meeting up again. Besides, he had something important to say to Ellie.

Alan made sure that Kerry was the last child to be dropped off, so that he could manage to have a brief word with Ellie.

"Thanks, Mr Thornton," Kerry said, as Alan deposited her outside the front door of Treetops.

"You're welcome, Kerry," he called, waving as the child rang the doorbell.

As the door opened, Ellie stepped outside. "It's very good of you to drop her home – thanks, Mr Thornton."

Alan nodded. "No problem, Ms Beckworth."

By now, Kerry had disappeared inside, and Ellie risked crossing to the car, leaning in and quickly kissing him.

"Careful!" Alan whispered. "That child of ours is very bright – let's not rock any boats just yet!"

Although he felt a surge of desire, he quelled the instinct to sweep her into his arms and make love to her on the spot.

"I have an idea," he told her. "I think it's time we got Kerry a bike."

CHAPTER 45

When an emotional Laura arrived back in the apartment, Kerry hastily threw on her dressing gown, and joined her in the kitchen.

"Has Steve done something to upset you?" she asked, looking worried.

Laura angrily told her friend what had happened.

"Why won't Jeff leave me alone?" she shouted. "How dare he interfere in my private life! How dare he think he can still tell me what I can do, or who I can go out with!"

"He's not just interfering in your life – he's wrecking it!" Kerry said grimly. "I presume your guy Steve will report the damage to the police?"

Laura was looking miserable. "He said he would. Unfortunately, he's not 'my' Steve any longer – Jeff's made sure of that! I'd just assumed that Jeff was still venting, and that eventually he'd stop his stupid carry-on. But what if he doesn't? What if he keeps hurting anyone connected to me? Even you could be next!"

Kerry nodded, unable to think of anything to say.

As Laura sat brooding, and staring into the cup of coffee that Kerry had just made, she was livid. "How on earth could Jeff know where Steve and I were tonight?" she whispered angrily. "Even if he was standing outside the apartment and saw us leave, he wouldn't know where we were going. He'd have needed luck to get a taxi straight away, and a cabbie who was willing to race after us . . ."

Kerry grimaced. "Maybe Jeff's employing other people to do his dirty work? He's certainly wealthy enough to pay for it."

Laura nodded. "Yes, I think you could be right. I'm positive he wasn't outside the apartment when Steve and I left here tonight. I took a good look around and there was no sign of him. So maybe he arranged for someone else to follow us –"

Kerry gasped and Laura turned quizzically towards her. Kerry quickly pressed a finger to her lips, then grabbed a piece of paper and wrote hastily on it before passing it to Laura. Now it was Laura's turn to gasp. Kerry was suggesting that there could be a listening device in the apartment!

In total silence, and using only hand signals, the two women began checking behind clocks and ornaments, in drawers and beneath cupboards, and in between books and CDs.

Eventually Kerry located a small device with a tiny blinking light attached to the underside of the coffee table in the living room. Gesturing to Laura to follow, she headed for the kitchen, where she dropped the device into the soapy water in the washing-up bowl. The blinking stopped immediately.

"Now you can't hear us any more, you bastard!" Kerry hissed. Then she turned to a horrified Laura. "So that's how lover-boy knew we'd be at the bar in Flower Street! And that you were annoyed with him for hanging onto the wedding presents. He'd also have known about your date with Steve, because we sat at that very coffee table talking about it!"

Laura shivered. "If he's trying to spook me, he's succeeding," she said. "How on earth did he manage to put it there?"

"He must have done it the night you were both here for dinner," Kerry replied. "Remember you helped me do the washing-up in the kitchen? He was alone in the living room for about ten minutes – that would have been more than enough time to attach it."

Laura let out a groan. "And to think I was on edge while we were in the kitchen! You know how Jeff hates being on his own, even for a minute, unless it's on his terms. I was actually relieved that he wasn't grumpy when we joined him again – now we know why he was looking so smug."

Laura was still finding it hard to take in the enormity of Jeff's deceit. "But why would he want to bug *your* apartment? It doesn't make sense – he and I were still together then!"

Kerry grimaced. "Obviously, being married didn't stop him wanting to spy on you," she reasoned. "He must have wanted to find out what you and I were talking about." She hesitated. "I don't want to worry you, love, but I'm beginning to think he probably even planted listening devices or cameras in the apartment you shared. He's obviously the kind of man who'd want to find out who visited or phoned you when he wasn't there." Suddenly, she shuddered. "Thank goodness you rang me from your bathroom the night you told me you were leaving him – he obviously hadn't planted any listening device in there."

Laura cradled her head in her hands. "How could anyone stoop so low?" she whispered.

"You said he was insecure – I guess men like him can't bear their women to be independent of them. And after you'd broken up with him, the device he'd planted here was even more useful, since he could now find out everything about your new life."

Laura shivered. "Why can't he just let me go? I'm never going back to him."

"I don't think Jeff can accept that you rejected him – he's convinced that you'll come back to him if he just pursues you enough. Either that, or –"

Kerry hesitated.

"Or what?"

"Or he's deliberately trying to drive you out of your mind."

Laura shivered. "Why would he want to do that?"

"Because if he can't have you, he wants to make sure you'll never be happy with anyone else."

Laura gave a heartfelt sigh. "I've been a fool, haven't I? Why did I try so hard to make it work with Jeff? I guess it was because I wanted somewhere to belong, and someone to belong to. I've been so lonely since I lost Pete and my parents." She looked earnestly at Kerry. "Our families give us our identity and history, don't they? I suppose I thought that Jeff could give that back to me. By starting our own family, we'd be building a family history of our own."

Kerry shivered. "Thanks goodness you didn't!"

Laura nodded. "When I miscarried, I thought it was the worst thing in the world that could have happened to me. Now, although I'm still sad for the poor baby, I'm relieved. If I'd had kids with Jeff, I'd never have got away from him." She stood up. "Maybe we should check out the other rooms – just in case?"

Kerry nodded. "Good idea – I suppose he could have crept around the flat while we were in the kitchen. Now that we know what he's capable of, we'll have to keep one step ahead of him."

As they checked each room, Laura was still reeling from all the bizarre events of the night. "The only caring thing that Steve said was that I should contact the police myself," she said.

Kerry looked worried. "I see the logic, but I'm beginning to wonder if that's a good idea," she cautioned. "I've been reading up on stalkers, and it seems they have a tendency to become even more violent after they've been reported." She put her arms around her friend. "I just don't want anything bad to happen to you."

Laura said nothing, feeling overwhelmed by Jeff's vindictiveness.

As they returned to the kitchen, having found no other devices, Kerry injected some positivism into their discussion. "Look, it might just be enough to change your mobile-phone number – tomorrow you should definitely contact your service provider."

"Yes, Steve said that, too."

Kerry squeezed her friend's arm. "Cheer up, love – before long, Jeff will get fed up with pursuing you. We'll just have to wait it out. Hopefully, by this time next year, he'll have moved on and we'll hardly remember his name!"

Laura smiled weakly. She knew Kerry was trying to cheer her up, but deep down she wondered if Jeff would let her go so easily. I won't allow him to get under my skin, she vowed. He's not going to win.

CHAPTER 46

"Ooooh!" *Kerry wobbled uncertainly and the bicycle juddered for a few seconds, then she fell headlong into the flowerbed.*

Alan ran to her and helped her up. "Are you okay? You did really well!"

Grimacing, Kerry wiped the clay from her hands. Her knees were stinging, and she felt certain she'd skinned them both. But she was determined not to cry. She was relishing every minute of her time with Mr Thornton – it was almost like having a dad of her own.

She'd been astonished and thrilled when Mr Thornton had kept his promise. He'd arrived at Treetops one afternoon after school with a new bike in the boot of his car, and it had been exactly the right size for her. "But you mustn't tell Laura, or anyone else, about the bike or the lessons," he told her sternly. That very afternoon, she'd had her first lesson.

"It's all about confidence," Alan told her, as he helped her to brush the mud off her knees. "You were doing fine until you got a fit of nerves, right?"

Kerry nodded.

"Now, hop up on that bike again, and let me see what you can really do."

Kerry grinned, climbing on, determined to show Mr Thornton that she was a worthy pupil. He'd already spent ages running alongside her, holding onto the bike as she pedalled up and down the Treetops driveway. It was only when she'd realised that he'd let

200

go – and she found she was actually cycling on her own – that she'd got such a fright and ended up in the flowerbed. At least the ground there was reasonably soft. So far, she'd managed to veer away from the holly bushes near the front gate.

As Kerry got on the bike once more, Alan held the back carrier and ran alongside her as she pedalled. "Keep going, Kerry!" he shouted, as she cycled down the driveway. "You're really getting the hang of it now!"

Kerry smiled as the bike wobbled. She knew he had just let go, but she was managing to keep steering straight ahead. Then she cycled around the grass in a circle, and came to a neat stop in front of him.

Alan's face was wreathed in smiles. "You were great that time! You've got amazing balance. You'll be ready for the Olympics in no time!"

Kerry smiled, wallowing happily in his praise. She so envied Laura having such a great dad! She was enjoying their secret meetings, and her mum seemed to like him too, because they were always whispering and laughing when they thought she wasn't listening.

However, Kerry had also worked out that once she learnt to ride, Mr Thornton wouldn't need to spend time with her anymore. So she was actually taking a lot longer to learn than was strictly necessary. The pain of a few bruises and scraped knees were worth it in order to have his undivided attention.

"I'm definitely getting the hang of it," she told him. "But I still need a few more lessons –"

"Yes, of course. I'll see you here at the same time next week?"

As she nodded, Kerry's little face was a picture of happiness. She had more of his visits to look forward to, and maybe she could fake a bad fall next time, and stretch out the lessons a little longer.

Alan was also enjoying the time he was spending with his secret daughter. Throughout the winter months and into the spring, he'd been giving Kerry a lesson once a week. Having spent the earlier part of the afternoon with Ellie, he was able to claim that he'd 'just arrived' at Treetops when Kerry got back from school. He was well aware that the child had already become a perfectly competent cyclist, but he didn't mind her little deception. He was flattered that she wanted to spend time with him, and the feeling was reciprocated. He'd also come to appreciate Kerry's determination and her courage, and he realised that she, too, was benefiting from their time together. She was a hardy little thing, so unlike Laura, yet their differences seemed to have cemented a surprising friendship between them.

Kerry's mother appeared at the door. "Would you like a cup of tea before you go, Mr Thornton?"

"Yes, please, Ms Beckworth – this is thirsty work out here!" Alan replied amiably. "But Kerry is doing brilliantly – she'll be a competent cyclist by the summer!"

Leaving Kerry to put away her bike, Alan headed inside to Ellie's kitchen, glad of the opportunity to spend even a few minutes alone with her. Seeing her, but not being able to hold her, was torture. And soon, their time together would be even more limited – summer was approaching, and the children would be on long holidays from school. So they'd be able to snatch only an occasional afternoon together when they were certain Kerry was occupied elsewhere.

Alan sighed at the thought of not being able to see Ellie every afternoon. For years, he'd led a charmed life, slipping away from the office for a late – and long – lunch with Ellie almost every working day. If any staff noted his absence, they didn't dare say anything, and his PA had always been paid well enough to warrant her covering for him while he was missing. Sylvia assumed he was at work all day, and during the evenings and weekends he'd been able to tell her that he had urgent factory business to attend to. But now that Kerry was growing older, things weren't quite so easy. Already he was unable to visit Ellie at weekends, and during the week he had to leave Treetops long before Kerry returned from school.

"I don't know how I'd cope if the school holidays were any longer," Alan grumbled, giving Ellie's hand a surreptitious squeeze. "As Kerry gets older, maybe we can send her to one of those summer camps for a week or two?"

Ellie laughed. "Luckily, she's old enough to join the junior tennis club this year, and she's really looking forward to it." She smiled at him. "That takes place every afternoon for most of the summer."

Alan winked conspiratorially at Ellie. "Then I'll buy her the best tennis racquet money can buy – after all, the more she likes tennis, the more she'll keep playing!" He sneaked a hand up Ellie's sweater. "And the more time we'll have to spend together!"

Alan was pleased. Maybe the school holidays wouldn't be such a problem after all.

CHAPTER 47

Having changed her mobile phone number the following day, Laura felt a lot more secure. She was still smarting from the events of the previous night, and the fact that Steve had effectively dumped her. It wasn't a nice feeling, but Laura decided that the best way to get over the ignominy was to throw herself into her work with a vengeance.

As the week progressed, she began to feel a lot calmer, and was relieved that there were no further calls from Jeff. She hoped that he'd realised that the daubing of paint on Steve's car had been a step too far and had finally decided to leave her alone. She'd also put off going to the police, reasoning that this unfortunate episode of her life was now over, and Jeff had probably learned his lesson – unfortunately at her and Steve's cost. She was also conscious of Kerry's warning about stalkers, and didn't want to antagonise Jeff if he'd already decided to leave her alone.

She was also reluctantly accepting that Steve hadn't been the man of her dreams either – otherwise, he'd have hung in there with her, and helped her to deal with Jeff's behaviour. She felt guilty about his car, but she'd offered to pay and he'd declined her offer. Hopefully his insurance would sort it out for him.

By Friday, Laura was looking forward to a night out with Kerry, Norma, Jack and several of their colleagues from Sea Diagnostics. One of the company's design teams had spent months working on plans for an estuary barrage. Now the plans had been submitted to the relevant authorities, and all they could do was wait, and hope it would be accepted. But in the meantime, they could party!

As her students left Laura's office at the end of her afternoon tutorial, she was looking forward to going home, showering and getting ready for her night out with Kerry and her colleagues. She then had the whole weekend ahead, and she intended doing some serious relaxation.

As she switched her phone back on, it began to ring. Laura guessed it was probably Kerry, phoning to see if she'd left work yet, so she picked it up off her desk and was just about to press the call button. Then she looked at the caller ID and she froze. It was Jeff's number! Quickly she pressed the red button and rejected the call. How on earth had he managed to get her new number already? She'd had it for less than a week! Anxiously, Laura looked all around her office, as though Jeff was likely to pop up from behind her desk or suddenly materialise beside her. She was shaking and furious. The gall of him, daring to contact her after what he'd done to Steve's car! Did he really think she'd ever want to speak to him again?

In a fury, Laura locked her office and proceeded down the corridor. Her excitement about the night ahead had already waned considerably, and she wondered if she should give the planned outing a miss. Maybe Jeff would turn up and spoil the night, since he seemed capable of finding her anywhere.

The door to the office of the department's secretary was still open, and Greta waved to Laura as she hurried past.

"Goodnight, Laura – I hope you're off somewhere exciting!" she called.

Laura stopped in her tracks, aware that she'd forgotten to say goodnight and wish her colleague well for the weekend.

"Oh, hello, Greta – sorry, I was miles away," she said apologetically, stepping into the office. "Shouldn't you be gone home by now?"

Greta smiled cheerfully. "I'm just printing off the programme for the seminar next week." She smiled. "I don't mind doing Darren a favour – there aren't many bosses as decent as him. I'll be gone in a few minutes, anyway."

Laura had a sudden thought.

"Greta, did you give out my new phone number to anyone?"

The department secretary looked vague. "No, I don't think so." Then she brightened. "Oh, yes, I'd forgotten – but then, I don't suppose your husband counts! Yesterday he rang to say he'd accidentally deleted your new number, and could he have it? He said he felt such a fool."

Laura nodded, feeling annoyed. "So you gave it to him."

"Of course. Why wouldn't I?"

Laura bit her lip. Greta was right – under normal circumstances, there would be no reason not to. But so far she'd avoided telling anyone in the department that she and Jeff had broken up. She'd been coming to terms with the situation herself, and hadn't wanted people's sympathy in case it made her burst into tears. Now that reasoning felt so childish and stupid.

"Well, I'd be grateful if you wouldn't tell him anything more about me," Laura said gently. "Jeff and I have broken up, and he's being difficult about it."

Greta's eyes widened. "Oh Laura, I'm so sorry!" she said, looking surprised and guilty at the same time. "If only I'd known –"

Laura nodded ruefully as tears threatened to form. "It's my own fault – I should have told you all before now. But I feel such a fool – I'm not even married a full year yet, and my marriage is over already."

"Well, I'm sure you've made the right choice," Greta said supportively. "Marriage isn't for everyone, you know." She looked at Laura grimly. "But I think maybe you need to change your phone number again."

Leaving Greta's office, Laura turned and went back down the corridor. Since she'd told Greta that her marriage was over, she felt it was only right to let Darren know as well. He was her boss, and as a matter of courtesy he should really have been the first to hear it.

Knocking on his door, Laura waited apprehensively. She hoped he wouldn't be overly kind to her, since she was likely to break down and cry if he did.

"Come in!"

Stepping inside, Laura stood in front of Darren's big desk, feeling awkward.

"Sit down, Laura – take the weight off your feet," her boss urged. "How did you get on with those statistics lectures?"

"Fine," said Laura dismissively. She never had any problem with her teaching schedule. It was in other areas of her life that things weren't going so smoothly.

"Well then, is this a social call?" he asked, smiling.

Laura sighed. She couldn't put off telling him any longer. "Jeff and I have split up," she said.

Darren's expression was grave. "I'm very sorry, Laura. But perhaps it's for the best."

Laura wanted to shout at him and ask him what exactly he meant by this last comment. But she was too emotionally drained by it all, and she knew what he meant anyway. There wouldn't be anyone in the Sociology Department who'd be sorry to see Jeff out of her life. Most of her colleagues had already made it clear that he wasn't their favourite person, and she couldn't blame them either. If anyone was to blame, it was her for being so stupid. Why hadn't she left him the first time he'd raised his hand to her?

"Do you want to take some time off?" Darren asked softly. "If you feel you need some space, I'm sure Maria could delay her break for a week or two."

Vehemently, Laura shook her head. "That's the last thing I need," she said. "I was going to ask you if I could do some extra hours – throwing myself into work is probably the best thing for me right now."

Darren nodded. "Well, I can't deny that I'd be delighted if you could take the second years for their social cohesion module. I'd been thinking of bringing in a substitute lecturer, but if you're sure you feel up to it –"

"Of course I do," Laura told him briskly.

Darren suddenly grinned, and Laura could see that his eyes were twinkling. "I presume we can now take down that dreadful plaque on your door?"

Nodding, Laura blushed.

"Good," Darren said briskly. "Can you take over from Monday week? That'll give you time to revise and update your lecture notes for the course. But don't worry about the first year tutorials – I'll get Timmy to handle them."

Laura nodded. "Thanks, Darren," she said, rising to her feet. She was grateful that he hadn't gone all maudlin on her, or tried to wheedle the details of the break-up from her. Right now, sympathy would be her undoing, and Darren seemed to know that instinctively.

"Laura –" Darren took off his glasses and polished them on his handkerchief. "Please don't forget that we're all here for you."

Laura nodded, a lump in her throat as she left the room and closed the door.

When she'd gone, a big smile appeared on Darren's face, and he punched the air in jubilation. At last, he'd got his Laura back.

CHAPTER 48

As the days began to get longer and brighter, Kerry cycled over to Greygates to play with her friend.

"Where did you learn to ride a bike?" Laura asked, outraged.

Kerry reddened. "Oh, a friend taught me."

Laura looked at her suspiciously. "What friend, and when did they teach you? You couldn't ride last summer, and you never said anything to me about learning – if you'd told me you were getting lessons, I could have come along and learnt to ride too!"

"Oh, it was just someone Mum knows," Kerry said dismissively. "And he only gave me a few lessons. I didn't need any more."

"And who bought you the bike?"

Kerry coloured as the lie formed on her tongue. "Mum did."

Laura felt hard done by. It was as though Kerry had moved on to a different level, and she was being left behind. She was always acutely aware of the three-month age difference between them – and it always seemed to give Kerry an advantage. And now that Kerry could ride a bike, Laura was suddenly afraid that she might move on to other friends, people who could ride bicycles and therefore could cycle to the woods or to the park on picnics.

"Will you teach me to ride?" Laura asked anxiously.

Kerry nodded. "Okay, but I don't want you falling off and damaging my bike."

"Huh!" said Laura, annoyed now, "I can see you're more concerned about your bike than about me."

Kerry grinned. "You're right – because once you've learned on mine, your parents will buy you a brand new one, and I'll be left with the one you've wrecked!"

Although still annoyed, Laura could see Kerry's point of view, but she was still determined to acquire this new skill.

"Okay, I'll strike a deal with you – if I damage your bike, I'll let you ride my new one when we go out cycling together. But I can't let Mum know, because she'd kill me!"

Grinning, Kerry nodded. "You've got a deal! Come on – let's get started!"

"And while you're here, could you fix my skateboard?"

Kerry nodded. "Of course. What's wrong with it?"

"I don't exactly know, but one of the wheels is definitely stuck."

"It's probably rusted up since last summer. I told you to oil the wheels before putting it away, didn't I? But I'll bet you didn't."

As she watched Laura's cheeks turn red, Kerry didn't need any reply.

"Dad, Kerry is teaching me to ride a bike," Laura said proudly, as she joined the family for their evening meal.

Alan felt a pang of guilt, realising that he should have been the one to do it.

"That's great, love," he told her enthusiastically. "Would you like me to help?"

Laura shook her head. "No thanks, I've nearly mastered it already. But you can watch me at the weekend – I should be able to do it perfectly by then."

"So I guess you'll be wanting a bike for your next birthday?" Alan said, smiling.

"You're not bad at all," Kerry conceded grudgingly, as they finished Laura's latest cycling lesson. "I think your dad was impressed, too."

"Thanks," Laura said, blushing. She was delighted with her progress, and thrilled that her father had come along to watch her ride successfully around the lawn.

Kerry and Mr Thornton had also shared a knowing wink and

Kerry knew he was grateful she hadn't told Laura about the secret lessons he'd given her. Kerry liked sharing a secret with Mr Thornton – in a way, it was almost like having a secret father of her own.

As Laura climbed off, Kerry inspected her bicycle. "You don't seem to have done any damage," she declared magnanimously, "so I'll let you off our deal. Just as long as you give me one go on your new bicycle when you get it?"

"Hmmm . . ." Laura murmured pointedly. "What sort of deal should we have, in case you damage my new bike?"

"You catch on fast, don't you?" Kerry said, grinning as she leaned her bike against the wall. "Anyway, I wasn't really going to hold you to it. And I've fixed your skateboard, too – it's in your shed."

"Oh thanks – that's brilliant!" Laura said, smiling.

"No problem," Kerry said gruffly, embarrassed by Laura's obvious admiration. "It only meant adjusting one of the wheel nuts where it had rusted."

"Well, I couldn't have done it," Laura told her. She was always in awe of her friend's ability to disassemble and put things back together.

"It's easy!" Kerry told her dismissively. "If you didn't spend all your time playing with those stupid dolls, you'd be well able to do it."

"I haven't played with dolls for ages!" Laura told her, annoyed. "On second thoughts, maybe I won't give you a ride on my new bike after all. In fact, you needn't bother coming to my birthday party, either!"

"Huh!" said Kerry disdainfully, "Do you really think I want to go to your stupid party? You're such a baby – and in case you need reminding, I'm three months older than you, and I always will be!"

The standoff lasted a few moments while they looked at each other uncertainly. Then they both started laughing, and the brief spat was over.

"Come on, let's go and get some juice from the kitchen," Laura suggested. "Riding a bike is thirsty work!"

"Okay," said Kerry, abandoning her bike in the grass and, arm in arm, they headed across the lawn towards the house.

CHAPTER 49

After several more phone calls from Jeff over the weekend – none of which she'd answered – Laura accepted that her ex-husband wasn't going to give up, and it was time to approach the police about his behaviour.

During her lunch break on Monday, Laura stepped into the local police station and hurried to the front desk.

"Officer, I want to report my ex-husband's unreasonable behaviour."

The grumpy-faced policeman looked bored as he sat behind a mound of papers. "Hold on, I'll see if someone is available to talk to you."

After an eternity, he returned with an officer in tow, who gestured for her to follow him into a dingy office down an equally dingy corridor.

As they sat on opposite sides of a table marked with cup rings and scuffmarks, the officer gestured for her to begin.

"I've recently left my husband because he turned violent after we got married," she explained, the words tumbling out. "But since I've left, he's been following me, turning up at the same places, and he even bugged my friend's flat – and when I went out with another guy, my ex-husband deliberately damaged his beautiful car!"

The policeman's steely grey eyes studied her. "How long are you separated?"

"Six weeks."

He raised his eyebrows. "And you're already seeing someone else? You didn't waste much time, did you?"

His contemptuous look made it clear to Laura that he considered her a loose woman, who had no regard for her marriage vows, and who was clearly the villain here.

"I'm not dating anyone!" Laura said indignantly. "I just went out for dinner with a friend. And I won't be seeing him any more."

The policeman gave her a sarcastic look.

"I hope you're not condoning what my ex-husband did to me?" Laura said angrily.

"Don't put words in my mouth," the officer warned.

Laura tried to keep her face expressionless and concentrated on the wall behind him. Otherwise, she was in danger of climbing across the desk and throttling him. And that wouldn't help her case at all.

"So you think I should stay with a violent man?"

"See, there you go again!" the policeman said, grimacing. "That's not what I said at all. I just think that young people today don't give enough thought to their marriage vows."

Laura stood up. "I wasn't playing away! And I don't want to be with him any more! He's a violent thug and he's not my husband any longer –"

"The law says differently, Ms Thornton. You're still married to the guy. Now sit down, and let's talk about this sensibly."

Laura sat down again, aware that she was on the verge of losing her temper, and knowing that such behaviour wouldn't work in her favour. So she made a valiant effort to put a non-threatening and pleasant expression on her face.

The officer became more interested when she told him about the writing on Steve's car, and about the listening device that had been planted in her friend's living room. She even produced the device for the officer to see.

The officer nodded as he looked at it. "Okay, I'll look into your claims. But it would be impossible to prove that your ex-husband planted the bugging device – I could have it dusted for fingerprints, but I suspect you and your flatmate have already handled it?"

Laura looked embarrassed. "I'm afraid so. And we dropped it into water to stop it working."

The officer grimaced. "The perpetrator probably wore gloves

anyway. Nevertheless, we'll send an officer round to Mr Jones' apartment to speak to him."

Laura nodded, relieved. "Thank you, officer," she said gratefully. She was glad she hadn't walked out earlier, although she'd been strongly tempted to do so. Now she was actually hopeful that a visit from the law would quickly cool Jeff's ardour. But she was also aware that it could increase his volatility. She'd made a point of reading Kerry's book on psychopaths and stalkers, and it was clear that being thwarted by police could send some stalkers over the edge and increase the danger to the person being stalked. She just had to hope that Jeff would regard the police visit as a turning point, cut his losses and decide to leave her alone.

That night in Kerry's flat, Laura brought her friend up to date with what had happened at the police station.

"It didn't start off very well," she admitted. "The police officer wasn't very impressed by the fact that I'd started dating Steve so soon after walking out on Jeff. He made me feel as though I was prostituting myself!"

"Here, don't fret," said Kerry, bringing a wineglass for Laura to the kitchen table. "You were just unlucky to get a cop who wasn't very sympathetic. He probably has marriage problems of his own."

Laura smiled. "But things began to improve when I produced the listening device – it was as though he suddenly started believing me!"

"Does he think it's any help?"

Laura shook her head. "But he's going to send an officer round to talk to Jeff."

"That's great," Kerry said, opening a bottle of wine. "Hopefully, that should bring an end to Jeff's antics – if he has any sense, he'll calm down and realise that it's pointless to keep hassling you. And even if he tries anything else, it'll be easier to make the police listen next time."

Laura nodded. "I hope so – but my problem must seem very insignificant to the police, given the horrendous situations they have to deal with on a day-to-day basis."

Kerry looked at her tartly. "I'd consider a mental ex-husband to be rather serious! Anyway, I'm sure the police will give your situation

214

the attention it deserves." She grinned mischievously. "Why don't you ring Steve and see if he's notified the police, too? It might help to strengthen your case, if you ever have to go back to them."

Laura shook her head. "Definitely not!" she said vehemently. "Steve was more worried about his car than about me! Anyway, I wouldn't want him thinking that I was trying to get back with him, which I'm not. He can take a hike as far as I'm concerned."

Kerry gave a mock grimace. "Okay, I get the message," she said. "Of course that means I won't get to meet any of Steve's gorgeous friends . . ."

"Oops, sorry!" Laura replied, grinning back apologetically. "I guess we'll just have to find you someone else. How about another trip to the bar on Flower Street on Friday evening? There were lots of good-looking guys there the last time we went! Jeff can't possibly know where we're going now that we've removed the bugging device, and we can go the long way round, just to be sure we don't bump into him."

"I'm not going the long way round," Kerry said sourly. "I intend wearing my new heels and I'm not walking an extra block for anyone!"

Laura laughed. "Okay, okay. But if we see Jeff and we have to run –"

"We're not running from him, Laura – we have as much right to be in a public place as he has," Kerry said angrily. "So please stop thinking like a victim – to hell with him! He's the one who should feel bad, not you or me!"

Looking at the strain on Laura's face, Kerry proffered a suggestion.

"Maybe you should visit your doctor, and get something to help you sleep," she said. "I've heard you wandering around the flat in the early hours of the morning."

Laura grimaced guiltily. "Sorry. I hope I haven't disturbed you? But you're right – this business with Jeff is causing me a lot of stress. I'll make an appointment tomorrow."

Kerry nodded approvingly, pouring them each a glass of wine. Then, as they clinked glasses, Kerry proposed a toast.

"Here's to a Jeff-free life from now on!"

CHAPTER 50

The afternoon sunlight shone through the closed curtains, illuminating the slick of sweat that covered their naked bodies. Both of them were dozing, made sleepy by lovemaking. Suddenly, a sound interrupted their post-coital afterglow.

"What was that?" Ellie asked anxiously, sitting up and checking her watch. "It couldn't be Kerry – it's far too early for her to be back from tennis."

Alan smiled at her. "Stop worrying! It was nothing – probably just a twig cracking as some wild animal went by."

He listened, but heard nothing. Ellie lay down again, and he took her in his arms.

"I hate living like this," she whispered. "Always afraid of being discovered, afraid of every little sound."

He silenced her with a deep kiss. "It won't be forever, love – we'll find a way to be together soon. I promise."

For a while, they lay together in silence, each listening for any other unfamiliar sound. But all they could hear was the sound of each other's breathing.

Ellie was the first to break the silence. "I think she should be told the truth. Kerry deserves to know that you're her father."

"Not now, love – she's still too young. When we're finally a couple, and can be together all the time, we'll tell her."

"I wish I could have you with me all the time," Ellie said wistfully, pulling the bedclothes over her naked body.

"So do I," he whispered, kissing her nose playfully. "And you

will *have me, very soon. But we can't afford to rock any boats just yet."*

"*That doesn't stop me wishing,*" she replied, brushing a tear from her eye. "*I wish I'd been the one who met you first. Then we wouldn't have to go through this charade all the time.*"

"*Oh love, cheer up!*" he said, now kissing her tenderly, and cupping one of her bare breasts in his hands. "*Let's not spoil the little time we have together. I want it to be joyful – I want to show you how much I love you!*"

He stroked her tear-stained face and tenderly kissed her nose. "*Now, I'm going to make love to you again, and that will let you know just how much you mean to me!*"

Groaning, she surrendered to his tender ministrations. He knew exactly how to excite her. Every touch, every look, turned her on. And she knew it was the same for him – they just couldn't get enough of each other. It had been like that for years, yet they'd never grown tired of being together.

"*I love you!*" he whispered, as their bodies fused together and they climaxed simultaneously.

"*I love you too!*" she answered him.

But no sooner had he finished than he changed position again, pulling her on top of him and entering her once again. Exhilarated, she felt the width and length of him once more. They were insatiable when they were together.

Afterwards, they lay in silence, exhausted but still savouring their delight in each other.

Eventually, he looked at his watch. "*It's time for me to go, love,*" he whispered. "*Kerry will be home from tennis within the hour.*" Climbing out of bed reluctantly, he stretched as Ellie admired his athletic physique from the bed. Despite all the business dinners he had to attend, he never seemed to put on any weight.

Now it was time for the final part of their afternoon ritual. They always showered together, grooming each other's bodies lovingly in the heat of the summer afternoon. Then he'd be gone again, back to his other life, with Sylvia and the family who had a legal claim on him.

After a final kiss inside the front door, and having checked that the coast was clear, Alan stepped outside. As his eyes adjusted to the strong sunlight, he thought he saw a sudden movement over near the outhouse, but when he looked again, he could see nothing. It was probably just his overactive imagination – Ellie's fears were making him jittery, too. His visits to her were always fraught with the fear of being caught. He strode quickly to his car, which was parked behind the house, well hidden from the road. His skin was now freshly smelling of shower gel and aftershave. He checked his watch again. With luck, he'd be home in time to join the family for dinner.

CHAPTER 51

A week of relative peace ensued after Laura's visit to the police. There were no more phone calls from Jeff and she was feeling upbeat about starting a new life again. Although Kerry was insistent that she could stay as long as she liked at her apartment, Laura had taken a day off work to search for a new place to live. It wasn't fair to her friend to have to share such a small and cramped space indefinitely.

As she sauntered along the street, surveying estate agents' windows, Laura felt happy and confident about the future. She'd made a dreadful mistake by marrying Jeff, but hopefully that was all in the past now and, if he'd just leave her alone, she could get on with her life.

She'd also been to visit her doctor, and been given sedatives to help her sleep. She hadn't actually taken any yet, since she was keen not to become reliant on tablets. Anyway, the mere fact of having them in her possession seemed to have acted like some sort of placebo – she'd been sleeping like a baby ever since!

She was also toying with the idea of actually buying an apartment – although she'd inherited a huge amount of money after her parents and brother died, she'd never touched it because of the guilt she felt. Now she was beginning to see the sense of owning her own place. It would make her feel secure and beholden to no one. But it was a big decision, and she was scared of tying up so much money in a property she might later realise wasn't suitable for her needs.

She was also greatly relieved that she'd never told Jeff about the money – and she'd Kerry to thank for that. Although Jeff didn't seem to have any financial worries, he did like to spend. So he might have been very happy to access her money, or he might now be pursuing her in the divorce courts for a substantial share of it.

In one of the estate agent's offices, Laura explained her indecision about buying to Avril, the young woman who'd elected to answer her queries.

"Well, we have a luxury apartment at the corner of Green Street – it's available for rent, but the owner is intending to put it on the market next year. If you rented it and decided you'd like to buy it, you'd be in pole position to make an offer when the owner puts it on sale."

"That sounds interesting," Laura said enthusiastically. "I like the Green Street area – when can I see it?"

"I can take you there now, if you like. It's got a concierge and dual aspect, so I think you'll really like it."

"Dual aspect?"

Avril laughed. "Sorry, estate agents' jargon. It means that it's got windows on two sides, so there's lots of light."

"And it's got a concierge too?"

Avril nodded. "Yes, there's someone on duty twenty-four hours. It's another security feature that many people like, especially single women."

Laura was pleased. It sounded perfect for her, especially in her present situation with a mad ex tailing her. She also liked the idea of being able to live somewhere before having to make any decision about buying it.

The two women walked the short distance to Green Street, Avril tottering along on six-inch heels, and on the way she pointed out several other rental properties that the agency had on its books. "If this one doesn't suit, there are plenty of others we can show you," she told Laura.

In the Green Street building, the uniformed concierge on duty greeted them, introducing himself as Jim to Laura and the agent, punching in the code for the lift and pointing out the emergency staircase.

The second-floor apartment in Green Street was bright and airy, and had extremely high ceilings, which Laura instantly loved. She was captivated by the sense of space they engendered, and even though it was only a two-bedroom unit, it had a wide hall, a large living space and two very large bedrooms.

She was also intrigued by the unusual layout – entry to the apartment was directly onto a mezzanine floor, where the entrance hall, kitchen and living areas were over the large bedrooms, luxury bathroom and built-in storage units downstairs. Access to the bedrooms below was via a beautiful staircase.

"What an unusual layout – I'll bet the architects have won prizes for this design!" Laura said, gazing around in awe.

Avril nodded. "This building was a major restoration project some years ago. The whole interior was gutted and redesigned. It's quite spectacular, isn't it?"

The rent was also high, and there was a hefty annual service charge, but Laura felt that the extra facilities were well worth it.

"I love it," she said happily, "But is it okay for my friend to see it before I decide?"

"Of course." Avril smiled. "But I get the feeling you've already made up your mind?"

Laura nodded. "I'm positive Kerry will love it too. It's just that I'd feel better having a second opinion – I've a tendency into rush things, and it's already landed me in lots of hot water!"

Kerry was just as impressed by the apartment as Laura was. "Wow!" was her immediate reaction as she stared up at the high ceilings and the large living room flooded with light.

"This is amazing!" Kerry whispered. "It's fantastic!"

Laura grinned. "I just needed your opinion first."

Kerry gave a mock gasp. "Have you had a personality transplant? Where's the impetuous woman I used to know so well?"

Laura grinned. "I guess Jeff taught me a few valuable lessons."

"Well, he's gone now and it's the start of a whole new life for you, love – congratulations! Let's go out tonight and paint the town red!"

CHAPTER 52

Alan was furious. He'd had to ask his father-in-law to bail out the factory for a third time, but the old man was refusing, claiming to be worried about tying up his capital in such a precarious business venture, and having to wait too long for a return on his investment.

"But Dick, how can you call it precarious?" Alan had bellowed. "This is one of the most viable businesses in the area, providing massive employment and giving a more than reasonable annual return. We just need to update some of the machinery – otherwise, we'll go under!"

But his father-in-law had countered with queries as to why obsolescence hadn't been written into the original business plan? And why should he bail out a business that should have been putting aside money over the years to deal with this very situation?

They'd parried back and forth all day, and finally Alan had seen red and stormed out of the meeting. Now he'd have to approach the bank for a loan instead, and even if they agreed, their conditions would be a lot more stringent. To hell with Dick Morgan!

The only advantage was that by now, most of the previous loan had been repaid. The man had been rewarded handsomely for his earlier investment – in fact, if he hadn't demanded such a high rate of return, the factory mightn't now need to ask for another loan! Alan was livid. The only benefit – if you could call it that – was that it was now the ideal time to ask Sylvia for a divorce. In a way, asking her now would be a way of punishing her father for his refusal to reinvest.

All day at work, Alan preoccupied himself with planning how to bring up the subject of divorce with his wife. His stomach was churning and he was developing a stress headache. At lunchtime, instead of visiting Ellie, he went out for a walk, hoping that the fresh air might clear his head, but he returned to the office feeling just as stressed. Every ten minutes he looked at his watch, wanting the workday to be over, yet perversely dreading it.

As he sat daydreaming, there was a knock on his door.

"Mr Alan, production's stopped on Number Three conveyor belt." Tony Coleman, the factory manager, stepped into his office. "We've already sent for Maintenance, but that order for Superbuys is going to be delayed by an hour or more . . ."

Alan sighed. Sometimes he was sick of his responsibilities. Everyone seemed to want a piece of him. Sylvia wanted him, Ellie wanted him, and he was charged with the responsibility of keeping hundreds of workers in their jobs. Sometimes, he just wanted to run away, perhaps to a desert island where no one could find him.

Alan got to his feet. "Okay, Tony – I'll be with you shortly."

He'd have to ask the workers to stay late, since Superbuys was an exacting client, and likely to impose a penalty for late deliveries.

As he left his office and headed downstairs to the factory floor, he wondered how it would feel when he was going home to Ellie after a day's work. They wouldn't be able to have quite as much sex, since Kerry would be there in the evenings. Would his life with Ellie become as boring and predictable as it currently was with Sylvia?

It would feel odd living with his eldest daughter. He'd grown very fond of her, although he didn't see her as often as he'd like, since of necessity his visits to her mother always took place when she wasn't around.

He was also considering, for the first time, the effect his divorce would have on his two children with Sylvia. How would Pete and Laura feel about seeing him living with their friend's mother? Would they still call to play? Would his relationship with Ellie drive a wedge between him and his other two children?

Alan's stomach was still churning, because he knew that as soon as he and Ellie went public on their relationship, she'd insist on letting everyone know that Kerry was his child, and that would have a devastating effect on poor Sylvia. Divorcing her was bad enough, but having her know that his affair had produced another child just before she'd given birth to their own daughter – well, that would be the ultimate humiliation. How could he do that to Sylvia? She loved him, and she'd never done him any harm, so how could he destroy her in this way?

Then he thought of his father-in-law, and his blood ran cold. This would be no amicable split – even though Sylvia would undoubtedly behave with dignity, Dick would rise to his daughter's defence and might punish him by demanding the balance of the money he'd ploughed into the factory earlier. Even though there wasn't a huge amount still owing, it was enough to tip the balance precariously, possibly leading to closure of the factory, with the loss of hundreds of jobs. Of course, that would affect Sylvia too, but people often behaved irrationally when in the throes of strong emotions. He simply couldn't do it – the price was too high for everyone concerned.

By the end of the day, Alan was physically and mentally exhausted. He'd had to beg his workers to keep the production line running until the order was finished, and promise them double time for doing so. Delays in production were becoming all too regular lately, and they wouldn't be happening if he could replace their outdated conveyor-belt system with some state-of-the-art equipment. His headache was pounding and his skull felt as though it was about to split open. One minute, he was filled with anger, and unwilling to let Dick – and by extension, his daughter Sylvia – hold him and the factory to ransom. The next minute, he was filled with remorse at the thought of altering so many people's lives for his own benefit. In truth, he was beginning to wonder if a divorce would indeed benefit him personally. If it did, it would be at the expense of so many other people's happiness and livelihoods, and that would ultimately ruin his own peace of mind. He wouldn't be able to live with himself if he hurt so many people.

By the time he got home, he still hadn't made up his mind about what he was going to do. He was relieved to discover that no one was in the kitchen or the living room – no doubt the kids were out playing somewhere, and Sylvia was probably at the golf club. He decided to go upstairs to his bedroom en suite and have a shower that would hopefully relax his aching muscles and soothe his thumping head.

When he entered the bedroom, he was surprised to see Sylvia sitting at her dressing table, since he hadn't noticed her car in the driveway. She was just putting down the phone extension, and she looked up happily when he entered the room. He felt a rush of remorse. How could he bring such devastation to this genuinely lovely woman? He cared for her very much, and if he hadn't met Ellie, with her sparkling eyes, luscious lips and voluptuous, accommodating body, he'd have been content to spend the rest of his life with her. Sylvia didn't deserve what he was contemplating.

His wife's eyes were twinkling, and he was momentarily worried. Had he forgotten some event they were going to that evening? Was it their anniversary? That would be ironic.

Conspiratorially, she turned to face him. "I'm not supposed to tell you, darling, but Daddy's just been on the phone, and he's had second thoughts about investing in the factory." She looked at him shyly. "You know, he privately thinks you're a wonderful businessman. He says you have a natural flair for business, and he doesn't want to see that flair limited by lack of capital. He told me confidentially that he's reconsidered his earlier decision, and has decided to be your backer for as long as you need him. Isn't that great, darling?"

Alan nodded, feeling the pressure removed for the factory's future, but knowing that now he couldn't possibly ask his wife for a divorce. In a way, he was relieved, since he genuinely cared about Sylvia. She was the mother of two of his children, and he didn't want to hurt her. He smiled bitterly to himself. If only it was acceptable for a man to have two wives! Maybe he should consider moving to Utah and becoming a Mormon . . .

"You'll pretend you don't know, won't you, darling?" Sylvia asked anxiously. "You know how Daddy loves to play his little power games. Let him have his fun first, then look surprised and grateful when he tells you."

Surprising even himself, Alan suddenly leaned forward and placed a kiss on the top of his wife's head. She, too, looked surprised at this spontaneous gesture of affection, and he could see that her cheeks had blushed crimson. She looked so pleased that he felt guilty at ever having considered hurting her so badly. She'd done absolutely nothing wrong – he was the one who was guilty of cruelly deceiving her. And his two children with Sylvia – how on earth would he have been able to tell them he was leaving?

As he stared at his reflection in the mirror, Alan saw a stranger looking back. What had he been thinking of? How could he – as managing director and someone regarded as a pillar of the local community – leave his wife and children? And if he'd gone to live with Ellie and his secret child, his wife and children would be humiliated daily as they drove or walked past his new home at Treetops. And how could he manage to see his and Sylvia's children regularly, without involving both families in stress and trauma?

He sighed. Ellie would just have to accept that there could be no marriage – now or ever. But he'd ensure that she and their daughter wanted for nothing.

Alan stood in Ellie's kitchen. But he didn't dare initiate any sexual contact, as he usually did on arrival.

"I can't leave now, love – I'm sorry, it's out of the question. I need her father's investment in the factory – but I love you, too. Can you please accept the situation as it is, since I'd rather die than lose you?"

Ellie bit her lip. She wasn't going to give in easily. For years, he'd dangled the carrot of marriage in front of her, although she'd known in her heart for a long time now that it was never going to happen. Since she'd already been married, the institution itself wasn't all that important to her. Of course, she'd have liked the public adulation of being Alan's wife, and of attending important functions with him, especially the factory Christmas party. She'd have enjoyed watching all the employees' faces when she walked in on his arm!

But she also knew that marriages were often simply tribal alliances, designed to keep dynasties and businesses together. And marriage to Alan might create far more problems than any joy it would bring. Alan wouldn't be the successful businessman without his father-in-law's money, and his father-in-law wouldn't invest unless Sylvia was happy. And without the factory, Alan couldn't financially support Ellie and Kerry. So they were all trapped in a spiral of need. A penniless husband would be no picnic, and slowly but surely she and Alan would gradually annihilate each other. So she was willing to sacrifice the legal niceties in order to keep Alan's love, since that was all she'd really ever wanted. But she'd extract her pound of flesh before giving in.

"Well then, you must promise me that Kerry will continue at her present school, and go on to university, or whatever college she chooses. I want her to have the same opportunities as your other two children."

"Of course, love – that goes without saying," Alan said eagerly, relieved that Ellie was accepting the situation so easily. "She's my child too, and you know how much I care about her welfare."

Ellie nodded, looking down at her diamond and gold ring. She did know how much Alan cared. Ironically, he'd become the father Kerry had never had. He'd taught her to ride a bike, and made a point of including her in his family's events whenever he could. They'd both had to accept that the two girls had become firm friends, but they'd managed to structure their own lives to accommodate it. In fact, it was astonishing and wonderful that they'd managed to maintain their secret lives together for all these years, without ever hurting anyone else.

Instinctively, Ellie rushed into Alan's arms. "I love you," she whispered, reaching up to kiss him.

Gratefully, Alan kissed her back. "We'll grow old together," he promised. "I know the situation isn't ideal, but we'll make it work for us. I'll never stop loving you, and I'll still be making love to you even when we're in our eighties."

"Will you be able?" Ellie asked tartly, grinning at him.

Alan grinned back. "As long as you still want me, I think I'll manage."

CHAPTER 53

Kerry awoke from her dream, her forehead clammy. At first she felt disoriented, then she looked at her watch. It was just before midnight. The streetlights outside provided backlighting for the trees as they blew in the wind, throwing bizarre shadows onto the glass. They seemed to be performing a macabre dance to some demonic rhythm that nature had imposed.

She suddenly realised that a phone was ringing somewhere in the distance. It had to be her phone, since Laura had gone to a movie with her colleague Maria, and was staying overnight at the other woman's house.

Leaping out of bed, Kerry hurried into the kitchen, feeling a chill of apprehension running down her spine. A late-night caller was never the bearer of good news.

"H-hello?"

There was no reply, although Kerry knew there was someone on the other end of the line. Breaking her own rule never to respond, she shouted angrily at the caller.

"Whoever you are, go to hell!"

Then she banged the phone down on the table. She was furious at being woken up just after she'd managed to drift off to sleep. If she hadn't known about the pervert lurking outside Sea Diagnostics, she might have been worried about this latest call, viewing it as part of some frightening scenario orchestrated by Jeff or his drug-dealer colleague. But thankfully, Norma had been able to put things into perspective for her. She now accepted that the call was probably just some random drunk calling a wrong number.

Since finding out about the local pervert, Kerry had seen him again several times, but now she didn't let it bother her. She was also relieved she hadn't told Laura about him. Laura would have made an even bigger deal of it – perhaps even impulsively challenging Jeff – and that would have proved hugely embarrassing. Kerry certainly didn't want to give Jeff the satisfaction of knowing he had the power to terrify her. And letting him know about an imaginary stalker might give him ideas! Yet again she'd proved the value of keeping her own counsel.

Deciding to make herself a cup of tea, Kerry turned on the kettle. She was wide-awake now, and unlikely to get back to sleep any time soon. If she couldn't drop off quickly, she might even help herself to one of the sedatives Laura had been prescribed but never used. There was an important meeting at Sea Diagnostics in the morning and she needed to be alert. Damn the caller, whoever he or she was.

Although she was now no longer frightened, these random incidents had nevertheless brought back long-forgotten memories from her childhood. She'd never told anyone about the man who used to hide in the shadows of the Treetops driveway and watch her as she played. Since she'd always prided herself on her no-nonsense attitude – even as a child – she'd refused to let it bother her, believing that by telling anyone she'd be making herself into a victim. There was also the distinct likelihood that her mother would restrict her freedom and insist she play indoors instead.

She'd never been able to see the man clearly, since he'd always stayed hidden among the trees. But she got a perverse thrill from knowing that he was there, and from knowing that he didn't realise she knew. At times, she convinced herself that this man in the shadows was her long-lost father. She became adept at weaving stories in which this father of hers had a starring role. Sometimes, he'd just returned from overseas, or from bravely fighting in some war or other, and he was unable to resist seeing how his daughter was getting on. But since he seemed unable to visit her openly, she eventually changed her story to one in which he'd been in prison –

wrongly convicted, of course – and that her mother had banished him forever from their lives. Desperate for a father of her own, Kerry had relished that particular story, and for a while she'd even unfairly resented her mother for keeping this noble man at bay.

In later years, she'd concluded that the man had probably been a paedophile and she could have been in extreme danger, and she was grateful that she'd heeded her mother's warnings not to talk to strangers. Now she understood what danger she could have been in.

Sighing, she rinsed her cup and headed back to bed. It was time to forget about perverts and silent phone calls. Sea Diagnostics was about to tender for yet another big project, and it needed her full attention the following morning. Within minutes of climbing into bed, Kerry was fast asleep again.

CHAPTER 54

"Syl – are you ready?"

"Coming, darling – I'm just putting on my earrings – I'm wearing those lovely diamond ones you bought me years ago, remember?"

Alan gave her a vague smile when she reached the bottom of the stairs, and it was clear from his expression that he didn't remember the gift, and she could have had Brussels sprouts dangling from her ears for all he'd notice.

All the same, she'd gone to considerable effort to look good. She was wearing a tight-fitting dark-green sheath dress that was expensive and well cut; and as an exponent of the theory that less was always more, she was wearing just earrings and her watch to set it off.

They were on their way to a prestigious business awards luncheon, and Alan had already been tipped off that he'd be receiving an award himself. He looks so handsome, Sylvia thought. I'm a lucky woman, even if our relationship has become a little tarnished over the years.

She'd sensed a change in Alan around the time her father invested heavily in the new machinery for the factory. Perhaps it was simply because her husband's money worries had been eased – he'd been preoccupied for months before the modernisation became possible. All she knew was that her husband had suddenly become more affectionate, and she'd also wondered if it could be because his affair had ended, and he'd finally realised the value of what he had at home. If so, she was very relieved, and glad she hadn't unburdened herself to any of her so-called friends, or challenged her husband about it.

She was still mortified by her moment of weakness all those years ago, when she'd blurted out her fears about Alan's infidelity to Ellie Beckworth. No wonder the woman had kept her distance ever since – she must have been deeply embarrassed at being drawn into the lives of her former boss and his wife! Nevertheless, Ellie's words of advice had proved invaluable, and clearly she hadn't betrayed her trust either. Sylvia had been terrified that Alan might get wind of her confession, and he'd be very angry at having his relationship with his wife discussed with a former employee.

It was ironic how, years later, their two daughters had become close friends, and Sylvia wished their friendship could have mirrored that of their mothers.

Sylvia had hoped that as their daughters' friendship grew, it might somehow bring herself and Ellie together more. But apart from an occasional foray into the village for provisions, Ellie didn't seem to go out much. Years ago, Sylvia had seen her in Tony Coleman's company one evening, but other than that, the woman seemed to be a veritable recluse.

Over the years, she'd made a special effort to show Alan how much she loved him, to look nice and be enthusiastic in bed. But the passion of their early years had never been rekindled. Clearly, the passing of time dulled such feelings – perhaps it happened in all marriages and long-term relationships.

"Do you think this tie is okay?"

Sylvia dusted a fleck of fluff from his shoulder. "It's perfect with your charcoal suit – you look very handsome, darling."

"Thanks. The taxi should be here shortly. Are the kids okay?"

Sylvia smiled to herself. How typical of a man to ask such a question about two minutes before leaving the house! "Yes, Alan, the baby-sitter's with them in the games room." She grimaced. "Of course, Pete is objecting to having a baby-sitter at all – he thinks he's too grown up to need supervising!"

Alan nodded. "Well, I can see his point of view – he's thirteen now, and Laura's almost eleven." He grinned at his wife. "Where on earth have the years gone? They seem to be flying by!"

"Well, I'm glad that at last your business acumen is being recognised," Sylvia told him, patting his arm as they headed out to the taxi. "You've kept that factory going, and kept hundreds in employment, against all the odds."

"Well, your father's been a big help – an essential help," he replied. "I wouldn't be getting this award if he'd pulled the plug on us."

"Daddy thinks a lot of you," Sylvia added. "He's always appreciated what a great businessman you are."

As Alan conversed with the taxi driver, Sylvia sat back and contemplated their situation. It amused and saddened her to think that she was the only one in the relationship who realised that anything had ever been wrong. Alan was probably still living under the illusion that she'd never suspected anything about his affair. At times like today, when they were operating well together as a successful couple, she liked to think that the affair had never happened. Since she'd never given voice to her feelings, it was easier now to put it all behind her. But she still wondered about the gold and diamond ring that Alan had bought all those years ago – her fortieth birthday had come and gone without any sign of the ring. Nor had Aunt Maud been given it for her seventieth birthday.

Sylvia sighed. Anyway, it was merely a bauble – albeit a very expensive bauble – and there was little point in getting worked up over it now. But she still occasionally wondered if it was the same ring that Janette claimed to have put on her gold card. Sylvia still felt a little jolt of anger every time she saw Janette wearing it.

Since she could hardly ask to see Janette's credit-card statements, she'd once tried to engage Matthew in a roundabout conversation about Janette's taste in jewellery. She'd commented on Janette's magnificent ring, but Matthew, who lived his life in a fug of alcohol, hadn't risen to the bait. "Janette does what Janette wants," he'd slurred. "And do you know what, Sylvia? I couldn't give a fuck. She leaves me alone, and that's all that matters to me."

"We're here, Syl – you okay?"

"Yes, of course," Sylvia said, stepping out of the taxi. "Silly me, I was just daydreaming. Here, let me straighten your tie – we can't have you looking anything less than perfect today, can we?"

As she reached up, Alan suddenly hugged her. "Thanks, Syl – for everything," he said softly.

Sylvia blushed, embarrassed and pleased all at once. Was it a hug that silently begged her forgiveness? Or a hug that simply meant he cared? Whatever it meant, Sylvia was not going to query it. Not today, of all days. This was a good day, and she intended making the most of it.

"Come on, let's get the Businessman of the Year inside," she said, taking his hand.

"I think you might be jumping the gun," Alan said frowning. "They haven't told me what particular award I'm getting."

Sylvia looked at him archly. "They wouldn't dare give you anything less, would they? Anyway, even if they don't appreciate you, you'll always be my hero."

CHAPTER 55

A week later, Laura decided it was time to return to the local police station. She was actually looking forward to her visit this time, since she was hoping they might have some news about their visit to Jeff. Hopefully, her ex-husband would leave her alone now that the police had been in contact with him.

In the police station, Laura waited eagerly as the duty officer on the front desk searched for the report, and then having found it hurried off with it to confer with a colleague.

Shortly afterwards, Laura was ushered into the office of a different police officer from the one she encountered on her previous visit. This one was a detective sergeant, and he acknowledged her presence with a nod, thumbing through the stack of papers in front of him, extracting several sheets of paper. "Hmm, yes, it says here that one of our officers went round to Mr Jones' apartment last week."

The DS looked up. "But according to this report, your ex-husband says you're making it all up." He looked down again at the wording in the report and read it aloud to her. "He says you're a vindictive woman who's determined to wreck his life. According to him, you're out for revenge because he kept some of your wedding presents."

While Laura sat open-mouthed, the police officer read from the papers again. "It says here that he offered them back to you, but you wouldn't accept them. He maintains that you refused to take them because you wanted to be able to keep hassling him."

Laura was aghast. "But that's exactly what he's doing to me! Can't you see that he's hijacking my story and using it against me!"

The detective sergeant looked at her cynically. "So you're telling me a story, are you? A story is usually a bit different from the truth –"

"What?" Laura screeched. "Are you saying that I'm lying?"

"Calm down, Ms Thornton – you're becoming hysterical. In fact, you seem to be proving the man's point – he said you've even been screaming down the phone at him."

"That's untrue – he's been the one hassling me!"

The DS looked at her cynically. "Well, he's got a sound alibi for the time you claim he damaged your friend's car, and he's given us a recording of you on the phone to him, and I have to say, it did sound as though you were the one hassling him."

Laura was speechless. Jeff had obviously recorded their last conversation, and then selected an example that would show her in as unfavourable a light as possible.

"So you obviously didn't hear the bits where I begged him to leave me alone," Laura said sarcastically.

"No need to get stroppy – I'm only doing my job."

The DS stood up, left the room briefly and returned with a small tape recorder. As he pressed the button, Laura could hear her own strident voice.

"You bastard, Jeff! I am sick to death of you – don't make me do something I'll regret! You're nothing but a pathetic loser!"

"I presume that's your voice?"

"Yes, but –"

"So you get my drift?"

"But it's been taken completely out of context! That was when I rang him back after he –"

"You were angry. I can hear that, ma'am. But it takes two to tango. Now, I suggest you calm down and look at the situation rationally. Your husband has a point, doesn't he?"

Before Laura could answer, the DS spoke again. "Your ex-husband has also filed a complaint against you – on the grounds that you're the one who's making his life a misery, that he's moved on but you just won't let him be!"

Laura exploded. "My ex-husband is from a violent, dysfunctional family – his father killed his mother, then hanged himself – yet Jeff saw fit to model our marriage on theirs! He's told me he works for MI5, but I've no way of knowing if that's true or not. I'm also fairly sure he's killed someone!"

The DS's eyes narrowed, and he made a quick note on the report. "Things tend to get nasty when couples break up," he said noncommittally. "And people have been known to make false accusations against each other."

"I'm not making this up –"

He rose from the table. "Ma'am, I don't think there's much more I can do to help you. If you don't want to see your ex, then surely you can just stay away from him?"

"That's what I'm trying to do – but he keeps turning up everywhere I go!"

"Well, haven't you left the marital home, and moved on? I'm sure things will settle down gradually."

"But how do I get him to leave me alone?" Laura shrieked, then took a deep breath, suddenly aware that she'd been shouting.

The DS looked exasperated. "Ms Thornton, I can see you're very worked up about the situation. And maybe you're reading more into it than it warrants? But by all means, call us if there are any further incidents –"

"Are you going to wait until he kills me before you do anything?" Laura screamed.

In tears of frustration, she stomped out of the police station. Yet again, Jeff had foiled her attempts to get help by pre-empting her claims. He was even more devious than she'd thought.

CHAPTER 56

The following week, Laura got the keys to her new apartment. She didn't have many possessions other than her clothing and the precious photographs of her parents and brother. When she left the apartment she'd shared with Jeff, she'd taken only the minimum of items with her, since her prime concern had been to get away to safety.

The new apartment came complete with beds, lavish kitchen appliances and two beige sofas in the large living room, but everything else Laura would need to supply herself. On the day she was moving in, she and Kerry spent several enjoyable hours traipsing around hardware stores trying to find basic items like cutlery and crockery, pots and pans. Armed with an assortment of purchases, and some staple foodstuffs, they entered the new flat.

"Will I stay with you for your first night?" Kerry asked as she filled the kitchen cupboard with bread, salt, tea and coffee. "I mean, it's bound to be a bit lonely until you get settled in. We could get a take-away . . ."

"Thanks, but there's absolutely no need," Laura replied cheerfully. "You must be sick and tired of me by now, and I'm sure you're dying to have your own bathroom to yourself again!"

"Well, if you're sure –"

"Of course. I'm quite looking forward to being here on my own. Not that I'm not grateful for all your help, and for putting up with me for so long –"

Kerry dismissed her thanks with a wave of her hand. "All for one, and one for all – isn't that our motto? You'd do the same for me."

Laura nodded. "But you'd never be so stupid as to get involved with someone like Jeff."

Kerry patted her arm. "What's done is done – you're starting a new life now, so forget about him. Anyway, I'm much too cautious to rush into anything – maybe that's a fault rather than a virtue. At least you followed your heart."

As Laura stood alone in her new apartment, she felt a surge of joy. The apartment was hers and she loved it! Right this minute, she wanted to buy it, lock stock and barrel! So it was probably just as well that she'd have to wait until next year, because she was being her usual impetuous self again. Living there would enable her to find out if the apartment truly suited her. But in her heart she knew it would.

A sudden wave of sadness swept over her. She'd never expected to be buying a home on her own. She and Jeff had planned on eventually buying a big home in the country, and she'd always imagined it would look similar to the house where she'd once lived with her parents and brother. There would be trees for their children to climb, and acres of garden where they'd learn about nature and have lots of space to let their imaginations run riot, just as she, Pete and Kerry had done all those years ago.

Sighing, she shook her head, as though to dislodge the memories of her past. She hoped she hadn't seemed too eager to get rid of Kerry. She owed her friend a huge debt of gratitude, and she wouldn't want to hurt her feelings. But she was really excited at being alone in her new home. She found herself repeatedly walking in and out of the different rooms, touching the walls and familiarising herself with each and every detail, and planning what would go where. She'd have to get a television. And some potted plants. And a few lamps to help create a cosy atmosphere.

As she walked from room to room, Laura made a list of all the things she'd need. Since she was already planning to stay in the apartment long term, she intended making it look exactly the way she wanted it. The existing lease didn't allow her to change the colour of the walls – which were all currently white – but she'd add warmth by using brightly coloured throws and bed linen. Next year, when she'd bought the apartment, she'd paint the walls varying warm shades of pink and orange. Only a few days earlier, in a city-centre store, she'd seen a beautiful rug patterned with pink and orange swirls and it would make the perfect focal point for the living room, and draw together the colour scheme she was planning for the future. Although it was terribly expensive, she could easily afford it.

Looking around the apartment, Laura made a vow to start spending some of the money she had stashed away in banks and investments. Rationally, she knew that the guilt she felt over her family's deaths was pointless, and whether she spent the money or not, nothing was ever going to bring her family back.

She could also assuage her guilt by giving some of the money to Kerry. Laura was aware that, divorced or not, her ex-husband was unlikely to be able to claim any of her money. But somehow, the legal ending of her marriage seemed like the right time to reward Kerry's loyalty and support over the years.

Checking her watch, Laura was astonished to discover that it was already quite late – how time flies, she thought, when you're enjoying yourself! Drinking a cuppa before heading downstairs to bed, she settled back into the comfort of one of the large cosy couches, and contemplated her future in the apartment. Since she'd arrived, she'd been walking around smiling to herself. Maybe, when she'd fully settled in and bought the items that would enable her to put her own stamp on it, she'd think about having a small party. Just for her work colleagues from the Sociology Department and, of course, Kerry and her colleagues from Sea Diagnostics. And she'd invite Avril from the estate agent's office as well.

She felt a brief pang of sadness at not being able to invite Steve to see the apartment. But he'd chosen his car's well-being over her safety, so she had no room in her life for anyone like that. Besides, there were lots more fish in the sea – if she ever again decided to get involved with another man, that is.

Climbing into bed, Laura was still smiling. She felt that at last she was entering a new and exciting phase of her life. No sooner had her head hit the pillow than she was fast asleep.

Laura awoke suddenly. Her sleepy and befuddled brain had registered an unusual sound somewhere in the apartment. She reached for her watch, and its luminous dial told her it was just after 3 a.m. In the dark of the room, she was unable to see anything, and realised how urgently she needed bedside lamps. Listening carefully, she heard nothing, so she assumed it had just been her imagination going into overdrive. It was probably just one of those creaky sounds that buildings made – she wasn't yet familiar with the Green Street building's quirks. Possibly it was the cistern? All the same, she now wished that she'd accepted Kerry's invitation to stay the first night with her. Her heart was thumping and her mouth was dry. She'd locked the front door, hadn't she? Stop it, she told herself crossly. You're behaving like an idiot. Anyway, there's a concierge on duty downstairs, so nothing bad can happen. That's why you took this apartment – so that you'd feel safe.

She was just about to go to sleep when she heard it again. It was a faint scraping sound that she couldn't identify, and it was definitely coming from somewhere upstairs. Someone was in her apartment! Terrified, she glanced around the dark downstairs bedroom. But there was nowhere for her to hide. There was no key in the door, so she couldn't lock herself in – had the estate agent forgotten to leave it? There was no space underneath the bed base either, and no other furniture in the room as yet. What was she going to do? Did she wait in the bed for whatever was going to happen, or did she try to escape?

Leaping out of bed, she dived behind the bedroom door and crouched down, listening all the while for sounds of anyone coming down the stairs. If only she had some kind of weapon! Her heart was beating so loudly in her chest that she felt sure that whoever was in the flat must hear it. She felt as impotent as a small child, and she remembered all the times she'd been terrified of the

241

monsters beneath her bed, whose tentacles might reach out and grab her leg if she tried to climb out. And she remembered how her father would get down on his hands and knees and confirm with a shake of his head that there were definitely no monsters lurking there.

Laura felt the tears filling her eyes as she remembered the father she'd loved so much. How she wished he was here now, to protect her! Angrily she brushed aside her tears – this was no time for self-indulgence and maudlin thoughts. She needed her wits about her if she was to deal with the present situation.

As the minutes ticked by with no further sound, Laura began to relax a little. Maybe she'd just imagined it? But she was still too terrified to leave the bedroom and investigate. By now she had cramps in her legs and one arm was numb from hanging tightly onto the doorknob for support. If only Kerry had stayed over!

Eventually the cramp proved too much to bear any longer, so Laura stood up as quietly as she could. Straining to hear, she waited anxiously, but heard no further sound. She could hear the noise of occasional traffic outside, and it lent an air of normality to things. Had she simply imagined the scraping sound? After all, the concierge down in the foyer wasn't going to allow anyone up to her apartment without good reason, and certainly not in the middle of the night. She was just being silly once again.

All the same, she was still too scared to check any of the other rooms. Sitting down on the bed, her head now resting wearily against the headboard, Laura stifled a yawn as she pulled the duvet around her. A wave of lethargy swept over her. She'd need to let each of the three concierges know about Jeff, and ensure that he was never allowed anywhere near her apartment. She'd do that in the morning. Right now she was feeling unbelievably tired – all the drama of the last half-hour had proved exhausting. Her eyelids began to flicker, and she was having difficulty keeping them open. Gradually her grip on the duvet relaxed, her eyelids gave up the fight to stay open and she fell into a deep sleep.

CHAPTER 57

Laura awoke to find the sun streaming in through her bedroom window, and for a moment, she forgot about her late-night intruder. She'd fallen asleep with her head still resting against the headboard, and her muscles now felt stiff and sore from lying in such a cramped position. Then she remembered the terror she'd felt the night before, but in the daylight things didn't seem quite so frightening. No one had murdered her during the night either. Jumping out of bed, she left the bedroom and tiptoed up the staircase onto the mezzanine floor, finding a bundle of keys for the various rooms resting on the console table in the hall. She also discovered what had been making the scraping sound the night before.

Lying on the floor just inside the front door was a large envelope. Clearly it had been stuffed through her letterbox with difficulty, and had been bent in the middle in order to get it through. Laura instantly felt rather foolish. But who would be delivering a letter at around 3 a.m.?

Tearing at the top of the envelope, Laura drew out a large *Good Luck in Your New Home* card. But when she opened it, her heart sank. It was signed: '*Jeff*'. Then her annoyance turned to anger. Jeff had cost her another night's sleep! And how on earth had the card reached her apartment? There was no stamp on it, so clearly it had been hand-delivered. Surely Jeff didn't have access to the apartment complex?

Dressing quickly, Laura left her apartment clutching the card and its envelope, and headed downstairs. She needed to catch the night-duty concierge before he finished his shift.

In the hall, the elderly concierge greeted Laura warmly, but she was in no mood for pleasantries. Quickly she told him her name and apartment number and showed him the card.

"Oh yes," said the concierge, beaming. "A very nice tall blond man called here last night. He begged me to let him deliver the card to your apartment, but naturally I couldn't allow him to do that. So he asked me if *I'd* deliver it." The concierge smiled at her. "When things were slack, around three o'clock, I managed to go up and put it through your letterbox. As you know, it was a bit on the large size, so I had to bend it a bit to squeeze it through – I hope the noise didn't wake you? But the guy was adamant that he wanted you to get it first thing this morning."

The concierge looked pleased with himself, thinking he'd done her a favour, and clearly expecting her to be grateful. But the smile was quickly wiped from his face when Laura explained the situation.

"Please – don't ever let him near my apartment," she begged him, "no matter what he says – believe me, I don't want my ex-husband within a million miles of me. And I'd be grateful if you could tell the other concierges – or do you want me to have a word with them?"

"No, it's okay – I'll let them know," the elderly man told her, looking concerned. "I'm sorry about the card, but please don't worry any further – we'll make sure you're safe here – that's our job."

Bleary-eyed, Laura returned to her apartment. She'd no doubt that Jeff had deliberately chosen to have the card delivered during the night, and he'd selected a large card so that the noise of it being stuffed through the letterbox was bound to frighten her. But more worrying was the fact that he'd discovered where she was living. Was she ever going to be rid of him?

Laura phoned the estate agent's office.

"Avril, it's Laura Thornton – I've rented the Green Street apartment?"

"Oh, hello, Laura – have you settled in okay?"

244

"Well, yes, but – did you let anyone know that I'd moved into the Green Street apartment?"

The woman thought for a moment. "Oh yes, now that I think of it – a man phoned yesterday, looking to rent an apartment in the same block, and I explained that we'd just let one there. He asked if it had been let to a Laura Thornton, and I said yes. I assumed he was a friend of yours? I told him I'd let him know if another apartment becomes available . . ."

"Do you remember his name?"

"Let me check for you –"

Laura heard what sounded like a desk drawer opening and the rustling of paper, then Avril was back on the line.

"Jeff Jones was his name –"

Inwardly, Laura was screaming. But outwardly she tried to appear calm. "Please – I'd be grateful if you'd let me know if he ever intends moving in here – because I'll be moving out."

"Why on earth –"

"He's my psycho ex," Laura told her.

Avril was immediately contrite. "Oh, God – I'm so sorry! I'll make sure he doesn't rent anything in Green Street through us – in fact, I'll cross his name off our list this very minute."

Laura heard the sound of a pen scraping across paper.

"Of course, if an owner puts up a For Rent sign themselves and he sees it – well, there's not much I can do about that," Avril added apologetically. "But I'll leave a note here in the book, and explain the situation to the other agents when I see them."

"Thanks," Laura said. "And I'd really appreciate knowing if he contacts you again."

Turning off her phone, Laura sat staring into space. Jeff was ruining her life! Clearly this was what he intended, because he'd given Avril his real name, no doubt hoping that his ex-wife would find out that he was intending to move into the same building! He was orchestrating a slow campaign of terror, yet she was powerless to do anything about it. Now, she'd end up leaving the apartment she already loved, since she wouldn't even contemplate staying there if Jeff had access to the building. How dare he think of moving into Green Street! Hopefully he'd only inquired about an apartment in order to elicit information from Avril, or to terrify his ex-wife. The idea of seeing Jeff on a regular basis was more than she could cope with.

Laura was also furious that Jeff had found out where she was living. She supposed it wasn't all that difficult – he, or someone he employed, could have been following her. In fact, finding her would hardly present any difficulty if he genuinely had MI5 connections. Alternatively, he might simply have rung all the local estate agencies, knowing she'd choose to live within an easy commute to her job. She could only hope that Avril would be true to her word and let the other estate agents know. Of course, Jeff might go to another estate agent, or see a private For Rent sign himself . . .

Laura sighed. There were so many imponderables! Already Jeff had robbed her of her peace of mind, filling every moment with fear. Everywhere she looked, she saw his face – in trains, buses, on the street, in shops. She had to stop letting him be such an all-powerful force in her life. He was only one person, although she was well aware that his money could buy him extra eyes.

Resolutely, Laura decided that the only way to cope with Jeff was to adopt a different attitude. She'd be the one to change. She'd stop letting Jeff dictate how she lived her life. She'd ignore his petty behaviour, and when he got no response to his actions, he'd get tired of playing games and go away. She wasn't going to let him drive her out of the apartment she loved. All the same, she was glad she hadn't actually bought it yet. Hopefully, by the time that option became available, the situation with Jeff would have resolved itself, and she could make it her permanent home.

CHAPTER 58

The duty concierge, beamed at Laura as she returned home from the university. "I hope you're settling in okay?" he asked.

Laura smiled. "Yes, thanks, Jim – I can't believe that I'm here two weeks already! I really love the apartment. But there are still a few things I need to get, like a rug and some lamps –"

The concierge nodded. "Yes, it takes a while to turn a place into a home, doesn't it?" He smiled cheerfully. "At least you've got your TV working now. So you'll be able to –"

Laura turned sharply. "Hold on – I don't have a TV – what do you mean?"

"Oh." The concierge looked puzzled. "I thought – I mean, the guy said he was here to fix your TV. He said you couldn't get any reception, and he was going to sort it out for you. He knew your name and apartment number, so I assumed –"

"You let him into my apartment?"

The concierge nodded, biting his lip.

"What did he look like?" Laura asked, her heart pounding.

The little man looked contrite. "Well, he was a tall, blond guy, wearing a dark grey uniform with a red and yellow logo – I think it said Ace TV Repairs?" Momentarily he looked confused. "No, maybe it said Domestic TV Repairs –" He hesitated. "Are you saying –?"

"Yes!" said Laura angrily. "You let my ex into my apartment!"

The concierge blanched. "Oh my God, I'm so sorry! Since the guy knew all about you, I guessed you'd probably booked an

247

appointment with his company and forgotten to let us guys at the desk know –"

"Would you mind ringing the police?" Laura asked frostily.

"Well, ma'am, if you're sure nothing is missing –"

"No, officer, everything seems to be there," Laura said dully. "And you're certain there are no listening devices or cameras in the apartment?"

The police officer looked mildly amused. "At your request, our people have checked thoroughly, ma'am, and we've found nothing." He looked at his notebook. "But we'll certainly be contacting this Mr Jeff Jones, to see if he can throw any light on the matter. I believe one of our officers has visited him before?"

Laura nodded, her voice shaky. "Yes, I've already reported my ex-husband for stalking me – he's been making my life a misery ever since we broke up. And it looks like he's determined to continue his campaign against me."

The officer gave her a sympathetic nod.

She appreciated the police presence, and she was grateful for their attention to detail. On the other hand, she was well aware that Jeff would probably have a sound alibi for the time her apartment was broken into.

The policeman looked at her closely. "Are you absolutely certain this couldn't be a mistake?" he asked. "Isn't it possible that the TV man asked for your apartment by mistake, but went to another apartment instead?"

Laura shook her head. "No, the concierge opened the door of the apartment for him. And, before you arrived, the concierge checked with all the owners of the other apartments," she told him frostily, "and no one else had booked, or was visited by, a TV repair man today."

The police officer looked puzzled. "It seems a little odd that someone would break into your apartment, yet steal nothing," he remarked. But seeing Laura's thunderous expression, he decided it was safer to say nothing more.

After the police had gone, Laura sat in her kitchen staring at the walls. She felt sick at the thought that Jeff had been snooping around in her apartment. She still wasn't convinced that he hadn't hidden a listening device or camera somewhere, although the police had assured her there was nothing present, and she had to accept that they were highly skilled in the area of detection.

Anxiously, she drummed her fingers on the kitchen table. On the other hand, couldn't they have missed a very sophisticated device? If Jeff really was in the secret service, he'd be an expert in this area. And if Kerry was right, and he was up to something illegal instead, he'd probably know a lot about surveillance anyway. He could also afford to spend money on a top-quality item – one the police mightn't be able to detect. Laura decided that just to be on the safe side, she'd make all her calls in the corridor outside her apartment or in the lobby downstairs.

Laura shivered. Despite the police's assurances, she no longer felt safe and secure in her own apartment. Looking around fearfully, she wondered if Jeff could have inserted a tiny camera into the light overhead. Or inside a picture frame? Was she being watched at this very minute?

Mentally shaking herself, Laura decided that she wasn't going to let Jeff dictate how she lived her life. This was precisely what he wanted – to drive her mad. He might have done nothing to the apartment, but he'd have known that the mere fact of him being there would be enough to set her nerves on edge.

Feeling very emotional, Laura went downstairs to her bedroom and sat on her bed. Then she opened the drawer of her bedside locker – this was where she kept the precious photos of her parents and brother. Like a comfort blanket, she always reached for them in time of stress. Connecting with her lost loved ones helped to calm her. Looking at their smiling faces always helped her to dispel the loneliness that often threatened to overwhelm her. It confirmed that she'd once been part of a loving family.

Reaching into the drawer, Laura expected to feel the plastic folder beneath her fingers. But it wasn't there. Frantically pulling out the drawer, she gaped inside. The precious photos of her parents and brother were gone! Staring into the empty interior,

Laura was unable, for several seconds, to fully comprehend what could have happened. Then it hit her like a ton of bricks. Jeff had taken the photos! He knew how much they meant to her, and he'd have known exactly where to find them – she'd always kept them in the drawer of her bedside table, even when she and Jeff had lived together.

As the enormity of what had happened began to sink in, Laura sat down on her bed and began to weep. She felt as though she'd lost her beloved family for a second time. Jeff had won yet again because he knew how much the loss of the photos would hurt her. She'd always meant to have copies of the photos made, or put onto her computer, but of course she'd never got around to it. Now it was too late.

Eventually, when she'd dried her eyes and washed her face, Laura made two phone calls – one to the police, to report her missing photos, and the other to Kerry, who promised to come over immediately.

A little while later, a red-eyed Laura opened the door to her friend. And on seeing Kerry, she burst into tears again.

"My life is a total mess, isn't it?" she wailed as her friend embraced her. "And I always seem to be calling on you to get me out of one bad situation after another. But there's nothing you can do this time!"

"Don't worry, love," Kerry soothed, "You've had a run of very bad luck lately."

"This isn't about luck, Kerry – this is Jeff, trying to unhinge me!"

"And you're certain you haven't just mislaid the photos?" Kerry asked tentatively. "If you like, I'll help you do a thorough search of the apartment –"

Laura looked distraught. "Surely you, at least, believe me? I've already been through this scenario with the police on the phone. They thought I might have mislaid them, too. But it's Jeff – I know he's the one who took them!"

Kerry hugged her friend tightly. "Look, I know it's awful, but that's what Jeff wants – to make you miserable. Please don't let him get to you – then he'll have won." She handed Laura a paper handkerchief from her pocket. "Here – wipe your eyes, love. I know you're devastated, but at the end of the day they're only photos – you'll never forget your family. You have them stored where they're most important – inside your heart."

Laura refused to be placated as she wiped away a fresh batch of tears. "But they were the only photos I had left of them!" she sobbed. "Sometimes, when I can't remember their faces, I panic, but then I always had the photos to remind me – now I have nothing left!"

The police officer sighed. "Look, I've spoken to Mr Jones about the photos – he denies knowing anything about them. He's even invited us to search his apartment if we don't believe him. And he has an iron-clad alibi for the time you say the TV repairman entered your apartment."

"Well, he'd make sure he had an alibi, wouldn't he?" Laura replied angrily. "And he's hardly going to keep the photos in his apartment. He's probably destroyed them by now!"

"Are you positive you couldn't have thrown them out accidentally?" the police officer asked. "It's an easy thing to do – we all make mistakes."

Laura was incandescent. "Officer, I'm hardly likely to throw out the one thing that means so much to me!"

The police officer looked momentarily annoyed. "Look, Ms Thornton, I don't know what else I can do," he added patiently. "You seem to have a vendetta against Mr Jones –"

"I'll bet my ex-husband himself suggested that word!" Laura replied angrily, and was pleased to see that the police officer looked embarrassed. Clearly, Jeff had put the notion of a vendetta against himself into the officer's mind. He was good at that sort of thing.

CHAPTER 59

During the first week of the summer holidays, twelve-year-old Laura found herself playing alone each day, since Kerry was busy cutting, shaping and planing pieces of wood in the outhouse at Treetops. She'd found an old crate in the woodpile, and had gleefully set to work on converting it and several disparate pieces of wood into a box-cart. It would be perfect, she told Laura, for whizzing down the sloping driveways of both Greygates and Treetops.

Bored with her own company, and tired of Pete's attempts to play tricks on her, Laura eventually decided to see what was keeping Kerry so preoccupied. In the gloom of the shed, she watched as her friend hammered different pieces of wood together, then planed them to smooth the surface and remove any splinters.

"Where did you get the wheels?" Laura asked, mesmerised as she watched her friend's clever little hands at work.

"I got them off my old baby buggy – Mum had dumped it in the shed. It was covered in spiders' webs, but the wheels are exactly the size we need."

Kerry gestured towards the workbench. "Hand me those axle brackets, would you, Laura?"

Laura gazed uncertainly at the various items laid out before her.

"See those right-angled metal pieces on the left? Yes, that's them."

Laura handed her friend the items and watched as Kerry nailed them to each end of a long narrow piece of wood.

"This is for steering the cart," Kerry explained, "The wheels will be attached through here, like this –"

Kerry was delighted to have an appreciative audience, and was eager to explain how she was going to attach the moveable steering bar to the front of the cart by adding another axle and washers underneath. That would make it possible for them to change direction when they needed to. Laura simply gaped in awe, unable to fully understand, but thrilled and looking forward to the fun they were going to have when it was finished. Wouldn't Pete be surprised to see what Kerry had made!

"Are we going to let Pete go on it?" Laura asked warily. "He's so rough he might damage it."

Kerry grinned. "This is going to be very sturdy, so you needn't worry about him! But I think we'll make him really jealous before we let him on it. After all, he wouldn't let us use his skates last summer!"

Laura gave a conspiratorial grin. "You're right – and we'll remind him of that when he starts begging for a ride on it!"

Kerry smiled, finally attaching the front wheels and spinning them upside down to ensure that they moved freely. Satisfied, she turned the box-cart over and both girls surveyed the finished product.

"What do you think?"

Laura gazed at it in awe. It looked very impressive!

"It's amazing," she said, smiling excitedly at Kerry.

"Did you manage to find some kind of rope?"

Laura nodded, producing a length of nylon washing line from her pocket. She'd no idea what Kerry wanted it for but, when asked to find some, she'd rushed home to do her friend's bidding, and found the length of abandoned clothesline in the scullery.

"Perfect!" Kerry said, unwinding it and cutting off a segment. Then she tied a knot in one end and threaded the length of clothesline through one of the holes she'd drilled at either end of the front axle. Urging Laura to sit in the kart, and placing the washing line in her hands, Kerry threaded the other end of the length of the line through the second hole in the steering bar. She then tried to gauge the distance required for comfortably steering it, and when she felt it was the right length she tied another knot on the underside of the steering bar.

"Does that feel comfortable?" she asked. "Pull the string to one side, and see if you can move the steering bar easily."

Laura nodded, pulling on the washing line and watching in awe as the axle moved the bar to one side.

"Now try the other side."

Laura obediently complied, thrilled to play even a tiny part in getting the project up and running.

Kerry cut off the surplus washing line, then turned and grinned at Laura. "Let's take it over to your place for its maiden voyage, shall we?"

Laura nodded, grinning back. She was so excited, and so proud of her clever friend!

As Kerry pulled the go-kart behind them, the two girls headed out of the Treetops driveway and walked alongside the road. "If Pete wants to go on this badly enough, I think he should pay us for it!" Kerry said, grinning, as they walked in the direction of Laura's house. "We'll make him use his pocket-money to buy us ice creams!"

"Great idea!" Laura said happily. She knew Pete would be pissed off to think that a mere girl could build such a magnificent and efficient structure. She was just a little worried in case he might try to sabotage it, but she didn't say anything to Kerry.

As they reached Greygates and hauled the cart up the driveway to the top, Kerry handed the washing-line steering-handle to Laura. "Go on – you can have first go," she said generously. "Just don't break your leg or bump your head. I don't want to get into trouble with your parents!"

Laura's face lit up. "Really? I mean –"

"Get into the bloody thing, Laura, and let's start having fun!" Kerry said gruffly. "Anyway, you're going to be the guinea pig – if anything is wrong with it, you'll be the one to discover it. Ready?"

Laura nodded, grinning happily as Kerry gave the box-cart a shove, and she found herself flying down the driveway. She gripped both sides of the washing line, steering herself as she built up speed. "Wheeeee!" she cried, loving every second of the experience. The wind was making a whooshing sound in her ears as she hurtled past the flowerbeds, barely missing the grocery store's delivery boy who was cycling up the driveway. Laura just had time to register his horrified face before his bike wobbled and he fell into the hedge. Chuckling to herself, Laura continued on, pulling on one side of the washing line to ease the cart round the bend in the driveway – just as her father's BMW was coming towards her. Now, there was just one problem to be faced – Kerry hadn't shown her how to stop!

"Aaaaaargh!" Laura tried to avoid the BMW, but she clipped the edge of its front bumper as she flew past, then the cart zigzagged and overturned, while Laura was thrown out onto the driveway. She skinned her two knees and the pain was excruciating, but she screwed up her eyes in an attempt not to cry.

"Laura, are you okay?" Her father came running back towards her, having abandoned his car in the middle of the driveway. He was followed shortly afterwards by Kerry, who was out of breath from running down the entire length of the driveway.

Having ascertained that she hadn't broken anything, Alan eyed Laura sternly. "Why on earth weren't you being more careful? You could have injured yourself! As it is, you've scraped the bumper on my car."

"Sorry," Laura mumbled. Then she turned to him accusingly. "But you're home early – if you hadn't been here, I wouldn't have had any problem!"

Her father looked amused. "That's because I'm going to collect Pete – he wants to come with me while I pick up my new car from the showrooms," he said mildly. "Just as well this one is leased, isn't it? If not, you'd be paying for the repairs out of your pocket money for a very long time!"

Kerry looked quizzically at Laura's father. "What does 'leased' mean, Mr Thornton?"

Laura gave Kerry a smile, grateful that she was distracting her father from chastising her. Her knees were badly hurting, and she was also hoping that Kerry wouldn't regard her as too incompetent to use the box-cart again. She'd absolutely loved the sensation of flying down the driveway at speed, and she was inwardly furious with her father for appearing at that precise moment and spoiling her fun.

"Leasing means that companies like Thornton Foods don't actually own their fleet of cars, but it's more tax-efficient for us, since we don't have the initial outlay. And if anything goes wrong, we don't have to fork out big money for repairs. The sales team, as well as Sylvia and myself, all have BMWs that are leased."

Kerry nodded although she didn't really understand what tax efficiency meant or how the leasing company made its money. But if Mr Thornton was happy, then Kerry was, too.

By now, Alan had turned his attention to the box-cart, which was lying on its side.

"Did you make this?" he asked Kerry, who was standing by Laura's side.

Kerry nodded, blushing.

"Wow! You're a very clever girl! This is amazing!"

Examining the box-cart, Alan was impressed by the well-designed axles that turned the buggy wheels, the washers and locking nuts that enabled the steering column to move freely, all perfectly in place, the wood pale and smooth from being carefully planed.

"If you can turn out this at the age of twelve, you've clearly got a great career ahead of you!" he said admiringly. "There's just a little damage to the bracket on the steering bar, but I'm sure a bright girl like you will sort that out in no time."

Kerry blushed again.

"What are you going to be when you grow up, Kerry?"

"I'll probably become an engineer," she told him.

"Really?" Alan was pleased. "That's great! You've certainly got the flair for it."

Kerry blushed again, lapping up the praise. She liked it when Mr Thornton complimented her.

Alan smiled to himself; it tickled him pink to think that she was taking after him, as he had trained as a mechanical engineer. At some time in the future, Kerry might even come to work at the factory, maybe running the entire maintenance department. Ellie would be pleased about that, and he'd enjoy working alongside his secret daughter.

"I'm going to be a teacher," Laura piped up, not to be outdone.

"Good for you," her father said, nodding approvingly. But he didn't expand the conversation, and Laura felt decidedly left out.

"I'm interested in how things work," Kerry continued, as though neither she nor Alan had even heard Laura's comment. "I want to designs things – maybe cars or toasters – and find ways to make them work better. That's what an engineer does, isn't it?"

Alan nodded. "There are lots of different careers in engineering," he explained. "But you're right – designing and perfecting products is a big part of it." He smiled over his shoulder. "You've certainly made a great start with that box-cart of yours – it's just a pity that Laura couldn't keep control of it!"

"It's fine – it only suffered minor damage," Kerry said dismissively. "And it's quite strong, so it can cope with a few knocks."

Laura smiled at her friend, grateful again for not being made to feel guilty.

"You're an engineer yourself, aren't you, Mr Thornton?" Kerry asked.

Alan nodded, pleased that Kerry was showing an interest in the professional aspects of his life. "Yes, I qualified as a mechanical engineer. Of course, our factory manager, Tony Coleman, takes care of the day-to-day running of the machinery and the timing of production lines. I mainly do the paperwork now, but my knowledge of engineering is a great help to me in understanding what's going on, and in making major decisions."

As Alan began walking back to his car, he suddenly turned back.

"Kerry, would you like to come to the car showrooms with me and Pete? They have a big repair department there as well – you might be interested in having a look around while I'm dealing with the finance department."

"Can I come too?" Laura piped up.

"Okay, come on, both of you," Alan said, grinning.

Having stored the box-cart behind one of the flowerbeds, the two girls eagerly hopped into the car. This was an opportunity too good to miss.

Up at the house, Pete was already waiting for his father at the front door, and his face dropped when he saw the girls already in the car. "What are they doing here?" he asked disdainfully, clearly annoyed that he'd have to share his time with such lowly and unworthy occupants. "Surely they're not coming with us?"

"Yes, they are," Alan said mildly. "And I expect you to behave yourself, Pete. Any rudeness to the girls, and I'll leave you behind."

Glowering as he climbed into the front passenger seat, Pete said nothing. He wasn't going to risk being ousted by a pair of twelve-year-old girls. He was fourteen now, and already considered himself an adult. Conversing with mere children was beneath him, and a waste of his valuable time.

The three children stared in admiration at Alan's new car as it stood on the garage forecourt. Its chrome glistened, and its dark-red body gave off such a sheen that it made them all want to run their hands over it.

Inside, the cream leather seats smelled new and luxurious, and the children smiled at each other as they tumbled inside. In the excitement of the moment, Pete seemed to have forgotten that he hadn't wanted the girls to accompany him and his father. They were all chattering nineteen to the dozen, and finally Alan had to beg for silence so that he could figure out which switches had been moved or altered on the newer model.

Eventually, they drove back to Greygates, and found Sylvia waiting on the doorstep to see the new car.

"It's lovely, Alan," she told him smiling. "What do you think, children?"

They all nodded enthusiastically as they stepped out of the car.

"Thank you, Mr Thornton," Kerry said solemnly. "I've had a brilliant time today!"

Alan felt a stab of guilt as he patted the child's arm affectionately.

"You're more than welcome, Kerry," he said softly, aware that she got so much less than his other two children, yet she seemed to derive so much enjoyment out of the little she got.

Sylvia herded them all inside. "You'll stay for your tea, won't you, Kerry?"

The child nodded shyly. She loved the rough and tumble of the Thorntons' house, and she wished more than anything that she could have a father like Mr Thornton.

CHAPTER 60

Laura was in the middle of a tutorial when Darren knocked on her door.

"Sorry to disturb you, but I need to speak to you – privately."

Smiling apologetically at the five students seated round her desk, Laura rose to her feet and left the room. Her heart was thumping, since she knew it had to be bad news. Darren had never interrupted a tutorial before.

"Laura, there's been a fire at your apartment," he told her without preamble. "I think you'd better get back there straight away – don't worry about your tutorial – I'll get Maria to fill in, or I'll take it myself."

"Thanks, Darren," Laura mumbled and, as he waited outside, went back into her room and apologised to the students, urging them to wait for a replacement tutor. Grabbing her coat and briefcase, she left the room and closed the door.

Outside, Darren was still standing there. "I've already organised and paid for a taxi for you," he told her. "It'll be waiting for you outside the main door."

Taking her arm, he led her down the corridor. "Let me know what's happened, won't you? And please don't worry – at the end of the day, it's only bricks and mortar. If you need somewhere to stay, you're always welcome at crash at my place."

"Thanks, Darren," Laura mumbled, wondering how much damage had been done, and knowing in her heart who was to blame for this latest disaster. Was it always going to be like this?

As the taxi pulled up outside the Sociology Department door, Laura stepped inside, waving gratefully to Darren who stood watching as the taxi drove off.

In a daze, Laura sat back and contemplated this latest outrage. How could Jeff have got into her apartment?

As she stepped out of the taxi in Green Street, Laura looked up and could see that the side wall of the building, where her apartment was located, was now blackened, and the window frame completely charred. Her heart was in her mouth as she contemplated Jeff's latest attempt to punish her. As least she didn't have to worry about her family photos, because he'd stolen those already.

As she rushed into the entrance hall, Laura was assailed by a variety of people, all waiting to speak to her.

"Ms Thornton, I'm the insurance company assessor –"

"Ms Thornton, I need you to fill out this form . . ."

Laura brushed them all aside, spotting Avril, the estate agent, on the other side of the vestibule, and heading across towards a familiar face.

Avril's face lit up briefly. "Laura! This must be an awful shock! You poor love – if you like, I can find you somewhere else to live – because obviously it's going to take a while to get the damage repaired. But the insurance company will probably cover those rental costs for you –"

Laura gulped. She hadn't even considered having to leave the apartment she loved.

Avril looked worried. "You must have left in quite a hurry this morning!" she added. "You obviously forgot to turn off whatever food you were cooking."

"W-what?" Laura was bewildered. She never cooked in the mornings – she always had a bowl of cereal and milk!

Avril gave her a sympathetic smile. "I'm afraid that most of your possessions are in a fairly bad condition – so I suspect they'll all have to be dumped. I presume you had contents insurance? Luckily, the fire brigade got here quickly –" She shuddered. "Otherwise, who knows what might have happened!"

Laura felt the colour drain from her face. This was even worse than she'd expected.

"Fortunately Albert, one of the concierges, was just arriving for duty, smelled the smoke, heard the fire alarm ringing and called the fire brigade," Avril continued. "Thankfully, the sprinkler came on, otherwise it could have been a lot worse. People might even have *died*."

Avril seemed to be enjoying this ghoulish aspect of the proceedings.

"But wasn't Jim already here on duty?" Laura asked, wondering why it had taken the arrival of the second concierge to realise what was happening.

"I don't know all the details yet – I only arrived just before you did," Avril explained. "Nothing like this has ever happened while I've been in this job," she added, looking around. "I hope the owner of your apartment doesn't decide to take his business to another estate agent . . ."

Later that evening, when she'd bought a few essentials and settled in her new, temporary apartment, Laura phoned Kerry. She hadn't wanted to do it earlier, since she knew her friend would invite her to stay, and she didn't want to impose on her any more than she'd done already.

"What?" Kerry screeched when told what had happened. "Oh my God! Where are you now? You're welcome to stay here, of course –"

"I'm fine – I've moved into a temporary apartment," Laura informed her. "But I'm going to go to the police tomorrow – I can't let Jeff get away with any more of this – someone could have been killed!"

Kerry sighed. "Look, I know we'd love to blame Jeff, but you can't really believe he could have done it, can you?" she said gently. "There's a concierge on duty downstairs, so Jeff could never get past him. All the concierges are aware of who Jeff is, so they'd never let him near your place." Her voice softened. "Laura, I think you have to accept that you must have done it yourself. I hate to say it, but if you contact the police you'll just look like an idiot."

"But I didn't do it! I know I didn't!" Laura shouted, dissolving into tears.

"Look, we're all capable of making a mistake," Kerry said quietly. "You're under a lot of pressure right now, so it would have been easy to forget to turn off the cooker –"

"I didn't forget!" Laura screamed. "I never use the cooker in the mornings! Why won't anyone believe me?"

Kerry sighed. "Okay, Laura, maybe you're right," she said eventually. "But I'd rather believe it was you – because then, we wouldn't have to worry that Jeff was still out to get you."

"I know it was Jeff!" Laura said stubbornly. "He's upping the ante because I went to the police – you were right when you warned me about stalkers reacting badly to police involvement. What the hell am I going to do?"

Kerry shook her head. "I don't know, love. I'm just worried that the police won't take you seriously. And if it is Jeff, then he'll try some other stunt once the police come after him again."

"Well, I'm going to them anyway," Laura, said stubbornly. Then she ended the call.

The police officer looked at her sternly. "Ms Thornton, according to the fire department, the fire was started by a pan of cooking oil left heating on the cooker. It overheated, caught fire and exploded, causing extensive damage to the walls and furnishings. How on earth can you consider that Mr Jones is guilty? The concierges have already confirmed that no one, other than residents, entered or left the premises yesterday morning." He looked annoyed. "You're very lucky the fire was caught before it spread to other apartments."

"But it *had* to be him!" Laura insisted. She was becoming more and more agitated.

The police officer put down his pen and stared angrily at her. "Ms Thornton, your insistence on Mr Jones' involvement makes me wonder if you're trying to cover up your own guilt."

"W-what?" Laura's mouth dropped open.

"Or perhaps you're so desperate to get your ex-husband into trouble, that you started the fire yourself?"

"You can't possibly –"

Laura closed her mouth. She was stunned that anyone could even think such a thing.

The police officer looked at her grimly. "I think, Ms Thornton, that you'd be well advised to leave the matter to your insurance company. Otherwise, you might find yourself in a lot more trouble than you bargained for."

Stumbling out of the police station, Laura was filled with rage and indignation. How was Jeff still managing to get away with his cruel vendetta? She could fully understand why women's groups were up in arms over the soft treatment of violent men like Jeff. Was it the prevailing ethos that allowed people like him to ride roughshod over the system – or was Jeff just too damned clever to get caught?

CHAPTER 61

Seeing Kerry coming up the Greygates driveway, Sylvia leaned her head out the window of her BMW.

"Hello, Kerry – I'm afraid Laura won't be able to play today – we're off to get new school uniforms." Sylvia grimaced, looking at her watch. "At least we will be, when Laura deigns to turn up. I've been waiting for ages for her."

Behind his mother's back, Pete was making funny faces at Kerry through the car window.

Kerry smiled politely at Sylvia. "I think I know where she is, Mrs Thornton – will I go and find her for you?"

Sylvia sighed, giving the child a benevolent smile. "Would you, Kerry? Thank you so much!" Sylvia said. "We're running late, and I really need to get going."

Setting off at speed, Kerry ran through the woodland that made up most of the huge garden at Greygates. She knew exactly where Laura would be hiding. Since Kerry had helped her and Pete to build a platform in their chestnut tree all those years ago, Laura spent a lot of her free time there.

Reaching the tree, Kerry stood at the base and looked up. She could see Laura's legs dangling over the edge.

"Laura!" she called up. "Your mother is getting very pissed off – you'd better hurry up and get in the car. Pete's already in the back, so you've no excuse for delaying any longer."

"Alright, alright," Laura called down tersely, "I'm on my way. I don't need you nagging me as well as Mum."

Kerry shrugged her shoulders. "There's no need to pick on me – I'm only doing what your mum asked me to do."

Laura was annoyed with her friend, since she'd been unable to find her the previous evening. "Where the hell were you yesterday evening?" she asked angrily. "I needed your help to sort out my skateboard – there's definitely something wrong with one of the wheels, and you're so good at sorting out that kind of thing."

Kerry kicked the base of the tree. "I can't be at your beck and call all the time, you know."

Laura was annoyed, but she said nothing.

Kerry looked up into the tree. "Since you're not free to play today, I'm going home. But you'd better get a move on – your mum really needs to get going."

"Yeah, yeah, okay."

Laura made a move to climb down the tree, but as soon as she saw her friend heading back to Treetops, she sat back on the platform again. She'd brought bread for the injured blackbird she'd found the previous evening, but it didn't seem interested in eating. Nor did its shiny orange beak look as bright as it had the day before, and Laura wondered if it needed water. Why hadn't she thought of that before? It was probably dehydrated. Climbing down the tree, she found an old bowl filled with rainwater. Carrying it up, she placed it in front of the bird, who blinked its eyes warily.

The bird seemed uninterested in the water, despite Laura encouraging it to drink. It made a feeble attempt at flapping its wings, but soon gave up.

"I'd better be going," Laura eventually told the blackbird apologetically. "Aren't you lucky you don't have to go to school, or wear a uniform? I'll check in with you later – maybe you'll have managed to fly away by then? I really hope so."

Sylvia's patience had finally given out and, just as she was preparing to drive off, her husband came hurrying out the front door.

"Hang on, Syl – since you're still here, I might as well take a lift with you," he said, settling into the front passenger seat. "If you can drop me off at the garage, you'll save me the bother of ordering and waiting for a taxi."

His wife nodded as she started the engine and began moving off.

"The mechanic said he'd have the heater in the car sorted out by mid-morning," Alan added. "I can't believe the damned thing has failed already – I only got the car a few weeks ago!" He rubbed his hands together, as if to warm them. "I'll be glad to have the heater working again – especially since the weather's starting to turn cooler already." He smiled at Pete, who was in the back seat, and looked quizzically at his wife. "I thought you were taking Laura today, too?"

His wife nodded. "That was the plan, but she doesn't seem bothered about getting ready for the new school term – but I might as well take Pete to get his uniform anyway."

Laura raced back through the undergrowth and headed in the direction of the lawns outside the front entrance to the house, aware that she'd been gone for ages, and knowing how annoyed her mother would be. Why did she need a new uniform anyway? The one she had seemed perfectly fine to her. Okay, so it was a little bit on the short side, but she actually liked it that way. Her mother would make sure the new one was several sizes too big – so that she could 'grow into it' – and she'd be mortified when all her classmates laughed at her.

Her breath was coming in gulps as she finally reached the lawns outside the house, just in time to see her mother's car disappearing down the driveway. Laura sighed, annoyed with herself. She'd missed the trip to town by seconds. There would be hell to pay later, when her mother lectured her about punctuality.

267

CHAPTER 62

Alone in her temporary apartment, Laura paced the floor into the early hours. How could she stop Jeff from continuing to make her life a misery? The police didn't seem to take her claims seriously, and Jeff had now neatly turned the tables on her, making the police think she was a demented and irrational fool. She was beginning to realise that her life could be seriously in danger. Jeff wasn't going to stop until he killed or seriously injured her.

She was well aware that quite a number of women had died at the hands of angry jealous exes over the years, and intervention was often too little and too late. Well, she wasn't going to sit around and wait until Jeff managed to finish her off. He'd already unintentionally indicated that he'd killed someone in the past, and she believed he was definitely capable of murdering her, too.

Finally, Laura reached a heart-breaking decision. She'd have to leave London and move to a place of safety, where Jeff couldn't find her. She'd ask for a transfer to another university if possible, and beg Darren, her boss, to keep her new location a secret.

While she'd no regrets about leaving her small temporary flat, Laura was filled with sorrow at having to give up the Green Street apartment, with its beautiful proportions, unusual mezzanine floor and rooms flooded with light. She loved the location and had fully intended buying the apartment when it went on sale, but now Jeff had ruined everything for her.

Where would she go? Having grown up on the outskirts of London and gone to university in the capital, she was going to miss the hustle and bustle of the city, the Underground, the theatres, the markets, the restaurants, the constant buzz of a city that rarely slept. On the other hand, she'd be starting a new chapter in her life, a new adventure that would at least bring her peace. She'd no longer be looking over her shoulder for Jeff or one of his cohorts, and she'd be able to sleep at night without worrying about the sound of the cistern or a creak in the floorboards.

Obviously, given her university career, she'd have to relocate to another university town, and Jeff would know that, too. But he was hardly likely to pursue her across the country, was he? Although he had the money, and probably the contacts, to do so, she hoped he'd forget all about her when she wasn't conveniently close to hand.

Laura felt apprehensive as she approached Darren's office. She knew he'd be disappointed to lose her, and she didn't like leaving him in the lurch, especially during term-time. But she couldn't risk delaying her departure any longer.

In the confines of his small office, Laura wrung her hands nervously.

"Darren, I don't really want to do this, but I have no choice but to hand in my notice. I'm sorry – I know I'm leaving you in the lurch, but I'm going to be brazen and ask if you'd recommend me for a lectureship at another university."

Darren looked stunned. "Dear God, why, Laura? I thought you were happy here! And I've always been pleased with your work –"

Laura bit her lip. "Thanks, Darren – I love working here too. But it's Jeff – he won't leave me alone. He's been stalking me for a while now, and some really bad things have happened – you know about the fire already. I'm afraid of him, so I've got to get away, because I believe he'll injure me eventually."

Darren rose from his chair in agitation. "Why on earth didn't you tell me?" he asked, his eyes like saucers behind his thick glasses. "Is there anything I can do? Do you want to stay at my place?"

Laura shook her head.

"But you can't let him bully you like that!" Darren said, appalled. "I presume you've been to the police?"

Laura nodded. "There isn't a lot they can do, because Jeff is too clever to leave any evidence that might incriminate him. I just need to get away – I'm hoping that once I break the connection, he'll leave me alone and eventually forget about me. And at that point, hopefully I'll be able to come back to London again."

Darren said nothing as he sat down again. "It seems a very drastic step to take," he said at last. "Is it really that bad? I mean, surely your ex will get tired of hassling you before long?"

Laura smiled sadly. "He's crossed the line too many times, and I don't want to give him the chance to kill me. For that reason, I want you to promise me you won't tell anyone else where I've gone. Assuming I get a job somewhere else, that is. I've more than enough money to live on, but I couldn't imagine not working."

Darren twirled his pen, then put it down on the desk. He sighed, looking closely at Laura before he spoke, and she felt he was trying to convince himself that what she was doing was truly in her best interests.

"I'm not sure if I'm helping you by telling you this," he said at last. "But there's a job available at Dorrington University – I only heard about it yesterday from a colleague who teaches there. Would you mind going so far north?"

Laura shook her head. The further away from Jeff, the better.

"Apparently, the present incumbent's been carted off to hospital – heart attack followed by surgery – and he'll be recuperating for quite some time. So they need someone to replace him immediately. It's a temporary junior lectureship in Sociology – so it won't pay as much as your current job here, but it would get you away from London." He looked at her directly. "But I don't want to encourage you to make a rash decision. I'd rather you took a bit more time to think things through –"

"Thanks, Darren," said Laura, smiling. "I'll take the job – if you can put a word in for me, that is."

Darren gave her a regretful smile. "Well, lucky Dorrington. But who am I going to get to replace you?"

"I'm sure Maria would be glad of the extra hours," Laura said. "And Timmy would take up the slack initially."

Darren sighed. "Well, you don't need to worry about any of that – that's my problem now," he said, looking at her sadly. "I'll be sorry to lose you, Laura, but needs must and all that and, if you really want to go, I'll ring Bill Maddison straight away. He's professor of the Sociology Department at Dorrington."

He caught her eye, and she detected the ghost of a smile. "I presume I'll be recommending you as Laura Thornton?"

Laura blushed and nodded.

Darren grinned at her. "Somehow, I never got around to changing your name in the department files. Other than my memories of that hideous plaque on your door, you'll always be Laura Thornton to me."

While Laura waited, Darren rang his colleague in Dorrington, and based on his assurances, she was given the job immediately. She would start the following week. Darren also astutely suggested that she might like to leave her job in his department immediately, so that she didn't need to face the other colleagues she liked so much.

"Thanks, Darren – you're the best!" Laura had said, hugging him as he stepped out from behind his desk to wish her goodbye. "I'd probably start crying if I had to tell them all personally, and it would be difficult to keep secret the reason why I'm leaving. It's not that I don't trust them – but all it needs is for one person to accidentally let the cat out of the bag. If Jeff found out, I'd be back to square one."

"I'll think of some excuse," Darren said sadly. "Maybe you had to rush off to take care of a sick relative?"

Laura had tears in her eyes. This minute she'd be grateful to have any living relative, sick or not.

"Anyway, I'm hoping that you'll be back again next year," Darren added. "I don't like letting go of good staff like you."

"I'm going to miss you all so much!" she told him.

"I'm going to miss you, too," Darren said gruffly. Then he hugged her solemnly. "I hope you're doing the right thing, Laura. No one should have to run away in order to survive."

Kerry's voice shook when Laura told her of her plans to leave

London. "Leave? My God, Laura – where will you go? I can't believe you'd do something so drastic! And you've packed in your job without even telling me!" She looked bereft. "Are you sure you're not being too hasty?"

"I'm sorry for not letting you know first, but I was afraid you'd try to dissuade me," Laura told her, tears in her eyes. "Anyway, I don't feel I've any other choice. Jeff has gone too far this time – it's clear that he wants to kill me. I'm not going to hang around until he makes his next move."

"But Dorrington? It's hundreds of miles away! I'll never get to see you!" Seeing Laura's eyes filled with tears, Kerry sighed. "Sorry, love – I'm being totally selfish. I'm only thinking of how much I'm going to miss you. But I see your point – maybe you don't have any other option."

Laura hugged her friend. "There isn't any other way – I'm never going to be rid of Jeff otherwise. And because I've no family, I'm in a position to make this clean break – I couldn't do it if Pete and my parents were still alive. At least Jeff can't hurt them." She clutched Kerry tightly. "I never thought I'd be grateful, even for a moment, to be all alone in the world!"

"You're not all alone – you have me, and we'll never lose contact, right?"

"Of course not, but I want you to pretend to Jeff that we're not in touch any longer," Laura said. "I want you to be safe, Kerry. We both know now that Jeff is capable of anything." Laura wiped away a fresh tear. "And please, list my phone number under another name, in case Jeff ever manages to steal your phone."

Kerry looked at her bleakly. "You've really thought this through, haven't you?" She hugged Laura tightly. "And to think I assumed you were just being your usual impulsive self!"

"No, I've been thinking about it for a while now," Laura said determinedly. "Having my apartment set on fire was simply the last straw. If I can just break the link with Jeff, maybe he'll eventually forget about me."

"I hope you're right," Kerry said fervently.

They agreed between them that Kerry would report any

sightings of Jeff to Laura, because as long as he was in London, she could feel reasonably safe.

Laura smiled at her friend through her tears. "I couldn't ask for a better friend than you," she said. "I just hope Jeff doesn't decide to target you when he can't get to me any longer."

"Let him try!" Kerry said stoutly. "Anyway, it's only you he's interested in – you dumped him and he can't get over that. He'll get nothing out of me," she added, "no matter how hard he tries. You have my word on that."

CHAPTER 63

On her train journey north, Laura acutely felt the loss of her old life. With every mile the train travelled, she was leaving behind the city of her childhood, where the memories of her parents and brother were most strongly rooted. She was also leaving her best friend Kerry, her colleagues and her career at the university – and the wonderful Green Street apartment. She'd been heartbroken when telling Avril, the estate agent, that she wasn't in a position to go back to Green Street after the fire. And by quitting the property, she was also losing her chance of purchasing it when the owner decided to sell. Yet again, she silently cursed Jeff for all the harm he'd done to her, and she wished she could be a fly on the wall when he discovered she was no longer within his reach. She wished she could see the shock on his face when he realised she'd foiled his plot to terrorise her.

As the train passed through station after station, Laura gradually began to take stock of her new life ahead. Despite her fears for the future, she was also excited. She had no doubts about her ability to do the job at Dorrington, and there was a certain buzz in being forced out of her comfort zone and into a whole new way of life. Would she get on with her new employers? Would there be in-fighting in the department? She was due to report to Professor Bill Maddison, head of the Sociology Department, and Laura hoped he'd be as easy to work for as Darren.

She'd booked into a hotel in the city centre, not far from the university, and would stay there until she'd time to find more permanent accommodation. She'd stay at the hotel for the first few weeks until she learned about the local areas, and discovered what areas of Dorrington were the best places to live.

Later that afternoon Laura approached the magnificent redbrick Dorrington University buildings with butterflies in her stomach. She was still reeling from her sudden departure from one university and arrival at another, all in the space of a week. Finding the Sociology Department proved relatively straightforward, and soon Laura found herself knocking on Bill Maddison's door.

"Come in!"

Bill was a warm, personable bear of a man, and Laura's hand seemed to disappear inside his large one as they shook hands.

"You're very welcome, Laura," he said, smiling. "Thanks for getting us out of a pickle. Darren tells me you're a Londoner?"

Laura nodded, feeling immediately at ease. She surmised that Bill was in his late forties. His tousled dark-brown hair was streaked with grey, and his brown eyes crinkled at the corners when he smiled. She warmed to him immediately.

"I'm grateful for the job, but I'm sorry to hear about your colleague," Laura said.

Bill nodded. "Yes, it was quite a shock. At the very least, he'll be out of action for the rest of the academic year. So I hope you'll be able to stay with us for a while."

Laura was relieved that he didn't ask her why she'd been able to step into the vacant post at such short notice, and she suspected that Darren had explained she had personal reasons for making the move.

"If you like, we can ease you in by getting you to mark some of last term's papers," Bill suggested. "Then, when I've given you the timetable for first year Sociology, you can start working out your lecture programme."

Laura nodded.

"I doubt if you'll have much preparation to do anyway," Bill added, smiling. "Darren tells me you were the bright spark in his department, and very popular with all the students."

Laura could feel herself blushing. Dear old Darren was always supportive.

"How soon would you feel comfortable about starting to lecture?"

Laura shrugged. "After I've marked the term papers, I'll get started straight away."

Bill nodded approvingly. "Good for you – that's the spirit." He smiled encouragingly. "I hope you'll be happy here, Laura. We work hard but we're an easy-going bunch, and we don't take ourselves too seriously."

Laura smiled back. She liked the laid-back philosophy that Bill Maddison was outlining. Having experienced Darren's easy-going way of running his department, she'd been worried that she wouldn't fit into a more structured and tightly controlled environment. But Bill's attitude seemed similar to her former boss's.

"Have you found somewhere to stay?" Bill asked.

Laura nodded. "I'm staying in a hotel for a week or two, until I find something more suitable."

Bill nodded. "Well, if you need time off to go flat-hunting, just let me know. Someone can usually cover for you if you need to go and view a place."

Laura thanked him, thinking that if everyone else was as nice as Bill Maddison, then she was going to enjoy being at Dorrington very much.

"Do you know anything about Dorrington?"

Laura shook her head.

"Then it's worth getting to know the different areas before you decide on where you're going to rent. Ayersview and Clipperfield both have a bus service that drops you right outside the university. On the other hand, some say that Bayside – which is further out – is worth the longer commute because of the views of the coast. But it takes two buses to get there from here."

"Thanks, I'll bear that in mind," Laura replied.

Bill went to the bookshelf behind his desk and handed her a local tourist guide. "You'll find a lot of useful information in there," he told her. "This isn't a big city, but it does have a big heart."

He handed her the keys to her new office down the corridor. "Let me know if I can do anything for you – my door is always open."

As he ushered her out of his office, he smiled down at her. "Tomorrow I'll introduce you to the rest of the Sociology Department staff. We usually have a weekly mid-morning catch-up in the canteen. See you there at eleven?"

Laura nodded.

Having moved her files and lecture notes into her new office, she left the college and headed back to the hotel, feeling pleased with how things had gone so far. Her new boss seemed kind, and he was allowing her time to settle in before imposing a heavier workload on her. All in all, it had been a seamless transition so far, and she felt a sense of peace gradually flowing over her. She was hundreds of miles away from Jeff, and he'd never manage to find her. Only a few trusted people, such as Kerry and Darren, knew where she was, and Jeff would never manage to extract that information from either of them.

CHAPTER 64

As Sylvia started the car and began heading down the driveway, her husband smiled to himself. Laura still hadn't turned up – no doubt she was up to mischief of some sort, as usual. He'd have been surprised if she'd been sitting meekly in the back seat! And how ironic that she'd become best friends with Ellie's child. He wondered what either girl would say if they knew the truth – that they were actually sisters.

He glanced at his wife. Even after all these years, he still felt guilty for deceiving her. Yet he'd been drawn to Ellie in a way that he'd never been to any other woman. Even now, after all their years of secret trysts and stolen hours of passion, she was still as exciting as ever to him. He was a lucky man to have a happy marriage and a mistress who was still as loving as the day they met.

And Kerry, his secret daughter – he'd need to ensure that she was provided for financially. He'd promised Ellie that he'd pay for her university education too. He'd sort all that out just as soon as he got around to visiting his solicitor. Lately, there was just so much to do at the factory – installing the new state-of-the-art sterilising unit had cost a packet, yet it had been necessary in order to keep the business competitive. And it had been possible only because of Dick Morgan's investment.

Poor Ellie – he felt guilty about her too, because he wasn't ever going to marry her now. He'd made rash promises to her when they'd been younger, and at the time, he'd believed them, too. But age and wisdom had made him realise – and clearly Ellie realised too – *that you couldn't always have what you wanted in life. If you got fifty per cent of it, you were lucky. And he was luckier than most. Anyway, he suspected that Ellie was content to be his secret wife, and to have him maintain his second family in a good standard of living.*

"Damn," Sylvia muttered, and Alan turned to her in surprise. His wife never used strong language.

"What's wrong, dear?"

"I'm not sure, but there's definitely something wrong with the car. It doesn't seem to be steering properly. It keeps pulling to one side . . ."

"Well, why don't you drive me to the garage first, and let the mechanics there take a look at it?"

Sylvia nodded, saying nothing more as she concentrated on making her way onto the motorway. But before long, she glanced at him again, her eyes now filled with concern. "Alan, the car won't turn properly. It's pulling to one side and I can't seem to do anything about it –"

"What do you mean?"

Sylvia's voice rose. "I can't steer the damned car!"

Aghast, Alan watched helplessly as the car crossed several lanes, heading towards the central barrier of the six-lane motorway, while cars all around them slammed on their brakes and hooted their horns angrily. It felt as though the car was drunk or on a suicide mission. They weren't going to make it. Alan was paralysed with fear as the central barrier loomed before them.

"Brakes!" he shouted, even though it meant they'd be hit from behind. But it might prove the lesser of two evils. But, oh God, Pete was in the back seat.

"I can't – the brakes aren't working either!"

Galvanised into action, Alan leaned across his wife, trying desperately to pull at the steering wheel, but it wouldn't budge. It was firmly locked in position. He glanced back at his son, who was just beginning to realise the seriousness of their situation. His face was white as he watched his two helpless parents in the front. Alan wondered briefly if he could save Pete by ordering him to jump from the moving car onto the motorway. But just as quickly he dismissed it. His son would definitely be killed that way, because of the fast-moving traffic in front and behind them. They were in a moving death trap and he was powerless to do anything to save them.

As Sylvia screamed, the car mounted the concrete barrier, briefly stalled then headed directly into the oncoming traffic on the other side. An articulated truck was coming towards them, and the last thing that Alan saw was the look of surprise and shock on the driver's face. After the impact, there was nothing but oblivion.

Since she'd avoided going for her new school uniform, Laura decided to make the most of her free day. She stayed out in the woods all morning, watching rabbits foraging and grasshoppers leaping through the long grass. When she tired of watching the local wildlife she'd checked on the injured bird again, but it was still sitting where she'd left it.

Realising she was hungry, she made her way back to the house, and let herself in through the kitchen door and made herself a sandwich of bread and cheese. It had been a novelty to spend the morning alone without having anyone telling her what to do. The silence of the house was a new experience too. There was no one there to nag her about spilling crumbs on the floor, or getting scuffmarks on the toes of her shoes.

She was enjoying the solitude and, as she chewed her sandwich, she decided she could use her remaining free time to play a trick on Pete. He was always the one who was playing tricks on her – maybe this time she'd give him the surprise of his life! If she dug a trench between the two big sycamore trees down by the stream, and camouflaged it with twigs and leaves, when he next ran after her, she'd skirt the trap but her unwary foe would fall straight into it! She chuckled at the thought of getting one over on her brother. She'd have plenty of time to dig the trench before the family got back from town.

Briefly, she thought of cycling over to Kerry's house and asking for her help with the digging, but Laura quickly changed her mind.

Her friend had been in a grumpy mood earlier that morning, probably because she hadn't been free to play with her. Anyway, she was enjoying being on her own.

After spending the afternoon laying her trap in the woodland, Laura returned the spade to the shed and headed back towards the house. She had no idea what time it was since she'd left her watch on the kitchen table, but it felt late, and she was beginning to feel hungry again. Inside the house, she looked at the kitchen clock, and was surprised to see that it was almost six.

A niggle of worry furrowed her brow. Where was everyone? Surely it didn't take all day to buy a school uniform? She wasn't looking forward to her mother's ire when she returned. She was now realising that her delightful day of freedom had been bought at a cost, and she'd still have to endure another day of shopping in town.

Debating whether or not to check on the injured bird again, Laura finally opted for the half-mile walk to Treetops instead. She'd check on the bird later. By now she wasn't annoyed with Kerry any more, and was actually looking forward to some company. She was smiling as she walked along the road, pleased about the trap she'd laid for Pete. She was looking forward to telling Kerry about it too – they were both agreed that Pete could sometimes be the most tiresome of boys, and he seemed to think that because he was fourteen, he could treat his sister and friend like they were babies. They'd enjoy seeing him get his comeuppance for a change.

Laura was chuckling to herself as she hurried down the road toward Treetops.

CHAPTER 65

Kerry, Norma, Jack and a group of their work colleagues were all celebrating in the Flower Street bar the following Friday evening after work. Sea Diagnostics had just been awarded the contract for the estuary barrage, and everyone was determined to have a good time before the actual construction work on the project began.

Kerry froze as she heard a familiar voice close by.

"Oh, hello, Kerry," Jeff said pleasantly, sidling up to her at the counter as she waited for the barman to get her another glass of wine. "I couldn't help overhearing that your company's just won a big contract – congratulations."

"Thanks," Kerry replied, turning her head away.

"Laura's not with you tonight?"

"Why do you want to know?" Kerry retorted, turning back to face him. "Haven't you done her enough harm?"

Jeff had the grace to look embarrassed.

"Anyway, she's gone," Kerry told him angrily. "She just upped and left. She didn't even leave me a note. It's all your fault that I've lost my best friend!"

Jeff looked confused. Clearly he hadn't expected this to happen. Then Kerry saw a momentary flicker of pleasure in his eyes as he realised how bereft she looked. But it was quickly replaced by a look of genuine shock and dismay.

"What do you mean – 'gone'?"

"Exactly that. She's left, and I've no idea where she is."

"You mean, she's disappeared?"

"Apparently so. I can't believe she could do that without even telling me!" Kerry pretended to look angry. "Anyway, what she's done is none of your business any more. And she's obviously decided that it isn't any of mine either."

"I hope she's okay," Jeff said humbly.

Kerry had to steel herself against the look of sorrow and concern on his face. She thought she saw a tear in his eye, and she had to remind herself that he was a vicious thug, whose tears were far from genuine.

"Will you let me know if you hear from her?" he asked in a subdued voice.

"No, I will not," Kerry said hotly. "You had your chance with her, and you blew it. Anyway, since she's left without even leaving me a note, I don't expect to be hearing from her anytime soon, if ever."

Jeff suddenly grinned maliciously. "Yes, she's dumped you, too. Surely you must hate her for that?"

Kerry looked at him witheringly. "We're not all like you, Jeff – thank goodness."

Paying the barman, she grabbed her drink, then turned and walked off.

Laura picked up her phone as it rang, pleased to see that the number was Kerry's.

"Guess who I met last night," Kerry asked without preamble.

"Jeff?"

"The very man."

"Where was he? What was he doing?"

"I was in the Flower Street bar with Norma and the gang after work, and he sidled up to me, bold as brass!"

"Did he ask about me?"

"Of course – it was the first thing out of his mouth. As arranged, I gave him short shrift. Told him you'd vanished, and that I'd no idea where you'd gone."

"Thanks, Kerry."

"How are you settling in? Do you like Dorrington?"

"Yes, it's fine. It'll take a bit of time to get used to all the changes, but I'm happy enough. I do miss London, though."

"Well, hopefully once Mr Vindictive focuses his attention elsewhere, you'll be able to come back."

Laura felt a sudden pang of remorse, realising that the authorities had been due to announce the name of the company that had won the contract to build the estuary barrage the previous day. And she'd forgotten to ask Kerry about it.

"Sorry, love – I forgot to ask you about the barrage project – were you, by any chance, celebrating last night?"

Laura could hear the pleasure in Kerry's voice as she replied. "Yeah, we won the contract. Everyone here is over the moon about it."

"That's wonderful news!" Laura told her, feeling guilty that the date had slipped her mind. "When will you actually start work on the project?"

"Hopefully, the preliminary work on site will get underway within the next few weeks. But there's still a lot of paperwork to complete first."

After the two friends had ended their call, Laura sat staring into space, livid with herself for having forgotten about Kerry's project and its importance to the Sea Diagnostics team. *She* should have been the one to phone, not Kerry. She'd been so preoccupied with her own problems that she'd forgotten to ask about it. Some friend she was. Buck up, Laura, she told herself, disgusted by her own self-absorption, you can't blame Jeff for everything.

CHAPTER 66

Laura was quite enjoying her search for a new apartment. She'd done most of her viewing in the evenings, since she hadn't wanted to ask for time off unless absolutely necessary. She'd seen several apartments of varying standards, but she hadn't found any with the wow factor yet. In fact, no place came close to the spectacular apartment in Green Street. She reluctantly accepted that she was unlikely to find anything in Dorrington that would measure up – after all, it was a much smaller but sprawling city with a totally different architectural style, and she'd no right to expect the place to conform to her notion of desirability. All she needed was a moderately comfortable place to lay her head – it wasn't as though she was going to be settling there permanently.

On the third day of her search, Laura found a pleasant apartment in Bayside. Although it was further away from the university than she'd have wished, she loved its closeness to the coast, and she planned to take long bracing walks along the seafront. She needed to clear her head and get her life back on track.

Having settled into a routine at the university, and into her new apartment in Bayside, Laura was relieved to discover that life in Dorrington was proving relatively stress-free. It was great being so far from Jeff, and it looked as though her troubles were finally over.

By her third week in Dorrington, Laura had assumed full responsibility for the previous lecturer's schedule. Bill was happy with her work and the students were welcoming and seemed invigorated by the new and different approaches she brought to her lectures and tutorials.

As the weeks went by, Laura began to feel secure again, and by the time she'd been in Dorrington for two months, she was feeling confident that Jeff and his antics were now firmly in the past. She still resented being so far away from Kerry, Darren and all her colleagues at the university. She missed them all, and longed to be back in London. Nevertheless, she was making friends with other lecturers in the Dorrington Sociology Department. Her new colleagues were all nice people, and before long she was joining them for occasional nights at the pub or theatre, something she hadn't been able to do for ages.

After an enjoyable night of stand-up comedy in a small city-centre theatre, Laura was still smiling as she bade her colleagues goodnight. She had an early start the following morning, so she'd reluctantly decided against joining them for a nightcap. Living in Bayside meant she had to leave early in order to synchronise her two buses. Nevertheless, the coastal location made up for the slight inconvenience. She loved its esplanade, and she'd been fitting in a brisk walk there every morning before leaving for work.

Deep in thought, Laura crossed the pedestrian plaza and stepped out onto the main road, intending to cross to the other side in order to reach her bus stop. The road appeared clear, but some sixth sense seemed to alert her to danger, and she suddenly noticed that a car had appeared out of nowhere and was bearing down on her at tremendous speed. Momentarily paralysed with shock, she barely made it to the pavement before the car shot past.

Shaking, Laura stared after the fast-moving vehicle, but it was too late to see the registration or make a note of any other detail. She shuddered. If she'd taken just a second longer to reach the pavement, she'd now be lying injured, or maybe even dead . . . Her heart was pumping frantically, and she wondered if what had just happened was simply due to her own stupidity. But she'd checked the traffic before she'd stepped out, hadn't she? The road had been clear, she was sure of it. It seemed as though the car and its driver had been waiting specifically for her . . . Laura desperately wanted it to be her own stupid mistake, because if not, she had to face the fact that someone had just tried to mow her down.

She shook her head. She was being paranoid. Why would some driver be out to hurt her? Then her heart plummeted as a picture of Jeff pushed its way into her brain. Had that been him in the car? Suddenly her peace of mind evaporated, and her eyes began to fill with tears.

Back in Bayside, Laura rang her friend's mobile phone, not even bothering with preliminaries. "Kerry – are you sure you haven't told anyone where I am?"

"Of course not! Why do you ask? Has something happened?"

Laura bit her lip. "I don't know – I'm not sure. Maybe I'm just being paranoid."

"For God's sake, tell me what's bothering you!"

"Look, I guess I'm just on edge, and starting to imagine things. It's probably nothing to worry about – I'm just being stupid, as usual."

"You're the least stupid person I know, so you've every right to be cagey," Kerry answered.

"Look, I'm sorry, love – I haven't even asked how you are. Or how the barrage project is going."

"Don't worry," Kerry said dismissively, "everything is fine at work. Now that our design has been accepted, the really hard work begins. But I'm worried about you – what's happened to make you so concerned?"

"Someone tried to run me down tonight."

She could hear a gasp at the other end of the phone.

"Oh my God," Kerry whispered. "What happened?"

"I was walking back from the theatre – I'd just said goodbye to some of the others from the university – and I was crossing the main road to get to the bus stop – and a car came out of nowhere and headed straight towards me. I barely got out of the way, and I know I wasn't imagining it."

"Did you go to the police?"

"What for? What on earth could I tell them?"

"Did you manage to see the driver?"

"It was dark and, anyway, I was too busy jumping to get out of the way."

"Was it a man? Do you think it could have been Jeff?"

"I don't know. It could have been, or someone he paid to do it for him. I just feel sick. I don't know what to do any more."

Laura's voice was close to breaking, and Kerry hurried to reassure her. "Look, it was probably just an accident, and completely unconnected to Jeff."

But Laura wouldn't be mollified. "You're trying to tell me that I came all the way to Dorrington, and the most dangerous and inconsiderate driver in the whole city just manages to find me?"

Kerry laughed. "Sorry, I know it's not funny, but there's no way Jeff could know where you are. There just isn't, Laura. It must have been an accident."

By now, Laura was beginning to calm down a little. "Yeah, maybe you're right," she said grudgingly. "But I got one hell of a fright."

"I'm sure you did, but just think about it – although Jeff knows you've disappeared, he hasn't got a clue where you've gone. Stop worrying, and enjoy your time in Dorrington."

When they rang off, Laura threw herself down on the sofa and cried. She didn't know if she was crying from fear or relief, or simply the stress of trying to second-guess Jeff. Kerry was right – he couldn't possibly know where she was.

CHAPTER 67

As Laura set off for work, she made her usual early-morning detour along the Bayside esplanade, breathing in the salty sea air and revelling in the glorious early morning sunshine before heading off for her bus. She'd been doing this since she'd settled in her new apartment, and had established a routine that enabled her to feel invigorated by the time she reached the university.

As she left the esplanade and headed up the already busy street to her bus stop, she suddenly sensed that she was being watched. Turning around quickly, she was just in time to see a pair of eyes lock onto hers before they looked away. Within seconds, the man who'd been staring at her had melted away into the crowd that was milling around waiting for the bus to arrive.

Laura felt a stab of fear in the pit of her stomach. She was positive she'd seen that man somewhere before. In fact, she knew she'd seen him before. But where? And why was he staring at her? Had Jeff sent him? Memories of her encounter with the speeding car the previous week now assumed massive proportions in her mind again. Could he have been the man driving the car? Despite what Kerry thought, it looked as though Jeff had found her again.

As she walked through the centre of Dorrington on her way home from the university that evening, Laura experienced another prickly feeling running down her spine. She spun around, just in time to see the same man staring directly at her again, before he merged into the throng of people crossing the pedestrian plaza.

As she headed towards her bus stop, Laura kept checking over her shoulder, but the man didn't reappear. This was the second time that someone in Dorrington had been watching her closely, and she didn't like it one bit. While she might have been mistaken the first time, a second time seemed to confirm her worst suspicions.

Laura was now feeling shivery and ill, and kept watching fearfully as she crossed the main road to the bus stop, conscious that this was the exact spot where she'd encountered the speeding car so recently.

Laura was relieved to see her bus approaching and quickly settled herself inside. She feared she was losing her marbles. Perhaps Dorrington was simply a place where people tended to stare at each other a lot! As a sociologist, she of all people should know that different cultures, and even people in different areas of the same country, could behave in very different ways. On the other hand, if this man had just been observing her casually, why had he looked so furtive as he slipped away into the crowds?

Laura wondered if she was becoming paranoid. Yet within a short space of time, someone in a car had tried to run her down, a man had followed her from the Bayside esplanade to her bus stop, and the same man had been tailing her only a few minutes earlier. Surely, after all these weird incidents, she was entitled to feel paranoid? Or maybe she was simply losing it. This was what Jeff was doing to her. He was twisting the knife and loving every minute of it.

CHAPTER 68

"Goodnight, Kerry – see you tomorrow!"

Kerry smiled as she slipped on her coat. "Goodnight, Norma. I hope you and Jack aren't going to stay too late?"

"Nah – we're just going to get a head-start on the plans for our new project. Another half an hour and we're both outta here."

Kerry nodded, wishing that someone else was leaving the building at the same time as she was. Although she'd learned to ignore the pervert, he still made her feel uncomfortable. She wondered what made a person behave in this way, and what kind of kick he got out of displaying himself. Although she had to admit he hadn't made any effort to expose himself while she'd been around – on the other hand, she hadn't exactly waited to find out! She'd spotted him twice in the previous few weeks, although she couldn't have described him since she'd never actually seen him up close. But she could recognise his walk by now, and the slight stoop of his shoulders, as though he was a tall man trying to look smaller.

At this point, it was embarrassing to remember how terrified she'd originally been, imagining all sorts of scenarios in which Jeff or his drug-dealer friend was the protagonist. Clearly it hadn't been anything to do with the estuary barrage project either, since the team at Sea Diagnostics had already been awarded that very lucrative contract.

As Kerry exited the building, it was starting to rain, and she wished she'd taken her umbrella from her office, but she wasn't going back for it now. She surreptitiously glanced around her for any sign of the local pervert, but there was no one anywhere in the immediate vicinity.

Purposefully hurrying along the street, her head down, Kerry walked in the direction of the Tube station. She was very conscious that there were few people about at this hour, and there were no crowds into which she could easily merge. The click-clack of her shoes on the pathway was loud and clear, enabling anyone following her to know exactly where she was heading . . .

Kerry's heart almost stopped as she passed a row of shops. He was there, lurking in a doorway! As she began to turn away, he stepped out of his hiding place. He raised his hand in her direction, and for a moment, she wondered if he was holding a gun.

"Wait!" he called after her.

But Kerry didn't delay to find out what he wanted. Filled with fear, she began to run. Stumbling along the rainy street and out of breath, she heard a crack and felt a searing pain, then she was falling, falling, falling . . .

CHAPTER 69

When Laura arrived at Treetops, Ellie was in the kitchen, and she gave Laura her customary warm smile. "Hello, love," she said. "I was just going to take a glass of juice out to Kerry, so you can save me the job. You'll find her in the outhouse – I think she's repairing her skateboard."

Laura nodded, waiting as Ellie filled the first of two glasses with juice from the fridge. When the phone rang, she had only filled one of the glasses, so she gestured for Laura to wait. As she answered and listened to the caller on the other end of the line, Laura was instantly alerted by the change in Ellie's tone of voice.

"W-what?" Ellie whispered, her hands gripping the landline phone until her knuckles were almost white.

Laura instantly knew that it was bad news, but she had no idea just how bad it would be. Lurking by the kitchen table, she pretended to be absorbed in pouring the second glass of juice, but instinctively she knew that Kerry's mother was too preoccupied to even notice that she was eavesdropping.

"Yes, she's here – how did it happen?" Ellie groaned.

By now, Laura was listening intently, and after a brief interval Kerry's mother spoke again, her voice quivering with pain.

"Oh my God. Is there any hope?"

Clearly the answer from the other end was negative, because Ellie burst into tears, sinking to the floor, having forgotten that Laura was still in the kitchen.

"What is it? What's happened?" Laura cried, running to Ellie and throwing her arms around her. She'd never seen anyone in such a distressed state before. Something really bad must have happened.

At first, Ellie seemed oblivious to Laura's presence. It was as though a mantle of pain had suddenly surrounded her, cutting her off from everything else. Then, realising that Laura was there, she crushed the young girl to her chest, her eyes brimming with tears.

"Oh Laura, I can't believe it!" she sobbed, cradling the confused girl in her arms. "It's bad news, and we'll all have to be brave."

Laura looked confused. "Bad news?"

It seemed an eternity before Ellie spoke, and her voice shook as she whispered the words. "Yes, I'm afraid so, love. There's been an accident . . ."

In trying to soften the blow, Ellie was actually making it worse for Laura.

"Who's been hurt? Tell me, please!" Laura screamed.

"I'm afraid it's worse than that – your mother's car crashed, and she, your father and brother –"

"Are they okay? Are they in hospital?" Laura realised that in her anxiety, she was digging her nails into Ellie's hand, but Ellie didn't seem to notice.

Ellie dissolved into heart-rending sobs again. "No, love, I'm afraid they're all – oh my God, how can I tell you?"

"Please!" Laura screamed, terrified now, and clutching at Ellie's arm.

Not even feeling the pain of Laura's grip. Ellie turned her tear-stained face towards the child. "I-I'm afraid they're all dead. I'm so sorry, Laura!"

Her words momentarily winded Laura, and initially the young girl was unable to speak. Then she broke free of Ellie's embrace and ran screaming out of the house. If she didn't listen, it wouldn't be true. It couldn't be true! Everyone she loved couldn't possibly be dead! It was all a dreadful mistake – Ellie hadn't heard the caller properly, or maybe someone was playing a nasty trick on them. Everything would be fine when Mum, Dad and Pete walked in the Greygates front door. She was going straight back to the house, and she felt sure they'd all be waiting for her there . . .

As Laura ran into the yard screaming loudly, her eyes blinded with tears, Kerry rushed from the outhouse, and looked at her in astonishment. "What the –"

Laura stopped, her eyes red and streaming. "I didn't go for my school uniform, and now they're all dead!" she wailed, her eyes momentarily blinded by tears.

"What? Who's dead?" Kerry's face was white.

Laura gulped. She was so emotional she could hardly speak. But Kerry grabbed her arm and shook her angrily.

"For God's sake, tell me who's dead!" she screamed.

"They're all dead!" Laura whispered at last. "Mum, Dad, Pete – they've all been killed!"

"Oh, God, no!" Kerry croaked, now crying too. "All your family? I don't believe it! Even your father? But why would he be in your mother's car?"

"Because I was late!" Laura screamed.

She was devastated, her heart was thumping and her head was dizzy. This couldn't be happening. Soon she'd wake up and find it was all a bad dream. Maybe Kerry's mother hadn't heard the caller properly. Maybe the message had been meant for some other family, not hers . . .

"I should have died too," she whispered, fresh tears streaming down her face. She was riddled with guilt that her brother had travelled alone with her parents, simply because she'd gone to check on the injured blackbird. If she hadn't delayed them, they'd have left earlier and might have avoided the cause of the crash. Right now, she desperately wished she'd been in the car with her family, since she couldn't envisage a life without them.

Suddenly, Kerry began running towards her own house, desperate for confirmation from her mother. Distraught, Laura wasn't sure whether to turn back to be with her friend, but more than anything she wanted to be back in her own house with her family around her. So she ran down the Treetops driveway and out the gate, and began running along the road towards her own home. Pete would be alive when she got there – she had to believe it – and she'd fill in that stupid trap and just hug her brother tightly . . .

Blinded by tears, Laura ran alongside the road, hardly aware of the traffic, except when a car tooted its horn when she veered too far off the pathway. But she didn't actually care if she was killed because it would ease the pain in her heart that was unlike anything she'd ever experienced before.

Behind her in the distance, she could hear Ellie calling her, but she ignored her entreaties and ran on. She had to get back to Greygates, because her family would be waiting for her. It was all a lie – they couldn't possibly be dead . . .

At last, she staggered up the Greygates driveway, running past the house and down into the woodland beyond. Any minute now, she'd see Pete's mischievous face peeping out from behind one of the trees. And if she filled in the trap she'd laid for him, everything would be all right, because she didn't really want to hurt him . . .

Scraping around in the dirt, her tears mingled with sweat and mucus, Laura tore at the twigs and leaves with her bare hands. Crazed with grief, she began dragging the clay from behind the tree and packing it back into the hole she'd dug only hours earlier. Her nails broke and caked with dirt as she tried desperately to fill the void.

Strong arms suddenly grabbed her and, as she tried to free herself and continue digging, Laura found herself being pinioned by an equally distraught and out-of-breath Ellie.

"Laura, stop!" Ellie cried, her own tears running down her face and now mingling with Laura's own. "There's nothing you can do to bring them back – whatever you think you're doing, it won't change anything!"

Collapsing into Ellie's arms, Laura finally gave up the struggle, all the fight finally gone out of her. Smoothing Laura's hair, Ellie cradled her, and the two clung to each other. In between bouts of tears, Ellie began softly singing a lullaby. It was there, a little while later, that they were found by Laura's grandfather and the police.

CHAPTER 70

As Kerry pitched forward and fell to the ground, her heart was beating so fast that she feared it would burst out of her chest. Initially, the stab of pain she felt in her shoulder made her gasp. She'd heard a cracking sound at exactly the same time as she fell, and she wondered briefly if she'd been shot. Tears filled her eyes and she gritted her teeth as her knees scraped along the ground. Fearing for her life, she scrambled to her feet again, and continued running as fast as she could. Somewhere in the back of her mind, she realised that her body was still functioning normally and that as far as she could tell, there wasn't any bullet lodged in her flesh. Now that she recalled it, the sound she'd heard had been more like the smack of something – or someone – hitting the wet cobblestones. Besides, she only knew about the sound of gunshot from movies and TV, and she was beginning to feel rather foolish. Fear had been putting her mind into overdrive.

Risking a quick glance behind her, Kerry could see that she was no longer being followed. By now, she could see the main thoroughfare ahead, where people, cars and buses were visible once again. Sighing with relief, she allowed herself a moment to catch her breath. She was seriously winded from her exertions.

Now that she could think clearly again, she wondered if the sound she'd heard had really been a bullet. If so, it had obviously missed her. Had someone else been shot? She'd definitely heard a groan somewhere behind her as she'd taken to her heels . . .

"God, you're a terrible wimp – he's just a sad old man!"

Norma was highly amused as Kerry told her about her nocturnal adventure the night before. She was still laughing when Jack arrived and joined them at the coffee machine.

"Well, from now on, I'm not leaving here unless there's someone to accompany me," Kerry said resolutely. "I thought you said the guy was harmless? He almost frightened the life out of me!"

"Look, I'll walk you to the Underground in the evenings, if you're that worried," Jack offered, smirking. He, like Norma, found the incident highly amusing.

Norma chuckled. "Maybe the poor guy thought you were so gorgeous that he couldn't resist following you!"

"Are you implying that I'm only attractive to old men? Thanks, Norma!" Kerry grumbled, eventually having to smile herself, as she looked from one amused colleague's face to the other.

Now, in the light of day, Kerry was also beginning to see the humour in the situation. She felt stupid for behaving in such a panic-stricken way the night before. She'd over-dramatised the whole situation, even going as far as thinking the man had been armed. She really needed to get a grip. Nevertheless, she'd tuned in to the TV news bulletin before leaving for work that morning, just to find out if there'd been any shooting reported in the vicinity of the Sea Diagnostics offices the night before. Needless to say, there had been no such mention.

She'd even begun to feel pity for the man who'd terrified her the night before. She'd started to wonder about the sad life that a pervert must lead, driven by some terrible compulsion to jump out of doorways and expose himself to women passing by. What tragedy might have contributed to his condition? She supposed everyone had something in their past that made them the person they were today.

Since she hadn't seen the man properly, she couldn't even tell if it had actually been the local pervert or not. It might just as easily have been a homeless person asking for a handout. Or someone looking for directions. She was a prize idiot. She'd let her fears overrule her common sense. Kerry prided herself on being sensible and independent, yet here she was, behaving like an imbecile.

"Come on, I want to show you the draft plans Jack and I worked on last night," Norma added, linking her arm through Kerry's. "Jack came up with a very clever idea, although I'm loath to give him the credit for it –"

Jack tagged along behind them. "Huh! Wait till you see it, Kerry – you're going to be blown away! I'm not one to brag, but –"

Kerry smiled at their enthusiasm, glad to be with colleagues who loved their jobs and who routinely stayed late because they enjoyed every minute of what they did. She also admired their 'live and let live' attitude. They wouldn't be so pathetic as to let a sad old man terrify them.

"Lead on – I can't wait to see what you two have been up to," she said.

Still smiling, she walked with her colleagues down the corridor towards the design department, where the drawing boards and computers were housed.

CHAPTER 71

Laura woke early, and for a brief moment she'd managed to forget the tragedy of the day before. But looking around, she realised she was in the spare bedroom at Treetops, and the horror of it all came flooding back. Creeping out of bed, her eyes once again streaked with tears, she tiptoed past Kerry's room, then Ellie's room, and down the stairs, where she left a note in the hall explaining that she was briefly visiting Greygates again.

Not surprisingly, she'd completely forgotten about the injured bird. Now she felt guilty for neglecting it. Hurrying down the road, Laura entered the big metal gates that gave Greygates its name. Then she made her way to the tree platform in the wood, praying that the little bird's wing would have repaired itself and that it might have managed to fly away. Somehow she felt as though its recovery would indicate that something good, no matter how small, might be garnered from the awful events that had occurred the day before.

But as she climbed the tree to the platform, her heart plummeted as she spotted the little bird's body. It lay stiff and unmoving exactly where she'd left it – it hadn't even attempted to fly. Seeing it tiny lifeless body seemed to open the floodgates once again, and Laura wept until she had no tears left. She felt as though she'd traded her parents and brother's lives for the bird's recovery, yet even that had been in vain.

Unable to see because of the tears, Laura caressed the bird's shiny feathers, wishing she had the power to inject life back into the little creature and into all those she loved, or to turn back time so that they could all still be together.

Eventually, she climbed down from the platform and, using a stick, dug a small grave in the soft damp earth beneath the tree. She cried again as she placed the tiny body in the trench. The bird had represented something wild, beautiful and untamed. But now, along with her parents and brother, it was no more. All the beauty, all the hope, had been destroyed.

Climbing up onto the platform again, Laura cursed her loss. How could she have been so overjoyed only the day before? While she'd been enjoying the pleasures of being alone and unsupervised, her beloved parents and brother had been dying.

Now she was filled with guilt, because clearly her delay had been responsible for her father's change of plan. If she hadn't kept her mother waiting in the car while she tended to the bird, her father wouldn't have been able to take a lift with her. It was all her fault, and she'd never be happy again as long as she lived. And she hoped that wherever her beloved brother was, he wouldn't know that she'd been planning to play a mean, stupid trick on him.

Tears trickled down her cheeks. How could she not have known? Why hadn't she felt something at the moment of their deaths? What had she been doing at the precise moment that the truck had ploughed into their car? She'd heard murmurings about what had happened, but adult conversations ended abruptly as soon as she appeared. She knew that people were only trying to protect her, yet she had a perverse need to know exactly what had happened. She wasn't sure if she was doing this to punish herself, or to simply understand the enormity of what had happened.

Later that afternoon, when she returned to Treetops, a gaunt and shocked Dick Morgan made a perfunctory visit, but he and Laura were unable to derive any comfort from each other's presence. She'd always viewed her grandfather as an aloof and child-phobic man, and nothing about his current visit gave her reason to change her mind. He'd had discussions with Ellie behind the closed door of her kitchen, and it soon became apparent that his granddaughter wouldn't be playing any major role in his life. It had been arranged between them that Laura would continue to reside with Ellie and Kerry until she was ready to go to university.

The only time she ever saw her grandfather again was on the day of her family's funeral. He'd aged dramatically in the two weeks since he'd visited Treetops, and Laura was shocked by how old he looked, and how unsteady he was on his feet.

As she stood beside him at the graveside, watching as the earth clattered down on the three coffins, she remained dry-eyed and remote from what was happening. It was impossible to believe that her parents and brother were here in these caskets in the ground. If she just let her mind drift away, she could believe they were still around somewhere, and any minute Pete would appear, up to devilment as usual, and try to tie her pigtails to a tree.

The thought of her brother brought a brief smile to her face. She'd always reacted with mock anger to his mischievous carry-on, but now she wished she could tell him how much she'd actually enjoyed all the tricks he'd played on her, and how much she'd learnt from just trying to outwit him.

All the factory workers were at the graveside, eyes downcast and shuffling embarrassedly as they tried not to stare at Laura and her grandfather. She could feel their confusion and concern. It was clear they had all liked 'Mr Alan' as they called him, and no one could comprehend how such an awful tragedy could have happened. Laura guessed that they were also worried about the future of the factory and their jobs, although, out of respect for her and her grandfather, they made sure that no hint of concern for their futures would blight the paying of their respects that day.

Laura risked a glance behind, to where Ellie and Kerry were standing. Both their faces were streaked with tears, and Laura found it strangely comforting to know that others were as deeply affected by her family's death as she was. While she didn't want them to suffer the agony she was suffering, she derived comfort from knowing that they cared.

CHAPTER 72

As the weeks went by, Laura began to feel more settled and secure. There hadn't been any further incidents, and she was beginning to accept that it had simply been an incompetent driver who'd almost mowed her down. Her rented apartment was comfortable and in a lovely location, Bill Maddison seemed happy with her work, and all seemed well in her world.

No one else seemed to be tailing her either, although she felt sure she'd spotted the same man only the previous day in downtown Dorrington. He looked harmless enough this time and wasn't even looking in her direction. By now she was embarrassed to think that she'd ever got her knickers in a twist over him. He was probably just a local man who'd happened to catch her eye on a day when she was feeling insecure.

By the time she'd spent three months in Dorrington, Laura had become fully acclimatised to life in the small city. In her free time, she was enjoying exploring the warren of small winding streets that led off the very modern central plaza. She was also proving popular with her colleagues, and often joined them for a night at the pub or theatre. Her lectures were always well attended, and Bill had been amazed at how many students were making the effort to get out of bed for her early morning lectures.

As she left the lecture hall one morning, Laura was feeling in exceptionally good form. She'd just given a lecture on Émile Durkheim's concept of anomie to her first year students, and there had been a definite buzz among all the young people in the hall. She loved it when they were genuinely interested in the subject, instead of regarding it as something to be regurgitated at exam time. As she headed back to her office, she was planning on reviewing some student papers in preparation for her afternoon tutorial. As she stepped into her office, she turned her phone on and noticed that there was a message in her inbox.

It said 'Number Withheld', and Laura's heart gave a little jolt. Hopefully, it was just a query from the bank, or another lecturer wanting to switch tutorials. Since Jeff hadn't bothered her for quite a while, she was a lot calmer now when her phone rang or she received a text.

Nevertheless, she decided that the sooner she opened it, the sooner she'd know what it was about, rather than leaving her overwrought mind to conjure up all sorts of scenarios.

As she opened the text and scrolled down, Laura wondered if she was about to have a heart attack.

'Hello Laura – I really did enjoy your lecture today. You know your subject so well! I was sitting in the back row, so I don't think you saw me. You didn't see me either when you were crossing that busy road, did you? I'm disappointed you left London, but glad to know where my dear wife is now living. J xx'

Frightened, Laura threw her phone across the room, feeling that it was now contaminated. How on earth could Jeff have got this latest number, and found out where she was working? Every time she thought she was simply being paranoid, something happened that confirmed to her that Jeff was behind everything that was happening to her. Was he here in Dorrington? Had he arranged for that man to follow her? It looked as though the man she'd spotted earlier wasn't so harmless after all! Jeff was also letting her know that he'd been the one who'd tried to run her down.

Laura shuddered, although she was trying to think things through sensibly. She couldn't just up and leave a job every time Jeff managed to find her. But she needed to file for divorce as soon as possible. Surely Jeff couldn't think she'd ever go back to him? While it was clear he hadn't wanted their marriage to end, surely he had to accept his own role in its demise? It was heartbreaking that his insecurity and penchant for violence had been transformed into such vindictiveness, and she wondered where it would all end.

Laura felt bad about ringing Kerry again, but there was no one else who'd understand how scared she was feeling.

"I've just received a text from Jeff – he said he'd attended my lecture today."

"Jeff? But how on earth –"

"I don't know," Laura said miserably. "I've already changed my phone number three times – how on earth could he get this latest number?"

"What exactly did it say?"

Laura read her the wording of the text.

"Look, he's just trying to scare you. He probably wasn't there at all, and his mention of the busy road is just coincidence and has nothing to do with the car that nearly ran you down. But I think you should go to the police anyway."

"What's the point? They weren't very receptive before."

"Well, the Dorrington police might be more proactive," Kerry reasoned. "Surely they can check the number, or use whatever modern techniques they have nowadays?"

"Have you got any idea where Jeff is now?"

"No, I haven't seen him for ages – not since that night in the bar." Kerry's tone softened. "Look, just because he texted you doesn't mean he knows where you are – he's just trying to unnerve you."

"Well, he's succeeding," Laura said dryly.

Kerry was beginning to sound exasperated. "Can't you just forget about him? Leave him in the past, where he belongs. He can't possibly find you in Dorrington!"

"Can't he? Then how could he refer to the 'busy road'? I wish I could believe you that it *was* a coincidence! And why was that guy following me? I'd conned myself into believing that he was just someone who lived in Dorrington. But now that Jeff has texted, I'm having to re-evaluate the whole situation."

"What? You never told me about a guy following you!"

"Yes, I've spotted him three times now," Laura said, pleased to have Kerry's full attention again. "Since Jeff texted me, everyone is looking a lot more sinister to me."

"Are you sure you weren't imagining it?" Kerry said eventually. "You are rather jumpy at the moment, so it wouldn't be surprising if you read more into situations than was really there."

"No, I caught him looking at me, and turning away quickly. Give me some credit, Kerry – Jeff hasn't caused me to lose my mind just yet!"

"Listen, I gotta go," Kerry told her. "Norma, Jack and the gang are meeting up to discuss the progress of our star project."

"This is the estuary barrage project?"

"Yeah. Now that we've won the tender, we actually have to get it built – it's a very big deal for us, and we're all very excited about it."

"Well, I wish you the best of luck," Laura told her sincerely. "Let's talk again soon."

As she rang off, Laura had the distinct impression that Kerry was losing sympathy with her, and she couldn't blame her. She had her own life to live, and who needed a paranoid nutcase for a friend? Laura made a vow to take more interest in the estuary barrage that Kerry and her team were working on – that way, she might be able to support her friend and repay a little of the kindness that Kerry had shown to her over the years. Her friend had been there for her through thick and thin, and it was time she got her own life in order. And somehow banished Jeff for good.

CHAPTER 73

A week later, Laura had an afternoon free of tutorials, so she'd decided to visit an antiquarian bookshop in downtown Dorrington. The bookshop, tucked away in a little side street in the city centre, was renowned for its range of old books, and she was looking for an out-of-print text she hoped to use in a lecture on how attitudes, language and fashions are changed through scientific discoveries.

As she headed for the bookshop, she made a point of walking through the pedestrian area as much as possible. She didn't want to give Jeff any chance to make another attempt on her life. Thankfully, there hadn't been any further texts from him, so she had to hope he just intended to unnerve her from time to time.

Suddenly, she had an uneasy feeling that she was being followed again. Her heart in her mouth, she spun around, and her jaw dropped in surprise. Was that Darren? Before she had a chance to offer a surprised and delighted greeting, he'd disappeared down a side street. Hurrying back the way she came, Laura stared down the side street where he'd turned off, but it was completely empty. Had she imagined it? She must have, since Darren would never avoid her like that.

Puzzled, Laura walked on, still uncertain as to whether she'd seen him or not. Common sense told her to accept what her eyes had seen, yet she couldn't think of any reason why her former boss would be in Dorrington. Then it crossed her mind that he could be there to see Bill Maddison. Of course, that made perfect sense. But she was still puzzled as to why he'd hurried away when she'd spotted him. She and Darren got on really well, and he'd always seemed pleased with her work. Why wouldn't he want to say hello? Then a horrible thought struck her. Was Bill unhappy with her work, and had he sent for Darren to discuss getting rid of her?

Now confused and bewildered, Laura no longer felt like browsing. Her whole world seemed to be disintegrating around her. Despite all Jeff's antics, she'd still had her career, and it had given her an identity and security. Was she now about to lose that too? Then another worrying thought occurred to her. Since Jeff claimed to have been in the university, could he somehow have caused trouble for her with the college authorities?

Laura found it impossible to deal with all this uncertainty, so she vowed to tackle Bill straight away. Although she herself had the afternoon off, she knew he'd still be working in his office. She couldn't bear the thought of Bill and Darren discussing her over a cuppa or a pint, and of her being unable to defend herself. If they'd something to say to her, she wanted it said to her directly.

With a face like thunder, Laura abandoned her trip to the bookshop and hurried back to the university. But when she entered Bill's office, he smiled warmly at her, and she was suddenly filled with misgivings. He didn't look like a man who was about to sack her.

"Bill, has Darren been to visit you, or is he planning on being here?"

Bill looked surprised. "Darren? No, why do you ask?"

"I'm sure I saw him in Dorrington town centre today."

Looking puzzled, Bill shrugged his shoulders. "I can't imagine why he'd be here – we talk on the phone from time to time, but rarely in person. Are you sure it was him?"

"Well, I thought it was," Laura said, now wondering if she'd imagined it. Since she was probably still stressed over Jeff's last text, maybe she'd simply let her imagination run riot. Perhaps in an effort to comfort herself, she'd conjured up an image of someone she knew had always been there for her. If it *was* Darren she'd seen, why would he hide from her? Surely he'd say hello? But the person she'd spotted earlier had clearly been trying to avoid her. Suddenly, she felt overwhelmed by loneliness and sadness. What did other people know that she didn't?

Laura sighed. At least her job wasn't in jeopardy. But now that Jeff clearly knew where she was, she didn't feel safe in Dorrington any more. In fact, nowhere was safe from him. Since Kerry had spotted him with a well-known drug-dealer, she'd been wavering in her belief that he worked for MI5. But regardless of whom he worked for, he clearly had contacts everywhere, and seemed able to find her no matter where she went.

"You okay, Laura?"

Waking from her reverie, Laura smiled. "Yes, of course, Bill. Obviously, I made a mistake about seeing Darren."

Bill grinned. "Darren on your mind a lot?"

Laura blushed. Her former boss was sweet and kind, but she'd never thought of him in that way.

"Sorry, I couldn't resist teasing you," Bill said, chuckling. Then his expression turned to one of concern. "But you look stressed – is there anything wrong?"

Laura nodded, suddenly feeling overwhelmed by everything and deciding to tell him the truth. "I'm not sure how long I can stay here, Bill . . ."

Pulling up a chair, Laura told him all about Jeff, and about everything that had happened since she'd moved to Dorrington.

Bill said nothing while she talked but when she'd finished he let out a long low whistle. "Wow! I'd no idea things were so bad – is there anything we can do here at the university?"

Laura shook her head.

"Then I think you need to go to the police – I've always found the Dorrington police to be very helpful – I'll come with you, if you like."

Laura shook her head. "The trouble is – I've nothing concrete to show them," she explained. "To an outsider, Jeff's text would just read like a message from an admirer. He's too clever – only I know the menace behind the message. As for the out-of-control car, and the man who seemed to be following me – it's all rather tenuous, isn't it?"

309

"Well, we'll bump up security round the campus – make sure no outsiders can gain access to the lecture theatres," Bill told her kindly. "I'll have a word with our security team straight away – don't worry, Laura, we won't let this guy get near you." He looked at her sympathetically. "Promise me you'll go to the police?"

Laura nodded.

Thanking him, she left his office. But as she made her way down the deserted corridor, she couldn't help shivering. It was all very well to be protected while doing her job, but what about at other times? Was she going to have to stay on full alert for the rest of her life? And now that Jeff had managed to track her down again, was there any point in staying in Dorrington? There seemed to be eyes watching her everywhere, and she wondered if she was really losing her mind.

Laura angrily brushed away a tear. On the other hand, if she'd really spotted Darren and he'd avoided speaking to her, it didn't augur well for returning to her job in London either. What was happening, and why did she feel that everything in her life was spiralling out of control? Bill was right – it was time to talk to the Dorrington police. And she'd do it right away.

CHAPTER 74

Ellie lay alone in her room, the blinds drawn. This was the only place where she could cry in peace. She was supposed to be the strong one, the competent one, the person now charged with helping Laura get through the loss of her family. But how could she go on, without her beloved Alan? That was the trouble with a secret relationship – there was no one with whom she could share her own distress. Her heart was breaking, and she pressed the pillow to her mouth to prevent the two girls from hearing her crying.

She wished she could die and be with Alan, but young Kerry needed her, and she'd promised Dick Morgan that she'd rear Laura on his behalf. She felt sorry for the old man – he, too, had lost his beloved daughter and grandson. Yet neither she nor he was able to share their pain with each other. Instead, she'd reached a very business-like arrangement with him, whereby Laura would reside at Treetops and he would pay her a generous monthly sum for the child's upkeep. Which was just as well, since otherwise she was virtually penniless. While Alan had been alive, she'd been assured of her monthly stipend, but now she and her daughter had little personal income any more. It also looked inevitable that Kerry would have to leave her expensive private school and start attending the local comprehensive.

Ellie wiped away her tears, fingering the gold and diamond ring Alan had given her all those years ago. She'd loved Alan too much to blame him for leaving them unprotected. He hadn't expected to die, had he? And she'd never given a thought to suddenly finding herself without him. She'd loved him more than life itself and, despite all her blustering, she'd been content to be the woman he loved in secret. In fact, being his secret wife had given her a special joy that had appealed to her sense of the dramatic, and had always kept their passion on the boil. Now, however, it was cold comfort. There was no one with whom she could share her special brand of pain. Society showed no kindness to the mistress – she was simply the woman who'd broken society's rules. She wiped her tears. Now, at least, her own secret didn't matter any more.

A week later, Ellie was surprised to find Dick Morgan on her doorstep. Inclining his head in an old-fashioned gesture of respect, he made it clear that he expected to be invited in.

"Mr Morgan, come in," Ellie said, trying her best to smile. "You're very welcome. Would you like a cup of tea?"

Nodding, he followed her into the kitchen, and Ellie hoped that he wasn't there to tell her that he was reducing the amount of her monthly payment for Laura. Any less money and they'd all be in trouble.

"Did you want to see Laura? I'm afraid she and Kerry have gone cycling into the village –"

Dick Morgan shook his head. "No, it was you I wanted to see. In fact, I'm relieved the girls aren't here, so I'll get to the point."

Ellie waited nervously, certain that a further disaster was about to be visited on them all. Since the factory was already up for sale, perhaps Mr Morgan intended going abroad and taking Laura with him? She'd certainly miss the child, of whom she was genuinely fond. And the absence of the monthly cheque for Laura's upkeep would mean that she'd have to consider finding some kind of work right away. Wouldn't it be ironic if she had to apply to the new factory owners for her old job back?

Dick Morgan took a sip of his tea before speaking.

"It's come to my notice that my late son-in-law had been paying a monthly amount for your daughter, as well as for her education."

Ellie felt as though her heart was about to stop. Her mouth dried up and she felt unable to say anything.

"I don't know why he's been paying it, and I don't want to know," he added sternly. "I have my own suspicions, but I'm not asking you to confirm or deny them. I just wanted to assure you that I'll continue to pay for your daughter until she's finished her education. I don't see that children should pay for the sins of others, and it's good for Laura to have such a close friend as your daughter."

Ellie nodded, hoping that her face wasn't as red as it felt. "Thank you, Mr Morgan – I really appreciate that," she said.

Since there seemed nothing more to say, Dick Morgan stood up from the table and made his way towards the door, leaving most of his tea untouched.

He paused for a moment, his hand on the doorframe.

"My daughter Sylvia really liked you," he said suddenly, his stern expression softening. "She once told me that she wished she could've had you for a friend."

Ellie lowered her head. "I really liked her too," she whispered, blinking away the tears in her eyes. "If things had been different, I think we'd definitely have become the best of friends."

Later that night, as Ellie contemplated Dick Morgan's generous agreement to pay Kerry's expenses and school fees, she felt the tiniest stab of guilt at taking his money. But she was doing it for Kerry, wasn't she? It wasn't as though she was hurting anyone – there was no one who needed to know anyway.

Surely fate couldn't have been so cruel? She'd never told anyone what had happened that awful night thirteen years ago, and she'd totally blocked it from her mind. That way, she hadn't needed to face any unpalatable truth. Because once she did, everything would change, and she refused to let it. But sometimes, as she watched her sturdily-built young daughter, her dark head bent over some toy she was dismantling, feelings of guilt and regret overwhelmed her.

Anyway, now that her beloved Alan was dead, it didn't matter any more, and Dick Morgan wasn't exactly short of money. She'd managed to keep everyone happy while doing the best she could for her daughter.

But try as she might, she could never manage to totally obliterate that night from her memory. But she'd made a decision, all those years ago, to deny it space in her head. But sometimes her mind played tricks, and the memories invaded her dreams at night, or caught her unprepared during the day. At times like that, she'd feel physically sick as she tried to quell the tide of revulsion that rose up inside her. It seemed that the more she longed to forget something, the more her mind wanted to keep reminding her of it.

Now, the pain of Alan's death was bringing that night back into focus. All the painful events of her life seemed to have relentlessly forced their way into her brain and were making her feel terrified as she faced a future alone. "Oh Alan," she whispered tearfully into her pillow. "I hope you knew how much I loved you . . ."

CHAPTER 75

Having visited the local Dorrington police station that very afternoon, Laura wasn't quite sure how she felt. While the police officer had been courteous, he didn't hold out much hope of nailing Jeff.

"Your ex would have used a throw-away phone," he told her gently. "And the SIM card will have been destroyed by now." He gave her a sympathetic smile. "I'm sorry we can't be more helpful, but these situations usually settle down over time. By your own admission, he isn't hassling you quite as much as in the past, so it sounds like he might be getting tired of bothering you."

"So that's it?" Laura asked peevishly. "He just gets away with it? He can try to run me down, hassle me any time he likes, yet nothing happens to him?" She glared at the officer. "And what about the two people following me? The same guy has followed me twice – and maybe at other times, too, for all I know – and I'm positive it's not a coincidence!"

The officer looked contrite. "I'm sorry, Ms Thornton, I'll make a note of it in the logbook, and if anything else happens, don't hesitate to let us know –"

"A note in a logbook won't help me if I'm dead!" Laura told him, flouncing out the door of the station.

When her mobile rang later that evening, Laura checked the number. It was one she didn't recognise, and at first she didn't bother answering it. It was probably a bogus call, or Jeff on the line, and she didn't think she could cope with any more hassle. But when the same number rang again later, she felt so angry that she grabbed the phone, took a deep breath and risked pressing the button.

"Hello?"

"Ms Thornton, this is Detective Sergeant Andy Sheeran, from Islington Police station in London."

Laura's heart began to thump uncomfortably. Was he really a police officer or was this just another trick that Jeff had thought up?

"The police in Dorrington have been in touch with us about some incidents you reported –"

"Yes?"

The man's voice was curt. "We'd like you to come here, Ms Thornton, as soon as possible. I have some information that may be of concern to you."

Laura sighed, wishing he wouldn't talk such gobbledygook. What on earth did 'of concern to you' mean? And why couldn't he just say what was on his mind, rather than dragging her to London, to be told something he could probably have said over the phone?

Laura sighed. "Look, if it's that important, why can't I just go to the local police station? I'm rather busy at the moment –"

"Ms Thornton, what I have to tell you is best said in person. I'd rather you came here, and please, make it as soon as possible."

"Okay, okay – I'll get to you tomorrow afternoon."

"Thank you, Ms Thornton. See you then."

Ringing off, Laura phoned her colleague Alison. Then she left a voice message on Bill's phone in the Sociology Department office: "Sorry Bill, but I'm afraid I won't be in tomorrow – I've already rung Alison, and she's agreed to take my lectures instead. I need to visit London urgently, so I'll be taking the first train in the morning."

Before she left Dorrington, Laura checked with the local police station, and they confirmed that Detective Sergeant Andy Sheeran really did exist, and that it was genuinely urgent she visit the

Islington police station as soon as possible.

As she sat on the train, Laura gazed pensively out the window. Something else was definitely wrong. She'd expected to stay at Kerry's apartment while in London, but when she'd rung her friend, she'd been distinctly evasive, fobbing her off with excuses. This offhand treatment was making Laura feel decidedly uneasy – why was her best friend giving her the brush-off? She was also still reeling from having seen Darren in Dorrington, yet he'd deliberately turned away when she spotted him. It made her feel sad and worried that the people she cared about most were now avoiding her. What on earth was going on?

At Islington Police Station, Laura was ushered into Detective Sergeant Andy Sheeran's office as soon as she arrived.

"Ms Thornton, please sit down."

Laura dropped into the chair facing the detective's desk. She now recognised him as the unhelpful officer she'd spoken to when she'd returned to the police station expecting to hear that Jeff had been rapped over the knuckles. Instead, he'd been downright rude to her, playing a recording of her own voice as she screamed at Jeff, and almost implying that he was the one who needed protection.

Laura now glared at him, still annoyed at being dragged away from Dorrington, especially since her earlier experiences at Islington police station hadn't been particularly helpful.

"Would you like a cup of tea?"

Laura's mouth dropped open. What was going on? Why was he suddenly being so polite? Had he been dragged before some disciplinary panel and challenged about his earlier lack of courtesy?

"No, thanks."

The officer shuffled some papers on his desk before eventually looking straight at her.

"I'm sorry to have to tell you this – but your ex-husband is dead. He died two months ago."

Laura's jaw dropped open. What? No, it wasn't possible! Then her eyes began to fill with tears. Even though she and Jeff had parted, she was still shocked and saddened. She'd once loved him deeply.

"Oh my God. W-what happened?"

The police officer cleared his throat. "Mr Jones got into a brawl while on remand in prison, and he was fatally stabbed."

Laura looked stunned. "In prison? What was he doing there?"

Momentarily, the officer's expression softened. "On your previous visit here, I was particularly interested in what you'd said about your husband's parents, his claims of being in MI5, and the fact that you thought he might have murdered someone." He twirled his pen between his fingers. "After you'd left the station, I looked up the files and discovered that there were a lot of question marks over his parents' deaths. I talked to the officers who'd worked on the case, and they all felt that Mr Jones definitely had something to do with his father's death, although they hadn't been able to prove it at the time." The police officer looked grim. "Thanks to you, we got the case reopened – and this time, the advances in DNA enabled us to get the evidence we needed to prosecute him. He was in jail awaiting trial for the murder of his father when he was killed." He looked at her closely. "Did you know that he strangled his father with his bare hands, then used a rope to make it look like suicide?"

Laura shivered, suddenly recalling Jeff's remark about threatening to kill her 'too'.

"No, I didn't. And I'm glad I didn't know that while I was married to him!"

"Although we only got him for one murder, we're fairly certain he was responsible for others too," the detective added. "Several witnesses who were due to testify at drug-dealers' trials conveniently disappeared, and we believe he was the one who killed them." He looked at her tentatively. "The Drug Squad were also running surveillance on your ex-husband, but the people at the top of the supply chain are always the most difficult to put away. Of course, we now know that you weren't aware that he was one of the country's major drug dealers."

The colour drained from Laura's face as she shook her head, suddenly understanding why Jeff had been so vehemently against the legalisation of drugs – it would have destroyed his own illegal business! So his MI5 claims had just been a cover to fool his gullible wife, and Kerry had been right all along.

"But you said he died two months ago – why on earth wasn't I told before now?"

DS Sheeran grimaced. "I'm sorry, Ms Thornton – we had our reasons. When you first disappeared from London, we wondered if your ex-husband had bumped you off. The chap at your university wasn't willing to reveal your whereabouts, but we checked your credit-card usage, and discovered that you'd been using it in Dorrington."

Laura gasped. "So that was *you* who was following me?"

DS Sheeran nodded.

"You scared the hell out of me – I thought you were one of Jeff's henchmen!"

The officer gave an apologetic smile. "After Mr Jones was killed, we wondered if your original complaints to the police had been part of an elaborate plan to distance yourself from your husband's drug empire, with a view to taking it over after his death."

"What? You mean you thought *I* might have planned his murder?"

DS Sheeran shrugged his shoulders. "Stranger things have happened. That's why I followed you to Dorrington – we had to find out whether or not you were involved. Obviously, we know now that you had nothing to do with your husband's death or with running his business."

Still in shock, Laura said nothing.

"But when you levelled further accusations against your ex-husband while you were in Dorrington – after he was dead – alarm bells started ringing, and we began to wonder what on earth was going on."

Laura slumped in her chair.

He closed the file on his desk and looked at her closely. "Do you realise what that means?"

Laura shook her head, looking blankly at him.

"It means your husband couldn't have been the person you claim was targeting you."

Laura's mouth dropped open. "W-what?"

"Someone else must have been trying to harm you. Do you have any idea who it might be? If you're prepared to register a complaint, we'll investigate this person or persons immediately."

The colour drained from Laura's face. If not Jeff, who else could it be? Her mind was rapidly racing through all the recent events that had happened, and the people she'd trusted to keep her whereabouts secret. She still didn't understand why Darren had been in Dorrington, but he wouldn't have any reason to harm her . . .

Then her eyes filled with tears. No, no – it couldn't possibly have been. No, definitely not. How could she even think such a thought? No, no, no – on the other hand, who else would have known all the personal details of her life . . . Laura shook her head angrily. How could she think such a thing, even for a second?

The police officer looked at her astutely. "I can see that you've someone in mind," he said gently.

Laura shook her head. No, she couldn't even bring herself to mention this person's name. Because if she said it, she'd be admitting that she'd actually given consideration, however briefly, to the ridiculous notion . . .

Jumping up, Laura grabbed her coat and rushed out of the police station, with the detective in hot pursuit.

"Ms Thornton, please come back –"

Tears now blinding her, Laura hurried along the road. Her mobile rang, but she didn't answer it, guessing that it was probably the police officer begging her to return to the station. Then she heard someone calling her name, but she ignored them. She didn't have time for pleasantries right now. She had to find out the truth, and there was only one way to do it.

Just as she reached the corner of the street where Kerry's apartment was, Avril, the estate agent, was coming out of a building on the other side. As usual, she was clutching her portfolio of leaflets and teetering on her six-inch heels. Waving goodbye to the clients who'd been viewing the property, she crossed the road to where Laura was now approaching.

"Well, hello! How nice to see you, Laura! I thought you'd moved abroad somewhere? What brings you to this part of the world?"

"I'm just on my way to Kerry's place," Laura explained.

Avril looked confused. "But she doesn't live here any more – have you forgotten?"

Laura's jaw dropped. "What do you mean?"

"Well, you know that she's taken over your old apartment in Green Street –"

"No, I don't," Laura said tersely. "When did that happen?"

Avril suddenly looked worried, sensing a potential problem. "Oh dear! After the fire, when you gave notice that you were leaving, your friend contacted me and said she'd like to rent it when it had been repaired and refurbished. And that she'd be interested in buying it when the vendor was ready to sell . . ." Her voice faltered. "I assumed you knew . . . you're saying she didn't tell you?"

"No, she didn't," Laura said.

"Oh dear, that was a bit rude, wasn't it?" Avril muttered. "I mean, it's a great place, so maybe she felt she had to snap it up before anyone else showed interest – but I do think she should have mentioned it to you –"

"Sorry, Avril, I've got to go," Laura said, smiling apologetically as she turned to leave, hoping that Avril wouldn't think she was in any way responsible for her ill humour.

"Okay, Laura – but let me know if you're looking for another flat around the Green Street area," Avril called after her. "I've got a really nice one on the books at the moment –"

But already Laura was hurrying down the street towards the nearest Underground station.

CHAPTER 76

In the lobby of the Green Street apartments, Laura rushed past Albert, one of the concierges, before he had time to react, waving to him and banking on the fact that since she'd once lived here, he'd remember her and would let her through without a fuss.

When Laura knocked at the door of the apartment, Kerry looked shocked as she opened her door.

"Laura! How did you –?"

"How did I find out you'd moved in here? It doesn't matter – aren't you going to invite me in?"

Kerry gave a weak smile, but it was obvious that she'd been caught out.

As she stepped inside, Laura could see that the apartment was already looking very different from when she'd lived there. The fire damage had been completely repaired, and Kerry's style was already evident in the different range of furnishings. It looked as though she'd been working on one of her projects at a big desk in the corner of the living room, which was piled high with books and papers.

"You didn't waste any time before putting your own stamp on it, did you?"

Kerry rallied. "Well, you were right – it's a fabulous flat," she said. "The amount of light it gets is wonderful, and I envied you so much when you moved in here. Why shouldn't I take it over when you left?"

"It would have been a courtesy to let me know – I'd have been pleased for you. But it never crossed my mind that you could afford the rent and the service charge, much less buy it."

Kerry smiled malevolently. "Well, I wanted to stake my claim, because I expect to have the money *very* soon."

As the two women stared at each other, Laura licked her lips. Her mouth was dry as she tried to find the words she wanted to say, but no sound would come out. As she stood there, Kerry went into the kitchen, returning with two glasses of juice. It was just the kind of thing that Kerry usually did, and it lent an air of normality to a bizarre situation.

At first, Laura ignored the drink, but her throat and mouth seemed unbelievably dry, and she wanted to be able to articulate her case clearly, so she took the glass and gulped the juice down rapidly. The whole situation still seemed unreal, but her mouth felt fresher and her tongue now seemed able to form the words she wanted.

"Jeff is dead – he's been dead for two months," she said. "He was killed while on remand in prison – they finally nailed him for killing his father – and you were right, he was also involved in drug-dealing." She took a deep breath. "So you know what that means, don't you?"

One look at Kerry's face told Laura all she needed to know.

Kerry shrugged her shoulders. "Oops, my mistake. It looks like the game is over," she said, giving an apologetic smile. "I'd hoped to have fun with you for a little while longer, but it looks like you've figured out what I've been up to . . ."

Laura's heart sank. She'd been desperately hoping that Kerry wouldn't be the one who'd been targeting her. She'd been positive her friend could offer some logical explanation for what had been happening to her.

"But how – I mean, Jeff was hassling me, wasn't he? So I don't understand –"

"Oh, make no mistake, your husband was a violent, nasty thug," Kerry added, finishing her own juice. "At first, I was really worried about him – I thought he'd make certain I lost all control over you. But I soon realised that Jeff was the icing on the cake – I loathed him, but he served my purpose admirably." She smirked at Laura's incredulous expression. "Think of your impulsive personality, Laura. I knew that if I said I didn't like Jeff, you'd fall for him like a ton of bricks, and find every reason to save him. I knew you'd eventually have to leave him. But by then I'd be able to ensure that Jeff continued to terrify you, long after you'd broken up."

Laura's voice was barely a whisper. "But why? What purpose did Jeff serve? I thought you were my best friend! I don't see why you'd want to –"

Kerry didn't answer, and Laura longed to hit her. Instead, she lashed out with her hand and sent all the books and documents on the desk flying to the floor.

"*Answer me!*" she screamed as both women surveyed the mess of papers now spread all over the floor. Simultaneously, their eyes were drawn to a pile of photos lying among the debris, but neither of them seemed able to move or speak.

At last, Laura found her voice, although it only came out as a squeak. "So you were the one who stole my family photos!"

She bent down and picked up a photo of her father, which had now been put into a frame. In it, he was smiling at the camera, looking carefree and happy. Laura stared at it, mystified. "Why did you put the picture of my father into a frame?"

"Because he's my father as well!"

"W-what?"

Kerry sneered. "Poor Laura – you thought you had the perfect family, didn't you? But all the time, your dad was doing it with my mum – and I was the result!"

"I don't believe you!"

Kerry shrugged her shoulders. "It doesn't matter what you believe. How do you think I could go to the same posh school as you? Because your father – our father – paid all my school fees. And he was planning on leaving you all, to come to live with Mum and me!"

"My father would never have left my mother!" Laura said angrily. She was finding it difficult to reconcile all this new information with what she remembered of her parents' lives. They had always seemed happy, but then, at twelve years of age, who could understand the nuances of adult conversation, gestures and glances, the heartbreak that could lie behind smiling faces?

Kerry sighed. "You may well be right – history doesn't show all that many successful transitions from mistress to wife. But I actually heard him tell Mum he was coming to live with us."

Kerry's face crumpled, and Laura thought she detected the glint of tears in her eyes as she spoke.

"You had a father every day of your life – I hadn't! Why should you have had everything? He was my father too, but I was never recognised. I was just his dirty little secret!"

Laura was experiencing a complex range of emotions. On the one hand, she hated what Kerry was saying about her parents, but she was desperate to understand, even if it meant learning unpalatable truths.

"H-how did you find out about this supposed affair?"

"It was easy enough – one day I came home early – tennis lessons had been cancelled – and I discovered your father's car hidden in the bushes behind the house."

Kerry looked steadily at Laura. "I could hear my mother and your father in her bedroom, so I crept up into the loft above her room, and was able to peep down through a crack in the ceiling – and I saw what they were doing."

"B-but what made you think you were his child?"

"I heard them talking about it," Kerry said triumphantly. "When they were lying in bed, Mum said that it was time I was told who my real father was. But he begged her to wait – he said the time wasn't right yet, and that they'd tell everyone I was his daughter once he'd left your mother. He promised Mum he'd do it very soon." Her voice trembled. "I crept back outside, and watched from the outhouse as he drove off afterwards. Then I pretended to come home at the usual time, and Mum never suspected a thing." Her voice rose. "I waited day after day, week after week, for him to make a public announcement about it. But when nothing happened, I figured it was time to help things along myself."

"W-what do you mean?"

Kerry's face contorted in anger.

"You were always impulsive and emotional, weren't you, Laura? That's why you weren't in the damned car when you should have been! You went off to save that injured bird – so you escaped the death I'd planned for you, and I lost my father instead!"

Laura was bewildered. "W-what are you talking about?" She suddenly felt as though the ground was giving way beneath her feet. No, it couldn't be true – no, no no!

Kerry grimaced. "Back then, I was young and naïve, and I thought I could create the perfect family. I figured that if you all died, my father would come to live with Mum and me, and we'd be a real family at last."

The colour had drained from Laura's face. "But I remember you crying your heart out when you heard about the crash!" Laura said, bewildered. "We cried together – were you acting then, too?"

Kerry gave a clipped smile. "I didn't need to pretend – I was devastated! Your father – my father – wasn't supposed to be in the car that day! If I'd realised that his BMW was being repaired, I'd have waited until another day!" Kerry glared at her. "So you see, I was genuinely crying because I'd lost my dream of a real family – yet somehow *you* managed to survive!"

A tidal wave of rage welled up inside Laura. She longed to use her fist to wipe the smirk off Kerry's face, but there was more she needed to uncover first.

"What did you do to the car?"

"I tampered with the steering the night before." Kerry smiled triumphantly. "Remember that afternoon when we all went to collect your father's new BMW from the showroom? Well, I learnt everything I needed to know from one of the mechanics in the workshop there!" She grinned. "He thought I was just a nosy kid, but I got him to answer some very pertinent questions! That's why you couldn't find me to fix your skateboard – I was in your garage, underneath your mother's car!"

"You merciless bitch – how could you!"

"Do you think I cared about you? I wanted a family of my own!"

Laura stared at her incredulously. "All the times that you were crying, I thought it was out of concern for me! And your poor mother – she must have been heartbroken, too!"

Kerry's eyes narrowed. "That day when we got news of the crash – my mother ran off to Greygates to comfort *you*! Even though my heart was breaking, there was no one there to comfort *me*!"

Laura said nothing, thinking how devastated Ellie would have been to know the lengths to which her own daughter had gone in pursuit of her dream family.

"I hope you know that my mother only took you in because she needed the money, and none of your relatives wanted you!" Kerry added spitefully. "My mum was left penniless when our father died – despite all his protestations of love, he made no financial provision for either her or me!"

"Well, he wasn't exactly expecting to die, was he?" Laura retorted. "We'll never know what he intended to do, because you killed him! And anyway, your mother was always very kind to me – you destroyed her life, too."

In the silence that filled the room, Laura felt as though her heart would break. Everything she'd believed had suddenly been taken away from her, and she felt as though a giant rug had been pulled from beneath her feet. A wave of nausea swept over her, and she leaned against the desk to steady herself. She was suddenly feeling very woozy. "But all those years we were friends, all those times you were so kind to me – were you really pretending?" she asked at last.

Kerry shrugged her shoulders. "You really *were* my best friend, up until the day I found out I was his daughter. Then everything changed." Tears formed in Kerry's eyes, but she wiped them away angrily. "There were lots of times when I actually forgot how much I hated you, and I genuinely found myself caring about you. I'm human, after all. But at the end of the day, it's hard to forget how unfair it was that I was never recognised as Alan Thornton's first-born daughter."

"Maybe he intended looking after you, but you didn't give him a chance, did you?" Laura retorted. "You killed him instead! You destroyed your own future!"

Thoughts were tumbling through Laura's brain, in no particular order. Her head was spinning, and she was feeling increasingly dizzy. There were so many things she wanted to find out. Surely this was all just a big silly joke – although nothing that was being said sounded particularly funny.

"You still haven't answered me about Jeff –"

Kerry laughed. "Poor gullible Laura! It was almost like taking candy from a baby!"

"But it was him stalking me, wasn't it?" Laura pleaded, "I know he made all those phone calls, and I had to change my number –"

Kerry looked exasperated, as though she was dealing with a particularly stupid child. "Oh, Laura – you really are a dolt, aren't you? You never really checked the number, did you? If you'd looked properly, instead of reacting so emotionally, you'd have seen that one digit was different from Jeff's number. It was me who was calling you. I bought a throw-away phone with a number as close to Jeff's as I could get."

Laura felt winded, as though Kerry had punched her in the gut. She felt as though she'd morphed into *Alice through the Looking Glass*, and that she'd stepped into some strange world where nothing was as it seemed.

"What about the '*Good Luck in Your New Home*' card? Surely that was Jeff?"

Kerry laughed. "No, it wasn't. I paid an out-of-work actor friend, no questions asked, who looked reasonably like Jeff. I knew that the concierge would describe him to you as tall and blond, and you'd jump to the conclusion I wanted you to."

"And the TV repair man?"

"Same guy."

"But Jeff did phone the estate agent –"

Kerry chuckled. "What a fool you are, Laura – you almost deserve to be deceived! No, my actor friend made the call and gave Jeff's name."

Laura was shocked, and another wave of nausea swept over her.

"So Jeff never wanted to live in the same apartment block?"

Kerry sniggered. "No, he didn't. I think Jeff actually got over you quite quickly. You've always had a tendency to overestimate your pulling-power."

Laura gave a jolt as another thought entered her mind. "The listening device under the coffee table – who put it there?"

Kerry smiled, pleased at her own ingenuity. "I did, of course! I bought it and installed it under the table – I just pretended to find it there, to scare you."

Laura's mind was still doing somersaults. "But the fire in my apartment – Jeff started that, didn't he?"

Kerry giggled. "Wrong. It was clever old me again! I used my out-of-work actor friend to set the scene. With his hair darkened and dressed as a barista, he arrived at the concierge's desk, offering Jim a free coffee of his choice, courtesy of a new, fictitious café opening shortly. Needless to say, I'd made it my business to find out Jim's favourite coffee in advance." She grinned. "I crushed one of those strong sedatives you got from the doctor into the coffee, so Jim was soon fast asleep. Then I was able to sneak past him, enter your apartment with the spare key I'd borrowed, then turn on the cooker and place the pot of cooking oil on it. I returned the key and sneaked past poor comatose Jim again."

"So I need never have gone to Dorrington."

Kerry nodded angrily. "You caused me a lot of hassle by your impulsive decision to move so far away. I had to take time off work to go after you –"

"So that was you in the car that tried to run me down?"

Kerry smirked at her. "I just wanted to scare you – and I did, didn't I? And when you rang me to whine about what had happened to you, you thought I was in London – but I was actually staying close by, in a Dorrington hotel!"

"And the text?"

Kerry nodded again.

"Oh God. Why would you do all that?"

"Why?" Kerry's lip curled. "Are you a total fool? Because you've always got everything you wanted –"

"Like my parents and brother dying?" Laura retorted. "You destroyed my life all those years ago! What can you possibly want from me now?"

Kerry grinned. "Your money, of course. If you're dead, it'll all be mine!".

As the two women stared at each other, Laura wondered if she could simply be having a bad dream. But if that was the case, why couldn't she wake up? She was also feeling very tired – perhaps the impact of all this horrific information was starting to addle her brain . . .

By now, Kerry's mood had darkened even further. "You self-centred bitch, you never gave me any of the money you got – yet half of it was rightly mine!"

Laura felt like exploding. "I never used any of the money because I felt guilty about inheriting it – I thought it was my fault that my family died – now I know it was you who was responsible!"

A thought suddenly occurred to Laura. "If you hated me so much, why didn't you want me to tell Jeff about the money? He'd have wheedled it out of me before long, or he'd have tried to get a chunk of it through the divorce courts. Then you'd have had the satisfaction of seeing me in very reduced circumstances."

Kerry's lip curled. "You still don't get it, do you? He'd have been spending *my* money! I wasn't going to let that happen. That money is rightfully mine!" She grinned. "Needless to say, I was very relieved when you miscarried – I didn't want anyone else muscling in on the money either!"

Laura was stunned by Kerry's casual cruelty. But her hatred had been building for so long that it probably seemed normal to her now.

"Okay, let me work this out," Laura said bitterly. "You killed my family, and now you're planning on getting rid of me. But how do you intend getting your hands on my money? How do you know I haven't left it all to a charity?"

Kerry looked pleased with herself. "I've sneaked a look at your will – I know you've left everything to me. Thanks, Laura – you've made things very easy for me."

"What do you mean?"

"You just gave me the idea yourself, when you said that Jeff had killed his father, but arranged the scene to look like a suicide." Kerry wrung her hands in mock horror. "I'll tell the police that you've been very depressed lately. That the deaths of your parents and brother have been weighing heavily on your mind, and that you've mentioned suicide several times."

She gave a sigh. "Jeff's death was probably the last straw – I mean, getting news like that would clearly unbalance your mind, wouldn't it? You were very upset when you arrived here, but I eventually managed to calm you down – or so I thought. Then I went off into the kitchen to cook us dinner, and you repaid my kindness by hanging yourself from the banisters as soon as I'd turned my back. I'll sob and tell the police that I feel responsible – if only I hadn't left that rope stashed in the cupboard beneath the sink –" She smirked again. "And I'll be distraught when I ring for help." Putting on a sorrowful voice, she mimicked calling the police. "Oh help, please – my friend has just hanged herself!"

"If you've felt so strongly about this for years, why didn't you kill me before now?" Laura asked, bewildered. "Why wait?"

"Since you escaped the death I'd originally planned for you, I decided to have some fun with you before finishing you off. Anyway, I thought it better to wait until you'd divorced Jeff, just to make sure that there couldn't be any complications over your will. I doubted that a dodgy character like him would risk challenging it anyway – but now that he's dead, I don't need to worry any more. Your money will soon be mine! Besides, if I'd got rid of you earlier, I'd have missed all the pleasure of taking revenge."

"But what have I done to you? I don't deserve your hatred!" Laura screamed. "It was our father and your mother who created this situation! They're the ones who had an affair! Why do you have to avenge yourself on me?"

Kerry gave a bitter laugh. "Because you were born with a silver spoon in your stupid mouth, that's why! You even got into prep school early, because your parents could pull strings for you! I should have been the daughter who had everything – I was born three months before you! But because my mum was only the mistress, you got all the attention! I knew he was my dad, yet I still had to call him 'Mr Thornton'!"

Laura's eyes filled up with tears again as she remembered her father, and for the blink of an eye she could empathise with Kerry's loss before the rage returned. Kerry's very existence confirmed that her father had had another secret life. Briefly she wondered if her mother had known about the affair, and if she'd been aware that Kerry was her husband's daughter? She felt an urge to cry, hoping that her poor mother had been oblivious to the situation.

"Oh my God." Another thought had just crossed Laura's mind. "Steve –?"

"Yeah, that was me – I wrote that stuff on his car, then headed home and waited until you arrived back in tears." Kerry laughed. "You should be thanking me, Laura. I saved you from that guy – he clearly thought more of his car than he did of you!"

Then Kerry's expression changed from mirth to anger again.

"It sickens me the way guys are always falling for your simpering charms. All your life, they've been fawning over you –"

"My God, you're jealous!" Laura had finally found Kerry's Achilles' heel.

Kerry shrugged her shoulders. "You're right – I've always hated you for your money and your looks. Well, you won't have either for much longer!"

Laura looked puzzled. "But you inherited Treetops when your mother died! How many people are lucky enough to be given a fine house with acres of land attached, on the outskirts of London? You got a million and a half when you sold it!"

Kerry shrugged her shoulders. "What's a million and a half when I should have had gazillions? It's ironic, isn't it? Because of me, you inherited the entire proceeds of the sale of the factory and your magnificent family home – you didn't have to share it with anyone!"

At this point, Laura could barely contain herself any longer. "You nasty, vicious bitch!" she screamed. "I'd have gladly shared the money with Pete – and even with you! If you'd told me you were my father's daughter, I'd have given you an equal share too! I'm not obsessed with money like you are!"

"Easy to say when you have so much, eh?" Kerry inspected her nails. "Anyway, you took your time about it, didn't you? How long were you going to make me wait?"

"Believe it or not, I'd actually decided to give you a chunk of the money as soon as my divorce became final. You knew I couldn't bear to touch the money earlier, because I felt so guilty! I thought I'd killed my family, whereas *you* were the guilty one all along!"

"Well, I could hardly tell you the truth, could I?" Kerry said, grimacing. "Just my luck that you developed a guilty conscience! Anyway, I no longer need any handout from you – I'll have it all soon enough."

Laura felt her eyes closing. Why was she feeling so tired just when she needed to be alert? "You're out of your mind . . ." she managed to say.

"Maybe I am, but you probably didn't realise that I slipped a sedative into your juice – the same one I gave to Jim, the concierge – and I can see that already you're beginning to feel drowsy. When you're comatose, it'll be easy for me to get a rope around your neck and throw you over the banisters."

Laura's eyelids were fluttering, and she was finding it difficult to keep her eyes open. "But the police will discover that you've filled me with sedatives –"

"Don't worry, I've thought that through as well," Kerry said, smiling. "I'll volunteer the information that you've been taking a lot of medication lately, to cope with all your stress. Remember those sedatives you got from the doctor, but never took? Well, I nicked them when I set your place on fire. Now I'll be able to produce the box from your handbag – with your name clearly on it – and show it to the police. I'll remove most of the tablets first, of course – proving that you'd been dosing yourself regularly."

Laura tried in vain to move towards the door, but she was already beginning to feel the effects of the tablets. She found herself struggling to stand, and she felt as though a terrible weight was pressing down on her, and she was finding it difficult to keep her eyes open. Although she willed herself to stay on her feet, she was overwhelmed by the desire to sleep, although her very life depended on staying awake . . .

"After you've topped yourself, I'll find you, and run screaming out the door," Kerry told her. "But not, of course, until I'm certain you're dead."

As Laura struggled feebly, Kerry laughed. "You're fighting a losing battle – those pills are pretty strong. Of course, I'll weep and moan when you're gone – that's what you'd expect from your best friend, isn't it?"

Kerry seemed possessed of inhuman strength just when Laura felt at her weakest.

"I hadn't actually planned on killing you today," Kerry added, as she dragged Laura along the mezzanine floor towards the banisters. "I'd intended having a bit more fun with you first. But since the news of Jeff's death, I don't need to delay my plans any longer. And as you've actually turned up at my door, we might as well get it over and done with."

Even though drugged, Laura tried to call out, but no words would come. Somewhere in the deepest recesses of her brain she realised that her organs were shutting down and she was falling into a deep sleep. And if Kerry had her way, it would be a permanent sleep . . .

"Laura! Are you in there?"

Unable to speak, Laura could only make a gurgling sound in reply. Dimly, she was aware of a banging sound. Perhaps it was coming from the entrance hall . . . Perhaps she'd imagined that someone was calling her name?

By now, Kerry had managed to tie the rope to the banisters, slip the noose around Laura's neck and tighten it. The banging and the shouting seemed to be reverberating in Laura's brain as Kerry redoubled her efforts to get Laura over the banisters.

"Goodbye, Laura!" Kerry whispered, as she heaved the top half of Laura's helpless body over the rail, then leaning down she grasped Laura's legs, intending to dispatch her headfirst over the banisters. Although she tried to grip the banisters, Laura felt like a rag doll, unable to move her limbs, and all she wanted was the oblivion of sleep . . .

"What the fuck –"

"Jesus Christ, what's going on –"

There was a lot of shouting and pushing, followed by a piercing scream and a thud as someone pulled her back from the abyss. Laura felt the rope being removed from her neck and found herself in Darren's strong arms, as he whispered endearments to her and held her tightly. Laura smiled sleepily. She must be dreaming, but it was such a lovely dream . . .

CHAPTER 77

Tony Coleman had insisted on driving her home after the cinema, although Ellie had assured him she was well able to make her way home by herself.

"Otherwise," he said gallantly, "I'd worry in case anything happened to you."

"Oh, alright," Ellie had replied, grateful for the company on the journey back. The movie they'd seen had been forgettable, but she'd enjoyed having someone with whom to spend a pleasant evening. Alan was away on a business trip, so the days were dragging more slowly than usual. Being on her own for days on end wasn't a very pleasant experience, so when Tony had invited her to the cinema, she'd been glad to accept his invitation to see the latest blockbuster in town. She'd also felt that Tony might prove a useful decoy – if people saw her out and about in his company it would never cross their minds that she could be involved with someone else.

Tony hadn't made any further declarations, and seemed to have accepted that Ellie was only interested in him as a friend. He was pleasant, if fairly dull, company, which was the perfect foil to the excitement Ellie felt when Alan was around. Of course, Tony had no idea that there was a special man in Ellie's life, and that was the way she intended to keep it.

"Thanks, Tony," Ellie said as they reached her doorstep and she prepared to go inside.

"Don't I get a cup of coffee?"

Ellie sighed. She was tired and longing to go to bed so that she could dream about her beloved Alan. But it would seem churlish to deny Tony such a small indulgence, especially as he'd gone to the trouble to make sure she got home safely.

"Okay, come in."

But once inside the door, Tony grabbed her roughly by the hair. "You've been leading me on for ages," he whispered, his breathing laboured. "Do you think you can keep playing games with my feelings? You're nothing but a tease, Ellie!"

"Leave me alone!" she replied, her eyes now blazing with fury.

But Tony was undeterred. "I like it when you're angry," he said smiling malevolently, still holding her by the hair. "You think you can put out all the time, but never deliver? I'm not waiting any longer, Ellie."

"Tony, I never led you to believe –"

"Oh yes, you did, but right now I don't care whether you believe that or not. I won't take 'no' any longer –"

Grabbing her hand, he pressed it against his erection.

"That's what I'm going to give you, Ellie –"

"Tony, please –"

Tony grinned, his breathing laboured. "I love when a woman begs for it – it's such a turn-on!"

"I'm not begging, you fool – I just want you to go!"

"I'll go when I'm finished with you," he said, his face too close to hers. "Come on, Ellie – you've been married, so you're no vestal virgin. You can't tease a man and not expect him to respond!"

Roughly he pressed his mouth to hers. Retching as she inhaled his stale breath, Ellie tried to pull away, but he was too strong for her. She was now very frightened. What had been a pleasant evening had suddenly turned very sour.

She looked around wildly for something she could use to hit him with, but there was nothing in sight. Silently, she cursed the isolation of her house – it was ideal for conducting an affair, but no one would hear her if she cried for help. If only Alan would call and save her! But of course he was away, and he knew nothing about her little trip to the cinema with Tony that evening.

Tony realised that she was looking for some kind of weapon,

and his desire turned to fury. Still gripping her by the hair, he slid across the bolt on the front door with his free hand, closing off any escape route.

"We don't want any visitors, do we?" *he whispered menacingly in her ear.*

"Get off me, you bastard!"

Dragging her into the drawing room, he lowered her unceremoniously onto the large rug in the centre of the room, knelt down beside her and began pulling her clothing off. As she resisted his attempt to remove her bra, he momentarily raised her up and deftly flipped open the hooks at the back. Then he bit her nipples as she cried out in pain and fear. How had she ever thought Tony was a nice man?

"Come on, Ellie – you know you want it!" *he panted.*

In a frenzy of lust, he pulled off her panties and spread-eagled her, using his knees to keep her legs apart while he quickly opened his trousers. Bucking and screaming, Ellie tried to push him off, but he was far too strong for her. Without preliminaries, he entered her, and Ellie cried out as she felt the searing pain as he thrust deep inside her. How different it was from when she was with the man she loved! Then her body was always ready for him.

With a final heave, Tony reached a climax, and lay spent on top of her. Ellie struggled to breathe, fearing that he was going to fall asleep on top of her. But instead, he opened his eyes and smiled at her. Now that he was sated, he was prepared to be civil again.

"How about that cup of coffee, Ellie?" *he asked, his eyes twinkling knowingly.*

"Go to hell!" *she said, her voice low and disgusted.*

"Didn't I satisfy you?"

"You raped me!"

Tony looked surprised. "For heaven's sake, don't be so dramatic! It's not as though I took your virginity."

"Don't you know that 'no' means 'no'?"

Tony grinned. "Well, you did need a little persuading!"

Her face contorted with disgust, Ellie pushed him off her and rose to her feet. Throwing on her clothes, she marched to the front door, unlocked and opened it. "Get to hell out of here!" she screamed, "and never come near me again!"

"Dear me, you do have a temper, Ellie!" Tony muttered as he sat up and rearranged his clothing. "Calm down – it was hardly a big deal, was it? Why don't we just forget about it, and go to the cinema again next Tuesday?"

"Get out."

This time, the tone of Ellie's voice didn't brook any argument. Smoothing down his hair, Tony buttoned up his trousers and left without a backward glance.

As soon as she'd locked the door after him, Ellie hurried to the shower. She felt sore, violated and unclean, and she desperately wanted to wash away any lingering connection to Tony Coleman. She felt suffocated by his smell, his touch, and his bodily fluids. How dare he think he had a right to use her body without her permission! She'd always believed him to be a dull but essentially mild-mannered man, but tonight he'd proved that she should never have trusted him.

In the shower, she scrubbed her body until it was almost raw, feeling that by doing so, she was obliterating every atom and molecule that might have come from contact with Tony Coleman. She longed to make him pay for what he'd done, but the cost for her would be too high. There was no way of knowing how Alan might react if she told him what had happened. He might feel she'd egged Tony on, remembering how she'd danced and flirted with him at her leaving party, and how she'd been entertaining him at her house on the day Alan had pretended to be delivering her holiday pay. She loved Alan desperately, but this rape might be enough to tip the balance of their relationship, and she wasn't prepared to take that risk.

At last, she felt cleansed and caressed by the hot cascading water, and her anger gradually began to fade. It was then that she came to a decision. Today was a day she'd wipe totally from her mind. She'd pretend it never happened. Only she and Tony knew what had transpired anyway, and he'd hardly have the nerve to come near her ever again. If he did, she'd threaten him with the police.

In the silence of her bedroom, and in the loneliness of her situation, Ellie wept until she'd no tears left.

CHAPTER 78

It had all been hushed up, for which Laura was very grateful. Albert, the concierge, had been fully in agreement with Darren that they should simply regard the event as a terrible accident. Albert hadn't wanted any further trouble associated with the apartments, since it could lead to him losing his job. Jim had nearly lost his when he'd been found asleep in the foyer while Laura's apartment was on fire.

Between them, Albert and Darren had agreed that the rope should disappear, and by the time the police arrived, they'd concocted a story in which Laura had taken a sedative and been resting at her friend's apartment, and while she was sleeping, her friend had apparently been cleaning the banisters but had somehow tripped and fallen backwards down the stairs. He and Albert slightly altered the timeline, claiming that Darren had arrived outside the apartment just as he heard the thud, then he'd gone downstairs for Albert and they'd entered the apartment and found Kerry's body on the floor below. Before the police were called, Darren managed to locate a cleaning cloth in one of the kitchen cupboards, which he'd dropped near Kerry's body.

Unhappy about her semi-comatose condition, the police had insisted that Laura be taken to hospital for a check-up. Darren had gone with her in the ambulance, and as soon as she was awake he'd explained that as he and the concierge were struggling to pull her and Kerry apart, Kerry had stepped backwards and tumbled headfirst down the stairs, breaking her neck as she fell to the floor below.

Due to the sedatives, Laura hadn't fully registered what had happened in the Green Street apartment. Now she was relieved and grateful to Darren for his help – and for his foresight regarding Kerry. Because despite what Kerry had done, Laura didn't want her late friend's name to be vilified. There were some things that were better hushed up.

Although still woozy, Laura did her best to fill him in on Kerry's secret vendetta, and how the death of her parents hadn't been an accident at all.

"So it's better this way," Darren whispered, glancing around the ambulance to make sure that the paramedic couldn't hear him. But the man was talking on a phone, and it was clear that he wasn't listening to them. "If Kerry had lived, you'd have wanted her to pay for what she'd done to your family. More than likely, your former friend would have gone to jail, and your whole life and hers would have been sifted through by both police and press – I don't think you'd have wanted that."

Laura agreed. "But how did you know where I was –"

Darren smiled as the ambulance pulled into the hospital grounds. "It's a long story – when you're home again, I'll explain everything that happened."

Laura nodded, suddenly wondering where home actually was.

As though he'd read her mind, Darren took her hand in his. "Come and stay at my place when you're discharged," he said softly. "I promise to take good care of you."

As she lay alone in her private room, Laura recalled the last time she'd been in hospital, and how her miscarriage had been the catalyst that had ended her marriage. Now, in the space of just a few months, so many of the people she'd once loved were gone – her baby, Jeff, and finally Kerry. And, of course, there was the loss of her parents and brother all those years ago. Since that fateful day when she was twelve, there had never been a day when she didn't desperately miss them, or feel remorse for her part in their deaths.

Now, in the light of Kerry's confession, she was free of the crippling weight of guilt that she'd carried with her since childhood. Knowing it wasn't her fault meant that her loss was no longer coupled with self-reproach. Her parents and brother had finally become real to her again, not simply reminders of her guilt. It was as though Kerry had given them back to her, releasing her from the pall of sorrow that had defined her relationship with them since they died.

On the other hand, she was sadly aware that all hadn't been ideal in her parents' marriage. But she'd made a decision to remember only the good bits, and they'd help to sustain her throughout the years. Would her father have left her mother for Ellie? It seemed unlikely, since he hadn't done so during all the years they'd been lovers. Had her mother known about the affair and tolerated it, or had she been totally unaware?

Laura sighed. There was little point in dwelling on what might, or might not, have happened. All the protagonists were now frozen in time, their earthly relationships over. It was all out of her control, and she had to learn to let go.

Wiping away a tear, Laura thought about dear, mischievous Pete who, because of Kerry's jealousy, had been denied the chance to grow up. For eternity, he would always be fourteen. She remembered Ellie with mixed emotions too. Kerry's mother had given her a home when her wealthy relatives hadn't wanted the responsibility. Maybe she'd done it in part for the money, but surely also in memory of the man she'd loved – his loss would have been devastating for her, too. And Ellie would have had to hide her own pain in order to keep Laura from knowing how much her late father had meant to her, and to prevent Kerry guessing about her connection with him. Of course Kerry had known already, and this must have added to the young girl's distress.

Laura sighed. There had been three very damaged and grieving women living together at Treetops all those years ago, each of them concealing her pain from the other two. How Kerry must have smouldered with resentment at the idea of Laura living there too, although she hid it well, no doubt at great personal cost. Kerry's plans had all gone awry, her father accidentally dead by her own hand, so her private grief would have been overwhelming.

Laura pulled herself up in the bed. Despite all that had

happened, she didn't want to hate anyone. When people were at the mercy of their emotions, reason flew out the window. Nor could she blame people for falling in love with the wrong person – she'd been the victim of an unwise and unsuitable relationship herself. How had she ever thought that Jeff was the man for her?

She'd also discovered that since she and Jeff had never got round to divorcing – and he'd never been formally charged with drug offences – all his possessions would eventually revert to her. But since she wanted nothing to do with them, she'd decided to have everything sold and the money given to charity.

Laura looked at her watch. It was almost visiting time, and Darren would be in to see her shortly. As she thought of him, a warm feeling pervaded her entire body. Darren was someone with whom she could always be herself. He'd never wanted to change her, unlike Jeff. And that fateful day at the Green Street apartment when he'd saved her life, he'd instinctively known how much Kerry had meant to her, and that she wouldn't want their friendship analysed and dissected by police and press. Darren had also been the one who'd made all the arrangements for Kerry's upcoming funeral. He'd been a tower of strength since Kerry's death, visiting Laura each day since she'd been admitted. In view of her recent miscarriage, the doctors had opted to keep her under observation for an extra ten days, but now they'd decided that all was well and she was free to leave hospital the following day . . .

"Hello, Laura – how are you feeling?"

Darren had suddenly appeared at her bedside, and Laura's heart did a tiny somersault. He smiled at her warmly, sat down beside her on the bed, leaning forward to kiss her cheek.

"I'm much better thanks," she told him. "They're letting me out in time for Kerry's funeral tomorrow – but I'm dreading it."

Darren squeezed her hand. "Don't worry," he said softly. "I'll be there beside you."

CHAPTER 79

When the two young women had finished university and begun their careers – Kerry in engineering, Laura in social science – Ellie felt able to let go of all the pretence she'd been maintaining for years. She was finally able to allow herself to grieve for the man she'd loved so deeply, and for the life they might have had together. During the intervening years, she'd needed to keep a cool head and a strong heart while her daughter and her friend grew to maturity. She'd sacrificed her own needs to ensure that both girls grew up healthy and secure, but now that her obligations were over, she could finally allow herself the indulgence of grief.

"Oh Alan," she whispered, in the silence of her bedroom at Treetops, "I don't want to live without you any more! Kerry doesn't need me now, Laura is self-sufficient too, and they'll always be able to depend on each other. I can join you now, knowing I've done my best for them both."

She wondered if she'd really see her beloved Alan again. And if there was an afterlife, who would be beside him – her or Sylvia? Perhaps earthly relationships wouldn't matter in the next world, and all the pain, jealousy and grief would be over, and the music of heavenly choirs would be enough.

As she reached for her sleeping tablets, Ellie suddenly smiled giddily, wondering why she was assuming she'd hear heavenly choirs anyway! How could she, after what she and Alan had done to Sylvia? And what she had done to Alan. But it was only a little deception, wasn't it? Hopefully, he wouldn't hold it against her in this next life of theirs, and that Sylvia wouldn't hate her or Alan either. Maybe Sylvia would be up in heaven on her own, and she and Alan would be down below together? It amused her to think that the flames of hell would ensure that their love stayed hot!

"Well, wherever you are, I'll find you, my love," Ellie whispered, although she truly doubted that there were such places as heaven and hell, or even an afterlife. It pleased her to think that she and Alan might meet again but, for her, oblivion would be enough.

"Sylvia, I did you a great wrong, but I couldn't help myself," she whispered, as she slipped the first of the pills into her mouth. "I really liked you, too, which made what I did even worse. I'll never know how deeply you loved your husband, nor do I know how much he cared for you. But I can assure you that what I did was done because of how deeply I felt for him. I put my right to love before yours, but I couldn't help myself. Alan was the love of my life, and while I know it's wrong to say it, I don't regret a minute of the time he and I spent together. Some people never experience those heights of love – but the reverse side of such joy is the loneliness and despair that I've lived with for years now."

As she swallowed another tablet, Ellie was feeling an almost childish glee at how she'd planned her demise. She'd already disposed of the pill bottle – it had gone in the refuse collection the day before. She wouldn't be leaving any note. And she'd cleverly visited her doctor several times lately, complaining of non-existent chest pains and accumulating sedatives to help her sleep. With no evidence of an overdose visible, she hoped her doctor would simply certify her death as a heart attack, and that Kerry might never know the truth. She didn't want to leave her daughter bereft and uncomprehending, but her own pain was so great that she couldn't stay a minute longer.

She glanced at the third finger of her left hand, now bare of Alan's ring. Idly, she studied the track of white that surrounded the finger with its darker skin. She'd already given the ring to a charity shop – she didn't want Kerry being given it after her death, and discovering the inscription 'Alan and Ellie forever' – of course

Kerry would wonder what had happened to the ring but that couldn't be helped. Besides, she didn't need the ring any more. It had served its purpose, reminding her, every day of her life, how much she and Alan had loved each other.

Reaching into her bedside table, she placed her original wedding ring back on her finger, wondering idly if John, her late husband, would be waiting for her in the next life, too? She chuckled to herself, thinking how crowded it was going to be!

The top of the bedside table was now bare, all the pills taken. Now all that remained was the glass of water, which Ellie quickly brought into the bathroom, emptied the remainder of the water down the sink, wiped it and placed it back in the toothbrush holder. Smiling, she returned to the bedroom and lay down, closed her eyes and waited for the end to come.

CHAPTER 80

As the graveside service ended, Laura, supported by Darren, began moving away from Kerry's grave. She'd gone through all the motions, sprinkling earth onto her erstwhile friend's coffin and behaving as though they'd been close right up until the end. Laura felt a fraud when Norma, Jack, and Kerry's other colleagues from Sea Diagnostics approached her, offering their shocked condolences at the accidental death of her dear friend. Nevertheless, she was genuinely heartbroken – despite what Kerry had done to her family, she'd been a major influence in her life.

Just as she stepped from the grass onto the pathway, an elderly man, leaning on a walking stick, approached Laura and extended his hand.

"Ms Thornton? My name is Tony Coleman – I used to be the factory manager when your father was alive."

Laura smiled. "Nice to meet you, Mr Coleman," she said, wondering why he'd bothered to seek her out, and why he was attending Kerry's funeral. Perhaps he was simply saying hello for old time's sake, or he was lonely and simply wanted to talk to someone?

As Darren stepped back and made way for him, the older man fell into step with Laura as she began following the other mourners through the graveyard and out towards the main gate.

"I was a friend of Kerry's mother," he told her, glancing quickly at her. "She was a lovely woman."

Laura nodded in agreement. She, too, owed Ellie a peculiar debt of gratitude.

He hesitated. "I'm glad she didn't know what happened to her daughter," he said, his expression bleak. "It's tragic when someone dies so young, isn't it?"

Laura nodded, still posing as Kerry's friend. Darren was right – it seemed pointless for anyone else to know the truth.

Suddenly, Tony Coleman stopped walking, and gripped her arm as his eyes stared unflinchingly into hers. "Did your friend Kerry ever tell you who her father was?"

Laura gave an involuntary shiver. Surely this old man couldn't know about her father's affair? And if so, why would he bring it up now? She shook her head, preparing herself for the worst.

"Well, Ellie and I –" The old man looked embarrassed. "We once had what – ahem – I think you young people call a one-night stand. And exactly nine months later, Kerry was born." His lugubrious face softened as he reached into his jacket pocket, extracted his wallet and took out a picture. "This is my mother," he said, handing it to Laura.

She gasped when she saw it. Kerry was the spitting image of the woman in the photograph!

The old man seemed pleased by her reaction. "Kerry was like her, wasn't she?"

Laura nodded, her eyes filling with tears as she handed back the photograph. She felt overwhelmed by sadness. Poor disillusioned Kerry – because of a chance remark all those years ago, she'd let her resentment grow out of all proportion. Now it seemed certain that there had never been any basis in fact for her lifelong resentment. Or for the destruction she'd wrought on Laura and her family.

Tony Coleman smiled at her wistfully. "Your mother approached me at the staff Christmas party the year Kerry was born, making veiled references about my 'responsibilities' to Ellie. The penny didn't drop until weeks later – then I realised that Sylvia thought – or maybe even knew – that Ellie's child was mine. I tried asking Ellie, but she always cut me off, and made it clear that she didn't want me having anything to do with the child."

Momentarily, he looked embarrassed.

"So I used to watch Kerry when she was small – I'd sometimes hide in the bushes at Treetops and watch her play. Even after she'd grown up, I'd still follow her from time to time. I liked to see where she was going and what she was doing. It confirmed for me – as I noted her mannerisms and discovered the things she was interested in – that she was definitely my daughter." He grimaced. "It was silly of me, I know, but I got her mobile number through her office, and I'd taken to phoning her recently, just to hear her voice." He looked sheepish. "Of course, I stopped doing that when it dawned on me that by not saying anything, I might be frightening her." He paused. "After Ellie died, I thought that Kerry might be pleased to know she still had a parent. But although I was still checking up on her from time to time, I could never pluck up the courage to speak to her. A few weeks ago, I finally decided that I had to tell her the truth – so I waited outside her office one evening, but I bungled it and she ran away. Clearly, I'd frightened her, so I left her alone after that." He gestured ruefully to the walking stick. "As I was trying to go after her that last evening, I tripped and fell, and broke my leg rather badly. It's never really healed, so it's become a constant reminder of that last time I saw her." His eyes filled with unshed tears. "Now, of course, I wish I'd made more of an effort to contact her."

"I'm so sorry for your loss," Laura told the old man.

Nodding, he accepted her condolences, shook her hand again and turned back the way they'd just come. Turning to watch him, Laura saw him hobbling slowly down the avenue again. Then he stepped off the pathway, kneeling with difficulty in front of what was now clearly his daughter's grave.

"Are you okay?" Darren asked as he helped Laura out of the taxi that had taken them back to his apartment.

She nodded, unable to speak. She was exhausted, but relieved that the funeral was over at last. She'd never forget Kerry, her one-time friend, or the extraordinary circumstances that had led to the build-up of so much hatred. But it wouldn't rule her life any longer.

As Darren paid the taxi driver and opened the door into the apartment block, Laura smiled her thanks. It was nice to be able to rely on someone to do all the day-to-day things that needed doing, because right now, all she wanted to do was rest. Darren had already rung Bill Maddison to say that Laura wouldn't be returning to Dorrington immediately, and Bill had been understanding as usual. Laura silently marvelled at how kind these two men were. They clearly understood how devastated she was, and were prepared to make whatever allowances were necessary.

In Darren's large but cosy apartment, Laura sank down onto one of the couches gratefully. There had been little opportunity to talk while she'd been in the hospital. Other than a brief explanation of what he and the concierge had told the police, Darren had urged caution any time Laura made even the slightest reference to what had happened at the Green Street apartment. But now, at last, she was longing to fully understand what had transpired that day, and how Darren had materialised just when she needed him most.

Having made hot drinks and brought them to the coffee table, Darren sat down beside her.

"Now, you'd better tell me everything," Laura said. "How on earth did you end up in Kerry's apartment?"

Darren smiled. "It's a long story, but I'll try to condense it as best I can. After you'd gone to Dorrington, I asked Bill to keep an eye on you, although I didn't tell him why. I was worried in case your ex found out where you were, and started hassling you again. Then some police officer rang me, trying to find out where you'd gone. I refused to tell him, since I wasn't even sure if he *was* a police officer. But the call got me worried. Why would the police be looking for you? Or was it one of Jeff's goons? So I decided to pay a quick visit to Dorrington, just to make sure that you were okay. I wondered if I'd done you a favour by telling you about the job there, or if I'd just made you more vulnerable. I was worried that in a strange town, you'd be more likely to stand out in a crowd. If anyone was trying to track you down, it would be easy enough to spot you. I decided to see who, if anyone, was tailing you. I knew Jeff could afford to hire a private eye, so I wasn't looking for him specifically – just anyone who might be hanging around you more often than they should be."

Laura tightened her grip on his hand.

"But all seemed fine when I got there," Darren confirmed. "I discovered that your friend Kerry was staying at the same hotel as I was, but I deliberately kept out of her way, since I'd have been very embarrassed if you'd discovered I was checking up on you. I found it odd that she wasn't staying with you, but I assumed your new accommodation wasn't big enough for guests. Then I saw her collect a hire car outside the hotel one day, and I surmised that the two of you were going off sightseeing. I was pleased for you – how wrong could I be! After that, I went back to London, never bothering to check with Bill if you were going on holiday."

"Some holiday!" Laura said wryly. "All I saw of that car was the bonnet heading towards me!"

Darren nodded, giving her hand a sympathetic squeeze. "Later, I decided to pay a second visit to Dorrington – that was when you spotted me!"

"I was really upset when you didn't want to speak to me – I thought I must have done something to offend you," Laura said accusingly.

Darren smiled. "You could never offend me, Laura. But how could I explain to you what I was doing? You'd definitely have me chalked up as an idiot!"

"But what about your job? As Professor of the Sociology Department, you can hardly disappear from the university on a whim!"

"I took time off. There was no problem – the others in the Department were well able to cope without me." Darren smiled, keeping a tight grip on her hand. "When you finally told Bill about the incident with the car, and the man who was following you, he rang me straight away. Then I remembered about Kerry hiring the car, and Bill confirmed you hadn't been away on any sightseeing trip at that time. That was when I realised you could be in real danger."

Now it was Laura's turn to squeeze Darren's hand comfortingly.

"Bill wasn't surprised to hear that I was in Dorrington – you'd already told him you'd spotted me earlier that afternoon. He and I then tried to contact you, but there was no reply from your phone. We now know, of course, that was because you'd changed your number again. Bill then checked the department files for your address, but unfortunately it hadn't been added yet."

Darren took out his handkerchief, took off his glasses and wiped his eyes.

"We were getting desperate at this stage, but thankfully, Bill discovered that you'd left a voicemail on his department phone. You said that you were heading to London by train the following morning, so we agreed that I'd be on it, and that I'd find you and warn you about your so-called friend." He grinned ruefully. "I had this stupid idea that I might get a chance to save your life – then you'd be grateful to me forever more. Pathetic, isn't it?"

"No, it isn't – you *did* save my life."

"Well, not in the way I'd imagined."

Laura raised an eyebrow. "How more dramatic could it have been? If you hadn't arrived when you did –"

Darren put on his glasses again. "I searched for you on the train, but I didn't manage to find you until we arrived back in London. I spotted you getting off, but somehow I lost you again in the crowds. Then I saw you heading for the Tube station, but you were moving so fast and the platform was very crowded. I could only hope that I'd got on the same Tube as you, and I had to keep sticking my head out at each station to watch for where you were getting off! When we got to Islington, you raced into the police station, so I waited outside until you reappeared. I almost missed you when you shot out of there like a bat out of hell – I called to you, but you were too focused on your mission to pay any attention to me. Luckily, that nice estate agent was able to tell me where you were going, and give me the number of the apartment."

Laura nodded, remembering the voice she'd ignored in her haste to confront Kerry.

"Albert, the concierge on duty, refused to let me up to the apartment," Darren continued. "But I pushed past him and headed for the lift. Thankfully, he came running after me, because I'd never have been able to open the door to the apartment myself. Luckily he carries a master key, and when he heard the strange noises coming from inside, he agreed to open the door." He shivered. "If we'd been a minute later, Kerry would have had you over the banisters . . ."

"I still don't understand why she hated me so much," Laura said sadly.

Darren grimaced. "I think her sense of injustice turned her mad. After all, she'd been letting it all fester since she was a child."

"The sad thing is – apart from leaving everything to Kerry in my will," Laura whispered, "I'd also decided to give her a sizeable chunk of the money just as soon as I'd divorced Jeff."

Trembling, and still finding it difficult to understand, Laura's eyes filled with tears again, and she was glad to feel Darren's comforting arms around her. Yet even though Kerry had professed to hate her, she couldn't feel that emotion herself. She had genuinely loved her friend. After Laura's family died, they'd grown up together in the same house. And all that time, Kerry had been a murderer, harbouring hatred that had grown like a tumour, and multiplying out of all proportion.

"I'm not very good at picking friends or husbands, am I?" Laura said, turning earnestly to face Darren. "I thought both Kerry and Jeff actually cared about me."

Darren smiled ruefully. "I'm sorry, Laura – I know it mightn't be politically correct to say so, but I was so glad to hear that you'd left Jeff. It allowed me to dream that somehow, once again, I might have a chance with you."

Laura felt a frisson of delight as he looked at her earnestly. Since that day when he'd saved her life, she'd come to appreciate his kindness, his generosity of spirit and his bravery, which counted for far more than being six foot two and having a handsome face.

"But why didn't you ever say anything?" she asked curiously. "We've known each other for years!"

"How could I? If you'd told me to take a hike, it could have made things very awkward for both of us. Apart from my personal feelings, you're a damned good lecturer, and very popular with the students. The university wouldn't want to lose you. And if I'd declared myself, you might have found it too embarrassing to stay on – then I'd have lost you twice over. At least if I said nothing, you'd stay on and I'd be able to see you every day."

What a sweet, sweet man, Laura thought, her heart brimming with affection for him. Darren was totally different from the kind of man she'd have chosen before – thank goodness. Now when she thought of Jeff, with his blond hair, good looks and suave demeanour, she felt sick to think she'd actually believed she'd loved him. She hadn't understood the meaning of the word back then. Jeff had never cared about her – he'd only wanted her on his terms. And Steve's vintage car had been more important to him than helping a woman in danger. Why had she always chosen such losers?

Now, she was seeing Darren in a totally different light. And with his glasses off, he had the most beautiful soft brown eyes. His black hair was thick and luxuriant, with just a few flecks of grey around his sideburns, and suddenly she longed to run her fingers through it. He had such strong, manly hands, and she felt a delicious shiver run down her spine at the thought of those fingers touching her body. While he wasn't conventionally handsome or tall like Jeff had been, he had a heart as big and brave as a lion. Why had she never noticed how totally gorgeous he was, or how wonderfully secure he made her feel?

Laura leaned forward and kissed his nose affectionately. "You're a wonderful man – I think I've always known there was something special about you – I just didn't realise how much you meant to me until you came to rescue me. If that wasn't an extraordinary decent and generous thing to do, I don't know what is."

Darren grimaced. "You're probably feeling a bit emotional right now," he said kindly, "so I'm not sure that you'd really want to settle for a plodder like me in the long run. I'm never going to do anything out of the ordinary, or set the world on fire."

Laura chuckled. "I've already come through one attempt at setting my world on fire, so it's not a trait I rate very highly! Besides, *you'd* be taking on a fool – why didn't I realise what a disaster Jeff was?"

Darren took out his handkerchief and wiped his glasses again.

"It's kind of you to try to make me feel better, but the truth is – I went to Dorrington because I couldn't bear not to have you in my life." He turned red. "To be honest, I was also terrified you might fall for Bill Maddison. He's available, and a good-looking, personable sort of chap – the kind I'm not."

"Which is why I didn't fall for him," Laura added softly. "Because he's *not* you."

Darren looked at her critically, as though he found it difficult to believe her. Then he smiled shyly, taking both her hands in his. "I had this daft vision of me as a James Bond-type character, arriving in some souped-up, spectacular car, and pulling you inside just before the baddies were about to harm you. Then we'd drive off, and you'd be so grateful that we'd immediately begin making love while the car was still moving."

"How could you drive and make love at the same time?" Laura asked in mock disapproval.

Darren grinned. "Ah, but you see, my James Bond car would be able to drive itself. I'd have already put it on automatic!"

"Hmm, I suppose we could try making part of that scenario come true," Laura whispered, her heart beating much faster than normal.

"Okay, you could start by kissing me," Darren said reasonably.

Laura was tingling with excitement. "And what happens then?"

"Well, I might totally lose control and have my wicked way with you."

"Sounds wonderful," Laura murmured breathlessly, marvelling at the fact that she no longer felt lethargic. "How soon can we begin?"

"Right now is fine by me."

"What a wonderful idea," Laura whispered, slipping back into his arms. "I suppose I should let Bill Maddison know that I won't be going back to Dorrington. Assuming, of course, that you'll give me my old job back?"

Darren's smile was beatific. "Bill's loss is my gain – I'll have you anytime, my dearest Laura!" He grinned. "And now that you've moved into my apartment, why don't you stay?"

Laura nodded, smiling back. "That would be great, at least for the moment –"

Darren looked worried until Laura kissed his nose again.

"I just meant that we'll eventually need somewhere larger."

Darren raised his eyebrows questioningly.

Laura blushed. "Well, if we're going to start a family some day –"

She had visions of a large country house like Greygates, with lots of space for children to play.

"A family with you would be more than I could ever hope for!" Darren said softly, hardly believing that his dream was finally coming true.

"I hope you don't mind me being very rich?" Laura added, holding her breath.

Darren grinned. "Why would any man object to a wealthy wife?" But then his expression turned serious. "But even if you had nothing, I'd still feel exactly the same about you. I love you very much, Laura, and I'll never let you down."

"Do you think you could take some more time off work?" Laura whispered, reaching up to kiss him again.

Darren nodded, smiling. "Okay, as long as you're going to be there to help me to make the most of it?"

"Of course I will, you wonderful man," Laura said fervently. "I can't wait for the future – our future," she whispered, as she held him to her heart.

Now that you're hooked why not try
Still Waters?
also published by Poolbeg

Here's a sneak preview of
chapters one, two, three and four.

LINDA
KAVANAGH

Still Waters

CHAPTER 1

A minute ago, everything had been fine in Ivy Heartley's life. Now her worst nightmare was coming true.

She'd been smiling happily as she'd opened the email from her sister-in-law, who was also a lifelong friend. She loved Peggy's newsy letters, filled with gossip about the village where they'd both grown up, and where Peggy still lived. Her emails had the ability to bring everything to life, and Ivy could almost see the events she described unfolding before her very eyes.

Ivy had been chuckling as she read what had happened the previous week in the Lincolnshire village of Willow Haven. Peggy told her about the fund-raising drive for a new roof for the church, the disastrous garden party at the vicarage, and the thief who'd raided the church's allotment. She'd been concerned to hear that Mrs Evans had just had a hip-replacement operation, and glad that her old school friend Clara Bellingham had got engaged to Bill Huggins from Allcott, a nearby town.

Ivy regularly visited Willow Haven. She and her husband – Peggy's brother – had left as soon as they'd finished school, and moved to London where Ivy studied at RADA. Now, almost twenty years later, they were both very successful in their respective careers, and Joseph, their son, was at university. She was a highly paid soap star, and Danny was founder and managing director of the Betterbuys supermarket chain. Their tiny rented flat in London was now a distant memory, and today they lived in a luxurious mansion in Sussex.

Ivy stretched, and decided to make herself a cup of tea before she continued reading Peggy's long email. While she boiled the kettle and placed a tea bag in a cup, she'd revel in the anticipation. She smiled as she thought of the garden party at the vicarage – those occasions were usually cringe-worthy, and she'd attended more of them than she cared to remember. As a celebrity, she was often called upon to open fêtes or lend a touch of glamour to community social events.

Returning to the computer, Ivy sat down again and scrolled through Peggy's email as she sipped her tea, reading about Peggy's husband Ned and family, and about her father-in-law Fred Heartley's high blood pressure. Peggy kept a close eye on him, for which Ivy was grateful, since she and Danny were hundreds of miles away.

Suddenly, Ivy's heart gave a lurch as she read Peggy's final words. *Since the village has been expanding so much lately, there are plans afoot for draining Harper's Lake. The space will be used for landfill, which means that eventually the land could be built on. Ned thinks it's a crazy idea, but the local council has voted in favour of it.*

Ivy's hands were now shaking, and she could no longer hold the cup. Putting it down, she covered her face with her hands. "Oh God," she whispered, "what am I going to do?" The past was finally catching up with her. The secret she'd kept hidden for most of her adult life was now about to destroy her. And not just her alone, but her entire family. Her career would be over, Danny would hate her for what she'd done. And Joseph – how would he react when he discovered his mother's heinous secret? Peggy, too, would want nothing to do with her. And all because she hadn't told the truth all those years ago.

Ivy found herself shaking from head to toe. If the Council's plan went ahead, the ripples from the lake would spread out and devastate many lives in the process. Just as they had on that fateful day when her own life had changed forever.

CHAPTER 2

Rosa Dalton was sitting at her desk in the classroom, busy writing in the front page of one of her schoolbooks, her fluffy blonde hair almost touching the desk as she leaned over it. Class hadn't yet begun, and she was deeply absorbed in what she was doing, which was writing her name as Rosa Heartley over and over again.

Everyone in the school knew that sixteen-year-old Rosa was crazy about Danny Heartley, and dreamed of marrying him and living happily ever after. He attended the local boys' school and was in the same class as Rosa and her friends. Every day she'd wait outside the girls' school in the hopes of engaging him in conversation when he passed by on his way home. But despite Danny's disinterest, Rosa refused to accept defeat. If Danny would only ask her out, she'd show him what a wonderful girlfriend – and later, wife – she could be. She just needed the opportunity!

As the teacher arrived, Clara Bellingham, who was sitting behind Rosa, gave her a warning dig in the back, and Rosa quickly hid the book she'd been writing in. Flashing Clara a grateful smile, she got out the correct book and turned to the page the teacher called out. It was Geometry today, and Rosa was bored before the class even began. All she could think of was Danny Heartley and his flashing eyes, and the shock of unruly blond hair that fell across his left eye.

"This morning, we're going to look at isosceles and equilateral triangles – please turn to page 47 of your texts," Mrs Jones announced, but Rosa heard nothing. She didn't see the value of all this theory – after all, when she and Danny were married, they weren't going to be discussing geometry over the breakfast table, were they?

As the teacher droned on about the importance of understanding the concepts of angles, equal and unequal sides, Rosa had a dreamy look on her face. Geometry had no place in her world view, and she regarded it as just another torment thought up by adults to keep young people from enjoying themselves.

She was having a lovely daydream about being married to Danny when the teacher noticed her gazing out the window with a faraway look in her eyes.

"Rosa Dalton, explain what I've just been talking about." Mrs Jones had a triumphant gleam in her eye. She'd caught Rosa out, and she intended to make the most of it.

At first Rosa didn't answer because she was too absorbed in her daydream, but the sudden silence and tittering at the back of the classroom gradually began to filter through to her consciousness and she glanced around, only to see Mrs Jones bearing down on her.

"Oh . . ."

"Stand up and repeat what I've just been explaining to the class for the last fifteen minutes."

"Oh er, I'm sorry, Mrs Jones," Rosa faltered, "I – I'm –"

"She didn't recognise her name, Mrs Jones!" shouted one of the girls at the back of the room. "If you'd called her Rosa Heartley, she'd have answered straight away!"

The classroom dissolved into laughter since everyone knew about Rosa's feelings for Danny Heartley. Angrily, Mrs Jones called for order as she returned to the podium.

"Sit down, you silly girl," she said haughtily to an embarrassed Rosa. "You'd better buck up and pay attention if you want to get decent exam results. There's more to life than boys, you know."

The other pupils began to snigger at the mention of boys, and Rosa turned puce.

Ivy Morton, who was sitting at the back of the class, felt sorry for her. Rosa was a daydreamer, but she had a bubbly personality and was fun to be with. Although they'd never been close friends, she and Rosa hung out with the same group of boys, and Rosa was usually the centre of attention because of her outrageous jokes and coquettish behaviour. It was impossible to dislike her, even though she always tried to outshine all the other girls and focus the boys' attention solely on her. She had a presence and a sense of her own importance and Ivy, who desperately wanted to be an actress when she left school, often wondered if Rosa wasn't more suited to the profession than she was.

Rosa heaved a sigh of relief as the teacher began the lesson again. She tried to look nonchalant and unaffected by the teacher's comments – she didn't want anyone thinking she cared about what Mrs Jones had to say. On the other hand, she was well aware that she needed to knuckle down and start studying. But it was difficult when Danny Heartley occupied so much of her thoughts . . .

Since childhood, Rosa had wanted to be a flight attendant, and she'd never tired of telling anyone who'd listen that she hoped to work for one of the big airlines. Everyone assured her that with her personality and looks she'd be a shoo-in, and in her dreams Danny was always waiting at the airport to welcome her home from the exotic locations she'd been visiting. He'd be so proud of his high-flying wife . . .

Rosa sighed. But first, she had to catch Danny, and convince him that she was the girl for him. She couldn't understand what he saw in shy, mousey Ivy Morton, who'd never amount to anything. Much to Rosa's annoyance, Danny was always trying to talk to Ivy, and she always ended up laughing at his antics as he tried to get her attention.

Rosa was relieved that Ivy didn't seem to return his feelings – or was the minx playing hard to get? Rosa's heart plummeted at the thought that Ivy might simply be pretending indifference in order to snare Danny. If Ivy started going out with him, Rosa knew she'd never live down the shame. Since everyone knew how much she fancied Danny, the other students would either feel sorry for her, or be delighted she'd got her comeuppance. Either way, she wouldn't be able to face them day after day in school. If only she'd kept her feelings for Danny to herself! But she'd confided in a supposedly trustworthy friend, who'd told her own circle of friends, and suddenly the whole school knew about it. Before long, everyone in the boys' school knew too. But ultimately, all the embarrassment would be worth it if she and Danny finally got together . . .

Suddenly the school bell rang, and Rosa was catapulted back to reality. She sighed with relief – another day of torment was over.

Clara nudged her. "Are we going to the lake?"

Rosa nodded. This was the most important part of the day, and a rite of passage for pupils in both the boys' and girls' senior school years.

"See you in five," she whispered, hurrying out of the classroom and down the corridor to the school toilets. She needed to check her hair, apply some discreet make-up and lip-gloss, and dab on some of the perfume she'd sneaked from her mother's dressing table. Hopefully, Danny Heartley would be at the lake too . . .

CHAPTER 3

"Hmmm, you smell gorgeous."

Danny Heartley, fresh from his shower, nuzzled the back of his wife's neck as she finished her make-up at the dressing table.

They were going to an important dinner and charity auction that evening, where the important people of the business world and minor nobility would be rubbing shoulders. Despite being a charity event, many lucrative business deals would also be concluded while the patrons were bidding ridiculously high sums of money for the ridiculously cheap items on offer, all in the name of flaunting their wealth.

"What are you wearing tonight?"

"I thought the long blue dress – what do you think?"

Danny grinned as he towelled himself dry. "I don't know why you bother asking me, my dear, because you take absolutely no heed of my opinion anyway!"

Ivy smiled back. He was right, but she still liked to ask his opinion, and she'd never wear anything he positively disliked.

Danny leaned forward and kissed her hair. "Whatever you wear, you'll look stunning," he whispered. "I'm so proud of my beautiful – and talented – wife."

Ivy smiled back at him, but he didn't notice the shadow of fear that had crossed her face as she wondered how long things might remain that way.

"Are you bidding on anything tonight?" she asked him, trying to sound cheerful.

"I suppose I'll have to – it's expected of me at this stage. I might bid on that awful painting by your friend Anton. If I'm unlucky enough to make the winning bid, I'll donate it to the children's hospital."

Ivy laughed. "I don't think Anton should give up the day job."

Danny nodded, looking amused. "You're right – I think he should stick to acting. Talking of which, did you say that Anton, Emily, Sarah and Dominic are coming for dinner on Saturday night?"

Ivy nodded. Normally, she'd be looking forward to an evening of shoptalk and gossip with her fellow actors. They were all cast members of *Bright Lights*, a hugely popular soap opera that aired five nights a week. Their schedule was gruelling, but it had made them all stars, paid them substantial salaries, and given them the adulation of millions of fans.

Luckily, Danny never felt out of place in their company, nor did he mind when they started talking about people he didn't know. But then Danny was a very successful businessman in his own right, and could hold his own in any company. He had nothing to prove to anyone, and he never felt remotely intimidated by the celebrities at his table.

As she brushed her hair, Ivy recalled their flight from Willow Haven all those years ago. While she'd trained at RADA, Danny had worked in a supermarket to pay for their accommodation and living costs. Since his flair and ideas were responsible for substantially increasing the company's turnover, he quickly climbed the ladder to senior management.

But Danny had always wanted to be his own boss. He hadn't wanted to run a small shop like his father's – his aim was to establish a chain of supermarkets offering something different from all the others. By the time Ivy was treading the boards in West End shows, they were able to afford a full-time nanny for young Joseph, and Danny was able to put down a deposit on a small supermarket that was going out of business. He'd had a hard time convincing the bank that despite his youth he could resurrect the failing venture but eventually he succeeded, and before long he'd acquired a second store. Then a third. Now, Betterbuys was the second largest supermarket chain in the UK, built up by offering the consumer organic and cruelty-free produce at reasonable prices, running regular lines of special offers, and paying his suppliers fairly, which ensured their cooperation and a constant supply of top-quality produce.

He'd also introduced special staff-training programmes that ensured customers were treated courteously, and that every member of staff was knowledgeable about all the lines they carried. Before long, working at Betterbuys became a status symbol among retail employees, and there were always many more applicants than there were jobs.

"Come on, love, get a move on! No time for daydreaming!"

"Oh, sorry," said Ivy, jumping up from her dressing table and slipping on her dress.

Danny stood behind her and zipped her up, taking the opportunity to kiss her bare shoulders as he did so.

"I love you, Mrs Heartley," he whispered, slipping his hand inside her bra. "Maybe we could . . ."

"I love you too, but there's no time for any of that," said Ivy, laughing. "We really need to get moving –"

Danny laughed. "You've a nerve – you were the one who was wasting time daydreaming a few minutes ago!" He slipped his arm around her. "You look wonderful! Every man at the dinner tonight will envy me. I'm the luckiest man in the world!"

Ivy smiled in acknowledgement, leaning forward to plant an affectionate kiss on his cheek, but she felt a cold stab of fear in her chest. How long would he love her if he learned the truth? Very soon, her whole life could come tumbling down around her.

Grabbing her sequinned evening bag, she hurried out the bedroom door and down the marble staircase after Danny. For tonight, at least, she'd act as though she'd nothing to lose.

CHAPTER 4

*Outside the gates of the girls' school, pupils from the local boys'
school had gathered to chat and flirt, and test out their
attractiveness on the opposite sex. There was a lot of giggling,
jostling and occasional touching. Rosa was centre-stage as usual,
laughing and flicking her halo of blonde hair at the boys, although
none of them took her flirting seriously, since they all knew that
Danny Heartley was the only one she wanted.*

*As Rosa, Danny, Clara Bellingham and groups of other boys and
girls walked in the direction of the lake, Ivy lagged behind, chatting
quietly to Joe Heartley. Joe was a year older than his brother Danny
and to Ivy he seemed much more mature. He was an interesting and
intelligent boy, and Ivy liked the way his freckles were flecked across
the bridge of his nose, and the way the sun glinted on the blond locks
of hair that curled around his ears. Ivy knew that a senior like Joe
would never regard her as girlfriend material, which meant she could
behave in a friendly and natural way with him, without feeling the
need to attract his attention by pushing out her chest, flicking her hair
or repeatedly licking her lips, as most of the other girls did.*

*Amazingly, Joe seemed to enjoy her company too, and they often
walked home from school together. While the other girls flaunted
their newly developing womanly charms, Joe was more interested
in discussing science, history and geography with Ivy. He was
taking his final school exams that summer, and was hoping to study
architecture at university. Unfortunately, his father had other plans
for him – he wanted Joe to study retail technology and eventually*

take over Heartley's Stores.

"No way am I going to spend my life in this village," Joe told Ivy vehemently. "I'm sick of fighting with Dad – it just seems to be one argument after another." Angrily he swung his schoolbag over his shoulder. "I'm not going to be stuck in Willow Haven forever! I want to be an architect, not run a grocery store – that may have been fine for Dad, but it's not what I want to do!"

Ivy nodded. She understood how Joe felt. She intended applying to RADA the following year, and she was lucky in having her parents' full support.

"What are you going to do?" she asked. "I mean, if your dad won't let you study architecture?"

"Then I'll leave home," said Joe determinedly. "There's a big world out there, Ivy – and I intend to see some of it!"

"Hey, you two – get a move on!" Clara called back, as the main group began walking up the steep incline in the road that ran beside Harper's Lake on the outskirts of the village. Further on, where the road sloped downwards again, there was an entrance to the lake that led along a well-worn pathway to a secluded area. It was quite a distance from the main road, and out of reach of prying adult eyes. All the senior school students in the area congregated there during the spring and summer months and, although it was now only February, the weather was already unseasonably warm. Which was a signal for all of them to head for the lake, where they enjoyed sitting in groups at the water's edge, chatting and flirting, as relationships began and ended amid the tranquil surroundings.

Signs warned of the danger of swimming, because there was a sheer drop into the water, which was close to thirty-five feet deep. But this element of danger made it all the more attractive to local teenagers. It was where they all liked to swim unbeknown to their parents. Splashing about in the water and doing dangerous acrobatics guaranteed attention, and increased the swimmer's chances of scoring with the opposite sex.

Today, however, the water was still far too cold to consider swimming, so everyone sat along the bank, chatting in groups.

Many of them had brought drinks or sweets, and banter flowed between the groups.

"Hey, Smithy – we saw you looking up the English teacher's skirt this morning!"

"Don't be daft – she's about a hundred!"

"Didn't look that way to me – maybe you fancy older women?"

Everyone laughed as the embarrassed boy turned a deep shade of red. They all found comfort in disconcerting someone else – it made them feel a little more powerful and a little less vulnerable themselves.

Ivy felt sorry for the boy who'd been embarrassed. She longed to be one of the crowd, but found it impossible to draw attention to herself by being nasty or embarrassing others, yet that seemed to be the preferred method of getting yourself noticed.

Ivy and Joe sat on the periphery of the groups, beneath one of the trees, a little further back from the shore. It was darker there, and Ivy felt comfortable leaning her back against the large sycamore, largely out of sight of the others.

Joe turned towards her. "Danny likes you, you know."

Ivy's cheeks flamed. "Don't be daft – he's just fooling around, to make Rosa jealous."

"No, he really likes you – he told me so. He's not interested in Rosa." Joe paused. "Do you like Danny, Ivy?"

Ivy shook her head vehemently. "No, not in that way. I mean, I like him as a friend, but I don't fancy him."

Joe nodded, and Ivy thought she saw him smile.

"Ivy –"

"Yes?"

Joe's cheeks turned the colour of beetroot and his voice came out as a croak. "I really like you."

"I like you too, Joe."

"No, I mean, I really like you, Ivy."

Ivy waited, holding her breath, hoping but not believing that Joe might be interested in her.

In the darkness of the trees, Joe took her hand. "Would you go out with me?"

She could hardly speak with excitement. "Yes, I'd like that."

The silence between them lengthened, and Ivy began to wonder if she'd said the wrong thing, or sounded too eager.

"There's just one problem, Ivy."

Her heart sank. She might have guessed that things weren't going to be plain sailing.

"Dad would have a fit if he knew I was seeing anyone. He thinks that when I'm not studying, I should be working in the shop."

Ivy said nothing.

"And Danny would be furious if he knew I'd asked you out. All that flirting with Rosa is only a distraction. He told me he was going to ask you out soon – I didn't know what to say to him, because I wanted to ask you out myself."

Ivy knew that Danny fancied her but, in deference to Rosa, she'd always been quick to dismiss his advances. She wasn't remotely interested in him, even though he was extremely good-looking, and lots of the other girls found him very attractive. She was also determined Danny wouldn't use her to hurt Rosa's feelings.

"Well, I suppose it's flattering to be so popular," she said with a shy smile. "So you don't want Danny to know?"

"Would you mind keeping it a secret for a while?" Joe whispered, slipping his arm around her. "If Danny found out, he'd be livid with me, and he'd tell Dad – then I'd be grounded and we'd never get to see each other."

"Of course," said Ivy, disappointed she couldn't trumpet their new relationship from the top of a mountain. On the other hand, she didn't want Joe getting into trouble.

Checking to make sure that no one was watching, Joe quickly kissed her. As their lips met, Ivy felt a surge of joy. Joe was the nicest boy in the village, and he wanted to be with her! Besides, there was something quite exciting about keeping their relationship a secret. One day, when they were able to go public on their relationship, Ivy would watch the incredulous faces of her friends as she revealed how long they'd actually been a couple.

"You're beautiful, Ivy," he whispered. "I can't wait to make you mine!"

Ivy found herself experiencing sensations she'd never known before and she shivered with excitement. It was wonderful to have a boyfriend of her very own, and especially a gorgeous one like Joe Heartley!

No one seemed to have noticed them kissing, since all attention was focused on Rosa and Danny. Rosa, as usual, was making herself the centre of attention by dancing around Danny and stopping at intervals to press up against him. Everyone was laughing at Danny's good-natured embarrassment, and cheering at Rosa's bravado.

As the groups disbanded, and everyone began heading home for dinner, Joe surreptitiously grabbed Ivy's hand.

"See you after school tomorrow?" he whispered, and Ivy nodded happily.

As she reached home and let herself into the house, she found her mother baking in the kitchen. The atmosphere was warm and cosy, and Ivy could smell apple-pies already cooking in the oven.

"Have a good day, pet?" her mother asked, rolling out pastry for an additional batch of pies. "You look a bit flushed – you're not catching something, are you?"

Ivy laughed. She supposed her feelings for Joe Heartley were a bit like a disease – she certainly felt as though she was suffering from a serious case of something or other. And it felt wonderful.

"No, Mum – I'm fine."

Up in her room, Ivy changed out of her school uniform and, as she stood in her underwear, she surveyed herself in the mirror. Joe had said she was beautiful, but she certainly couldn't see it. She was reasonably well proportioned, with a pale, slightly freckled face and long straight blonde hair. What was beautiful about that? Yet inside, she could feel an inner glow that filled her with joy and made her want to smile all the time – maybe being Joe's girlfriend was what made her beautiful.

Ivy longed to tell her mother and father about her new

boyfriend, but she had to respect Joe's wishes. Still smiling to herself as she dressed in jeans and a sweater and went downstairs, she hugged her secret to her like a warm cosy blanket.

In the kitchen, her mother surveyed her daughter's flushed smiling face again.

"Are you sure you're all right, Ivy?" she asked, looking worried.

Much to her mother's surprise, Ivy threw her arms around her and hugged her.

"Mum, I'm fine – in fact, I've never felt better."

Her mother sighed, recognising that faraway look on her daughter's face. Could Ivy be in the throes of first love? She could only hope her daughter would come through it unscathed. First love could be so painful, and she hoped the object of Ivy's affections would treat her kindly.

Eleanor grimaced. It was probably time to remind Ivy about contraception – on the other hand, would it seem that she was condoning teenage sex if she did? Maybe it would be better to say nothing – after all, Ivy had received sex education in school, and mother and daughter had had several rather embarrassing discussions about condoms and the pill. As a result, she felt confident that Ivy was too sensible to ruin her chances of an acting career by getting pregnant . . .